The Flaming Chalice Trilogy

By Peter Williams

Version 5.0

Copyright © 2012 Peter Williams

All rights reserved.

ISBN 978-1-291-08944-8

Coming Soon...

Prologue

Billowing black dust stung the creature's eyes as it looked out onto a ruined world. Pain emanated from every part of its body, not least the dull ache from its decaying tooth. Fear gripped it and it slunk deeper into a crevice in the surrounding rubble. Feeling the cold, it looked down at its body as if for the first time and pulled clumsily at the remaining fragments of clothing still clinging to its frame. It was relatively comfortable in the crevice, which was still warm from its previous existence as part of the café's kitchen. Soft material lay on the ground, although even as Glyn Cooper, he would never have recognised the remains of cotton tablecloths that had been stored in a now disintegrated metal locker. Devoid of colour and substance, the cotton had degraded into its original form; a material grown naturally by gradually absorbing energy from the sun and nutrients in the ground, its natural formation immune from the entropic reaction that had obliterated the objects forced into existence by man. All around the creature, other unaffected materials lay amongst the black dust. Rubble from demolished buildings lay everywhere, timber from the roof members were scattered as far as the creature could see, and fragments of leather and natural textiles from interior furnishings lay among the debris. None of the objects meant anything to the creature, but he recognised instinctively the warmth and comfort offered by the soft cotton so he pulled it greedily about his body.

    The creature looked out from his new lair onto a terrifyingly unknown world – he had no memory of the things that met his gaze but instinct warned him to be wary of the other creatures that moved amongst the rubble. He also knew to be fearful of the flickering orange light that grew, then faded, then grew again behind a pile of nearby timbers. A strong unnatural smell hurt, almost burnt, his senses – the creature knew nothing of the precious liquid that had powered road vehicles across this very place only a short while ago. Petrol from destroyed cars soaked into the ground having been unaffected by the catastrophe. Along with other fossil fuel products, the energy stored within its chemical composition had been captured in prehistoric times and was not easily released by the sudden entropic reaction.

'Yak, Yak, Yarik,' an unseen, living thing barked from the creature's right, making him shrink back once again into its shelter. Directly in front of the crevice, across the open space that had once been Oxford's George Street, a hairy four-legged animal fed upon a bloody carcass. The canine had no memory of its human masters and instinct told it to feed, so it ripped savagely at pieces of leather, originally designed to protect the motorcyclist from road injury, and gorged upon the corpse's belly.

The creature in the crevice watched excitedly as it spotted another of its own species suddenly appear, crouching behind a nearby wall and apparently stalking the four-legged animal; this creature was skinny and shivering and apparently intended to take a share of the animal's spoils. Then another of its kind – instinctively recognised as female - appeared beside the first. The female was pale and much smaller and the creature in the crevice noticed that five small, pointed shapes decorated this new creature's naked rear as she offered it to the shivering male in front of her. Uninterested, the male shoved her away with a snarl and returned his gaze to the feasting animal.

'Yak, Yak, Yarik,' the female barked and turned away so that she was now facing her hidden observer. Apparently sensing his presence, she slunk towards the crevice, crawling mainly on all fours but rising occasionally into a stumbling walk. Every few strides, the female paused and turned to display her rear, instinctively offering the only gift she had, in return for the protection a male of the species could provide.

The creature with the toothache had little interest in the food that was the source of conflict across the way. His stomach was full from a fried breakfast consumed in another world and topped up by a blueberry muffin eaten less than twenty minutes ago at the café. The female fascinated him though - there was a strange stirring in his groin and a previously unknown need started to develop. The creature's fear gradually abated until this new need became suddenly dominant and, without forethought, he sprang from the crevice, grabbed the female and pulled her back to the warmth of his shelter. The female did not struggle; apparently resigned to the larger male's dominance and once inside the cramped confines of the shelter she immediately turned and raised her rear to display her genitalia to the male. Intuitively, the creature pushed her flat to the ground and entered her cruelly from behind. The pair copulated like the animals they now were, without affection or even very much pleasure; they experienced only a terrible frantic, lustful release.

Book 1 - Degenesys

"It has become appallingly obvious that our technology has exceeded our humanity."
Albert Einstein

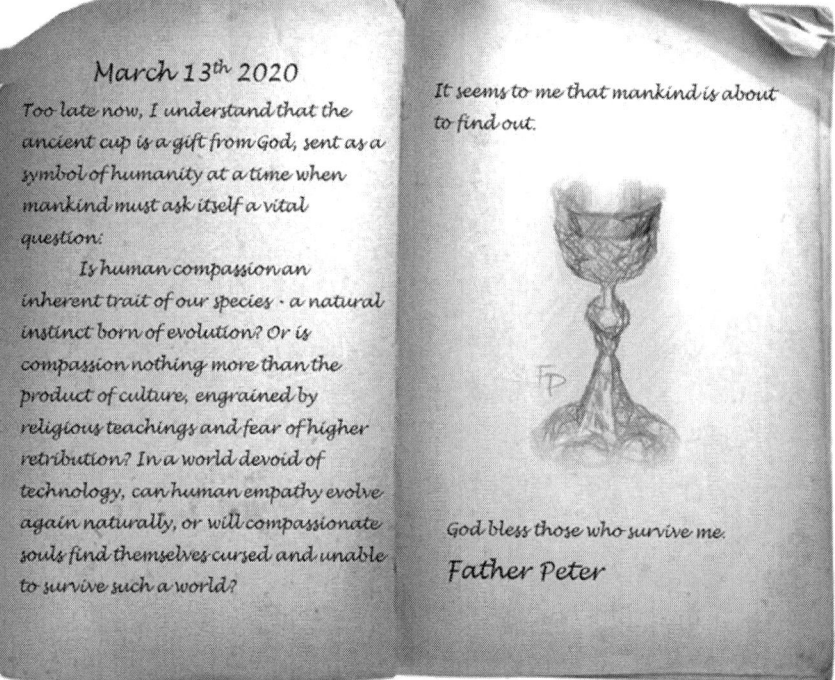

March 13th 2020
Too late now, I understand that the ancient cup is a gift from God, sent as a symbol of humanity at a time when mankind must ask itself a vital question:

Is human compassion an inherent trait of our species - a natural instinct born of evolution? Or is compassion nothing more than the product of culture, engrained by religious teachings and fear of higher retribution? In a world devoid of technology, can human empathy evolve again naturally, or will compassionate souls find themselves cursed and unable to survive such a world?

It seems to me that mankind is about to find out.

God bless those who survive me.
Father Peter

Chapter 1

Matt Campbell glanced out of the tinted bay-window of the power plant's control room and saw the Mercedes van draw up to the security building outside. The van's driver jumped out of the vehicle, his dark skin accentuated by the gleaming white paint of the driver's door as he slammed it. The man looked to be in his early twenties and his braided hair bounced as he jogged into the security gatehouse to sign in. Matt studied the huge vehicle; the Merc was clean and white, on an eighteen plate and had the blue and red logo 'TVUK' emblazoned across its side. He tried to see who sat in the passenger seat, but the sun reflecting off the windscreen prevented him from doing so.

A few moments later the young driver left the security building and swung athletically back into the driver's seat. As Matt watched the barriers rise to allow the van to enter the Degenesys site, it struck him that such diesel guzzlers were becoming a rare sight on the roads lately. The bloody media must have money to burn, he thought.

'The press are here Eddie,' he said, turning away from the window to face a gangly, white-coated engineer who sat sheepishly behind one of many VDU screens that filled the room. 'You'd better wish me luck.'

Eddie gave a thumbs-up. 'G…Good luck,' he stuttered through an awkward smile as Matt turned to check an array of monitors for any unusual alarms. Dr Edward Coleman, although not one of the original Degenesys scientists, was the most senior engineer left on the project and was far more capable of answering the difficult questions the reporters would inevitably ask, but Matt had volunteered to conduct the interview because he couldn't bear the thought of watching his lanky friend stammering his way through the television report.

Matt tapped the shoulder of a third man; a young technician who also scrutinised the monitors. 'My radio's off for about an hour Jim,' Matt said. 'Watch those alarms – I could really do without any embarrassing distractions while the press are here.'

'Don't worry – everything's steady,' the technician replied, making a note in the control room log. The journalists would be long gone before he handed over to the night shift, but their visit still had to be recorded.

Matt left the control room and made his way down the stairs and along the first floor corridor to a conference room. Turning on the lights, he went straight to the overhead projector's controls to check it was working – he planned to show the standard promotional films if things started to get heavy. He examined the room for any disorder, but it was impeccably tidy. There was coffee prepared on one of the side cabinets and chairs were placed symmetrically around the main boardroom table. He scanned the walls where pictures, depicting the Degenesys plant at the various stages of the waste-to-energy process, hung straight and uniformly spaced around them.

Matt sat down next to the phone and waited for reception to call to announce the visitors' arrival and for the first time tendrils of panic began to creep around his gut. The thought of facing the media again after so many years had stirred memories of a traumatic intrusion into his childhood grief. He experienced a flashback of the terrible guilt and loss he had felt as an eleven year-old boy being pulled through a horde of journalists relentlessly pushing cameras into his tear-strewn face. The violent death of his entire family had been his fault, he knew, but the media's reaction to those tragic events had left Matt with a deep-rooted aversion to responsibility and a fervent mistrust of the press. Eddie had better appreciate this, he thought bitterly, but deep down he knew that his stuttering friend was unaware of the sacrifice he was making. Matt felt some semblance of control returning as if acknowledging his good deed had somehow averted his rising panic. He took a series of slow, deep breaths and turned his attention to how best to play the interview.

Hopefully the reporters wouldn't be technically minded enough to grill him on entropic reaction theory. Matt knew the Degenesys plant well enough and he had a reasonable knowledge of thermodynamics, but was far from an expert on the science behind the new technology. Eddie was closer to the theory, but the real boffins were back at Cambridge Laboratories, already working on the next generation of entropic power stations. Degenesys was just a small-scale prototype and the project scientists had lost interest almost as soon as it was operational, but to Matt, the technology was still pretty sexy, especially compared to the gas-fired power stations where he had learnt his trade. The gas sites rarely ran now - priced out of the market along with all of the fossil fuel power stations by the on-going fuel crisis. A new generation of nuclear power stations had been thought to be the answer and, despite environmental concerns, several had been commissioned. Unfortunately, although the sophisticated computerised protection systems built into the nukes kept them safe, they also kept them off-line for most of the time and before long, the country had been reliant on the intermittent qualities of renewable energy systems. Matt recalled the fateful night, five years ago when, in the midst of one of the coldest winters on record, the national grid had finally collapsed and most of the country was blacked out for over three days. Now, electricity rationing was introduced at times of high demand, but unplanned power-cuts were still commonplace – today, working in the power industry made you about as popular as earning a living as a tax inspector.

Of course, it was the politicians who had really taken the flak; the tragedies witnessed during the early blackouts had spurred the government to introduce lucrative incentive schemes for new power generating technologies. Huge investment resulted and soon all sorts of innovative systems came out of the closet. Most of these had been under development for decades but were never going to be commercially viable without major funding.

Sir Richard Harvey, an infamous business magnate renowned for never missing a lucrative investment opportunity, had immediately snapped up the patents behind the entropic generation technology. His corporation had funded the construction of the Degenesys plant and was already investing in a much larger, sister complex in the United States. As the first of the new technologies to realise its potential, Degenesys was a media hot cake. Despite its limited scale, every minister wanted to visit and every newspaper wanted to run a story. Sir Richard, now CEO of Degenesys Ltd, promoted the new technology as the saviour of the power industry and promised the public and politicians alike that electricity rationing would soon be a thing of the past.

A rivulet of sweat ran from Matt's neck and was absorbed by the white collar of his shirt. It wasn't just his previous media exposure that was making him nervous - Matt was one of the few that knew the truth about Degenesys; the prototype plant was suffering a series of small, but potentially critical problems; problems that were bringing into question the very feasibility of the technology. Very few people outside the company were aware of this and today Matt was under clear instructions to try and keep it that way.

Matt jumped when the phone eventually rang and he picked it up to be informed by one of the receptionists that Ms Fox and Mr Boateng were here to see him. He asked for them to be shown up to the conference room and felt a strange, irrational relief that the reporter was a female. Unfortunately for Matt, he had never experienced the journalistic scrutiny of the indomitable Tanya Fox.

The receptionist showed the visitors in and Matt immediately recognised the woman; he'd often seen her reading the news; for some reason he didn't expect an actual newsreader to be interviewing him – but, of course, how else would it work?

Ms Fox strode in and introduced herself, followed by the young man who beamed a smile at Matt as he carried in an array of bags and cases. Tanya Fox was stunning – even more so in real life than on the screen. Her long brown hair was perfectly styled to compliment the shape of her face. Her eyes met his own with a confidence that only truly beautiful people achieved. As she spoke, her lips revealed perfect white teeth framed by an assured smile. Her voice, which of course was her career, was strangely enchanting.

'I'm very pleased to meet you Mr Campbell, my name's Tanya and this is Nic Boateng, my cameraman and assistant. As you know we're here to talk to you about Degenesys.' She swept both hands around in dramatic acknowledgement of her surroundings.

Matt welcomed them both and shook Tanya's hand. 'Please call me Matt.' He said.

'Okay Matt,' she smiled. 'Nic will start setting things up while we have a brief chat. Then I'll ask you a few questions on camera before we have a look around if that's okay?'

Nic had already started work - tripods, lenses, recording equipment and cameras were being assembled and interconnected with speed and dexterity, and all the time the young man kept looking up and smiling so enthusiastically that Matt couldn't help but warm to him.

'So what's your role here Matt?' Tanya asked, studying the room.

'Er, I'm the Production Manager,' Matt said, eyeing the cameras nervously. 'I'm responsible for operations - you know, keeping the plant running.'

'Is it difficult to keep running?' she smiled her bewitching smile again.

'Well, sometimes – we're still commissioning really,' he avoided her eyes. 'Can I get you both a coffee?'

'Not for me,' Nic replied with a distinct African accent. 'Never touch the stuff; caffeine screws up my brain, man.'

Tanya also declined. 'No thanks, I'd rather get on – we've got a lot to do.' She strode around the room admiring the pictures. 'Is it making electricity now?'

'Yes we're generating about fifty megawatts. That's about half full load; unfortunately there's a conveyor out for maintenance.'

Tanya led the conversation for a few minutes, asking questions that Matt guessed were designed to put him at ease. He wondered if she was purposely avoiding anything contentious until she had the cameras on him, but she seemed amicable enough. He expected the reporter would be looking for an angle to spice the story up; nobody was going to be enthralled by a documentary about a power plant, however innovative the technology.

Nic turned away from the camera, stood erect, saluted and smiled his infectious smile. 'Ready for action, guys!'

'Okay, Matt, if you can stand near the wall just to the side of this picture I'll stand here and ask you a few questions about how the plant works and such like. Just relax, try to ignore the camera and look at me.'

No problem there, Mat thought as he assumed his position; the newsreader was beautiful.

'I'm told you have some promotional footage on disk that we can use?'

'Yes, it's ready to run if you want to have a look.'

'Let's do the interview first and see how it might fit in afterwards - are you ready?'

Matt straightened his tie. 'As I'll ever be, I guess.'

The young cameraman gave Tanya the thumbs up and winked.

Tanya faced the camera and made her introduction. 'Today, TVUK visits the first of a new breed of power generating units designed to help solve the on-going energy crisis. The Degenesys plant, near Aylesbury, has recently been awarded the Thomas Edison award for innovation in the power industry. The station has been operating for over three months and we're told it's already meeting the generating needs of over ten thousand homes with no detrimental impact on the environment.' She paused for effect, and then continued. 'I'm Tanya Fox and I have with me today, the plant's Production Manager, Matt Campbell.' She turned towards him. 'Matt, what can you tell us about this new type of power station?'

Matt wiped another bead of sweat from his brow. 'Well, it's more of a recycling plant actually; it's powered by waste material – mainly scrap metal and recycled stuff.' Matt cringed – Stuff? It was only his first sentence and he was already coming across as illiterate. He caught a glimpse of his reflection in the camera lens and saw what looked like a football hooligan staring back – all angular face and shaven head. This is going out on national television, he thought in horror - Matt Campbell, ignorant moron, meet the world!

He pulled himself together and continued. 'The waste is brought in by rail and unloaded into hoppers where conveyor belts deliver the material via a processing plant to the reactor room.'

'Reactor room?' Tanya interrupted. 'Nuclear power had some pretty bad press lately.'

'Nuclear energy is in no way involved; this is a different sort of reaction and there's not even much heat dissipated during the process.'

'So how does it work then - magic?'

Matt was momentarily unnerved by the sarcasm in the reporter's question and suspected she was trying to provoke an unguarded response from him. 'Not exactly,' he replied more carefully, 'although you might have thought so a decade ago.' Matt played safe and quoted the textbook definition. 'Energy is released by entropic-reaction: A process that accelerates the degeneration of materials to their natural state, thereby releasing the energy that was originally used to create them.'

'So how exactly does that happen?' Tanya somehow managed to sound both curious and patronising at the same time.

'Well, the laws of thermodynamics are well understood…'

'Not by me,' she said, looking to the camera and raising her eyebrows.

Matt flushed; his anxiety was slowly giving way to a simmering annoyance. 'Well, by technologists they're pretty well understood,' he countered a little too abruptly. 'One of the laws says that the universe is in a natural state of disorder and apparently it seems to like it that way. Then man comes along and tidies things up. He digs things out of the ground and refines them; he heats things up, melds them together and forms all sorts of wonderful materials and products. However, nature wins in the end because these materials gradually degenerate back to their original components and as they return to their natural state of disorder they slowly release the energy that was used to create them.' Matt worried that it was his turn to sound patronising so he changed track. 'Take the van you arrived in - incredible amounts of energy went into making it – iron ore was mined, then refined to remove the oxides and impurities and then made to react with carbon to form the steel used for the van's body and chassis. Other metals go through an even more complex process to form alloys and super-alloys for the wheels and engine components. However, from the very moment the van rolled off the production line it started to degenerate. Over the next twenty years the body will oxidise, corroding away, back to its original state. The alloys degenerate too, but at a slower rate.'

'So Degenesys makes things rust – that doesn't sound very innovative!'

Her comment interrupted his train of thought for a moment and he glanced nervously at the camera before continuing. 'The reaction's not limited to metal corrosion,' he said. 'Other materials can degenerate and release energy, but as a rule, metals give a better reaction and produce more energy.'

'How exactly does rusting metal create electricity?'

Matt sensed that the newsreader was becoming impatient at his rambling responses and he refocused his mind. 'The natural process of material degeneration is so gradual that the energy transfer rate is negligible. What the entropic-reaction does is simply speed things up. The ability to trigger such rapid degeneration was discovered by scientists working on plasma-confinement techniques. They found that if you create a strong enough magnetic-field at exactly the right frequency, an activation-energy is achieved which initiates the entropic-reaction; we call it a flash – you'll see why later.'

'And that produces electricity... how?'

'Sorry, I am coming to that,' Matt said. 'You see, it was discovered that the reaction itself creates a powerful electromotive-force that can be used to induce an electrical current in a coil. Unfortunately the amount of electricity generated is so small in comparison to the energy used to produce the original magnetic field, that the importance of the discovery was at first overlooked. That was until further experiments showed that the reaction also radiates a reactive wave, which can trigger a chain reaction with other materials and so maintain the process long after the initiating field is turned off. In fact the reaction can be self-maintained indefinitely as long as it can be contained and there is sufficient reactive material available to feed it.' Matt paused, realising that he had probably lost the newsreader in his flurry of jargon. He looked to her for some sort of response.

'This flash…' she began, her eyes scrutinising him. 'How do you know it's safe?'

Matt had anticipated the question. 'The reaction is completely harmless to living creatures,' he said. 'I can show you some footage from the development labs if you want. It shows entropic-reaction reducing a biscuit tin to dust in the blink of an eye. Then, amazingly you see a small white mouse, which you then realise had been inside the tin, wander off unhurt and totally unaware of his ordeal. Apparently it went on to lead a long and normal life. It's a great clip.'

Tanya frowned, clearly unconvinced. 'What about this chain reaction?' Her tone feigned genuine concern. 'Couldn't it get out of hand?'

Matt knew she was pushing for a defensive reaction which might discredit him, but he was determined to stand his ground. 'Outside the confines of the process the reaction will just dissipate - in the worst case scenario I guess your nice Mercedes van in the car park would be failing its next MOT.' Matt immediately realised that such a flippant remark was playing right into her hands so he quickly tried to recover the situation. 'Safety is our primary concern,' he assured her. 'It's been proven that the reaction quickly disperses if it encounters a large mass of entropic material, so an uncontrolled reaction is quite impossible. It has to be contained of course, but compared to nuclear power this is much easier to achieve and far safer. Why not save that question until you see the reactor room – I think you'll be convinced.'

'Fair enough,' she said nonchalantly, apparently satisfied at having achieved her goal, 'What happens next in the process?'

Released from her scrutiny at last, Matt felt he had weathered the storm and some of his confidence returned. 'That's the clever part. The amount of electricity produced from the reaction is small and unsuitable for connecting to the distribution network so we store it in regenerative fuel cells. The electrical energy produced in the reactor room is converted into chemical potential energy by charging two liquid electrolyte solutions and then the energy is released via a converter and transformer when we need it. The amount of stored power is only limited by the volume of the electrolytes. You probably noticed the two storage tanks as you drove in, one contains sodium polysulphide, the other…'

'Sodium bromide,' Tanya interrupted. 'Quite a nasty substance; exactly how much do you store here?'

Matt felt as if his face had just been slapped – the newsreader had done her research all right - she might even know more about the plant than he did. Then he remembered the cameras and continued with as much composure as he could muster. 'I can assure you the chemicals are safe,' he said. 'Double skinned tanks and full bunding; every precaution has been taken...'

She interrupted again. 'I understand that you suffered incidents of sabotage during commissioning,' her brown eyes pierced him. 'Tell me, Matt - at any point was the integrity of the main protection systems at risk?'

Suddenly, Matt felt like a caged animal, as if the cameras were bars and this woman was teasing him with a stick. He was digging himself a hole and she knew it. 'There were a number of problems during commissioning, but that's to be expected with a prototype technology. The only incident of sabotage was when we first energised the plant and found some cables had been vandalised.'

'You mean nails had been driven into just about every high voltage cable on site – I heard the short circuits even caused an explosion?'

'There was a small fire,' Matt corrected, 'but there was never a risk of it escalating and nobody was ever in danger...'

'The question is - who was behind the incident? What if next time the bromide tank is targeted? We're only a mile from Aylesbury aren't we?'

'That's ridiculous,' Matt countered. 'Sodium bromide is hardly the most dangerous substance on earth. They store chlorine at the local swimming pool and that's a far more hazardous chemical.'

'But they probably don't have terrorists operating there, do they Matt?'

'We're not talking about terrorism here,' Matt felt his voice rising and his shirt collar was clinging to his neck. 'The cables were spiked on the day that our electrical contractor laid off most of its workers. A cable-puller with a grudge almost certainly caused the damage.' Matt sensed the camera's lens boring into his very soul. 'Can we have a break? I need a coffee.' He walked away from the camera and poured himself a cup.

Tanya joined him. 'Matt, you'll have to forgive me for pushing the safety issue but it's what the public are interested in. I promise the report won't over-dramatise anything. TVUK is a responsible network and I guarantee you'll be happy with the final cut and if you're not, we can edit it. I do need to ask the questions though.'

'Okay, but I want a chance to comment before the final film is submitted and I might need to have it cleared at a higher level, Sir Richard even. If that's not acceptable, it stops here right now.'

'It's a deal.' Tanya smiled. 'Now let's have a look around.'

Chapter 2

Twenty-five miles away in a café called the "Seven Spires" on Oxford's George Street, Glyn Cooper sipped a cappuccino and looked out onto the damp pavement at the miserable masses shuffling by. Glyn longed for the warmer weather to return so that he could sit outside on the terrace again and watch the people strolling along in the sunshine. It seemed to Glyn that nobody in the city ever looked happy, but he supposed somebody out there must be content with their lives even if they didn't show it.

Glyn was feeling far from content; he was still hacked off at being overlooked for the Production Manager job at the new power plant in Aylesbury. Having to swallow his pride and settle for a Team Leader position; a job he was clearly over-qualified for, still rankled him. Not that he had anything against the guy who had been selected; Matt Campbell seemed technically competent and was a decent man in Glyn's experience. In fact, he had even come to think of Matt as a friend, despite the bitterness he felt. Not a close friend of course, because Matt was his manager and tended to keep his personal life to himself, but they'd had the odd drink together and Glyn trusted the guy, which is what mattered in his opinion. What really niggled Glyn was the nature of Matt's appointment - despite having the least experience of all of the applicants; Sir Richard had taken an immediate shine to him and had appointed him on the spot. Glyn suspected it was Matt's "come-what-may" attitude that had impressed Sir Richard. The pompous idiot had mistaken Matt's nonchalance for some sort of self-assuredness or strength of character, but that couldn't have been further from the truth. Glyn knew that Matt had never really wanted the responsibility of such a senior position and hated the thought of managing people, Glyn was aware of this because his senior colleague had confided in him after one too many shandies after their first public exhibition. 'I'm just not that trustworthy,' Matt had slurred. 'I don't intentionally let people down, but it always seems to happen, I don't know why. My last girlfriend said I suffered from "commitmentphobia", before slamming the door never to be seen again.'

Of course Matt had taken the job once offered, but Glyn suspected he was regretting it now. The Degenesys project was in serious trouble and when the crap eventually hit, Matt would undoubtedly take the lion's share of the blame. At this very moment "Mister Come What May" had the unenviable task of trying to convince a TV crew that everything was fine and dandy at the plant. The poor guy must know that whatever he says on camera is bound to come back a thousand times to haunt him; Glyn smiled at the thought and felt immediately guilty, but why should he? Strong leadership was needed at times like this and everyone could see that Matt lacked leadership qualities – surely Sir Richard and his cronies could see that? Still, they had missed their chance and they wouldn't get a second one; it was time for Glyn to move on and find a job where his talents would be properly recognised.

He glanced at his watch – five past two - less than six hours until the next shift and Glyn still hadn't had any sleep yet. Still, if things worked out, this might be his last set of nights at the plant. Not that he hated the hours; starting the first shift on a Wednesday night wasn't too bad after a four-day weekend. The rota at Degenesys was one of the best that he had worked; the mixture of twelve-hour shifts - mornings and nights - gave him plenty of days off in between. But, whatever the perks, Glyn had made up his mind. He was going to leave; it was a matter of principle - pure and simple.

    Glyn scanned the street again; he was waiting for a man called Frank Veron, apparently some sort of head-hunter who had had the audacity to call the control room one evening and ask for Glyn personally. He wondered if the timing of the approach had been something more than a coincidence; Glyn's frustration was common knowledge and everybody knew how ambitious he was.

    A pretty young waitress moved from table to table, smiling and chatting with customers as she served coffee. Glyn noticed she paid particular attention to a table by the door where two young men were unashamedly flirting with her.

    Glyn looked out of the window again and spotted a man walking across the road from the direction of the cinema, heading towards the café. He was immaculately dressed in chinos, a cord jacket and an open necked shirt. Glyn had not met Frank before so he did not know exactly what to expect, but the man's clothes looked expensive, if a little too casual for such a meeting. However, for some reason he knew the person striding towards the Seven Spires was indeed the mysterious Frank and he was soon proved to be correct. On entering the café, the man caught Glyn's eye and immediately came over offering his hand. Glyn, a naturally suspicious person, was curious as to how the guy had so quickly selected him from at least half a dozen potential clients sitting in the café, but the intuitive recognition had been mutual and any dubious thought left him as soon as the man spoke.

'Nice to meet you Glyn, I'm Frank Veron from CEA consulting; it's a bit like the CIA but a lot more exciting!' He grinned confidently and sat down. 'So what's happening my man?'

Frank's jovial manner immediately irritated Glyn; he was tired and didn't need to be with some guy with flash clothes and an over-enthusiastic smile. 'What's happening is I'm on nights and should really be in bed, so what do you want to talk about?

'All in good time my man.' Frank spotted the waitress and caught her attention, 'When you're ready sweetheart,' he called over to her, flashing his annoying grin before returned his attention to Glyn. 'So, how's Degenesys going?'

'Pretty good,' Glyn lied. 'A few teething problems, as you'd expect, but nothing we can't handle.'

'Really, that's not what I heard,' Frank looked bemused. 'When's the reliability run due to end? It must be well behind schedule.'

Glyn was surprised at the question. The man might be a bit showy, but he was obviously well informed; perhaps he had something to offer after all. 'You're right,' Glyn conceded. 'To be honest I don't think we'll ever get the plant running properly; there's just too much to go wrong.'

'Perhaps you need to consider your exit strategy before it's too late,' Frank lowered his voice. 'You know why I'm here; I represent an international energy group who've seen your CV and liked what they saw.'

'Who is it?'

'I'm afraid I'm not allowed to discuss my client at this stage but if I give you some details about the position you'll probably be able to put two and two together.' Frank handed Glyn an envelope.

The pretty waitress appeared at their table and asked what Frank would like. Glyn anticipated some sexist comment but it never came; instead Frank just smiled at the girl and ordered an orange juice – the man was in business mode. The waitress wiggled herself off to the kitchen and as she passed her admirers' table she giggled at some unheard comment. As soon as she disappeared into the kitchen the two young men exploded with laughter.

Glyn opened the envelope and unfolded a single sheet of paper. On it was a brief job description and a summary of terms and conditions. Glyn couldn't believe his eyes; the salary was twice his current one, and for what looked like a very similar role. 'Where the hell is this job? Iran?'

Frank smiled; Iranian power stations were regular targets for Israeli air strikes of late and any engineer with a death wish could earn a fortune over there. 'No not Iran - nice location on the south coast actually. Are you interested?'

'It's tempting, but unfortunately I have a contract with Degenesys.' Glyn said. 'I can't let them down just because things aren't going so well.' This might be a once in a lifetime opportunity, but he wasn't going to give flash Frank an easy time of it.

'Look, it's a bit difficult because I'm not allowed to say too much until we know you're on board, but you've probably guessed from the description that the job's on a new-build nuclear plant.'

'I'm not surprised, for that money,' Glyn said. 'I didn't think the government had sanctioned any more nukes.'

'Well, all consents are currently on hold, but the plant in question was nearing completion when the government pulled the plug. The investors are in turmoil; they're banking on a policy change otherwise they face financial disaster. In the mean time they have to keep their options open and that includes attracting and retaining key staff to commission the plant quickly if and when the constraints are lifted. That's where you come in.'

'So it's a might be job,' Glyn said, annoyed that this whole charade was turning out to be a waste of his time - time when he could be getting some much needed sleep. 'If and when the project gets the go ahead, your people will expect me, and others I suppose, to immediately jump ship and get them out of trouble.' Glyn wanted out of Degenesys now, not in six months' time.

'Degenesys will fail,' Frank said with a certainty that Glyn found a little disconcerting, 'and when it does, my man, you'll be out of a job.' He leaned forward and lifted the unlit candle from the table. 'We're turning into a third-world country, Glyn. For Christ's sake, we're having to rely on candles again! You don't see the bloody French investing billions of euros in renewable energy or tinpot technologies like Degenesys. They've made nuclear power efficient and reliable and now their economy's the strongest in Europe. Sir Richard Harvey and his corporation are getting rich on government grants, while the country's going down the pan. Face it Glyn, if you're not part of the solution, you're part of the problem – join us and help us keep the bloody lights on!'

Glyn was taken aback by Frank's passion. 'So what's the deal? He asked.

'Well, as you already know the terms are very good,' Frank replied, 'but the offer's actually much better than you think.'

'Go on - don't tell me there's a might be company car with the package?'

Frank didn't seem to register the sarcasm. 'Actually they're offering a substantial down-payment.'

The waitress suddenly reappeared and placed Frank's fruit juice on the table in front of him. 'Can I get either of you anything else?' she asked sweetly.

'Nothing thanks,' Glyn snapped; he was impatient to know more about the offer.

When the girl had gone, Frank continued. 'In fact there are two down-payments, one now and one if the consents are granted and you start work.'

'How much?' Glyn asked. Things were definitely getting interesting.

'Ten thousand pounds when you sign up, followed by a further ten thousand when you commence employment. You have no commitment unless the plant is sanctioned and as soon as it is - the job's yours!'

'Ten grand for doing nothing - no commitment at all? They must be insane!'

'Not insane, my man – desperate! There's a lot at stake; it makes sense if you think about it.'

'I don't need to think about it, where do I sign?'

'Okay, let's meet here again on Monday morning after your night shifts. I'll bring your contract and ten thousand good reasons for you to be happy.'

Frank was grinning again, but now Glyn didn't find it at all annoying and grinned back heartily. 'Okay,' he said, 'Great... see you on Monday then.'

Frank stood up. 'Have a good day, my man' he was already making for the door, but then he paused and turned round with a quizzical look on his face. 'I suppose this puts you in an unusual situation; if you manage to get Degenesys through its reliability run and make it a success, then the government won't be under any pressure to sanction my client's plant. On the other hand, if you fail and things continue to go wrong, you'll probably end up in a better job. Ironic isn't it?' That grin again. 'Still I suppose either way you can't lose.' At this, Frank turned one last time and left the café.

As Glyn watched Frank cross George Street and head back towards the cinema, he was left with the unpleasant feeling that he could in fact, very easily lose. He could lose out on one of the best opportunities he had ever had. All of a sudden the prospect of tonight's shift left Glyn completely deflated; he badly needed some sleep and time to think. Glyn finished his coffee and got up from his chair. He dropped a few coins into the saucer, picked up the envelope and left the café.

Back in Aylesbury, the news crew had left the Degenesys boardroom and now that they were touring the site, Matt's home territory, he was feeling much more in control. Tanya Fox had shown polite interest in the conveyor systems and material processing plant but hadn't asked any searching questions. They now looked down from a gantry onto the vast array of fuel cells that stored the electricity. Matt explained that each one consisted of a latticework of chambers through which the two electrolytes flowed, separated in each cell by a special membrane through which electrically charged ions could pass. He said that the modules were connected electrically in series to provide the necessary voltage and additional strings were added in parallel to give the power rating of the plant. The newsreader was clearly impressed by the complexity of the interconnecting electrical bus-bars and the intricately meandering lengths of hydraulic pipe-work, but thankfully hadn't questioned the reliability of such a complex process. Matt was well aware that the system didn't need saboteurs - it was complicated enough to create its own problems.

    They moved on to the control room where Nic took some footage of the operating staff and monitoring equipment and then Matt led them through double doors into the main reactor hall. In the centre of the hall stood a huge dome with a large convex viewing window built into its surface. Computer monitors surrounded the window and to its side, a short tunnel protruded and ended in a hatch, which allowed entry to the dome's interior. It would have resembled a giant igloo if it hadn't been for the myriad of conveyor systems, ventilation ducts and power cables that fed the dome like a thousand umbilical cords.

    Matt led them to the viewing window and Tanya was visibly surprised when she spotted a technician actually inside the dome, filling out what looked like a pink check-sheet on a clipboard. Behind the technician was the most amazingly impressive machine.

Matt described what they were seeing. 'As you can see the reactor consists of a bed-plate which supports a slowly rotating ring of ceramic chambers each one connected to its neighbour by a conduit. As the device rotates, the chambers enter the fuel hopper system at one end and the field generator at the other.'

The field generator was massive and looked incredibly complicated. Seven laminated frames, golden in colour, protruded from a central sphere so that from the top it would have looked like a seven-pointed star. Each frame's many laminations were clamped together by hundreds of metallic looking bolts. Cooling pipes and cables projected from every angle.

'Do you want to go inside?' Matt asked. 'It's perfectly safe, but I'm afraid you'll have to change into some special clothes and leave the cameras outside.'

'Why can't we film inside, man?' Nic whined. 'I mean, if that thing's as safe as you say?'

'Against procedure, I'm afraid; you see the outer dome acts as a secondary containment area. The reaction takes place within the ceramic modules but as a precaution the dome's walls are made of the same insulating material as the modules and are designed to contain the reaction if for some reason one of them should fail. As a further precaution, no reactive materials are allowed into the dome. That includes ordinary clothing which could be damaged by the reaction; the overalls worn by the technician are made of special inert materials, but we have spare suits for visitors.'

Tanya decided that footage of her entering the dome taken through the viewing window would make a good shot so, despite some apprehension, she accepted the offer. Nic was left to position the cameras whilst Matt and Tanya disappeared into nearby changing rooms and soon returned wearing the special overalls.

Matt pressed a button to the side of the access door and it slid open with a hiss. 'The doors are pneumatically operated and interlocked with each other, a bit like an air lock.' Tanya followed him into the first chamber and Matt pressed a second button. The door behind them closed, something beeped and a second door hissed open. As it did, Tanya was clearly taken aback by the sudden, albeit subtle, change in the atmosphere. The air felt charged somehow, as if an electrical storm was brewing. The door was obviously well soundproofed because the increase in noise was surprising. The equipment's loud steady hum was interrupted by a repetitive whooshing noise, like the sound of waves on a beach.

'I can smell …coffee,' Tanya remarked, raising her voice in order to be heard.

'It's a result of the entropic-reaction; nobody seems to know why,' Matt shouted. 'The humming noise is coming from the reactor coil. It's de-energised now, but electrical power is being induced into a secondary winding by the reaction – that's what charges the fuel cells. It's much louder on start-up and we have to wear specially made ear defenders before entering.'

'Is that whooshing sound the entropic-reaction?' Tanya asked.

'Yes, if you look at the capsules as they enter the coil you can just make out red pulses in phase with the sound. A healthy reaction emits a dull red flash, which can be seen through the opaque ceramic material of the capsule.'

'Some flashes seem stronger than others,' Tanya observed. She had noticed that although the red glow was synchronised with the sound and quite regular, the brightness and the amplitude was far from uniform.

'Well spotted,' Matt shouted above the din. 'The size of the reaction depends upon two things; the mass of the fuel fed into the module and its specific entropic value. The processing plant does more than transform the scrap material into a suitable form for module delivery; it continually scans the conveyors to monitor the composition of the material being delivered. It's designed to convey only the correct amount of fuel to each module. However, there's another factor that affects the reaction, and one that can't easily be measured. For some reason, much more energy is released from a material that has only recently been manufactured - older materials trigger a much smaller entropic-reaction.'

Tanya looked intrigued. 'Why would that be?'

'Don't ask me, even the scientists can't explain it; it's as if energy gets locked into a substance after a period of time. For this reason fossil fuels don't react at all, despite having high entropic values, simply because they were created so long ago. Sometimes, even old metals pass through the process completely unscathed - this inconsistency is the cause of the fluctuating reaction. However, it makes no difference to the process because the released energy is stored in the fuel cells before distribution.'

'What if too much fuel is delivered to one of the capsules?' Tanya asked. 'Is there a risk that the module could overload?'

'No - we can safely degenerate even newly formed super-alloys, which are highly reactive. Each module is designed to contain a reaction even when packed with a material of the highest entropic value and don't forget, in the unlikely event that a failure did occur, the outer dome is designed to confine the reaction and even if the dome itself were somehow breached, the reaction would simply dissipate in the mass of the surrounding building.' Matt smiled his most endearing smile. 'Believe me, the process is completely failsafe!'

Tanya's face was expressionless as she scanned the interior of the dome and Matt knew she was struggling to find fault with the sophisticated protection systems on display. She looked out of the viewing window at the cameraman and Nic smiled back, giving her the thumbs up; then he pointed to his watch and Tanya took one more look around before reluctantly nodding in response. She turned to Matt and said, 'Okay, I think we've got enough interior footage, can we wrap up with a final session outside the dome?'

'No problem,' Matt replied and he felt an overwhelming relief as he initiated the door sequence.

As Matt watched the Mercedes van draw up to the security building on its way to leave site, he wondered whether he could really trust the newsreader to give an unbiased report. Tanya was obviously no fool and had given him quite a hard time in the conference room, but her inquisitive personality had somehow grown on him during the site tour. Matt could tell that she had been fishing for something contentious to report, but he didn't think he had given her any unnecessary ammunition. He was just glad that she had not delved any further into the reliability statistics, but perhaps she had already read between the lines. Nobody outside of the company knew that it took so much power to start the process that the plant had to operate at full load for at least a week before it achieved a positive energy return. So far Matt's team had failed to achieve more than five days continuous operation before something had failed, meaning the whole system had to be restarted. Operating costs were escalating and if reliability didn't improve soon, the Degenesys plant would be closed down and the project terminated. Matt wondered if the pretty newsreader suspected this and whether Tanya Fox would return one day soon to delve a bit deeper. Then he realised that some part of him almost hoped that she would.

Chapter 3

Arthur Wiseman studied his reflection in the mirror. The eyes staring back at him might well have belonged to a stranger; they were dull and lifeless - like a shark's. His long straight hair was greasy-dark and his beard was matted with filth but his lean face, despite the scarring, still looked regal to Arthur - akin to Aragorn in Peter Jackson's film version of Lord of the Rings. Arthur had never seen the movie of course (too many voices), but he remembered being drawn to a poster in one of the towns he had visited before his imprisonment. That was a long time ago now, but Arthur still remembered feeling great affinity for the character on the poster. Ironically, the title of the film was - The Return of the King.

'You know there are men behind the mirror.' The voice came from inside his head.

'Yes, I can feel them,' Arthur whispered. 'They have no respect.'

'They are scared of you – what you might do.'

'No, they do not fear me - they feel only pity.'

'Your time is coming Arthur; soon they will pay.'

Arthur knew this to be true; for as long as he could remember, he had lived under the influence of others - people in control who had no concept of his real identity or the gifts he possessed. He craved for his day of destiny, when he would come to power and have dominance over these people. He felt something was about to change around him, something big. He had always been able to sense such things; changes in the weather, floods and earthquakes, sometimes even wars. This time the change was closer and would affect him personally; when it did, whatever it was would finally return his dignity.

He turned away from the mirror and walked across the small room towards the only window. He looked out onto the spacious grounds of Hareford House, which were laid out as gardens. Beyond a neat drive, a large cricket green extended to a distant line of trees. Through a gap in the trees he could make out a field with horses. The horizon was tinged with orange; it would rain today but the night had been clear and the grass still showed the signs of an overnight frost; it was still very cold for March. Arthur yearned to be outside, to be able to walk free under that sky, or better still to ride. He loved horses; in a happier time he had worked with them, tending stables for a local landowner. Horses had dignity and Arthur respected them, but when he rode, he had mastery over them and they followed his commands without question. Horses did not judge him and their thoughts never dishonoured him – unlike their masters.

Arthur turned back to the room; a single table with two chairs stood in its centre. He visualised taking one of the chairs and throwing it at the mirror but he knew that the furniture would be secured to the floor and the mirror, like the small window behind him, would be specially reinforced. Arthur sat down on one of the chairs and waited.

Eventually the door opened and a man in a white coat entered. 'Good morning Arthur, how are you feeling now?' The doctor sighed when Arthur didn't respond and sat down opposite him. 'Look, when you refuse your medication you become very ill - you know that!'

Arthur ignored the words, but listened instead to the man's thoughts as he studied his face. Dr Hollins didn't look like a psychiatrist; he must have been in his fifties but was still a powerful man. His trim moustache was dark, as was the line of hair, which ran from his bottom lip to just below his thickset chin - too fine to be classified a beard. His glasses, apparently not required for this situation, were parked high up on his head. The skin around his eyes crinkled as he smiled, but Arthur was not fooled by the doctor's kindly face or by the fact that his mind appeared to radiate genuine concern. He had learnt that the doctor was cunning and capable of disguising his true thoughts. The man knew that Arthur was dangerous and he planned to use the medicine to disarm him. Arthur felt the urge to grab the doctor's fat throat and squeeze the life out of him; he nearly made his move, but just as he tensed his body to attack, the inner voice spoke to him again, urging caution.

'Others are watching from behind the mirror Arthur, and you remain weak from the poison they feed you – you must bide your time.'

The voice of Merlin had been guiding Arthur for most of his life and he feared the day that it might eventually desert him. One by one, the other voices had left over the years, but Merlin had remained. Some of the others used to antagonise him and encourage him to do bad things; sometimes they urged him to kill himself, but Merlin was loyal to Arthur and had driven them away. The wizard had stayed with him because their relationship was special, spanning many centuries, for surely he was Arthur, son of Uther Pendragon, King of Britain and Merlin had helped him survive a world where those around him plotted to prevent him from gaining his rightful throne. The poison they forced down him banished Merlin from Arthur's mind and also prevented him from understanding his captors' real intentions, their true thoughts. This made Arthur vulnerable.

'You hurt Lindsay very seriously Arthur, do you remember?' the doctor tried again.

Arthur suddenly lurched forwards. 'She took my books!' he snarled, spittle spraying from his mouth.

The doctor jumped back and Arthur felt the feigned compassion turn to fear. He sensed movement behind the mirror but it quietened again when Arthur settled back into his chair, smiling.

'The books were not helping you, Arthur,' the doctor continued, his cheeks flushed and his voice unsteady. 'Medieval torture and ancient warfare is not exactly suitable reading material for someone with your condition; Lindsay was trying to help you.'

'She poisons me!'

'The medicine is important - do you really want to go back to the high security hospital?'

Arthur knew the doctor was trying to mislead him, they had already decided to transfer him; it was inevitable from the moment he had bitten the nurse's face. All they wanted was for him to accept their so-called medicine without a fight.

The inner voice spoke again. 'They are going to drive me away again Arthur, but I will return, I promise,' Merlin said. 'Take your chance when it comes - remember who you are.'

Arthur looked at the doctor with his dead eyes and smiled as he silently told the man that soon he was going to eat his heart. Perhaps the doctor's subconscious mind registered the threat, but he only heard the spoken words, 'I'll take your medicine if you return my books.'

Doctor Marston hoped to God that he wasn't going to puke. He hadn't suffered from travel sickness since he was a child, but being cooped up in the back of this van, sitting opposite a man whose obvious attributes did not include personal hygiene was nothing less than a living nightmare. He hoped that once they were off the moors there would be a few less bends in the road and he would start to feel better. When Marston was a boy, his father used to tell him that fixing his eyes on a point on the horizon would stop him from feeling unwell, but for obvious reasons this particular vehicle was devoid of windows.

The large, sweating man sitting opposite was from hospital security and the ignorant oaf had not said a single word since leaving Hareford's psychiatric ward. At first the man's size had made Marston feel more comfortable because the patient they were escorting had a reputation for violence. Now, he couldn't help thinking that the amount of odour a body emits must be directly proportional to the same body's surface area. Someone should really tell this guy he has a problem – although Marston admitted that that someone would have to be extremely brave to do so. He thought about starting a conversation with the man, but the guard's eyes kept closing as if he were about to fall asleep so Marston thought better of it and turned instead to check on the patient. Arthur Wiseman was still slumped in his wheelchair, a line of spittle running down his scarred chin into his beard. The patient rolled his head and muttered something unintelligible before falling still again. Marston realised the sedatives were beginning to wear off. Not that it mattered, they would have completed their journey long before he regained full consciousness and anyway, the man was well strapped in. Nonetheless the young psychiatrist was on edge - he was still learning the psychiatric ropes at Rampton, Nottinghamshire's High Security Hospital, and this was the first time had had been asked to escort such a volatile patient. He looked down at his medical case and considered its contents; if the worst came to the worst he would use the extra sedative. It was normal procedure to carry a pre-loaded syringe, but he also knew an overdose could seriously harm the patient so he would only use it as a last resort.

Marston had travelled to North Yorkshire yesterday evening and although the hotel had been comfortable enough he hadn't slept particularly well; he never did in hotels. He opened the case, removed a folder and tried to read the patient's notes but looking down just made him feel worse. He was so nauseous now that he wondered if the prawns he had eaten the night before had been okay. He even thought about buzzing the driver on the intercom to ask him to steady his driving but decided that it wouldn't look very professional. Marston closed his eyes and tried to remember what he had been told about the patient.

Dr Hollins had briefed him thoroughly on Arthur Wiseman's condition. He was a forty-two year old psychopathic schizophrenic, extremely intelligent, but with delusional tendencies and was first sectioned under the mental health act at the age of nineteen following a dramatic suicide attempt. The young man had soaked himself in petrol at a village firework display before running full bore to meet Guy Fawkes on the bonfire. Luckily there were enough people there to pull him from the fire and douse the flames, but he had been seriously burned all the same. Once he had recovered sufficiently from his injuries, Arthur was sent to a psychiatric hospital where he was prescribed various anti-psychotic drugs. His condition had at first responded well to the medication and, during his twenties, Arthur had been released on several occasions, but each time he had ended up back in hospital following some setback or another. The problem was not an unusual one with schizophrenics, when feeling better they didn't feel the need to take their medication and those of a paranoid disposition rarely believed their psychiatrists had their interests at heart and so mistrusted any prescription. Initially Arthur had been sectioned for his own safety, but his condition had deteriorated until eventually the internments were made to protect the public. Over the years Arthur's tendency to violence had increased in line with his delusional fantasies. Now, even on heavy doses of medicine, he was a frightening and very dangerous individual.

  Procedures for transporting high-risk inmates between hospitals are well established and Marston was well versed in the safety and security section of the National Health Service Act. Following protocol, after the initial briefing, Doctor Marston had been introduced to the patient and it was explained that, with the patient's consent, Arthur would be searched and then sedated for the journey. The patient, as expected, had not responded in any way to this request, but instead had unsettled Marston throughout the induction by staring at him with his dull expressionless eyes. Hollins' warning that the patient was extremely perceptive had not prepared Marston for the uncomfortable feeling that Arthur Wiseman was analysing him, almost as if he were reading his mind.

The refusal of consent, implied by the patient's silence, meant that the Responsible Medical Officer, in this case Doctor Hollins, had to justify and authorise, forced-sedation and deliver it with regard to the patient's dignity. Doctor Hollins had filled out the necessary forms and personally administered the injection in a private room.

Following Arthur's sedation Hollins had sat down with Marston and together they reviewed the standard risk assessment for patient transfer and agreed the controls necessary to ensure the safety of both the patient and his escorts. The senior doctor had been strangely subdued during this process and at least once had paused, looking bemused. It was the sort of look Marston's mother used to have on holiday when trying to remember if she'd actually turned the cooker off before leaving home. In the end, Marston, the junior psychiatrist had taken the lead and completed the assessment himself. The process was intended to establish procedures for control in the event of breakdown, road traffic accident, attempted escape or unforeseen violent acts. Unfortunately they hadn't considered chronic travel sickness.

Marston was on the brink of dozing off when another powerful bout of nausea caught him. He opened his eyes and to his horror he noticed Arthur was now fully conscious and staring directly at him - glaring with a menace that he had never before witnessed in a human being. Marston, at first couldn't look away, transfixed like a rabbit caught in headlights. The young doctor remembered his training; never stare them in the eye, never touch them and don't ever turn your back. With an effort he averted his eyes and leaned over to the guard intending to wake him. He never made it though, because a terrible stomach cramp caused him to double over in pain. His head swam and he realised he was finally going to puke. He stood as best he could in the moving van turning one way and then the other not knowing quite what to do. Marston's movement was enough to rouse the security guard just in time for Marston to spray vomit all over him. The guard was horrified; he jumped up with an incredulous look on his face and without thinking, backed away towards the front of the van where Arthur sat in his wheelchair. Marston just had time to see the huge man fall backwards into Arthur's lap before he was crippled with another cramp. Kneeling on all fours on the floor of the van, Marston retched uncontrollably. Despite this, he still had the presence of mind to crawl towards the intercom and was about to press the emergency button when the huge mass of the security guard hit him full in the back and crushed him to the floor. The nausea suddenly disappeared, but Marston was badly winded and struggled to move under the weight of the man on top of him. The driver must have felt the commotion because Marston could feel the van braking hard and vomit ran past his face towards the wheels of Arthur's chair. Mixing with it in alarming quantities was what he could only assume to be the security guard's blood. Twisting further, Marston saw that the side of the guard's throat had been ripped open, apparently by the patient's own teeth. He turned his head towards Arthur and caught the terrifying sight of the lunatic frantically struggling against his straps. Amazingly, one of his hands was already nearly free and Marston realised that they were both in a terrifying race to see who would be first to escape from his individual predicament. Marston guessed that the consequence of him losing the race was immense - but unfortunately, losing seemed inevitable. Arthur was struggling with the strength of the madman he was and Marston was still winded, too weak to escape from under the massive body that trapped him. He stopped to think, trying to keep calm; his only hope was that the driver would somehow intervene, but he knew that procedures would be followed and the rear doors to the van would not be opened without due consideration. Then Marston saw his medical case and without any real plan he pulled it towards himself and opened it, spilling the contents onto the floor. Paperwork quickly soaked into the putrid, bloody mess. Plastic zip ties - used to restrain patients, but useless in this situation - fell around him, and the syringe primed with sedatives bounced on the metal floor and came to rest just out of reach.

Time stood still.

Arthur paused in his frantic struggle and Marston stopped to catch his breath. Both competitors looked towards the syringe. Then Marston managed to lever his foot against one of the wheel-arches and slowly pushed forward. As his outstretched hand closed upon the syringe, Marston thought that he caught the sound of church bells ringing in the distance. Perplexed, he looked back towards Arthur; the madman was still motionless, staring at the syringe as if mesmerised. Then

Arthur's eyes refocused on Marston, boring into his soul and freezing his spine, their evil intent almost unbearable. Then the nausea returned and for the first time Marston realised that Arthur had somehow been the source all along. The dull lifeless eyes stared unrelentingly and Marston's head began to ache. He tried to turn away but couldn't; then he noticed that his own hand, the one holding the syringe, was moving uncontrollably towards him. Marston started to panic, staring now, not at Arthur but at the needle moving steadily towards his face. His whole body shook except for the advancing arm, which might easily have belonged to another person. Helplessly, Marston felt the needle sink into his own neck and he remembered no more.

Chapter 4

Glyn Cooper forced a smile as one of his colleagues meandered his way towards the inevitable punch line of the story he was telling. Jim Brown was a fellow Shift Team Leader at the Degenesys Plant and was quite popular with the other staff, but Glyn liked to avoid him when he had a drink in his hand. Any kind of alcoholic potion seemed to transform the guy into an attention-seeking bore. He was describing how he had ruined his best pair of trainers one night, having forgotten to change them for inert footwear before entering the entropic reaction dome. It was one of those stories that seemed to go on forever but Glyn held on, half listening and half planning how he would make an excuse to leave as soon the story ended. Jim's audience comprised half a dozen shift workers from the plant and the two girls who worked in reception. Glyn scanned their faces for signs that they too were weary of Jim's epic yarn, but every pair of eyes were glued to the animated story-teller as they patiently awaited the climax.

'Honestly, it was sole destroying!' Jim brayed as the group erupted in laughter, but Glyn's mind was elsewhere and he missed the punch line. Having never been successful in delivering a convincing false laugh, he just smiled and shook his head, as if Jim's humour never ceased to amaze him.

'Come on Glyn,' Jim said to him. 'Cheer up! We're supposed to be celebrating here!' This morning had ended the twentieth problem-free shift of continuous operation at Degenesys, which finally marked the end of the reliability run and the impromptu party was inevitable after the pressure they had all endured over the recent weeks.

'Sorry Jim, I've still not recovered from my night shifts,' he said, downing his beer. 'Honestly, I've never known tension like it. Still, it all came together in the end! Who wants a refill?'

Nobody was quite ready for another drink so Glyn made his escape towards the bar; on his way he paused at the digital music station and viewed the play list - a mixture of chart hits and retro classics as was the fashion. Bob Marley was currently banging out "Stir it up", a hit from way back in the eighties. Glyn punched in his ID and downloaded a couple of his own favourite tracks, then pressed the shuffle button before wandering over to join a small group of men at the bar. Among them, Matt Campbell stood holding a bunch of empty glasses whilst Eddie Coleman, the Engineering Manager, tried to attract the barmaid's attention. Glyn could see that Eddie was not having much luck so he moved alongside to help draw the girl's attention.

'Hi G...Glyn,' Eddie said. 'Assuming I ever g...get served - can I g...get you a drink?'

'Yeah, thanks - I'll have a pint of lager.'

'I bet you never thought we'd see the day,' Matt said. 'How many re-starts on your shift?'

'Twenty-four in total! Not that I'm counting,' Glyn laughed and this time it felt more natural; perhaps his mood was finally lifting. He was at last coming to terms with Matt's dubious appointment and despite some of the terrible things Glyn had done over the last few days, he still felt part of the Degenesys team and proud of its achievements. He offered

Matt a fist in a gesture of camaraderie and Matt followed suit so that their knuckles met. 'We've snatched victory from the jaws of defeat.' Glyn declared.

'And you, my friend, are one of the heroes,' Matt grinned. 'As of today, Degenesys is officially a success!'

Glyn was already resigned to the fact that Frank Veron's lucrative contract would now be terminated and although he had clearly missed a great opportunity, Glyn was kind of relieved. He still had the ten grand in his bank account, but he had already decided that he would return the other envelope – the much, much thicker one that Frank had offered him the next time that they had met.

Their second meeting at the Seven Spires had not turned out quite as Glyn had expected. Frank had arrived at the George Street café immaculately dressed as before, but this time carrying a military-style Goretex rucksack. From the bag, he had pulled a contract of employment and an envelope containing twenty, crisp fifty-pound notes.

'Here's your retainer, as agreed,' Frank had said. 'Read the contract, sign it and return it to the address on the envelope.' Franks grin had been nowhere to be seen. 'Now, my man, how about really being part of the solution?'

When Glyn had asked what he meant, Frank had drawn a second envelope from the rucksack and pushed it across the table. 'Another fifty grand for you to hurry things along.'

It turned out that the rucksack had contained more than just envelopes. Inside had been what had looked like three small thermos flasks. 'Don't worry,' Frank had said in response to Glyn's reaction, 'they're not bombs, just some clever little devices to cause a bit of a disruption.'

Frank had explained that the flasks contained some harmless, but extremely reactive material that couldn't be detected by the processing plant's scanners because of the special containers. All Glyn had to do was occasionally drop one into a waste hopper so that it would find its way through to the reactor where it would inevitably overload and damage one of the modules. Glyn knew that if a module failed, the repair time would be anything up to a week, plus they only carried a single spare module and the lead time to manufacture more would be several months at least.

Glyn was not entirely sure why he had accepted the envelope and taken the Goretex rucksack. He couldn't imagine purposely sabotaging the plant for all the money in the world, but somehow it had seemed the right thing to do. There was absolutely no rule preventing staff from dropping material in the hoppers; in fact it was encouraged as an environmentally friendly thing to do. Glyn surmised that if Degenesys was so vulnerable, then the point should probably be proven earlier rather than later. It was in everybody's best interest - well, apart from the pompous Sir Richard Harvey perhaps!

Glyn returned his attention to the bar where Eddie was ordering drinks from a barmaid who waited patiently for him to overcome his stutter. Glyn liked Eddie; he had consulted him on numerous occasions during commissioning and the guy was nothing short of a genius in Glyn's opinion; Eddie knew Degenesys inside out and had probably worked harder than anyone in making the plant a success. For Eddie's sake, if nothing else, he was glad that Frank's strange flasks had failed and that the Degenesys team had finally achieved its goal.

Glyn had dropped one the three devices into a waste hopper several days ago now; he remembered how he had nearly retrieved it again, but knowing that his own team could be monitoring the CCTV, he had decided to let things run their course rather than arousing any suspicions. The next night Glyn had returned to work after a sleepless twelve hours to find nothing had happened at all; the reliability run was still on track and everything was as it should be. Glyn was glad that the other two flasks were now sitting at the bottom of the River Thames.

'Here's to success!' Glyn said, and gulped at the beer he had just been handed.

'To success!' Matt repeated with Eddie stuttering in unison.

As they downed their pints, someone's pager bleeped.

'No rest for the wicked,' Matt said as he headed out of the bar thumbing the buttons of his mobile phone.

'Bloody thing's p…probably tripped again,' Eddie said. 'Tonight of all nights.'

'At least it's not on my shift,' Glyn smiled, but he was suddenly feeling uneasy.

'What's your m…money on?' Eddie asked. 'I bet it's the s…static frequency converter.' A "SFC Thryristor Failure" alarm had been standing for two days now - another component failure on the same leg and the SFC would single-phase and trip the plant.

'Interesting theory,' Glyn replied nodding reflectively, 'Personally, I'm going for fuel cell over-temp; the standby coolant pump's been cutting in all day so something's wrong with the control system.' Whatever the problem, Glyn prayed it wasn't linked to his deed with the mysterious flask. He looked over to where Matt had left the room, hoping he would hurry back and put him out of his misery.

'You okay?' Eddie asked.

'Yeah, of course,' Glyn said, displaying his pint in evidence of the fact. Then he gazed into the amber liquid and paused thoughtfully. 'I put in for Matt's job you know?' He said softly. 'I didn't even get a bloody interview!'

Eddie smiled sympathetically. 'There'll be other chances,' he said. 'M…Matt's done a pretty good job – deserves the s…success after what he's been through in his life.'

'Yeah, I heard that something bad happened to his brother,' Glyn said, 'and both his parents died didn't they?'

'He n…never talks about it…' Eddie began, but then they both saw Matt re-enter the room and Eddie paused mid-sentence. 'S…Something's wrong,' he stuttered.

Glyn watched Matt push through the crowd towards them and could see that his colleague's face was the colour of chalk. When he reached them, Matt's voice sounded like it was sticking in his throat.

'Eddie, you'd better come with me; there's been an incident at the plant,' he said. 'I think someone's been hurt.'

Chapter 5

The following day, Matt spent most of the morning at the plant where a panel of inquiry had already been established. This was normal procedure in the event of an incident resulting in injury and staff from the previous night shift, with the exception of Jill Davies who had suffered the accident, had been asked to stay back in the morning to make statements. The only news from the hospital was that Jill was improving and had enjoyed a reasonably comfortable night. Matt had asked if he could visit her, but was told he would have to wait until the afternoon because a specialist was due to examine her later that morning. As to the kind of specialist she was seeing, the hospital wouldn't say, but they were obviously still concerned about her condition.

     Matt was eventually allowed to enter the reactor room, which was the scene of the incident and was surprised at how little damage there was. One of the ceramic modules had ruptured and the field generator's surfaces were badly tarnished with a strange green patina, but other than that, there was little evidence of anything out of the ordinary. The shift crew couldn't add much either; other than that at around nine forty-five the lights had suddenly dimmed and the control room had been inundated with alarms. The CCTV footage gave the best clue as to what had happened - it showed Jill entering the reactor room, presumably to take readings as normal. There was really no need to do so because all parameters were retransmitted to the main control room, but it was common practice all the same. The technicians had learnt that their eyes, noses and ears had proved to be much more reliable than the computers in picking up potential problems, so they religiously walked round the plant at least twice each shift. Looking at the film there was nothing to suggest that Jill had been concerned about the equipment in this particular instance; she seemed relaxed as she took readings inside the enclosure. Then suddenly the film showed the dome's viewing window light up in a red flash of such brilliance that the camera struggled to adjust itself to the brightness - so much so, that there followed a momentary blackness before the image re-focused. When the picture returned, everything appeared as it was before the flash, except Jill could no longer be seen through the dome's window.

Jill's shift team said they found her slumped on the floor of the reactor room, evidently in a state of shock. They said she couldn't stand properly or respond to their questions; otherwise she had seemed unhurt apart from a bruised forehead, apparently caused by her fall. They thought she might have been suffering from concussion, so had immediately called an ambulance. Only when pressed for more information did they mention that the poor girl had messed herself as a result of her ordeal.

That afternoon, the waiting room of the John Radcliffe Hospital was bringing back painful memories for Matt and he hoped that he would be allowed to see Jill soon. This is exactly why he shouldn't have taken the job at Degenesys; technical problems he could deal with, but responsibility for other people's safety was another matter. Let's face it, his track record wasn't particularly good in that area. If Jill was seriously hurt, the Health and Safety Executive would leave no stone unturned investigating this incident, especially as a new technology was involved and it was only a matter of time before they would ask to interview the Production Manager. As the most senior person in the operations department any criticism would surely be aimed at him and he wasn't sure he could handle the guilt, let alone being hounded by the press who, in the form of the tenacious Tanya Fox, was already on his case.

Matt's phone rang for the umpteenth time and the receptionist gave him a disapproving look; he noted the caller and shook his head in disbelief as he turned the phone off. He had given Tanya his business card, secretly hoping that one day the attractive newsreader might phone him, but now he seriously regretted doing so. She had been calling all day, obviously having heard about the accident at the plant. The woman was like a vulture and Matt was determined not going to give her the satisfaction of answering her calls. As Matt buried the phone in his rucksack, he did not see the doctor approach him.

'Mr Campbell?'

Matt flinched. 'God, you made me jump!' He stood up. 'Sorry – yes, Matt Campbell. I'm waiting to see Jill Davies.' Had it not been for the white coat, Matt might have mistaken the doctor for a young girl. He guessed she was no more than five feet tall at best and her face, devoid of any make-up, was captivatingly child-like, but behind her rimless glasses, the woman's eyes told another story. They were keen and intelligent, and the faint wrinkles in their corners suggesting that the doctor might be older than she first appeared.

'I wonder if we could have a word in private?' she asked. 'I'm Doctor Knight, the specialist dealing with Jill's case.'

'She's okay isn't she? Why hasn't anyone been allowed to see her?'

'She's fine; her family are with her now,' the doctor said. 'She's actually making very good progress. I understand you are her employer?'

'Thank God!' Matt replied. 'Yes, I'm her manager but she's also a friend, we've known each other for over three years.'

'Please come with me. If you don't mind, I'd like to ask you about her accident.'

Matt followed her to a side room and from behind, he couldn't help noticing how the white coat failed to conceal what was obviously a very athletic, if tiny figure. The doctor directed him to a seat and then closed the door leaving them alone, before sitting down opposite him. Matt guessed that the doctor, despite her young appearance, was probably in her late twenties, perhaps even thirty. Her boyish face was pretty despite the absence of make-up. Her fair hair was tied back in a neat pony-tail with just a few strands dangling free and framing her face all the way down to her pointed chin. Her face was sombre, almost stern, but again, the eyes told a different story; Matt thought that they were the sort of eyes that were more used to laughing.

'What exactly is wrong with Jill?' he asked.

'Physically not much, but it's a rather unusual case all the same,' she replied. 'I'm a behavioural psychologist and the hospital called me this morning because they were having problems diagnosing Jill's condition.'

'She's not mentally ill is she? She always seemed very stable to me,' Matt said. 'Hey, you're not suggesting she caused the incident on purpose are you, because…'

'No, nothing like that,' she interrupted. 'It's just that the shock of what happened to Jill has apparently caused a loss of memory and I could do with understanding a bit more about what she would have experienced when the incident happened; it must have been a severe trauma to have such an effect.'

Matt bit into his bottom lip as the doctor spoke; he had heard lots of stories about amnesia but he had never actually met someone who had experienced it. 'I'm afraid I can't really tell you too much, you'd be better off speaking to the guys at the Cambridge laboratories; that's where all the tests were done.'

'Tell me about the process anyway,' she said, 'anything might be useful in helping us understand her condition.'

Matt told her everything he knew about entropic reaction and how Jill had inadvertently been caught in the flash when the module failed. He explained that, despite the seriousness of the incident, the reaction shouldn't really have caused her any harm. The doctor listened to everything Matt said without interrupting him and took notes whenever she thought something might be significant. When he finished the doctor thanked him, but Matt could tell by her creased brow that she was still none the wiser for the additional information. 'Perhaps it was the blow to her head,' he suggested, but the doctor looked doubtful. He thought back to the footage of the mouse in the biscuit tin and wondered.

'Please call me if you think of anything else that might be of use,' she said, offering her card.

'Well, there's an investigation underway as we speak, I'll keep you up to date with anything we find,' Matt replied. 'Look, I know I'm not direct family or anything, but I do feel responsible for what happened; please would you call me if there's any change in Jill's condition - anything at all?'

'Of course,' she said. Then she smiled for the first time and her eyes wrinkled just as Matt had imagined they would.

She got up to leave but Matt reached out and touched her arm. 'Jill will be okay won't she?' He asked. 'Recover her memory, I mean?'

'I'm sure she will, amnesia is not uncommon following extreme trauma, it's just that Jill's symptoms are very unusual. Normally such cases involve only short-term memory loss; in Jill's case it's as if she's forgotten everything she ever knew. She doesn't even remember how to use a knife and fork let alone how to hold a conversation – it's really strange.' The doctor's frown returned for a moment, but then her face brightened and she smiled at him again. 'The good news is she's making rapid progress. I've never seen anyone so enthusiastic to pick herself back up; she's already re-mastered quite a few words.' Then the smile faltered once more. 'The poor girl still doesn't recognise her family,' she said. 'The problem is, although she's making progress, she's not actually remembering things, she's just re-learning them.'

The next day, for the first time in weeks, Matt drove to work - he only lived about five miles from the Degenesys site and would normally cycle, but today was Friday and he needed an early start. He would be expected to submit a repair programme to the board before the weekend and the extent of the damage to the reactor module was still uncertain. Plus, what happened to Jill was a reportable incident and he had to inform the Health and Safety Executive within twenty-four hours of the occurrence. Approaching the site entrance, Matt flashed his security pass at the guard and the barrier rose, allowing his Toyota Hybrid onto the Degenesys site.

Immediately, he realised that something was amiss - the cycle shed to his left was empty and the small parking area in front of reception was packed of vehicles – it was usually the other way around. A number of large, black vans were parked haphazardly in the car park along with a few other vehicles, one of which was a highly-polished silver limousine.

Matt parked the Toyota as best he could and made for the entrance to reception. In his rush, he nearly smashed into the double glass doors that normally opened automatically on approach. He pushed the palms of his hands against the darkened panes and tried to peer in, but could see nobody at the desk so he circumnavigated the building to a side access door, which served as a fire escape. Swiping his security pass against the reader, he pushed open the door, ascended the stairs and headed directly for Eddie Coleman's office.

The lanky engineer was stood at his desk, shuffling a mess of documents and schematic diagrams across its surface; he looked up anxiously as Matt entered the office. 'Matt, Thank God!'

'Sir Richard's here!' Matt exclaimed – it wasn't a question.

Eddie nodded. 'In the boardroom; he's s…set up an office there.'

'What's going on Eddie? What the bloody hell's he doing here'

'Matt, they've s…stood the shift team down, and m…maintenance. I'm the only one left – apart from s…security.'

'Why? Who do those vans belong to?'

Eddie slumped down into his chair and rubbed his eyes, precariously dislodging his glasses. Then he looked up again, his face grim and ashen. 'Th… They're closing us down, Matt – there's people f…from the labs all over the place.' Eddie paused, shaking his head. 'It's all over, Matt – S…Sir Richard's pulling the plug!'

Matt turned and strode along the corridor towards the boardroom. When he reached the door, he shoved it open without knocking. Sir Richard was sitting at the huge table, behind a laptop and talking into his mobile phone. When he saw Matt, he calmly ended the call and put the phone into the top pocket of his expensive Fioravanti suit. Then he rested his arms on the boardroom table, his solid cufflinks tapping its mahogany surface in unison, and greeted Matt with a voice, long turned to gravel by an overindulgence of fine cigars.

'Ah Matthew,' he growled. 'Very good to see you again…' His keen grey eyes stared out in contrast to his waxy face. 'Even in these unfortunate circumstances.'

'Why the hell are you doing this?' Matt asked, his voice shaking with anger. 'Is this because of Jill Davies? Her condition?'

Sir Richard shook his head. 'The girl's ailment has nothing to do with what happened at the plant – this is a business decision.'

'You're closing the plant a day after Jill's accident and you're telling me that your decision is coincidental?'

'Exactly that! The girl's condition is unrelated to the incident in the reactor room. We've had news from the hospital; apparently she's suffering from a condition called Encephalitis – acute inflammation of the brain - brought on by viral meningitis. She's very sick, but they think she'll make a full recovery.'

'But I was only with her…'

'Matthew, please believe me, the girl has nothing to do with this. Degenesys has failed; in business you sometimes have to make these decisions. Go home, have a long weekend and call me on Monday; I promise to sort something out for you.'

'But, we're so close…' Matt began to argue, but he was interrupted by the ring-tone of Sir Richard's phone. The older man retrieved the device from his pocket and held it unanswered, staring at Matt, waiting for him to leave. Realising that further argument was futile, Matt spun on his heel and stomped back towards the door. Before he reached it, Sir Richard's voice stopped him in his tracks.

'Matthew, please don't discuss this with anyone. I trust I can rely on your discretion?'

Matt, without acknowledging the question, strode out of the room, leaving the business magnate to answer his phone.

The next morning Matt woke with a hangover that he knew had no intention of leaving in a hurry. The power was off again and he stumbled down the dark stairs turning on his mobile phone as he descended. He had ignored the calls from the determined Ms Fox who had continued to hound him incessantly throughout the previous day and when the phone rang immediately on being powered up he assumed the worst. Here we go again he thought, answering the call. 'Matt Campbell speaking,' he said, bending to pick up the post from the floor.

'Mr Campbell? It's Doctor Knight. We met on Thursday at the hospital.'

'Of course - how's Jill?'

'No idea I'm afraid, she's no longer at the hospital.' The doctor's voice sounded different somehow - sort of shaky, but it may just have been the phone. 'I'm sorry to call so early on a weekend but I really need your help.'

'Jill's been released already?'

'No, she was moved to another hospital not long after you left - private I assume. Her records have gone with her – it's very peculiar.'

'That is strange, but I don't think I can help you - I know nothing about it, I'm afraid.'

'It's not that,' the doctor said. 'You see, I've just received results from the tests we carried out before Jill was moved. Matt, I really need to talk to someone in authority at your company.'

'About the meningitis thing? They told me it's completely unrelated to the incident at the plant.'

'Meningitis…? The doctor sounded surprised. 'Jill didn't have meningitis. Mr Campbell, I think something strange is going on - perhaps we could meet.'

'Sure,' Matt said. 'How about the Ferryman on Canal Street? They serve breakfasts on a weekend; I sometimes eat there.'

'I know it,' she said. 'I can be there in an hour, is that okay with you?'

'See you there,' he replied. At least it would keep him occupied even if it meant yet more bad news.

Chapter 6

Matt was first to arrive at the Ferryman, a picturesque little pub situated on a bridge overlooking the canal. It mainly catered for tourists on hire boats and due to the fuel shortage was often quiet at this time of year. As Matt expected, the pub was nearly empty and he was able to sit at his favourite spot in an alcove by a window overlooking the towpath. A waitress came over and he ordered a coffee, and then looked out towards the canal as an intermittent stream of joggers passed his window. He was amused at the number who, on seeing him, glanced at their watches as they passed as if by doing so, he would somehow be convinced that they were taking their exercise seriously.

When Doctor Knight arrived, Matt was surprised at the transformation in her appearance. She was dressed in jeans and a roll-necked jumper under a denim jacket. She had let her hair down and it was fairer than he remembered, almost blonde. Also she was wearing a small amount of make-up, which somehow brightened her face. Matt assumed that this was typical weekend garb for the doctor, but part of him hoped she had made just a little extra effort on his behalf.

'Thanks for agreeing to meet me, Mr Campbell,' she said. 'I really needed to talk to someone about Jill's condition.'

'Please call me Matt.'

'Okay, my name's Melissa, but only my mother calls me that - I prefer Mel.'

'Okay Mel,' Matt said. 'What's on your mind? I think I've had about as much bad news as I can take in one week.'

'Well, we decided to run a brain scan on Jill on Thursday afternoon, before they transferred her. I've just seen the results; I've never seen anything like it.'

'That sounds bad,' Matt said. 'My company was told that her condition was brought on by inflammation to her brain.'

'Impossible, there was no inflammation – or viral meningitis, but the test results are extremely concerning all the same. You see; the scan is designed to show amplitude of activity in different parts of the brain. We've learned a lot about cranial mapping over the last decade and brain scans have become an invaluable tool in diagnosing cases such as Jill's.'

'So what was so unusual about Jill's scan?' Matt asked.

'Well it actually answers a lot of questions about her unique condition,' she said. 'You see, memory failure normally involves the patient losing the ability to retrieve information. Usually, as a result of trauma, the brain sort of crashes and is temporarily incapable of retrieving information from certain areas of memory.'

'And in Jill's case?' Matt prompted, urging her to get to the point.

'In Jill's case,' Mel continued, 'it seems there's no data to retrieve. Her brain is functioning completely normally, but it's as if her memories - everything she has ever learned - has been wiped completely.' She looked at Matt waiting for him to register the implications of what she was saying. 'It appears that this entropic reaction of yours, apart from degenerating inanimate objects, also has the potential to reformat people's brains!'

Matt was stunned. 'How can that be? Surely someone would have discovered this before now.' He rubbed his temples and tried to think. 'Jesus, I have to tell someone,' he said.

'My thoughts exactly, but who?'

'I should call Sir Richard, I suppose.' Matt said, pulling his phone from the pocket of his jeans, but then he remembered the chilling tone in the businessman's voice when they last parted and hesitated. 'Look, are you sure about this? You realise that if you're right it's going to have serious implications.'

'As sure as I can be about anything,' she said. 'I think you need to warn your people in case someone else gets hurt.'

'Don't worry, the plant's been closed. Even if it was the reaction that wiped Jill's memory, it can't happen again – not at Degenesys anyway. Why don't we wait and…'

'Matt; we can't sit on this.'

'All right, let me call Eddie; he might still be on site.' Matt was about to dial the Engineering Manager's number when the phone rang in his hand, making him jump; uncannily it was Eddie's number that appeared on the LCD display.

'Eddie, I was just about to call you. I'm afraid I've got some disturbing news.'

'Tell m…me about it,' Eddie said. 'Where are you? We've g…got to talk urgently.'

'What wrong, Eddie?' Matt asked, not liking the tone of his friend's voice, but Eddie seemed reluctant to elaborate over the phone so Matt suggested he join them at the Ferryman.

Eddie arrived in little under twenty minutes, but when he saw the doctor he appeared reluctant to say anything at first. 'Matt, we need to talk alone,' he said, raising his eyebrows in a mixture of anxiety and frustration.

'This is Melissa Knight; she's the specialist looking after Jill.' Matt said. 'I guarantee whatever you've got to say is nothing compared to what she's just told me.'

'Don't count on it,' Eddie replied. 'There's a serious problem at the plant!'

'Whatever it is, I think we can confide in Mel, she's done so with me,' Matt said. 'Sit down for Christ's sake Eddie, you're freaking me out.'

'Okay, if you're s…sure,' Eddie said, finally sitting at their table.

'So what's happened now?' Matt sighed.

'I've just come f…from the plant,' Eddie said. 'Sir Richard's gone now, but engineers are still crawling all over the place and some m…menacing characters in suits have joined them. My presence wasn't exactly welcome and they wouldn't let me anywhere near the reactor, so I was pretty much confined to my office. There wasn't much I could do s…so I thought I'd review the CCTV disks, the ones s…showing the incident with Jill. That's the problem Matt, the disks have been corrupted.'

'Is that all…' Matt started.

'Just listen, will you,' Eddie interrupted. 'The disks were corrupt because they've been tarnished with the s…same s…stuff that we s…saw on the reactor coil.'

Matt knew he was obviously missing the point. 'What are you saying, Eddie?'

'Don't you s...see, the camera was outside of the dome, the reaction is outs...side of the dome?'

'I still don't understand....' Matt began, but again Eddie interrupted.

'If the disks have been affected, s...so's the camera. Other things will be corroding, Matt - the chairs, the f...filing cabinets, even the bloody roof members, they'll all be affected.' Eddie appeared to be on the brink of cracking up and looked desperately to Matt for a sign that he understood the implications.

Matt still didn't get it. 'So the dome was breached – incredible, I admit, but surely it's no big deal. The reaction has dissipated, absorbed by the building just as we knew it would. What's the problem?'

Eddie shook his head, his face pallid, his eyes never leaving Matt's.

'Oh, shit...you know something...'

'What? What does it mean?' Mel pleaded.

'How serious is this Eddie?' Matt already had a feeling that it was pretty damn serious indeed.

Eddie's eyes flittered from Matt to Mel and back again. 'There was always a risk, Matt – infinitely s...small perhaps, but never completely disproven. Now I believe it's real and manifesting itself as we s...speak.'

'What do you mean?'

'I'm afraid there's going to be a s...second flash, but this time much bigger.' His voice was speeding up again as his panic started to return. 'We can't s…stop it Matt, it's out of control!'

Despite the time of day, Eddie swallowed some of the brandy that Matt had bought him and at last appeared to calm down. Despite their very different personalities, the two men were very good friends and they knew each other inside out. Eddie was undoubtedly the cleverest person Matt had ever known but he was bloody useless in a crisis. What a pair, Matt thought, one of us shuns responsibility and the other can't handle it; now, if Eddie was right, they might both be facing a bigger crisis than most people did in their whole lifetime. He and Mel watched patiently as Eddie drank his brandy and slowly started to regain his composure.

     Matt thought back to the private game that he used to play with his unwitting friend during the long, boring hours of plant commissioning and wondered if Eddie had ever suspected his motives. The Engineering Manager was one of those people who continually experimented with hobbies and interests and was forever trying out new things in an attempt to satisfy his incessant appetite for knowledge. So every day, just for fun, Matt would ask Eddie a different question in an attempt to find a pastime that had so far eluded him. One day it would be; 'Eddie, have you ever been hang-gliding?' The next it would be, 'I'm thinking about growing bonsai trees, Eddie. I don't suppose you know anything about the subject?' To Matt's amusement Eddie had never failed to demonstrate at least some level of expertise in every topic he could think of and his friend would usually go on to deliver a tedious, stammering lecture on the subject. Matt wondered if such extensive knowledge could help them to get out of the mess they now found themselves in, but somehow he doubted it.

Mel looked at Matt and nodded imperceptibly as though she thought Eddie was finally ready to continue; he trusted her judgement - after all, she was the expert.

'Okay, Eddie, you're telling us that we're on the brink of some sort of serious incident, but nothing's actually happened has it?' Matt said. 'So let's not overreact, all right? Have you told the guys at the plant?'

'They already know – it's obvious. That's why they're there – trying to find a way to s…stop it. Look at this email to all s…staff.' Eddie pressed a few buttons on his handheld and read the message aloud, surprisingly without a single stutter.

'Scientists are currently investigating the recent failure at the Degenesys plant and are considering options to minimise further loss. Staff are not permitted to convey details of the problem to external bodies at this stage; we will be informing the relevant authorities as soon as investigations have been completed.'

'There you go then,' Matt said. 'The experts obviously don't consider the situation serious.'

'But that's just it - I think they do,' Eddie said. 'The way they're reacting s…suggests that they probably know even m…more than we do.'

'I think there's something they might not know,' Mel suggested. 'Nobody seems to realise that your entropic reaction is actually a lot more dangerous than any of you think.' She went on to explain to Eddie, her diagnosis of Jill Davies and her suspicions based on the unusual brain scan.

Despite his obvious anxiety and growing impatience, Eddie listened to Mel's story, but his body language betrayed his frustration. When she finished, he challenged her. 'Look, we've got a serious problem here and we can't afford to be distracted. You may be right about Jill, I'm not an expert, but surely you can't make such an assumption based on a single incident. Jill's condition is irrelevant at the moment; the effects of an uncontrolled entropic reaction could be devastating!'

'You're wrong,' Mel argued. 'I think Jill's condition is extremely relevant – if you're right, those people at the plant are in serious danger.'

'I think we should all calm down and think,' Matt said quietly. He was aware that the Ferryman had filled up since their conversation had started and people were beginning to show an interest in their increasingly raised voices. 'Eddie, I think Mel might be right – Sir Richard knows all about Jill's condition; that's why he moved her. They're covering something up – playing for time. Eddie, what do you think is going to happen at the plant?'

'It's impossible to s…say for sure, but people could get hurt, Matt. If a reaction occurs in such a built up area, all reactive m…material in the vicinity will be obliterated – the buildings could collapse!'

'Shit! How long have we got?' Matt could feel his heart pounding.

'I don't know yet but I can probably w…work it out. I've already started to m…measure the rate of degeneration from the corrosion s…samples and from that, I'll be able to calculate exactly when the activation energy will be reached. I'll know for s…sure later today, but I guess we've got somewhere between twenty-four and forty-eight hours before the first flash.'

'The first flash? Matt hissed, leaning forward. 'How many are there going to be?'

'Don't you s…see? There's going to be a chain reaction. When the Degenesys complex goes up, there'll be a s…surge – the reactive wave could travel for miles and there'll be further flashes every time it encounters enough material to feed another reaction – which is just about everywhere nowadays. And every flash will result in another s…surge – who knows? It might not stop!'

'How do you know this?' Matt whispered. 'I thought the whole process was fail-safe.'

'Nobody really believed… God, n…nobody ever thought…' Eddie's voice trailed off. 'I'm so sorry,' he mouthed.

'Matt, what if your people *are* covering this up?' Mel whispered. 'What if they're gambling – hoping they can resolve the problem before it manifests itself?' The young doctor looked pale and afraid. 'It might be too late then - we have to warn people.'

He took her hand, 'I don't know, I'm not sure that anyone will believe us and even if they do – then what? If we go public on this we'll be detained for sure. If Eddie's right, I don't want to be locked away in an interview room when the shit hits the fan. Before we do anything, we need somewhere safe where they won't be able to trace us; then I'll contact Sir Richard. If he can't convince me that things are under control, we'll start making phone calls, okay?'

'What about my flat?' Mel suggested. 'It's only half an hour away.'

Matt shook his head 'Once they know about Jill, you're going to be one of the first people they'll want to trace.'

'How about Hayley's house?' Eddie said. 'My… er… girlfriend. Her f…father owns a mansion on the outskirts of town.'

'Your girlfriend?' Matt was astounded. 'I thought you and her were just…'

Eddie looked embarrassed. 'I'd have to t…tell her anyway.' Eddie paused. 'I guess we've all got people close to us that w…we'll want to warn,' he said.

'Not me,' Mel said. 'My ex-partner deserves everything he gets and all my family and friends are safe in Australia…' She trailed off when she saw a strange look materialise on Eddie's face.

'Hayley's house sounds ideal,' Matt said. 'Her father's a politician isn't he? I think we might need his help before this is over.'

'A magistrate, but he's retired now,' Eddie replied. 'Let's take my car, it's parked just outside. We can p…pick up Hayley on the way.'

'No, you go with Mel,' Matt said. 'I need to speak to someone first.'

'I hope it's a good lawyer,' Mel said.

Matt laughed without humour. 'Actually, it's a priest!'

Chapter 7

Half asleep, Father Peter drew his dressing gown tight to his neck and shivered; the electricity had only been cut for an hour, but the cottage had already chilled despite the fire curling in the hearth. As his body slumbered in the faded armchair, the old priest's mind wandered in a strange and ancient land.

In his dream, Father Peter looked down onto the waters of the River Rhine, which flowed through the Grand Duchy of Baden. On this side of the river, the cobbled road was awash with people all heading towards the distant gates of the city of Constance. On the road, most of the travellers wore tattered, linen tunics; the women's reaching all the way to the ground, but the younger men had coarse, baggy pants as protection from the morning air, which was surprisingly chilly despite the time of year. Among the crowd a few noblemen rode horses, their garb distinguishable by its quality and cleanliness and they had woven tights instead of the scruffy pants worn by the peasants.

Father Peter knew that he was dreaming, but his surroundings seemed as real as everyday life - more resplendent in fact. Every leaf of every branch of every twisted tree lined the road with blatant reality and on the roadside, mud-spattered blades of grass appeared vividly alive in their struggle to escape the sodden earth below. In the fields, patches of bluebells glowed in the early morning light and swifts circled the sky in dark contrast to the pale clouds, which now seemed spent of the rain that had fallen through the night. Church bells rang in the distance as the priest passed thatched dwellings of wattle and daub and further out, a scattering of primitive farmhouses stood amidst fields of crops tended by kneeling women and teenage boys swinging scythes. Among them, an old man led a horse in an attempt to plough depleted crops back into a muddy field. Beyond the river, grey steeples rose from behind fortified walls and a great cathedral spire adorned with a huge, ornate cross towered above them all.

    The road gradually widened as it approached the city. It was better maintained here, with more uniform stonework and improved drainage, so there were fewer puddles on the ground and Father Peter's muddy feet at last began to dry. Eventually the road crossed the gently flowing river in the form of a solid stone-arched bridge. Beyond the bridge, battlements overlooked the main gate and along the opposite river bank, high walls with windowed towers formed the city's perimeter. A number of archers sat amongst the battlements chatting lazily and seeming to pay scant attention to the excited crowd below.

    As Father Peter passed through the city gate, the road fell into relative darkness and a feeling of dread washed over him – it was not the first time he had dreamt of this place. He followed the crowd for a hundred yards or so before pausing in the shadow of a large doorway. Inside the building, a blacksmith's hammer rang the air like a bell tolling his doom. Father Peter surveyed his dream-world surroundings; lining the road, street vendors displayed an assortment of goods including honey, spun wool and chickens hanging from wooden frames. One stall sold an array of foul smelling sausages, buzzing with flies. The crowd slowed and became turbulent as people stopped to examine the various stalls and the confusion was compounded by the convergence of two more roads. The majority of the crowd however, continued to move in one general direction - towards the centre. Two nuns strode past, seemingly not noticing him; they were dressed in garments similar in style to those worn by the other women, but their tunics were black and neatly made.

    Father Peter set off again following the nuns until he lost them once more in the crowd. Eventually the busy street opened out into a vast square and the crowd gradually thinned as it dispersed into the wider area. Around the square, travelling preachers stood screaming their faith into the faces of those who gathered around them. One spouted an apocalyptic warning with such emotion that he had drawn a large audience.

    'Where four towers rise from the western sea,' the preacher bellowed, 'an impostor will climb from the ashes of a broken land and drink from God's holy cup. On that terrible day, the spirit of Christ shall be lost for a thousand years.' As Father Peter pushed through the crowd, he caught the preacher's eye and the ardent lament paused as the man's gaze followed his passage. Suddenly the preacher's voice boomed out again, this time louder and even more passionate than before. 'Protect it with your life!' he screamed. 'For he will come to claim it, leaving chaos in his wake!'

    Somehow, Father Peter knew that the preacher's words were aimed at him and even more unnerved than before, he hurried away into the crowd. Suddenly his eyes were drawn to another commotion at the convergence of yet another road; this one joined the square from the west. Father Peter saw a group of militia moving towards him. He watched as the soldiers led a tall man through the crowds, which clamoured excitedly around them. A mounted guard wearing a chain mail shirt and a tall polished helmet led the group. A great sword hung at his belt as a warning to the crowd, which parted reluctantly in front of them. The other guards were armed with long pikes decorated with blue banners each depicting a white cross. People in the crowd shouted angrily at the host, but the soldiers were well-built and looked powerful in their leather armour. They strode with such authority that the agitated people backed away as they approached. As they came closer, Father Peter realised that the man in their midst was a prisoner; bound at the wrists, he was being jostled forward by his wardens. The prisoner was also a priest and appeared calm as he acknowledged those in the crowd who shouted encouragement or offered support. He wore a dirty red robe over a white tunic and he raised his hands as if blessing the people as he passed. The man had obviously suffered an uncomfortable time recently; his thin grey hair was matted and his closely cropped beard did little to conceal an ugly bruise on his right cheek.

  The party continued to the north end of the square and Father Peter followed at a distance, wondering what crime the imprisoned priest had committed. As Father Peter crossed the square, the crowd once again grew dense. Ahead, he could hear the booming voice of another man, which although distant, dominated the sound of all others with its strident command.

  'By the authority of the king, on this day, July sixth, fourteen-fifteen, at this, the second Council of Constance, I call all citizens to witness the third and final hearing which will end the trial and bring final sentence to the accused, Jan Hus.'

Father Peter shoved his way through the crowd and he saw the speaker standing upon a temporary, but elaborately furnished platform. The man wore a long black robe, which matched his dark pointed beard. Church bells rang as the bearded cleric held his hand aloft and announced the prisoner's arrival.

'Bring the heretic forward,' he cried. At this, the prisoner was escorted up wooden steps to the top of the landing where he was made to stand in front of a solid looking wooden table. On the table were two burning candles, a large open book and a number of religious artefacts including a wooden crucifix and … Father Peter's eyes were suddenly drawn to an object that gleamed in the morning sunshine. There it was! The mysterious relic that haunted his dreams; the same golden chalice that, six hundred years from this dream place, was locked away in the vault of Father Peter's own church. The old priest stared in awe at the gleaming cup and he knew then that he had to recover it from the clutches of the dark-robed cleric. But it was hopeless - there were other men on the platform; two more guards carrying crossbows stood at each end of the platform and four stone-faced clerics were seated on a row of thrones at the rear, facing the prisoner. The dark-robed cleric stood behind a podium which was set to one side; he made a slight bow of the head to the prisoner before continuing.

'Jan Hus,' his voice rang out across the square. 'The high clergy have found you guilty of heresy against the Catholic Church and sentence shall now be passed. Before this judgement I call upon you to denounce, once and for all, your anti-papal teachings before the citizens of Constance.'

The prisoner turned to the crowd and scanned the many faces staring silently upwards. Then he straightened and proclaimed in a clear voice, 'I denounce only the prodigal wealth and corruption that continues to dishonour the holy Roman Catholic Church.' The crowd murmured and there were one or two shouts of approval. Father Peter noticed two of the escort guards push off into the agitated people behind him.

'Burn the blasphemer,' a woman called out and more raised voices followed. A localised commotion ensued from where the woman had shouted.

Hus, the prisoner, moved forward to the front of the platform and once again addressed the gathering. He raised his bound hands as if to calm them. 'Do not fight among yourselves,' he shouted 'All of this luxurious wealth, these city walls, the noble's castles, they all come from your efforts - the work of the poor labouring people.'

At this, the dark-robed cleric made a signal and the two guards suddenly moved to the prisoner, restraining him and pulled him back to the table. 'You are a proven Wycliffite Heretic,' the bearded man declared. 'You have been found guilty of corrupting your students with rights of blasphemy and for this, there is only one sentence the council can pass.' He turned to one of the guards and nodded; the guard raised a horn from his belt and blew a signal.

Father Peter felt a growing agitation in the crowd and further disturbances erupted behind him. More and more guards were appearing all around them.

The prisoner lowered his head and shook it slowly whilst quietly responding to those near the front who could still hear his words. 'Why is it a sin to advocate the doctrine of clerical purity and to condone Holy Communion for the laity and clergy alike? Should not ordinary people celebrate the Lord's supper?' Then he raised his head and once more looked into the faces of the frenzied mass. He caught sight of an old woman that stared at him with compassionate eyes. He pointed at her while turning to face his accuser. 'See this woman, a peasant who may be poor but who lives a virtuous life; to me she stands higher before Christ than any noble man, prince or even king, and certainly higher than any of you!'

One of the members of the high clergy rose angrily from his seat and shouted. 'Blasphemer, I command you – denounce your sins!'

The people grew uneasy again and the clamour returned. A gap emerged in the jostling crowd and Father Peter saw for the first time a high tower wall a short distance behind the platform. A cart drawn by a single white horse was being led to part of the wall where built-in steps led up to a small stone dais about ten feet above the cobbled square. Two bronze rings were attached to the wall each side of the dais and one more above it. To his growing horror, Father Peter noticed that the wall was dark around the stonework, blemished by flame and smoke from previous burnings.

The dark-robed cleric's voice rang out once more. 'By the power vested in me by the holy council, I hereby sentence the accused to be burned at the stake for heresy against the Catholic Church.'

Screams of denial emanated from the restless crowd.

'The execution will take place immediately for the people of Constance to bear witness in the knowledge that every heretic shall meet the same end.'

Two guards grabbed the prisoner and dragged him down the platform's wooden steps and off towards the stone dais. The dark cleric then picked up the crucifix and gold cup and followed the prisoner. Holding them aloft, he called out as his dark robes flowed behind him. 'Bear also witness to these relics of heresy, which shall be cast along with the heretic's ashes into the waters of the Rhine.'

'No! Father Peter cried as the crowd dragged him along following the dark cleric towards the place of execution. He was horrified with the events unfolding before him, but there was nothing he could do to save the prisoner or the precious cup from their respective fates. As they neared the wall, a ring of guards prevented the angry crowd from getting any closer. The people were now on the point of riot, but they all knew there were archers atop of the tower with bows at the ready to dispel any disorder.

They led the prisoner up to the stone dais and his wrists were bound to the brass rings as faggots of fuel were unloaded from the wagon and placed on the ground around the steps below him. One of the executioners tied a string of small copper containers around the prisoner's neck and then the ends of the rope were attached to the upper bronze ring. The imprisoned priest struggled against his captors and screamed at the dark cleric.

'The prime endeavour of all my deeds has been to turn people from their sins,' he pleaded. Then as if finally accepting his fate, his voice dropped again. 'So be it - the truth that I have written, taught and preached in accordance with the holy doctrines,' he said. 'I will willingly seal with my death today.'

The dark cleric ignored his captor. 'I call upon you one final time to repent of your sins,' he cried. 'Recant once and for all, the heretic creeds, before you meet God in final judgement.'

The prisoner, now seated alone on the dais, struggled against his bound wrists. Fear now filled his eyes and all composure finally deserted him. 'It is you who sin before God and these people,' he gasped in a voice strangled by the ropes around his neck. Then he shrieked at the crowd. 'The church is corrupt – you must revolt, revolt against your feudal masters!' Ignoring his plea, one of the guards lit the faggots at his feet and flames suddenly leapt high around the prisoner. In his panic Hus raised himself from the chair, pushing up from the steps and strained against his bonds. 'Revolt!' he screamed in his agony as the flames rose further, licked at his thighs.

The horrific scene finally stirred the crowd into action. They surged forward against the soldiers who stabbed back at them with their pikes, but the long exploited people would not be contained as they pushed past the guards in an attempt to free the tortured prisoner. The dark-robed cleric fell amongst the surging crowd, still clutching the crucifix, which he held aloft as he drowned in the sea of bodies. The golden cup fell to the ground and bounced once before coming to rest upright at the base of the steps. Father Peter also fell amidst the jostling people and began crawling forward through the turmoil of kicking legs towards the cup. He made it to within a few feet of the steps when the first arrows rained down. Almost immediately, he was struck in the back of the neck and collapsed to the ground. Reaching out to the cup in an attempt to retrieve it, his arm stung as flaming drips from above fell around him and burned into his skin. To his dismay, he realised that these were drops of burning fat, the source of which was still screaming above him. He looked imploringly once more at the golden chalice, which was just out of reach of his outstretched hand. The cup's surface gleamed, reflecting the scenes of riotous horror from all around him. Then with wonder, he saw that the cup itself was aflame; the repulsive burning drips had fallen within its bowl and were still alight. This sight impregnated itself upon Father Peter's mind as a vision that would haunt his waking conscience.

Just as the strange image started to wane, he heard above the clamour of the frenzied crowd, a series of retorts from above. The containers of gunpowder around the prisoner's neck exploded with a 'rap, rap, rap,' and the blasts signalled the decapitation and final demise of the heroic martyr, Jan Hus.

Chapter 8

Rap, rap, rap - Father Peter awoke from his dream with the vision of the golden chalice still burning, literally, in his mind. For a moment he was disorientated, then he realised that he must have dozed off after his lunchtime session at the Rose and Crown. Somebody was at the door! The old priest rubbed his eyes with the palms of his hands and reaching for his glasses, rose wearily from the worn and faded armchair.

Matt knocked again at the door of the old house, which was one of five terraced cottages at the oldest end of the village. Matt's own house was only half a mile away, but the ambience here was so different he might have been in another age. Matt's house, inherited from his parents, was on the relatively new estate built in the eighties, which had grown over the years and now engulfed pretty much the whole village. The house was too large for Matt really, but he couldn't bring himself to sell up and move somewhere smaller. However, this end of the village remained a throwback to a time when life in the country was very different; a refuge for the older generation of villagers who still remembered such a life. Matt had known Father Peter since the mid-nineties and without the priest he probably would never have survived the early years that followed the accident. In fact, it was Father Peter who had helped Matt think of it as an accident rather than some sort of divine punishment for his own selfish irresponsibility. He thought back to the day when the first in a terrible chain of events had changed his life forever. It had been Matt's eleventh birthday and he still remembered the anger he had felt towards his parents for forcing him to look after his brother, Aaron on what was supposed to his special day. His parents never seemed to understand how important and precarious popularity was to a boy of his age. Matt had not been the most confident boy in the village and he constantly trod the fine line between group acceptance and social expulsion. A simple thing like always having your six-year old brother in tow was sometimes all it took to make the difference.

After the accident, the problem of his ever-present brother had suddenly disappeared; so too had the problem of his inconsiderate parents, so his grandmother had been left the unenviable task of bringing him up. She was supposed to be the one to take him by the hand and explain that life was sometimes cruel and that his anger and guilt would only result in further hurt in his life. Unfortunately she had not been up to the job, being too immersed in her own grief to understand how much the boy was suffering. So Father Peter, the village priest, had taken Matt under his wing and had offered him the comfort and guidance that he had so desperately needed in those early years. In fact, to his credit, he had done so ever since.

Father Peter opened the door and Matt guessed immediately that he had woken him. 'God, you look rough,' he said. 'Guess you had one too many in the Rose and Crown at lunchtime.'

'Don't be cheeky, boy,' Father Peter growled, his stern face betrayed by the hint of a smile. 'And don't take the Lord's name in vain,' he said, turning to make his way back to his armchair by the fire. 'I'm afraid the power's off again, so mind your head.'

Matt, needing no invitation, followed the priest into the darkened cottage and closed the door behind him. He had to stoop as he entered the room because the ceiling was quite low and the exposed beams sometimes caught Matt out now that he was taller. Matt loved the atmosphere of the old cottage; it made him feel safe – especially in the company of the old priest.

'Father, I've got to talk to you, I need your advice about something quite serious.'

'Sounds very dramatic,' Father Peter replied. 'You'd better sit down and tell me what you've got yourself into this time.'

Matt had visited Father Peter for two reasons: one, because since his grandmother's death, the priest was the only person in the world that he truly cared about; and two, because now more than ever, he needed some sound advice from his trusted childhood mentor. Matt's head was still spinning from Eddie's conviction that they were all heading towards some sort of major incident. If anybody else had concocted such a story Matt would have laughed it off, but this was Eddie! The Engineering Manager was just about the most level-headed person on the planet; he was never wrong about anything and he was certainly not prone to delusional fantasies. But even so, the whole thing seemed so absurd – how could the innocuous incident at the Degenesys plant result in a catastrophe of the proportions Eddie was suggesting? If it was true, then Matt had a moral duty to warn people, but the repercussions would be immense and he wasn't sure he could endure the media scrutiny that such a revelation might bring. Matt desperately needed to share his burden with someone he could trust, so slowly and calmly, he began to talk.

Father Peter already knew about the accident at the plant and about Jill Davies' apparent amnesia, so Matt just filled him in with everything he had heard from Mel and Eddie at the Ferryman that morning. Then he explained their plan to hide up somewhere safe whilst deciding what to do.

Father Peter listened to Matt's story without so much as raising an eyebrow and his lack of emotion made Matt feel even more uncomfortable. An incredulous response would have been better, even ridicule from his old friend would have put things back in perspective, but Father Peter's passive acceptance of the story unnerved Matt even more than ever.

'I'm sure that Eddie must be overreacting,' Matt continued. 'But he's a pretty clever guy you know? What if he's right? What if people really are in danger?' The old priest just nodded slowly and his rheumy eyes looked like they were somewhere else, but Matt was desperate for a response. 'Tell me what you think Father, has Eddie lost the plot?'

The old man's eyes returned to the room and focused now on Matt - his whole manner seemed to suggest that the incredible story was indeed no great surprise. The priest had been around for many years and had probably heard quite a few stories of impending doom in his time, but his lack of scepticism still surprised Matt; it was as if his news had just confirmed what the old man already somehow suspected.

Father Peter rose stiffly from his chair and in the shadows of the old cottage his face looked even more haggard than ever. 'My boy, I have a horrible feeling that your friend might be right and that something very bad is going to happen – for that reason I think I need to come with you.'

Rupert Ward stood in front in front of the huge bay window of his study and roared with laughter. 'Preposterous, absolutely preposterous!' he boomed. 'Get a grip people, your imaginations are running away with you.'

'Daddy, please!' His daughter, Hayley pleaded. 'I'm sure Eddie knows what he's talking about...'

'Don't be ridiculous child, this stuttering buffoon of yours brings a bunch of complete strangers into my house with stories of Armageddon and you expect me to drop everything and run to the hills? This is the stuff of childish fantasies – for God's sake, grow up girl!'

Eddie came to Hayley's defence. 'I know it's d...difficult to accept Mr Ward but there really is no...'

'So, you're a scientist now are you?' Rupert Ward's eyebrows raised in incredulous humour. 'Are any of you?' He looked at each of his uninvited guests in turn and when his gaze fell on Father Peter, he snorted with mirth. 'Surely this is a little far-fetched for you, Father? Or have they managed to convince you that the day of judgement has finally arrived?'

Father Peter remained silent, but he returned the gaze without faltering. The magistrate's furious face suddenly looked flustered and he turned back to his daughter with a glare that demanded an apology.

'Daddy, can we just talk about it? At least listen to what Eddie's got to say, please.' Hayley, like the priest, had taken no convincing about the impending disaster – if Eddie believed this was happening, then it was – end of story. She adored Eddie and had total faith in everything about him - her father though, was another matter.

'I'll tell you what I'll do,' Rupert replied, his amusement once again giving way to anger. 'I'll go and walk Baxter and leave you lot to your delusional fantasies. Hopefully, by the time I return, the apocalyptic horsemen will have been and gone.' He turned and left the room and they heard him guffaw once more as he walked down the impressive hall.

They sat in silence for a while and Matt wondered whether Hayley's father had a point. After all, Rupert Ward was a distinguished magistrate, annoyingly pretentious perhaps, but he was no fool. Why should he - or anybody for that matter, take such an incredible claim seriously? Father Peter's lack of scepticism had astounded Matt; for some strange reason, the old priest had accepted the story without question, but Matt realised the vast majority of people just wouldn't believe them. If they went public on this without thinking things through, they would be subject to ridicule or even suspicion and he somehow doubted that Sir Richard and his cronies would back their story.

'So, what are we going to do?' Matt asked the group.

'Tell the authorities,' Mel suggested.

'Who? the police?' Eddie asked. 'S…Some local politician? Who's going to believe us? I can tell even you people aren't convinced.'

Hayley sat on the side of Eddie's chair and put an arm around his shoulders in a show of support. She was so thin that she almost made the lanky engineer look brawny. 'I believe in you Eddie,' she said.

Eddie sighed, 'Look, I've calculated the rate of degeneration and everything points to an uncontrolled reaction occurring around f...forty hours from now. We can s...sit around and w...wait for it to happen or we can do something proactive, it's up to you.'

Matt looked to Father Peter, but the old man seemed lost in thought, so he made his own decision. 'Eddie's right, it doesn't matter how crazy this all sounds, it makes sense to assume the worst. Okay, if we're wrong, we're going to look bloody stupid, but if we don't prepare ourselves and Eddie *is* right, we might not be feeling anything at all - especially if Jill's condition is anything to go by.'

'Let's phone the press,' Mel suggested. 'That woman who's been hounding you ever since the accident – she'll listen surely.'

Matt looked uncomfortable. 'She'll listen all right, but that doesn't mean she'll believe us. They'll probably even run a story - but more than likely they'll make us out to be delusional fanatics and, even if we could convince her, what difference will it make, Eddie says it can't be prevented?'

'Perhaps the people at Degenesys will be able to find a way to stop it,' Hayley said. 'There must be something they can do.'

'I'm s...sorry, but I'm not s...sure there is,' Eddie said 'There's s...so much material in the early stages of degeneration, including the s...structure of the Degenesys building itself, that it would be impossible to encase.'

'What if all affected material was taken down and enclosed in the dome?' Matt suggested.

'Impossible, the whole b...building would have to be demolished around it and the dome's just not b...big enough anyway.'

'Is there any more insulating material available?' Mel asked.

'The ceramic material is state of the art, developed from nano-technology by the Ministry of Defence; it's difficult to m...manufacture and hellishly expensive. We carry a s...spare module in the national s...stores but that's it.'

Father Peter spoke for the first time. 'I'm afraid I'm not very technically minded,' he said. 'Assuming this event cannot be prevented, what exactly can we expect on Monday? In layman's terms I mean.'

Eddie took a deep breath and glanced nervously at the priest. 'I was involved in a HAZOP s...study early in the project's development stage,' he said. 'The risk of something like this happening was thought s...so improbable that it hardly warranted consideration, but a number of potential scenarios were modelled all the same. At the time it was made abundantly clear I was not to discuss it with anyone outside of the s...senior development team and their advisors.'

Mel's face reddened. 'I can't believe that you knew all along that something like this could actually happen?'

'There's always a risk with new technologies and the consequences of s...such a failure were of course evaluated, that's why every precaution was taken in protecting the s...system. The chances of an uncontrolled reaction were considered infinitely low.'

'Were they really?' Mel snapped. 'So what worst case scenario did the study conclude?'

Eddie looked even more uncomfortable. 'The rate of current degeneration is very slow but it will increase exponentially until, at around ten o' clock on Monday morning, a critical point will be reached, and then it's possible that the Degenesys plant's infrastructure will s...suddenly... just disintegrate.'

All eyes fell on the engineer - some compassionately, some accusingly, but all implored him to continue. Eddie swallowed with an audible gulp and then he went on. 'Perhaps that will be the end of it, but it's also possible that the consequential energy wave will travel for miles triggering more flashes and more waves whenever it encounters enough reactive m...material. In the worst case, Aylesbury will be hit inside a minute and the reaction will spread in all directions, p...probably until it reaches the coast.'

More silence, broken this time by Hayley. 'And will it stop there?' She asked, shakily.

'Probably... possibly... I don't know - it depends upon density of shipping and hundreds of other variables - you s...see, it's possible that s...seagoing vessels could act as s...sort of s...stepping-stones and there's a lot of other reactive material crossing the channel s...such as cables and rail links. However, if the s...surge doesn't encounter any reactive material in a few miles, it will probably dissipate.' Eddie looked into Hayley's eyes for some sign of encouragement, but his girlfriend seemed petrified. He turned back to the others and cleared his throat again before continuing. 'In the worst case s...scenario we have to assume that the reaction will reach the continent, and from there... who knows?'

'So what happens to anyone caught up in it?' Hayley's voice trembled.

'As I've already s…said, buildings will probably collapse and anyone driving a car…'

Mel interrupted. 'I believe,' she started, glaring at Eddie as if daring him to challenge her, 'that anyone in the vicinity of a flash will end up like Jill Davies - completely devoid of memory or reason, they won't have a clue how to survive their predicament.'

'In affected areas,' Eddie continued, ignoring her. 'There might be limited sh…shelter, and a lack of tools to rebuild anything,' Eddie said. 'And it's going to be cold; I know it's nearly April but the forecast is for another really cold s…spell – even s…snow! It's possible that synthetic clothing will also disintegrate with the reaction - it might even trigger one!'

'People could freeze to death!' Mel said and the room fell quiet as each of them tried to visualise the terrifying scenario

'Okay,' Matt said, counting with his fingers. 'It's four o' clock now, so if we warn people, they've got thirty-six hours to prepare - what could they do?'

'The best thing would be to get away from built up areas, find somewhere devoid of any reactive material and just sit it out.'

'You mean reactive material like clothing?' Mel sneered. 'You suggest people should freeze to death, half-naked on some hillside? I think I'd rather take my chances here.'

Matt could see Mel's anger rising - in her eyes Eddie was to blame for their predicament. He decided to interject. 'Natural textiles might not be affected,' he suggested. 'Or old stuff. Remember, old stuff doesn't react.'

'It would have to be very old, hundreds of years to be s...sure its material was inert,' Eddie said. 'Not the s...sort of thing you find in the average wardrobe. You'd have to raid a m...museum.'

'So, it seems we're all going to be in the crap whether we're caught in a flash or not,' Mel said.

For a while the only sound came from the fireplace where trapped moisture within the burning logs crackled and snapped as it vaporised in micro-explosions. Eventually, Hayley spoke with a subdued, faltering voice. 'What about us?' She asked 'Where could *we* go to be safe?

'S...Somewhere remote,' Eddie said, 'and s...somewhere away from...' He trailed off, as if reluctant to continue.

'There's something else isn't there?' Mel demanded. 'Something you're not telling us.'

Eddie paused before replying. 'Well, the HAZOP considered every possible eventuality, no matter how remote - we had to ensure the protection of the public...'

'Well you did a bloody good job, didn't you?' Mel interrupted.

'Leave him alone,' Hayley said, 'It's not Eddie's fault this has happened.

'She's right,' Matt said. 'Eddie, go on – there is something else isn't there?'

'Well, it's just that… there are f…far more dangerous processing plant around; if the reaction hits them they might also be destroyed. There'll be f…fires, explosions…'

Matt stood up, 'Shit, the nukes!' he said. 'The nukes might blow - there'll be devastation.'

'Most of the nuclear reactors have been decommissioned s…so devastation's a bit s…strong,' Eddie said. 'You're right though, in the worst case there'll be a s…significant local radiation hazard. We need to get as far away from them as possible, and we need to think about prevailing w…wind directions.'

Mel got up from her chair and stormed out of the room.

Chapter 9

It was early evening and the roads through Oxford were busy with pedestrians either coming home late from shopping, or going out on the town early. The spicy aroma of Indian food filled the interior of the Toyota as Matt followed Mel's directions through the damp city streets. Yet another power cut had forced them into the city to seek takeaway food to take back to Hayley's house where the others had been left planning their best course of action. Matt had tried to call Sir Richard several times earlier, but he hadn't answered, so Matt had left a lengthy message, which in hindsight had probably sounded more than a little crazy. He guessed that Sir Richard's promise to "sort something out" for him would now probably not be fulfilled whatever the outcome on Monday. He squinted at the rear-view mirror where headlamps from the vehicle behind, were dazzling him. The road was almost devoid of cars, but the person following was obviously in a hurry and apparently frustrated at being held up. Arsehole, Matt thought, some people didn't give a damn about conserving energy. He glanced down at his own fuel gauge, which was just over half full. Still, if Eddie was right, the energy crisis might not be a problem for much longer.

'Are we nuts or what?' he said to Mel. 'Do we honestly believe that on Monday morning this whole area might be destroyed? It's just bizarre!'

Mel repositioned the plastic bag on her lap, which was becoming uncomfortably hot. 'I know exactly what you mean,' she said. 'I keep running it over in my mind; one minute I believe it, the next I don't; I really don't know what to think.'

Matt had taken the young doctor with him because he realised that she had been on the brink of exploding back at the house and thought it best to put a distance between her and Eddie for a while. 'It's not Eddie's fault, you know. I'm sure nobody dreamt that such a thing could actually happen.'

'You heard him Matt – they foresaw the risk and chose not to disclose it in case it jeopardised the project. If your friend's right, and this turns into a disaster, I say he's as much to blame as anybody and if people get hurt and we didn't warn them, then we'll be guilty too. I know you said we should wait until we've heard from Sir Richard, but time's not on our side, Matt. We have to tell people what we know, and we need to tell them now.'

'Okay, I'll call Tanya Fox as soon as we get back.'

'No, pull in somewhere now and get it over with.'

'Alright, I'll turn into a side street,' he said, indicating left. 'Anyway, this guy behind's really starting to annoy me.' Matt took a left into a narrow residential road, which was lined on both sides with cars, some of which looked like they hadn't been driven for months. 'Shit, he's only coming the same way,' Matt said, looking again in the mirror. For a moment the headlights were no longer directly in his eyes as the following vehicle turned into the side street and, for the first time, he made out its shape and colour. It was a large, black van, just like those he had seen parked up at Degenesys the day before.

'Mel, I think we're being followed,' he said accelerating in an attempt to lose the larger vehicle in the narrow street.

'Are you sure?' Mel, asked, glancing nervously over her shoulder. Matt swung into another side road; again the vehicle followed them 'God, I think you might be right!'

Matt accelerated again and the distance between the two vehicles increased momentarily, as the van's size hindered its progress along the narrow street, but then it closed again as the road widened. Suddenly the Toyota lurched forward violently as the van rammed them from behind. Mel screamed as she was thrust back in her seat and cartons of Indian food spilled from her lap.

'Christ, did he just hit us on purpose?' she yelled.

Her questioned was answered when a second impact caused the Toyota to swerve alarmingly. There was a loud 'thwack' as the vehicle's wing mirror struck a parked car and shattered. Matt struggled to regained control and accelerated again until the two vehicles were careering at a reckless speed along the narrow street.

'Matt, be careful!' Mel shouted as the parked cars on either sided blurred past them at an alarming pace.

'Hold on!' Matt yelled. 'There's a junction ahead.' Suddenly, icy wind filled the car as the sunroof opened. 'What the hell are you doing?' he shouted.

'Just spicing things up for our friends behind,' she screamed back and tossed a carton of Beef Madras up through the opening.

Glancing at the rear view mirror, Matt saw the carton splatter against the van's windscreen and its wipers immediately started, smearing greasy food across the glass. Matt accelerated again as Mel slung another carton of curry through the sunroof. The van slowed and the distance between them started to increase again. Suddenly, they were at the junction and tires squealed as Matt swung the Toyota out onto a main road narrowly missing a taxi, which swerved, blaring its horn at them. Matt accelerated away and, for the moment, could see no sign of the van following.

'Over there, on the right.' Mel pointed at the entrance of a small car park. A sign read "Natural History Museum". Matt immediately swung into a dimly-lit car park, pulled up behind one of the few cars already parked there and quickly extinguished the Toyota's lights. They both ducked down and peered out into the darkness.

'That was quick thinking back there,' Matt said, looking in admiration at the young doctor.'

'I think we've lost them,' Mel whispered. 'Who the hell were they?'

Mel's face looked pale and scared in the car park lights and it suddenly struck Matt how beautiful she was. He had an urge to lean across and hold her; tell her how attractive he found her, but he quickly pushed such thoughts from his mind. He didn't want to get involved - relationships meant commitment; commitment meant responsibility and that was the last thing he wanted – now more than ever.

'I've a feeling Sir Richard's finally picked up my message,' he said. 'I reckon the bastard's sent his suits out to try and stop us from telling anyone else.'

'If you're right, it's probably best if we stay put for a while; we can't risk being followed back to Hayley's house. Make the call Matt - while you do, I think I'll have a look around the museum – see if there's anything we could use.'

Matt studied her face, wondering if she was serious. 'What do you want to do, rob the place? It's full of stuffed animals and dinosaur bones from what I remember.'

'Don't worry, I'm not going to ransack the museum, just have a look that's all. I took my sister there when she came over last year. That stuff you were saying about old things – I remember that there's some sort of exhibition in a separate part of the building. Artefacts collected by some explorer – all sorts of interesting stuff. I don't know – it might give us an idea that's all.'

'Suit yourself,' he said, 'but don't do anything to draw attention to yourself. Hey, are you sure I'm all right to park here?'

Mel smiled at the absurdity of his question, 'Look, if you get a ticket, I'll pay,' she said, getting out of the car. 'Make the call, I won't be long; the place closes soon.'

'Remember the food's getting cold,' Matt shouted after her. 'Or what's left of it,' he mumbled to himself. Then he grabbed his phone and dialled the number Tanya Fox had given him. When she answered, the newsreader's voice sounded as harmonic as ever, despite being on the phone.

'Finally!' She said. 'We were beginning to think you'd left the country. So, what's the story with Jill Davies, Matt?'

'Tanya, listen. There's a serious problem at the plant and people need to be warned…'

Tanya remained silent as he told her everything he knew about the predicted disaster and when she eventually did speak, there was a subtle difference in the tone of her voice. 'Thanks Matt, now tell me what's going on with Jill.'

Matt wasn't surprised; after pestering him all week for information, she didn't believe his story. She obviously thought he was winding her up - revenge for her incessant phone calls. 'Look, go to the plant and see what's happening for yourself,' Matt said. 'Or contact Sir Richard Harvey, he knows what's going on for sure!' Exasperated, he hung up, got out of the car and shaking his head in dismay, headed towards the museum entrance to find Mel.

The interior was pretty much as he expected it; he entered a brightly-lit hall, displaying row after row of exhibits. There were stuffed mammals depicting signs encouraging children to touch and feel their fur, and there were huge reconstructed dinosaur skeletons with signs warning the same children not to. The museum had very few visitors this late in the evening and there was no sign of Mel at all. He wandered in and out of the various displays following what he thought must be the planned route without paying too much attention to the exhibits. Then to his left he saw an alcove leading to another room. A sign read: "The Pitts River Exhibition".

Matt followed the directions and entered a second hall, smaller than the first, but which was in total contrast to the main building. Low lighting, row upon row of old cabinets and a distinctly musty smell gave him the impression of being in the library of some old mansion. As his eyes adjusted to the relative darkness Matt realised that larger exhibits were suspended from the walls and ceilings. Old pieces of furniture, boats, suits of armour, even a couple of huge Native American totem poles, were displayed. He spotted Mel disappearing behind a row of cabinets displaying voodoo memorabilia and hurried to join her before he lost track of her again. When he reached her, Mel was opening and closing cabinet drawers, full of displayed items protected by locked glass tops.

'Did you make the call?' she asked.

'Yeah, but I don't think she believed me – still, I know the woman; however sceptical she is, she'll soon uncover the truth and when she does all hell's going to break loose. Come on - we need to go, the food's getting cold.'

Mel shrugged her shoulders and continued to pull open drawers. 'It would be easy to take something, don't you think?' She whispered.

Matt noticed that her hands were shaking and wondered if she was all right. 'Don't be stupid, there's bound to be alarms, CCTV, you name it!'

'I don't think so, none of this is really valuable, and these drawers have flimsy locks, no alarms as far as I can see.'

Mel cracked her knuckles and Matt started to feel strangely nervous. 'Don't even think about it!' He said. 'There's nothing here of use anyway - come on, let's get back to the others.'

'Don't be so impatient. Look over there – some old guns, they might be useful!'

'Not old enough I'm afraid, and anyway what are you planning to do - stick them down your jumper? Come on, the place is closing…' Matt was interrupted by a beep from his phone alerting him to a received text; he read the message.

'pls call – urgent!' It read.

'Looks like Eddie's having another crisis,' Matt said. 'I'll have to phone him, but not from in here - let's go back to the car.'

'You go; I haven't finished looking around. I'll be out in a few minutes.'

'Okay, but don't go doing anything stupid,' he said. 'There's nothing here of any use to us, honestly.'

'I promise!' she said, raising her eyebrows, feigning innocence.

Reluctantly, Matt left her to peruse the various drawers and headed back to the museum car park. As he reached his car he glanced back at the impressive architecture and wondered what had got into Mel; it was almost as if she was purposely trying to get into trouble. Perhaps it was a desperate attempt to rid herself of the terrible responsibility that he was also feeling. Matt put the thought out of his mind and dialled his friend's number.

Eddie answered almost immediately. 'Matt, we're on the news, the police are looking for us – in connection with the incident, they s…say. You'd better get back here as s…soon as you can.'

'Damn, that's all we need. Okay, I'll get Mel and head back – I'll see you in half an hour.'

'No, I've got to go out – there's s…something I need to do,' Eddie said. 'Get back here and keep an eye on Hayley for me, Father Peter's gone home for the night and her f…father's being a right arsehole'.

'When will you…?' Matt suddenly noticed the museum doors were closing and there was no sign of Mel. Christ, where the hell was she? 'I've got to go Eddie, see you later.' Matt ran to the doors and pushed them, only to find that they had already been locked. Museum staff were leaving now; some were looking at him suspiciously. A young man rode past on a mountain bike. 'It's closed mate, you'll have to come back tomorrow,' he shouted.

Matt nodded and wondering what to do for the best he wandered back to his car. Mel was obviously still inside; hiding, he supposed – he had no idea what she hoped to achieve, but he couldn't ring her in case he gave her away – he supposed he would just have to wait for her to appear - stupid bloody woman!

Matt turned on the car radio and tuned into Radio Oxford. He had missed the beginning of the local station's six-o-clock news and a male newsreader was currently reporting an escaped mental patient in the north of England.

'…a vehicle escorting the mentally ill man failed to arrive at a secure hospital in Nottinghamshire yesterday and it is feared that the patient, Arthur Wiseman, may have escaped. The forty-two year old paranoid schizophrenic was being transported to Rampton High Security Hospital from another psychiatric clinic in Yorkshire. North Yorkshire Police have issued a warning that the patient has a history of violence and should not be approached by members of the public.'

The newsreader paused and a female colleague continued. 'Meanwhile, Thames Valley Police are trying to trace two engineers from the Degenesys energy recycling plant in Aylesbury. A woman was injured at the site on Wednesday evening when a reactor module failed. The plant has suffered a number of unexplained breakdowns recently and police have not ruled out industrial sabotage. Matthew Campbell and Edward Colemen are senior members of the Degenesys staff who police believe may be implicated in an attempted terrorist act.'

'The bastard,' Matt muttered, guessing Sir Richard had made the implications.

'In other news,' the male newsreader started, 'the visiting Joan of Arc exhibition in London has suffered...' Matt turned off the radio. He looked nervously around at the now empty car park and then towards the museum. Rows of arched windows were built into the impressive sandstone walls. The huge oak doors, closed now, were framed by another arch, which served as the base of a central tower section. This stood higher than the rest of the building and supported one end of the apex of the glass roof. Somewhere in there, Mel was on a mission to steal useless artefacts while he, already a wanted man, waited conspicuously in the empty car park of the closed museum. This is ridiculous; he thought and getting out of the car, marched towards the closed entrance. Without considering the consequences, he pressed the button of an intercom mounted close to the doors. There was a buzz, then silence. Matt waited for a minute or so before stepping back and starting to shout.

'Mel, its Matt, where are you? What the bloody hell are you up to in there?'

Suddenly a deep voice spoke from the intercom. 'Who are you? What do you want?'

'Hello – my friend is... er... missing; I think she may have been trapped in the museum when you closed.'

A pause, then the deep voice returned. 'Wait there – I'll come and let you in.'

Matt couldn't place the accent but the owner of the voice sounded foreign. Almost a minute passed before Matt heard heavy locks being operated. Then one of the oak doors swung noisily open to reveal the largest man he had ever seen. The oriental guy standing over him was so wide that he almost filled the doorway through which two men could normally pass with ease. The giant's long black hair was tied in a ponytail at the back of his massive head and his one good eye looked down at Matt disapprovingly. The other was hidden behind an eye patch, which along with the ponytail made him look like some sort of far-eastern pirate. Matt couldn't help thinking that something about this huge man was familiar, but where he had seen him before escaped him.

'Come!' The man growled, stepping back from the doorway to allow Matt to enter, then closing and locking the door behind them both. Without another word he turned his back on Matt and walked into the museum's entrance hall.

Matt paused before reluctantly following the massive man into the main hall and through the displays now eerily shrouded in darkness due to the subdued lighting. The man's bulky frame was somehow compressed into a pair of clean blue overalls, which were almost bursting at the seams as he walked. Eventually, Matt was led through a door marked private and through a short corridor to another door. The man unlocked this door and gestured for Matt to enter. When he did so, he saw Mel sitting sheepishly at a table set in the centre of a small utility room. Before Matt had time to react, the door closed behind him and he heard the key turn in the lock; they were both alone in the room.

'How did you get in?' Mel whispered.

'Just rang the doorbell – how do you think I got in? What have you done Mel?'

'Sorry – a moment of insanity I'm afraid.' Her eyes filled up and she stood up from the chair and moved towards him. 'I'm so sorry Matt; I think I'm going out of my mind with all this…'

Matt wiped her eyes with his thumbs and then held her; her small, firm body felt so good against him that he almost forgot their predicament. 'Who is that guy?' He whispered close to her ear. 'The man's a giant!'

Mel regained her composure and looked up at Matt with eyes smudged with makeup. 'I hid inside an old boat until everyone had gone, then I stole a compass – well nearly – I forced one of the drawers but he caught me. I didn't see him until he grabbed me from behind. He scared me to death – he's so strong.'

'I guess he's a caretaker - security or something. Where do you think he's gone?'

'Gone to call the "Creator" apparently, whoever that is.' She smiled through her tears and suppressed a giggle.

'Perhaps he's religious,' Matt suggested, smiling back. 'We've got to get out of here, the police are…'

Suddenly the door reopened and the huge oriental man re-entered with a tray laden with mugs and a teapot.

'You want some tea?' he asked, setting down the tray and started pouring from the large white pot'.

Matt looked at Mel who screwed her face quizzically at their bizarre situation, then he looked back at their host in an attempt to try and figure out what this giant meant to do with them. The man handed Mel a steaming cup and his single dark eye locked onto hers. 'Who are you lady? Why did you try and take the clock?'

'Look, this is all a big mistake,' Matt interrupted. 'Mel isn't a thief, it was just a joke… you know, a prank. Anyway it wasn't a clock; she was trying to take a compass.'

'Tell me why you took the … compass.'

'Perhaps we should introduce ourselves,' Mel said and handed him her business card. 'My name's Melissa Knight, I'm a doctor at the John Radcliffe Hospital and this is Matthew Campbell, he's from...'

'Yes, I just seen him on TV.'

Matt's heart dropped. 'Have you called the police?'

'Creator will decide – I left message on his phone.'

'Look, Mel is a respected medical consultant,' Matt said. 'You can see she's no thief.'

'We say in Japan that the reputation of a hundred years can be ruined by the conduct of one hour.'

Matt realised that although their captor was unlikely to be attending many Mensa seminars, he was not going to have the wool pulled over his eyes either. Their only chance was to convince him that their intentions were honourable, and perhaps the best way would be to confide in him - but not yet, he decided. Maybe they could win him over without taking that particular risk, but first they had to persuade him not to call the police.

'What's your name?' he asked.

The big man stood up and, to Matt's amusement, bowed formally. 'My Japanese name is Josuke Tanigaki, but people here call me Joe Sumo.'

'You're a wrestler!' Matt exclaimed, at last remembering where he had seen the man, 'You had bouts on that Friday night sports programme – Slamdown was it?'

The big man smiled and nodded. 'Smackdown,' he corrected. 'Yes Joe Sumo was a wrestler once, but not since…' he pointed at the eye patch. 'Now I work for the Creator – it doesn't pay so much but I guess it doesn't hurt so much either. Wrestling is a game here, not like in Japan, but there are still accidents.'

'What happened to us tonight was a sort of accident, Joe,' Matt said. 'We really didn't mean any harm.' But the big man appeared to be lost in thought and didn't seem to hear him; he just sipped his tea and stared into space.'

'Did you have a wrestling career in Japan?' Mel asked.

Joe Sumo blinked and he seemed to return to the room. His one eye stared proudly at her. 'Sumo wrestling is not occupation in Japan; it's way of life. I had no choice in the matter; at thirteen I was sent to special school because I was big and very strong for my age; I was taught the Sumo culture, history and technique and was made very big – two-eighty kilos. I dedicated my life to Sumo for ten years before I come to Britain.'

'How did you get hurt?' Mel asked.

'Never mind,' the big man looked uncomfortable and obviously wanted to change the subject. 'Tell me why you want the compass.'

Matt and Mel looked at each other and somehow without communicating came to a mutual agreement. 'All right, I'll tell you,' Matt said, 'but you probably won't believe me. We think something bad is about to happen.'

Joe Sumo listened intently as Matt told their story with Mel interjecting at regular intervals. Their tale ended with the events at the museum and they both waited for some sort of response from the ex-wrestler. Joe Sumo just sat in his chair staring at the floor shaking his head slowly.

'Stealing the compass was a ridiculous idea,' Mel said, standing up again. 'I don't even know why I did it; I think it I just wanted to... I don't know...' She started to cry again.

Joe Sumo watched in silence as Matt held her in his arms and then finally spoke. 'It is better to wash your old kimono than steal new one - you should remember that!' He paused again and studied them. 'You seem honourable people and there is no deception in your eyes, but that is not the same as believing you myself. You should not have come here. However, a Sumo believes he should not add trouble to those who are already troubled, so I will not do so to you. He got up, walked to the door and unlocked it. 'You can go,' he said, 'but don't come back'.

Chapter 10

'Thank God,' Hayley said as she opened the door. 'I've been going insane stuck here on my own. Eddie's not answering his phone and daddy's still in a strop; he's gone to bed.'

'Sorry Hayley,' Matt said. 'Mel and I had a bit of trouble - it's been sorted, but I'm afraid the food's cold.'

Hayley took the plastic takeaway bag and made off towards the kitchen. 'Don't worry – the power's back on so I can heat it up; there's only us to eat it now anyway.'

They followed her into the house. 'Are you sure we're alright to stay the night?' Mel asked.

'Of course, you both look exhausted, we've got loads of room and Father Peter won't be back until the morning.'

'Is he okay?' Matt asked.

'Father Peter? He's fine - nothing seems to surprise him, does it? Oh, he's decided to come with us by the way.'

'Good!' Matt said. 'Er…come with us where?'

Hayley loaded foil cartons into the oven. 'There are some maps in the dining room,' she said. 'Eddie said I should take you through our plan; apparently we're going to Wales. Come on, I'll show you.'

In the dining room the large table was awash with cups, maps and sheets of paper. A battered Ordnance Survey map lay open amongst the chaos and Matt could see that Hayley had been copying meticulous details from the map onto a large piece of pink paper.

'Hey, that's from the plant,' Matt said. 'The paper we use in the reactor chamber.'

'Apparently it has low entropic value – Eddie says he's thought of a way we can protect the original maps from decomposing but it's too risky to have them with us. It's possible normal paper might be destroyed by the reaction so he's asked me to make a copy of one of them.'

'This must have taken you hours,' Mel said, picking up the sheet of strange paper, amazed at the detail of the reproduction.

Hayley smiled proudly and pointed at the original map. 'This is where Eddie says we should sit it out.' She was pointing at a pale-green patch amidst a swirling fingerprint of close-knit contour lines. It depicted a copse with a tiny stream running through it to a small lake to the north. A single black word was printed in ominous contrast across the pale-green copse.

'Ruins!' Mel said. 'I don't like the sound of that,'

'Apparently it's an old Abbey, Eddie says he slept there last year when he was hill walking.'

One of Eddie's undiscovered hobbies, Matt thought. How did I ever miss that one?

'Eddie says the place is ancient so it should be safe; despite its age it still offers good shelter and it's never been renovated as far as he knows. Unfortunately the doors are gone but the roof is intact over a couple of the rooms and there's even an old fireplace - it sounds quite cosy!' Hayley seemed excited at the prospect at staying in the old Abbey. 'He says it should be warm enough for us to sit out the reaction and then we should try and find something more suitable, er... that's if there's anything still standing – his words, not mine!'

Hayley's anxiety seemed now to have been replaced by manic enthusiasm and Matt wondered again at the absurdity of their situation. This woman wasn't preparing for catastrophe – she was planning a bloody camping trip. Apart from Eddie, it was only Father Peter who seemed convinced of the gravity of the situation – the rest of them, he realised, were still hedging their bets.

'Eddie wants us to leave by tomorrow lunchtime,' Hayley said. 'There's a lot to prepare - I think we should all turn in.'

Matt's room overlooked the courtyard. He peered out of the leaded window into the darkness and wondered where the hell Eddie was. He turned to the dresser, where his mobile phone was charging and picked it up. If his friend was right, this might be the last charge it would ever receive. He dialled Eddie's number but it went straight to answer so he hung up. He was about to return the phone to the dresser when he paused and for some reason thought of Mel. Impulsively he typed 'u ok?' and sent the text message to her number. Then he felt strangely embarrassed and got into bed. Laying there in the darkness he thought of the young doctor, probably asleep in one of the other bedrooms and hoped his text wouldn't wake her. He wondered what she might be wearing - if anything – but realising that such thoughts were not going to help him get to sleep, he forced his mind to focus on the day ahead. How would they manage the logistical nightmare of getting everybody safely to the ruined abbey and far enough away from the dangerous manifestations of modern life including the very vehicles they would travel in? His thoughts were suddenly interrupted by an incoming text alert from the phone; he picked it up and read the message.

'can't sleep' it read.

'me neither' He typed and pressed send, before lying back down in his bed still holding the phone. He thought about calling her but the last thing he wanted was for Mel to feel awkward about him in the morning with everything else that was going on. Frustrated, he returned his phone to the charger, lay down again and closed his eyes. Sleep was a long time coming but eventually his mind started drifting, conscious thoughts being replaced by meandering dreams. He imagined a wave of crimson flashes sweeping the country like a lightning storm from hell. The world was crumbling to dust around him, but in his dreams his bed was immune from the devastation around him. He was warm and safe in its sanctuary and then, in his mind, Mel was suddenly there with him, holding her warm body close to his, kissing his neck from behind. 'You're gorgeous...' he sighed.

'I had to come,' she whispered back into his ear and Matt, feeling her breath on his skin, realised that he was waking now and this was no longer a dream - Mel was there in the flesh, her nakedness pressing against his back. She had come to his room and climbed into bed as he slept. Half asleep, but fully aroused now, he turned to meet her kiss and she gasped with pleasure as he found her.

It was daylight when they were awoken by the crunch of tyres on the gravelled drive.

'That must be Eddie!' Matt said, jumping from the bed to look out of the window. Mel followed him more slowly pulling the duvet to her slim body.

'Shit, get down!' Matt hissed. 'It's the bloody police!'

They both cowered below the window, Mel wrapping the duvet around them both as they peered from behind the curtains like two nosy neighbours. Two police officers, a man and a woman, strode to the front door and rang the doorbell.

'What are we going to do?' Mel asked.

'What can we do? Just wait and see what happens.'

They waited for what seemed like an eternity before the two police officers left the house and returned to the car. Apparently satisfied for the time being, they drove off down the long drive.

Mel kissed Matt gently on the lips and said, 'I'm going to get dressed, see you downstairs in a minute.'

Matt felt a surge of trepidation – he shouldn't get involved with this woman. He had managed to avoid serious relationships so far in his life and now here he was getting attached to someone the day before… Jesus - he really should stop this now! He studied the young doctor as she pulled on her clothes and felt a surge of nervous excitement - who was he kidding? He felt more alive now than at any time in his adult life. He was as excited as a teenager - the teenager that he had never been.

'They were asking about Eddie,' Hayley said, cracking an egg into a frying pan. 'I just told them the truth – that I didn't know where he was or when I would see him again. They seemed to believe me, then one of them received a call and they couldn't get out of here quick enough.'

Matt and Mel were sat at the kitchen table eating bacon and eggs as if they had not eaten a proper meal for weeks.

'You both seem in a better mood this morning,' Hayley said, smiling. 'Last night you each seemed at the end of your tether.'

'Amazing what a good night's sleep can…' Matt began, but was interrupted by the kitchen door being swung open.

Rupert Ward stood in the doorway, his mouth open and with an incredulous look on his pale face. He pointed back the way he had come and made as if to speak but couldn't seem to find the words.

'Daddy, what is it?'

'The… the news?' Rupert said, as if asking a question. 'The… they're evacuating Aylesbury - for God's sake, what have you people done?'

Hayley pulled out a chair and led her father to it. He sat down reluctantly and ran his hands through his grey, coifed hair.

'Good grief! Everything you described is going to happen isn't it?'

'Eddie's convinced,' Hayley replied, rubbing her father's back. 'The rest of us believe him too, I guess. We've decided we have to… just in case.'

'No… no, your friend's right, they don't evacuate a large town unless they're sure of a problem - something's going to happen all right! Dear God, are we safe here?'

'We don't think so, Mr Ward,' Mel said. We've decided to go west, into Wales. Eddie thinks we'll be safe there - please come with us?'

'Can Baxter can come too?'

The inflated ego of the conceited magistrate was disappearing right in front their eyes; Matt had a vision of the over-privileged public schoolboy the man had probably once been. Suddenly there was a sound of a heavy engine from the front of the house.

'Eddie!' Hayley cried, running out of the kitchen towards the front door. They all followed and were greeted by the sight of a huge vehicle with a Hi-Ab trailer pulling up in front of them. On the trailer a tarpaulin covered what appeared to be a large crate and a number of cardboard boxes strapped to wooden pallets. Eddie jumped down from the cab, beaming.

'The Unimog's the best industrial f…four-wheel-drive in the world,' he shouted above the sound of the chugging engine. 'The company used to use it for pylon work and I've just s…stolen it!'

'Christ Eddie, what do we want that prehistoric beast for?'

'And that's not all I've stolen,' he said, ignoring the question. 'Just wait and see what's on the back.'

Once the tarpaulin was removed, Eddie cut the boxes from the pallets and passed them down one at a time to Matt and Rupert. The first box was labelled 'EXTRA LARGE - BLUE', the second 'FOOTWARE - VARIOUS.'

'Inert clothing!' Matt exclaimed. 'For working inside the reactor.'

'I'm not s…sure how many there are; I cleaned out the whole s…stock from the central stores.' Eddie was now manoeuvring the large packing case using the HIAB hoist. 'Wait till you s…see this baby though!'

When the case was safely on the ground, Eddie unclipped a hasp and swung open the crate lid. Inside, a wooden frame supported a large opaque ceramic cylinder.

'The spare module!' Matt yelled. 'Eddie you're a genius.'

'Genius - yes,' Eddie said raising his eyebrows smugly. 'Actually, you gave m…me the idea yesterday when you suggested using the reactor dome as a containment area.'

'I don't think any of us will fit in that thing,' Hayley said.

'No, but we can put other things in it!' Matt said.

'Exactly,' Eddie grinned. 'We need to get it out of the case so that w…we can open it up. See the star shaped m…mechanism at the end of the cylinder; we need to be able to turn it. There's an inner cylinder that rotates within the outer body in order to align openings at the top and the bottom of the m…module in turn.'

'I'll leave you to it,' Matt said. 'I promised to pick Father Peter up - I'll be back later.'

When Matt and Father Peter returned, they brought with them a large bundle of maroon velvet drapes from the church and a small bag of the priest's belongings. As they entered the dining room Matt sensed an uncomfortable atmosphere had developed and guessed that they had interrupted an argument. The priest explained that the drapes were over a hundred years old and might serve as blankets or cloaks for their time at the abbey. Hayley looked relieved at their arrival and immediately set to work on the ancient material. Matt and Father Peter joined Mel, Rupert and Eddie at the dining room table. Baxter, Rupert's old beagle, lay by the fading log fire, seemingly oblivious to their mood. Rupert was apparently making a list, which already had a number of crossings out.

'Can't decide what should go in the module?' Matt asked, guessing at the cause of the disagreement.'

'There's just not enough room for everything we might need,' Mel said.

'And s…some people aren't being very practical,' Eddie grumbled.

'So penicillin and bandages aren't practical, now?' Mel snapped.

'M…Maybe, but do we really need to include toilet rolls?'

'So wipe your arse on the grass – see if I care!'

'All right, calm down', Matt interrupted. 'What have we got so far, Mr Ward?'

'Seeing as we're to be wiping our arses on the grass together I suppose you should really call me Rupert.' The magistrate said this so seriously that even Eddie smiled.

Rupert read from the list. 'We've agreed we should take some tools - knife, axe, hammer and nails. We need those…' he pointed to the ordinance survey maps that were now neatly stacked on one of the chairs. 'Then there's the medicine the young lady mentioned, a first aid kit, some rope, walking boots, extra clothes…'

Eddie interrupted. 'It's a s…small ceramic module - a m…metre across at most, not the bloody Tardis.'

'We should probably take a gun,' Matt suggested. 'Do you have one Rupert?'

'Only a shotgun – it might just fit in the module.'

Father Peter, who had so far remained silent, looked troubled - slowly he stood and retrieved his bag from the side of the room, then placed it on the table and carefully opened it. The others watched curiously as he removed first a small leather-bound bible and then an ornate golden cup.

'I'm afraid these also have to go with us,' he said quietly. 'At least the cup – it's very important.'

They all looked at the goblet he was holding; the flames of the log fire reflected from the polished gold onto their faces and Matt felt the room's ambience immediately change. The hostile atmosphere dissipated as those around him appeared mesmerised by the dancing flames on its surface - flames that slowly grew in intensity until they finally disappeared in a flash of crimson.

Matt felt as if he had been released from a trance; he turned towards the log fire and was astounded when he saw that the flames had long since died. He wondered what the cup meant to the priest but didn't ask; instead he just nodded, accepting without question that it should go with them. Somehow he knew that the golden goblet might prove to be more important to their quest than any map, gun or bandage.

Chapter 11

Arthur Wiseman fingered the plastic zip-tie as he watched the man chop vegetables on a slate countertop. The kitchen's décor was of traditional farmhouse style, but the multitude of expensive appliances contrasted its rustic charm. The aroma of roast beef sparked a rare feeling of nostalgia in Arthur's mind, but the only emotion it triggered was that of bitter resent. Classical music filled the kitchen – its source a digital music player, tastefully concealed in the antique pine surround. The chopping man hummed happily to the music, oblivious to the intruder's presence.

Arthur was amazed at how effective the doctor's zip ties had been in debilitating people, but the three men in the van outside had died far too quickly for his liking. Each time, in his excitement, he had applied the noose with unnecessary force and their struggles had only lasted a few minutes - this time he would try to be more careful.

The humming man turned and reached for a saucepan and Arthur stepped casually to one side to avoid being seen. The man tipped two handfuls of carrots into the pan and turned his attention to a colander of sprouts next to a chopping board. Arthur advanced on his prey, the plastic zip-tie held high and ready to snare his victim's throat, but one of Arthur's heavy boots scraped the flagstone floor and the man suddenly swung round in horror at the fearsome sight of his predator. He reacted quickly, grabbing Arthur's upraised arm with one hand and his throat with the other before a frenzied struggle ensued. Arthur shoved the man backwards, jamming his spine against the cold, slate countertop and snarled in his opponent's terrified face. The victim arched backwards in an attempt to avoid Arthur's slavering teeth and kneed his attacker hard in the groin. Arthur doubled over in pain and the man took his opportunity - grabbing the saucepan full of carrots he swung it with all his might at Arthur's prone head. The pan crashed into Arthur's temple, knocking him sideways into the countertop. Stunned by the blow and swimming in fiery pain, Arthur pushed against the slate surface in an attempt to steady himself, but as he did so his hand closed on something hard and wet. The man swung the saucepan again, but Arthur pushed himself backwards, dodging the blow. The saucepan clanked against ceramic tiles as Arthur grabbed the unbalanced man's collar with his left arm and shoved the kitchen knife into his victim's eye. Hot blood sprayed onto Arthur's hand as it forced the blade deeper into the struggling man's brain. Arthur stepped away and watched the dying man mouth something unintelligible before he slumped to the blood-soaked flagstone floor. Arthur rubbed his temple with one gory hand before reaching down to recover the zip-tie noose; then he staggered out of the kitchen to explore the rest of the house.

  As he left the kitchen Merlin spoke to him. 'There must be others in the house,' the inner voice said. Arthur climbed the stairs knowing the wizard was probably right; he knew from experience that people rarely cooked such a meal if they lived alone. This was a family house and the pictures on the walls confirmed the assumption. He examined one of them – a middle-aged woman held the reins of a horse, on which sat a pretty, blonde teenage girl. The farmhouse was in the background and the mother and daughter were both laughing. To Arthur, it looked as if they were laughing at him.

At the top of the stairs, he caught the sound of a voice from behind a door to his left. He edged the door open and steamy air engulfed his face. When it cleared, he saw the naked back of a girl sitting in a large claw-footed bath. The girl, whose damp, blonde hair was wrapped in a high bun, sang tunelessly along to the tinny music emanating from her iPod. Arthur slunk into the room and knelt behind the girl, listening to her voice for a while. Her eyes were closed, so he carefully lowered the plastic noose over her head – this time he would be careful not to over-tighten it. Like a child trying to guide the metal ring over the electrified wire of some fairground game, he knew that one slip would set off the alarm and end the contest. When it was in position, he slowly tightened the zip tie; the clicks of the plastic ratchet failed to penetrate the sound of the music and the girl didn't react until the moment she felt the plastic close around her throat. Suddenly her eyes sprang open and she immediately felt for her neck – Arthur pulled one more click. The zip tie was not particularly tight, but the reaction was spectacular. The horrified girl erupted from the bath and Arthur stepped back to watch the performance unfold. The girl stood in the centre of the bathroom, naked except for the plastic tie and the headphones clamped to her neck. The white leads dangled around her body as she span in circles clutching desperately at her throat. Arthur knew that she had seen him now, but apparently his intrusion was low on the girl's list of priorities. Then, despite the fact that her neck was starting to swell around the plastic, she somehow regained some composure. Running to the bathroom cabinet, she pulled open the door and swept the contents onto the floor. Arthur knelt with her as she rifled through the assortment of medicines, plasters, razors and grooming products. Arthur pointed at a pair of nail clippers, which she immediately grabbed and raised to her neck in an attempt to cut through the zip tie with its blades. She stood up and faced the mirror, but her hands were shaking and the blades wouldn't open far enough to get a purchase on the plastic. Arthur smiled at the girl's reflection and noticed that her lips were turning blue - he hoped she wasn't going to pass out just yet. For a moment she caught his eyes and he sensed that she was pleading with him to help her, then suddenly he felt her anger and she pushed past him, stumbling out of the bathroom and down the stairs. Arthur followed her into the kitchen, admiring her naked form and he started to feel aroused. He wanted to take her right then, but didn't want to ruin the show, so he decided to wait until she was more docile. The girl hardly paused when she saw her father in the pool of blood on the kitchen floor, but Arthur saw tears in her eyes as she stooped to pick up the gory knife from beside the body. She desperately tried to prise the point of the knife under the plastic tie but her throat was now swollen to a point that made it impossible, so she started to randomly slice at the plastic, oblivious to the damage she might do to herself. Her neck started to bleed badly from her actions so Arthur gently took the knife from her, whilst shushing at her to calm down. Arthur sensed that the girl realised she was at his mercy; if he didn't help her now she knew she was going to die. He smiled compassionately and pulled her to her feet. She was hardly able to stand, so he supported her as he led her back up the stairs and into the bathroom. There, he pushed her back against the wall and, taking another zip tie from his pocket, raised one arm high above her head and strapped her wrist to the radiator pipe. He repeated this for the other hand while the girl just stared into his eyes, silently pleading with him. Her face was turning blue now and as he let her go she slumped onto bent legs supported only by the zip ties around her wrists. Arthur kissed her gently and ran his hands over her body as he felt her mind slip into unconsciousness.

Caroline Stone dismounted the steaming horse and led it into the stable. Birthday Girl stood all of seventeen hands and towered above the forty year old woman but Caroline held complete dominion over the animal. She had been a natural with horses from an early age and was now considered one of the most accomplished equitation trainers in North Yorkshire. Caroline briefly rubbed down the animal with a handful of hay and kissed it's nose before securing the stable door. Birthday Girl was hot and needed grooming, but Caroline was intrigued by the white van that was parked in the rear courtyard so she decided to investigate first then return to the horse later. She walked to the van and looked through the passenger window but there was nobody in the cab, she thought about opening the rear doors but guessed they would be locked. In the week, John, her husband, had called a plumber to service the boiler but she doubted a visit on a Sunday afternoon was likely. She set off for the house feeling strangely unnerved. Passing the kitchen window, she peered in but couldn't see her husband who should have been preparing dinner by now. John always cooked the Sunday roast - Sundays were Caroline's day off.

Caroline Stone entered the house through the double doors of the conservatory. A well-established vine clung to the ceiling supported by wires and hooks. In a few months the vine would be heavy with fruit, but now it was devoid of leaves and to look at it the plant might have been dead except for the tiny green buds in the elbows of its branches. Two double-glazed doors led to the kitchen and dining room respectively, the kitchen door stood ajar.

'John, where are you?' Caroline called. 'Whose van is that in the courtyard?'

There was no reply so she opened the second door and entered the dining room, which was a shortcut to the hall where stairs led to the upper floors. For some reason she was shaking; she knew that her fear was unfounded but intuitively sensed that something was wrong all the same. She crossed the room to the fireplace above which, one of John's antique swords hung in symmetry with its matching steel combat scabbard. The sword was an old cavalry sabre from the Napoleonic Wars, which John had picked up in an antique shop in York. Quietly she lifted the weapon from its mountings and held it in front of her. The sword was heavier than she expected and she had to use both hands - one on the worn leather bound hilt and one, just in front, at the cold steel root of the blade. She crept into the hall with the sabre waiving unsteadily in front of her.

'Rebecca? ... John? ... Where are you?' Her voice, almost pleading for an answer was greeted only by silence.

Suddenly there was a thump from upstairs and Caroline's head swung towards the stairs immediately followed by the sword. Shaking uncontrollably now, she moved towards the impressive stairway, which curved out of sight as it rose. Her feet were silent on the deep carpet but she was conscious of the sound of her breathing, which was becoming heavier with her growing conviction that something was seriously wrong. She started to climb the steps unsure whether to call out again – she decided not to, but hated the silence just the same. As Caroline neared the top of the stairway she caught a sound from the bathroom and felt immediate relief; Rebecca would be listening to her music and John had probably just slipped out somewhere. Suddenly feeling foolish, she propped the sabre against the wall and strode over to the bathroom door and knocked loudly.

'Rebecca, are you all right in there?' Silence - She knocked again.

She tried the door thinking it would be locked but, the latch clicked and the door opened an inch. 'Rebecca? May I come in?' She pushed the door fully open and then she saw her daughter. Rebecca's slumped, naked body was bruised and bloodied; it hung from grey bloated hands, which were bound to the radiator pipe above her. Rebecca's eyes seemed to stare at her mother accusingly; the look on her daughter's face was a mixture of dismay and horror. Caroline screamed - not a scream of terror that you might expect from the witness of such a horrific sight, but an unnatural, growling sort of scream that was more animal-like than human. At that moment she felt no grief - just an intense hatred for the creature that had done this thing. She swung round with an irrational, but uncontrollable intent to hunt down and exact revenge upon the person responsible. But as she turned, her anger diffused at the horrifying sight that met her eyes; all thoughts of hatred and revenge just dissipated and were replaced by those of pure terror. No more than six feet away, Arthur Wiseman stood facing her, his scarred naked body steaming and dripping with bath water. His swollen penis pointed threateningly at her, as did the ancient sword he held at his side.

Arthur grinned at the woman, totally engrossed with the evolving emotions emanating from her mind - at first bathing in the intense hatred and then wallowing in the fear that replaced it. Tears ran down his face - Arthur had never been so happy.

    Caroline Stone groaned and slumped unconscious to the floor.

Chapter 12

Unaware of the violent atrocities occurring far in the north, Melissa Knight shivered on a cold stone floor as she watched Hayley wrap one of the velvet drapes around her father; they were all freezing despite the fire that Eddie had lit in the huge fireplace of the ancient building. They had expected the old abbey to be quite cosy once the fire had been lit, but that was not the case. The old building was a place of solitude, uninhabited for centuries, overgrown with thorns and fit rather to be the lair of wild beasts than the home of human beings. It was dark now and the only light was from the fire and the candles placed sporadically around the stone walls' many alcoves. A sack of potatoes, carrots and onions was stashed in one corner - the only food they had allowed themselves to retain. Four of the potatoes were now baking on a flat stone that lay amongst the flames. In daylight the old abbey had been impressive, if not quite what they (other than Eddie) had expected. The building had once been huge judging by the remnants of walls, which still covered quite a large area of the hill right up to the edge of the copse. A small, clear stream ran out of the trees and followed the track down the hill. The water was clean and drinkable but they had no containers to store it so they had to drink directly from the bank whenever thirst took them. The only part of the building remaining intact was the old dormitory where presumably monks had once slept; a stone arched doorway led to the first of two rooms inside which, ornate decoration could still be made out in the stonework. The first room of the dormitory had most likely been used for general storage, though probably also contained the parlour and warming room where the brethren would have been allowed to warm themselves by the roaring fire during the winter months. Further in, through a second smaller arch, was a single long room which would have once been the sleeping area set out with beds stretching down each side, possibly with a chest for each monk's change of habit, pen, knife and needle.

Devoid of even such meagre possessions, the party now sheltered in the first room where they could benefit from the fire. They had hung velvet drapes across both doorways in an attempt to keep out the cold but it seemed to have little effect. The cold stone walls would probably take weeks to warm through despite the fire. They all wore several layers of the special inert clothing that Eddie had salvaged from the plant, but it was not designed for warmth and the church drapes were the only things that kept them from freezing to death. They had all repeatedly thanked the Father Peter for thinking of them.

The old priest had spent the afternoon scratching away at sheets of inert paper with a small piece of charcoal he had found, but now he had given up on the task. He seemed to think it was important that the unfolding events were recorded somehow, but he had eventually given up, annoyed with himself, but glad that they had included some writing material with the other possessions stored in the ceramic module. Father Peter now sat with his back to one of the cold walls and seemed lost in thought as he silently stared at the fire. Mel wondered what was on his mind, but she was more concerned about the raking cough the old man had developed as the day had progressed. Mel was sitting in the centre of the room with

Baxter, who alone among the party seemed in high spirits. The old dog seemed to be enjoying the adventure and had spent hours running around the ruins, sniffing out rabbits and barking at crows. For the humans though, this was a depressing place; not only were they extremely cold, but they were also very tired.

Since arriving, they had spent the afternoon loading the Unimog with anything in the vicinity that might be reactive and driving it to be dumped into an old quarry that lay almost a mile down the track. Even the barbed wire fence that was designed to keep the sheep out of the abbey had been pulled down and disposed of. It was even more depressing because some of the very objects they were discarding would have made them much more comfortable in their current situation.

Mel stared with contempt at the man that she blamed for their uncomfortable predicament. Eddie was curled up asleep on one of the red blankets because he planned to leave in the early hours to meet up with Matt. The two men had agreed to rendezvous at first light on a quiet road to the south where they would leave the Unimog and Matt's Toyota behind, along with the rest of civilisation, and return by trekking back across the hills on foot.

Hayley caught her glare. 'This isn't Eddie's fault you know,' she whispered.

Mel raised her eyebrows, but didn't respond, so Hayley came over and sat next to her. 'Are you all right, Mel? You seem agitated.'

'I just wish Matt was here, that's all,' she said. 'I wish I'd gone with him rather than sitting in this dump.' Deep down, she realised that it wasn't the cold that was bothering her; Matt was the first man she had slept with for some time and she was already missing his company. Somehow he made her feel safe, despite his reluctance to talk about his past.

'You really like him don't you?' Hayley asked.

'He's nice, but I'm not looking for a relationship.' She glared again at Eddie. 'I've had my fill of men, thank you very much.'

'Have you had… many relationships? I've only ever known Eddie.'

'A few – I even had a husband once,' Mel said. 'When I was studying in Melbourne I fell for a British author who had been researching a novel there. That's why I came to England; I left my family in Australia to get married and start a new life.'

'How romantic,' Hayley sighed. 'An author – was he famous?'

'Famous? No, but he was romantic all right – he made a living writing chic lit. A strange genre for a man, but he was reasonably successful and ambitious and I loved him.'

'What happened?'

An ironic smile touched Mel's lips. 'He travelled a lot with his work; that's what happened. It was several years before I discovered just how seriously he had taken his research. When I challenged him, he hadn't even tried to deny it; it was as if he expected me to accept that infidelity was inevitable in his line of work. After we separated, I had a string of unhappy relationships with men who inevitably cheated on me. I soon came to the conclusion that no man can be trusted, so I engrossed myself with my career and became resigned to the fact that I'm better off single.'

'Not all men are the same,' Hayley said. 'I don't think Matt's like that.'

Somehow, Mel felt that Matt might be different; he seemed strangely insecure and this made her comfortable somehow. Now that he was gone she realised that she might be falling for him and it worried her. No, it was just her circumstance that was making her feel vulnerable, that's all. Matt was probably just like the rest of them and she was not going to make a fool out of herself again. 'You're wrong,' she said. 'They're all potential bastards – trust me.'

Hayley shook her head and instead of answering she moved over to where Eddie lay and snuggled down next to him to go to sleep.

Mel felt immediately guilty and wondered what Matt was doing. Originally, the plan was for him to travel with the rest of the party but just before leaving Rupert's place, Mel had received an unexpected phone call. She had forgotten all about Joe Sumo from the museum and she had certainly forgotten leaving her business card with him. Apparently, Joe had been watching the news and the developments in Aylesbury with growing interest and it must have dawned on him that their story might not have been so far-fetched after all.

'A man should never stay close to danger trusting only in miracles,' he had said on the phone. 'Better to seek safety with people you trust.'

Despite the ordeal at the museum, Mel had taken a shine to the massive Japanese wrestler and the way he constantly spouted obscure proverbs amused her. So, she had managed to convince Matt to pick Joe up at the museum on the way to Oswestry, the Welsh border town near to where Matt had agreed to rendezvous with Eddie the next morning. Mel had not heard from Matt since leaving Oxford and she was worried that something might have happened to him; he was a wanted man and she had the unnerving feeling that she might never see him again. Feeling lonely, Mel raised herself stiffly to her feet and made her way over to where Father Peter was sitting. She sat next to the old man, leaned back against the cold stone and crossed her legs in front of her.

'Do you think we're crazy, father?" She asked. 'Coming half way across the country to hold up in some freezing ruins on the advice of one man?' She glanced at Eddie. 'It just doesn't seem real somehow – like we're in a dream.'

The old man's eyes never left the fire, but his smile acknowledged her question. 'I'm sure some people would think us deluded, but for me… for me it seems right.' The priest's smile faded but he continued to stare at the flames. 'You see, I've been feeling uneasy for some time now; on edge and strangely unsettled. My sleep has been troubled and I've been having bad dreams - premonitions of impending doom. When Matthew came to me with his story I suddenly knew their meaning. Have no doubt child – tomorrow is going to reshape all of our lives.'

Mel followed the old man's example and stared at the fire through her misty breath. She thought about the events that had brought them together and after a while she plucked up the courage to ask a question that had been preying on her mind.

'That old cup you brought from the church has got something to do with it, hasn't it?' She pointed at a bundle of velvet by his feet.

Father Peter's eyes turned towards her and she felt uncomfortable under his scrutiny, then he seemed to make a decision and returned his gaze to the fire as he answered her question. 'The cup always appears in my dreams,' he said. 'A focal point as it were.' The old priest tapped the velvet bundle. 'It's quite an heirloom, you know,' he said. 'It's been in the church for a very long time; they say it was brought there by the son-in-law to James the First, back in 1619. It was presented as a relic from the bohemian wars and is said to date back to the fifteenth century. Some believe the cup originated in Czechoslovakia and was a personal possession of Jan Hus, a professor of theology and a priest from the region. Others say that the cup is much, much older and that the Czechoslovakian priest was just one of its many possessors over the centuries'

'Jan Hus? Wasn't he executed by the Catholic Church?'

The old man nodded. 'Jan Hus was a celebrated martyr, one of the greatest personalities in Czech history because he was devoted to serving the common people. He challenged the material greed of the church and yes child, he eventually paid with his life.'

Mel was silent for a while, not sure whether to say what had been bothering her since earlier that morning. 'Father, this is going to sound really weird, but earlier… earlier in Rupert's dining room I noticed something strange. I… I'm sure I saw flames reflected on the cup's surface but when I looked at the fire it had died; I know I didn't imagine it.'

The priest continued to scrutinise her. 'The others saw it too, I'm sure,' he said.

'What if it's a bad thing? What if the cup's cursed?' She felt suddenly embarrassed and looked down at her feet. When she continued, her voice was low and its tone more urgent. 'Sorry, I know that sounds irrational, but think of all the bad luck we've had. It's like we're cursed or something!'

'There are many evil things in this world child, but I don't believe the chalice is one of them; in fact I'm convinced it's here to help us in some way.' Father Peter returned his gaze to the fire and his brow creased as if he were concentrating. 'Chalices, cups and flagons have always represented good; as religious symbols they can be found on ancient manuscripts and altars dating back to the earliest times. A chalice used by Jesus at his last Passover became the Holy Grail sought by the knights of Wales and England.'

'But why did I see flames? What do you think it means?' Mel asked.

'A flaming chalice has been a symbol of faith for many religions throughout history. For instance Unitarians believe that a flaming chalice has the power to change history. You see, the symbol of the chalice flame is a metaphor for the lives of human beings, both as individuals and in community. A cup is a familiar object made to be held and passed around - for sharing. A flame, by contrast, is not an object. It cannot be weighed or measured. It is no static thing, but a dynamic, changing process.'

'You mean the flame represents humanity?'

Mel could tell by the priest's eyes that he was impressed by her perception. He continued ardently. 'Not just humanity – but all the elements of society in the right balance. Fire itself needs three elements and the first of these is fuel. Fuel is material - like the human body, like the treasured objects that modern society relies upon. If a fire lacks fuel it is said to be "burning low" like a candle in its final moments when the flame shrinks to a feeble glow. Many of today's problems are brought about our reliance on the fuel of physical things.'

As the priest spoke, Mel continued to stare at the fire and for the first time it dawned on her what they all might be about to lose. The old man, sensing her fear, took Mel's hands in his own.

'The second element is heat. Think of the heat of life itself, distinguishing the living from the dead, the spark of intelligence, the warmth of human encounter, even the friction of disagreement.' He glanced at Eddie, before continuing. 'If a fire lacks heat, as when you dampen a flame with water, it is said to be guttering. To develop as human beings, people also need heat - the vitality of others. The warmth that supportive communities can provide sustains society.' At this point Father Peter cleared his throat and the action triggered another coughing episode. Mel put her hand to the old man's shoulder and waited for him to compose himself. Eventually the coughs died and with watering eyes Father Peter continued.

'The third element is air,' he wheezed. 'Human spirit has often been compared with air by most religions. If a fire lacks air, we say that it is smouldering. There is much heat and thick black smoke, but little or no light. Modern life is too often like this. To develop, people need air - or spirit: the inspiration, or breathing in of that invisible, yet vital element - the movement of the heart when affection is shared with another human being.' He smiled knowingly at Mel who reddened slightly. When he spoke again, his voice was little more than a whisper. 'Keep this to yourself, child; I wasn't going to tell anyone, but the cup has shown me unexplained images on many more occasions than this morning. I've seen things reflected in its surface that have disturbed me and I've seen things that have confused me, but I'm sure that all of these images are important messages. I'm convinced we have with us a very powerful artefact that has been brought to us at a time when society has become unbalanced and is degenerating into a culture of greed, selfishness and depravity. It has come to us at a time when humanity is about to suffer a sudden blow to the heart and one that it might not survive. The flaming chalice is to many a symbol of love, brotherhood and human fellowship; only such sentiments can prevent society degenerating into primitive malfeasance. The gold chalice is not cursed, child! I think it's here to remind us of the importance of balancing the essential elements of society. I'm not sure what other part it might play but I'm convinced we're carrying something of great value, something that perhaps may prove to be nothing short of a modern day miracle.'

Chapter 13

Less than fifteen miles away Matt and Joe Sumo were also deep in discussion. They had booked into a small hotel in Oswestry and despite the prospect of an early start had stayed up late in the bar talking about their lives. Matt was surprised to find his Japanese companion extremely good company – he didn't say much, but when he did speak he usually said something that made Matt laugh, especially when he quoted one of his irrelevant Japanese proverbs. Not once did they talk about what might happen the next day – all that had been said at the museum, but during the four-hour journey into Wales the news on the car radio had continued to report on the events at Aylesbury. The local area had been evacuated because engineers had discovered severe corrosion of chemical tanks at the plant. Experts were concerned that, in the event of a leak, toxic gasses might be released into the local atmosphere. Despite the controversial news story, Joe had no doubt that seeking refuge in Wales was the right thing to do. He trusted the media no more than Matt did and had already drawn the conclusion that the authorities were covering something up.

    Matt realised that this was his last chance to relax, talk about nothing in particular and just enjoy a drink in good company. And Joe could drink all right - he downed pint after pint of the local Welsh bitter without seeming to feel any effect. Matt tried to match him round for round but soon gave up. Even so, by the end of the evening he was definitely feeling the worse for wear.

'One last pint before bed,' Matt slurred, getting up and heading for the bar. The bar tender was a large Welshman, sporting a bushy beard. He stood behind the gleaming mahogany surface, polishing a pint glass. Apart from the Welshman, the room was empty.

'Same again, is it?' he asked. 'That'll have to be the last round I'm afraid - I need to be shutting up shop.'

'Thank God,' Matt said. 'I can't keep up with my friend over there.'

'He's a big lad, isn't he?' The barman said. 'But I'm glad of the custom, the place is bloody dead tonight.'

'Where is everybody?' Matt asked. 'Don't people round here drink on a Sunday?'

'Haven't you heard, boyo,' the man boomed. 'The world's going to end tomorrow!'

'What?' Matt was stunned. 'Who's saying that?'

The Welshman laughed. 'I wouldn't be worrying, sir. It's just the internet – those social network things are full of it apparently. Nobody knows who started the rumours, but they're saying something bad's going to happen tomorrow. A terrorist attack perhaps – they say something's been leaked by a militant group. Others reckon it's got something to do with that power station over in Aylesbury. They think we're all going to be poisoned by a gas cloud or some such rubbish. Load of bollocks, I say!'

'Are people believing the stories?'

'I doubt it really, but you know how people enjoy a panic – remember twenty years ago at the end of the millennium? We all convinced ourselves that planes were going to drop out of the sky at midnight. So some people are staying indoors just in case. It say's on the internet that you should stay inside and put damp towels round the doors and windows, some of the hotel staff have already called in sick. Bloody ridiculous!'

Matt picked up the replenished glasses and made his way back to Joe Sumo who was half-asleep at one of the tables.

'Joe, there are stories going about and people are staying indoors.' Matt whispered. 'If Eddie's right, that's the last thing they should do.'

Joe opened his eyes 'Good choice or bad choice,' he said, sleepily. 'Neither is defence against fate,'

Matt drank his beer and considered telling the barman what he knew, but he guessed the Welshman would take some convincing. Anyway, deep down Matt couldn't believe that the destructive wave, even if it did occur, would ever reach such a remote part of the country. 'Come on Joe,' he said. 'Let's go to bed.'

When Matt eventually staggered into his room, he picked up his mobile and without considering the implications, dialled the number of Tanya Fox. There was no answer so he left a message urging her to phone him. Leaving the mobile turned on in case she called back, he slumped onto the bed and immediately fell asleep.

That night he dreamt that he was eleven years old again. In his dream he was lying in his boyhood bed listening to his parents muffled voices from downstairs getting louder and more heated. He heard the front door open and slam closed again - it was par for the course – they never quarrelled in the house, always taking their dispute to the family car where they would be out of earshot. They didn't argue often, but when they did, he would wait anxiously in bed hoping that Aaron wasn't feeling the same anxiety in the next bedroom. Tonight was different though for two reasons, firstly because this time he knew what they were discussing and secondly, because Aaron wasn't there anymore. The accident was three days ago now and he knew his parents hadn't slept since. They didn't seem to care how Matt was feeling, offering no comfort or support to ease his suffering and he knew why – because they blamed him. It should have happened to him! Matt started to cry again. He tried to sleep but couldn't; the terrible guilt continued to torment him, just as the press had done after the accident. He wanted to die – to be with Aaron – to say sorry.

In Matt's dream, time passed and his parents still hadn't returned to the house. Suddenly, he couldn't stand the waiting any longer – he had to face them and try to make them understand. Matt climbed out of bed and wandered down stairs; the place was a mess – bottles and glasses were strewn across the kitchen table – washing up stacked high in the sink. He walked to the front door, opened it an inch and peered out. They were still in the car; the engine was running, but the interior was dark. Matt walked out of the house and his slippers crunched gravel as he made towards the car.

'Mum? Dad?' He called. 'Can you come in now, I don't want to be on my own.' There was no reply, so in complete darkness, Matt edged around the car to try the driver's door – it was locked. 'Dad, please! I'm scared!' He felt his way round to the other side of the car and tried the passenger door. It opened with a clunk and the interior light momentarily dazzled him. Something heavy fell to his feet as vicious nauseating fumes engulfed him. He looked down at the blue, bloated face of his mother, her swollen tongue lolling grotesquely large against her cheek and he screamed.

Matt jumped up in his bed, sweating and nauseous – where was he? Then he remembered, and realising it was morning already, climbed unsteadily out of bed to face his day of reckoning.

An hour later Matt's head was still pounding as he drove along the lightly frosted road towards the prearranged meeting place - a remote visitor's centre approximately eight miles west of the town. Next to him, Joe was in high spirits despite the previous night's alcoholic consumption and chattered incessantly along the route. They eventually pulled up at a small parking area outside a tiny stone building with a sign that read "Mynydd Duon Heritage Centre." The place was deserted but was exactly as Eddie had described it. The gravel parking area stood between the narrow road and a fenced off cliff edge with views of low valleys to the South. On the opposite side of the road, a steep hill rose up northwards into the mist.

'That's where we're heading, Joe,' Matt said groggily. 'Due north to the Abbey where the others are waiting.'

'A journey of a thousand miles must begin with a single step,' Joe said, staring into the mist.

Matt laughed, suddenly feeling better despite his headache. 'Don't worry my friend; we're not exactly crossing Antarctica.'

Joe gazed at the imposing hills and didn't look convinced. 'You know the way?' He asked, dubiously.

'We'll follow Hayley's map – it won't be a problem.'

'Men get lost on the straightest road,' Joe had a strange look in his eyes. 'You must wish you had that old compass, now.'

'We don't need a compass,' Matt said. We'll follow the tree lines – it'll be fine.' In his younger days, Matt had taken up orienteering and to his knowledge his sense of direction had never let him down. Suddenly, they heard the sound of the Unimog struggling up the steep road. Eddie, as usual, was bang on time. The massive vehicle pulled into the parking area and out jumped the lanky engineer followed by Baxter, Rupert's beagle. Eddie shouted a greeting and pulled a bundle of inert clothing, footwear and red velvet capes from the cab onto the ground.

'How are things at the Abbey?' Matt asked. 'Is everyone okay?'

'It was a bloody cold n…night and Father Peter's developed a nasty cough, but they were all s…sleeping peacefully when I left.'

'And Mel? Is she all right?'

Eddie nodded. 'Fine,' he mumbled, avoiding Matt's gaze. Then he introduced himself to Joe Sumo who grabbed his bony hand and shook it enthusiastically.

'Not s…sure how well these are going to f…fit a big guy like you' Eddie said dubiously, handing Joe a pair of overalls. 'You're just going to have to make do I'm afraid.'

The ex-wrestler bowed politely and Eddie raised his eyebrows. 'Are you f…for real?' He asked.

'Guess so,' Joe said as he accepted the strange clothing.

Ten minutes later they left their vehicles behind and set off on foot, heading north up the hill. Eddie led the way with

Baxter repeatedly bounding enthusiastically ahead before returning impatiently as if to encourage the others to pick up the pace. Joe Sumo followed closely behind Eddie, looking like some sort of overweight action hero with the inert overalls impossibly tight to his body and the red velvet cape billowing out behind him as he climbed the steep hill. Matt, who was last to leave the car park, looked ahead at the absurd sight of his companions and was immediately overwhelmed by the comedy of the moment. What started as an inaudible snigger, soon developed into full-blown laughter. The sound was so unexpected that Eddie turned around to locate its source only to find Joe Sumo, whose one good eye was momentarily obscured by his cloak, blindly bearing down on him. Eddie squealed but failed to prevent the huge man stumbling into his own gangly frame, causing them both to fall to the ground in an ungainly heap. Baxter, of course, started to leap around their prone bodies barking insanely at the unexpected development. Behind them, Matt fell to his knees in hysterics; tears ran down his face and he probably would have stayed there laughing until he wet himself had it not been for the unexpected sound of another vehicle on the gravelled road behind him. He turned to see a white van draw up alongside Matt's Toyota; its darkened windows obscuring those inside, but Matt immediately recognised the vehicle.

'Holy crap,' He said under his breath. 'This is all we need.'

The vehicle stood with its diesel engine rattling for what seemed like an eternity before the passenger door finally opened. Matt, Eddie and Joe Sumo knelt on the frosty ground staring silently as Tanya Fox climbed elegantly out of the vehicle.

'Well, well,' she said, smiling at the three disadvantaged travellers. 'That must have been one hell of a fancy dress party!'

The van's other door opened, Nic Boateng climbed out and immediately set about recording their predicament with a small hand-held camera.

'What... how... the hell did you find this place?' Matt asked, incredulously.

The newsreader sauntered towards him waggling a mobile phone in her hand. 'You're lucky I got here before the police,' she said. 'They'll be tracking your mobile too, I expect.'

'W...What do you want?' Eddie asked.

'I want to know what you're up to; it's going tits up back in Aylesbury and nobody seems to know what's happening – except possibly you guys.' She walked over to Matt and stood directly over him. 'Where are you going and why are you dressed like that?' Her voice was serious now, meaning business.

Matt rose angrily to his feet. 'I've already told you what's happening, but you won't listen and you still haven't warned anybody' he said. 'In a short while a wave of energy is going to cause a chain of reactions that will result in a devastation that might even reach us here. Anyone in the vicinity of reactive material could end up like Jill Davies, or worse! That's why we're dressed like this and that's why we're heading into the countryside.'

Tanya laughed, 'I'm sorry,' she said. 'But you must admit it is a little amusing. Just like all the other stories on the Internet.'

Matt's frustration erupted. 'So why don't you just turn round, clear off back the way you came and go and do something about it?'

'Because you might even be right.' Tanya shrugged. 'I don't know, maybe there's something strange going on. I couldn't even get close to your people at the plant. Either way it's a great story! You do realise we're going to have to come with you?'

Matt shook his head. 'Sorry, make your own plans,' he said. 'You should be back there warning people!'

'I don't really see how you can stop us. We'll just follow you – as you can see we're better equipped for walking than you are, we're probably fitter and we're hardly going to lose sight of you in those ridiculous outfits!'

'You can't follow us dressed like that – your equipment's reactive – You'll put us all in danger.'

'What do you suggest then?' The newsreader asked.

Matt turned away from her and walked up to Eddie and Joe. 'What are we going to do?' He asked. 'She's right, we can't stop her following us - not without getting physical anyway.'

'Look, we've g…got plenty of inert gear,' Eddie said. 'Dress them up and let them come if they w…want; what harm can it do?'

'You don't know what she's like Eddie, she's nothing but trouble…' Matt paused with exasperation, and then continued dejectedly. 'Oh, I suppose you're right, let them come. What harm will it do?' He walked back down to the Unimog and pulled a bundle of inert clothing and velvet drapes from the cab.

'Get changed into these or you're not going anywhere and don't think we couldn't stop you,' Matt warned, glancing over at Joe Sumo.

Nic followed his gaze. 'I think he's got a point boss, the big dude's packing some muscle.'

Tanya, clearly frustrated, snatched up the inert garments and stomped off behind the van to change. Nic was already dressed in the strange clothing by the time she returned. It seemed that Tanya's composure had also returned.

'Okay, lead the way,' she said, picking up one of the cameras and smiling.

'You c...can't bring the cameras!' Eddie said.

'Sorry, you're not getting off that easily,' she replied.

'You don't understand,' Matt said. 'There might not be any warning - the cameras could put us all in danger.'

'I'm not walking into those hills without them,' Tanya said, stubbornly.

Matt could tell the newsreader was used to getting her own way. 'Then, as I said, you're not coming with us!'

'You're going to have to tie me up then; of course, I'll probably freeze to death.'

'Jesus!' Matt sat on the ground, exasperated at the situation. Eddie, obviously realising they were in a stalemate, walked back over to where Matt sat and knelt beside him. Joe Sumo, seemingly felt that the argument had nothing to do with him and walked over to Nic to introduce himself with his typical courtesy.

'Look, Matt,' Eddie whispered. 'It's not essential we get to the abbey before the reaction hits – we probably won't m…make it now anyway. The important thing is to get f…far enough away from anything reactive. I think we can compromise.'

'Be my guest,' Matt sighed.

Eddie approached the newsreader and introduced himself. 'We've not m…met, but I imagine you know who I am,' he said. 'We are in serious danger if we get caught with those cameras when the entropic s…surge hits us. Trust me; your life depends upon it.'

'I'm not leaving them behind,' Tanya replied as stubbornly as ever.

'How about we leave your equipment in your vehicle and walk half a m…mile or so up the hill? Find s…somewhere safe and wait there. When the reaction hits, you'll be convinced. If not, if there's any doubt at all, we'll come back down and retrieve the cameras. You can f…film our humiliation or you can go home or do whatever you want to do.'

'What's to stop you just carrying on walking when we get there? We'll never catch you if we go back for the cameras.'

'Here's the keys to the Unimog,' Eddie said. 'That beast will g…go anywhere, f…follow us if we do a runner. You'll s…soon catch us up.'

'Okay, I'll agree to sit up there in the wild, freezing my bits off for two hours, but two hours only. Then I'm coming back for the cameras and I'll be on your tail!'

'It's a deal,' Eddie said. Now for God's s…sake let's get going before it's too late.'

Chapter 14

The guard leaned against the security barrier at the site entrance and looked onto the Degenesys complex at the turmoil of activity in front of him. Dozens of men in white paper overalls, masks and goggles milled around the reactor building carrying all sorts of equipment he didn't even start to understand. The men in their suits reminded him of human sperm, circling some embryonic egg in a sex education film he had once seen. Cherry pickers and man-lift baskets also surrounded the building and carried other sperm-men who were all busy spraying the structure with a liquid chemical, which dried to leave the building's surface grey and strangely shiny. The activity had started yesterday – on Sunday, at around lunchtime - not long after the police had started evacuating the local residents from the fifty or so dwellings that lay closest to the plant. Truck after truck had rolled into the power plant without any warning or explanation and once at rest, they had ejaculated the sperm-men who immediately went about their strange business.

    The security guard looked down at his watch and was disappointed to see that it was only ten-thirty. It didn't seem fair that the other Degenesys staff had been laid off on full pay whilst the security team had all been retained. It wasn't that he was scared of being close to the plant – he had seen all the crap on the Internet, but he didn't believe any of it. The risks had been explained to him and he was satisfied that things were under control. However, he was envious that his more fortunate colleagues were sat at home while he was stuck here bored out of his mind. What he really needed was a cigarette and he wondered if he could sneak behind the security building for five minutes without being missed. He was no use here anyway; the local police were covering the roads into the evacuated area and were turning away any vehicles that were not part of what they called the "preventative maintenance" operation.

The security guard absently scratched his thumbnail against the flaking paint of the barrier and decided that he would take the risk and leave his post briefly for a smoke. He was oblivious to the fact that beneath the barrier's paint, an atomic-scale tug-of-war was already taking place between a myriad of positively-charged ions and negatively-charged free-electrons. Within the barrier's mild-steel body, energy was being produced at an exponential rate as ions rapidly dissolved into surrounding electrolytes including the very sweat left by the security guard's hand. Accelerated corrosion processes were causing electrochemical changes within the metal and were about to destabilise the its delicate thermodynamic equilibrium. The guard was unaware that a critical activation energy level was about to trigger the very first, of what would be many, uncontrolled entropic reactions.

The security guard released his grip on the barrier and ambled towards the rear of the security building. Out of sight, he pulled a packet of Benson and Hedges from his rear trouser pocket and removed a single cigarette. He sniffed it lovingly before placing it in his mouth. The smell of the cigarette was as satisfying as he had expected but it was interlaced with another unexpected odour - the unmistakable smell of fresh coffee. This struck him as strange because his partner, who was monitoring the CCTV cameras inside, never drank coffee - or tea for that matter, just can after can of diet coke. He put the thought out of his mind, removed the lighter from his top pocket and imagined he felt it vibrating strangely within his grasp. In fact he thought that he could almost feel the air around him vibrating somehow, as if it was charged with electricity. Distracted by these feelings, he failed to notice the strange green patina that now coated the metallic part of the lighter. As he brought it towards the cigarette, his right thumb span the flint wheel and the resultant spark ignited the gas now emanating from the lighter's open valve. The guard watched the pale yellow flame being drawn to the cigarette as he inhaled, but felt absolutely nothing as the flame suddenly turned a vivid red and completely engulfed his body in a burst of crimson energy that looked born of fire, but was devoid of heat. The entropic reaction immediately dissolved the lighter he was holding, part of the cigarette he was smoking and even most of the uniform he was wearing. The guard slumped unconsciously to the ground as the security building collapsed onto his numb frame and crushed all life from his body.

No sooner had the army of sperm-men turned towards the sound than they too were engulfed in the entropic flash. The main reactor building collapsed into a pile of dust and inert debris, as did the cherry pickers and man-lifts that had previously surrounding it. Only the bodies that fell amongst the devastation seemed physically unaffected by the reaction - most now lay motionless amongst the rubble, but the few who were still conscious attempted to raise themselves clumsily from the cold ground. Even the concrete and other road material had degenerated into the very substrate that supported it leaving only ash and broken masonry on the surface.

The terrible entropic surge travelled out along the access road, which continued to feed the reaction, leading it towards the heavily populated areas of the town. The speed at which the reaction travelled was incredible - so much so that the whole of Aylesbury was engulfed within a minute and from that moment, the town was unrecognisable. The majority of building's roofs collapsed as fixtures and support ties crumbled; cars disintegrated, leaving fragments of leather, rubber and cloth lying amongst dusty soot in the road. When the devastation eventually reached the town's outskirts, the surrounding countryside finally dampened its vehemence. The red flashes were diminished but not totally extinguished. The reaction continued to travel where it could follow roads, power lines and the like. However, even where the reaction died through lack of fuel, the invisible reactive surge continued unabated through the atmosphere, triggering occasional red flashes into the distance whenever a building or other man-made structure was encountered.

Ryan Bradley gave up on Harry Potter for a moment and closed the book. His father's agitation was making it hard to concentrate and he was bursting for a pee. It had been over four hours since they had taken off from the Reykjavik airfield and although his father's twin-engined aircraft had every optional extra, it was devoid of one important piece of equipment - the D42 Twin Star lacked a toilet. Ryan looked down at the swirling clouds below, but the strange red pulses that had previously illuminated them had disappeared; now everything below them was grey.

'Control, are receiving me, over?' His father's voice was anxious. 'I wish to join I.L.S. for approach.' The digital audio system just crackled in response.

'Perhaps the radio's broken,' Ryan suggested.

'Maybe,' his father said, trying to sound calm. 'The airfield should be right below us; I'm going to take her down.'

They had been flying at seven thousand feet above the cloud to avoid icing and at this altitude the Welsh landscape was completely obscured from view. Ryan watched as his father selected V.F.R. for a visual landing and felt his stomach lurch as the aircraft started to descend. They aimed to land at an airport near Welshpool in mid Wales, where Ryan's mother waited to collect them. His father, a Canadian, was a member of the International Arctic Science Committee and had been working in Iceland on a research project to evaluate climate variability and its link to increased ultraviolet radiation. His mother was a teacher and Ryan had not seen her for nearly a month; they were not poor, but the cost of flying was taking its toll on their visits. He missed his mother terribly, but all Ryan could think about now was his aching bladder.

The cockpit dimmed as they entered the clouds and turbulence rocked the aircraft, increasing Ryan's discomfort.

'Dad, I've really got to pee!'

'I know son, we'll be landing soon.' But his father's face didn't look convinced of the fact. They were descending at five hundred feet a minute and the instruments displayed their heading at $180°$ due south. Their altitude was less than a thousand feet now and the swirling cloud was still as thick as ever. Ryan sensed his father was scared and he had never experienced that before; he couldn't ever remember him landing on Visual Flight Rules in such poor conditions. The cloud broke momentarily and Ryan at last caught a glimpse of the grey-green landscape below, but the sighting was brief and was immediately obscured again. Seeing the ground just made his need all the more unbearable and he crossed his legs in desperation. Then, suddenly the aircraft broke free of the cloud.

'Christ Almighty,' Ryan's Father shouted on seeing the airport and the twin diesel turbo-charged engines screamed as he pulled the aircraft up, out of its descent.

'What is it, dad?' Ryan asked. He was feeling scared now.

'The airport's... gone!' Well, it's still there... but it looks like it's been demolished or something.'

'I don't understand – where's mum?'

Something must have happened - that's why they're not responding. Look, were going to have to make a detour, okay?'

'I thought we were low on fuel.'

'We'll be fine. There's a disused airfield northwest of here, at Llanbed near the coast. I'm going to fly below the clouds and land there. Can you hold on for fifteen more minutes?'

'I don't know dad – I'll try.'

As they flew over the gloomy landscape, Ryan's anxiety grew with every passing mile. His father gazed downwards, first one side and then the other and beads of sweat appeared on his brow. Below them, the topography was devoid of buildings - instead, sporadic ruined husks of stonework jutted like broken teeth from the countryside. They followed a road, heading northwest; it was the colour of soot and empty of cars.

'What's happened dad? Has there been a war?'

'I don't understand – we've only been in the air for a few hours... Hey look there's the airfield!'

The two runways were the same colour as the road they had followed, but from the air at least they looked intact. Broken masonry and other debris surrounded the runways - the control tower and hangers had apparently collapsed into ruin. A red light started to flash on the avionics system, but Ryan's father ignored it and started to descend.

'Nearly there, son,' he said as the runway loomed ever larger in front of them.

Ryan always enjoyed the point of touchdown; the sudden lurch as the tyres grabbed the tarmac, the fierce braking moment before the steady taxi towards the landing bay. This time though, the sensation was terrifyingly different – as soon as the wheels made contact, clouds of black dust erupted and engulfed the plane. Its nose suddenly dipped as its tyres sank beneath the runway's surface and impacted on a hidden hard-core of rubble. The aircraft bounced violently before crashing back down again with a horrible graunching of twisting metal. Ryan flew forward, restrained by his seatbelt as the undercarriage sheared off beneath the plane. Ryan saw his father's head hit the windscreen as the plane careered sideways along the runway, spinning uncontrollably towards the ruined buildings. The last thing Ryan remembered was a warm sensation between his legs.

Glyn Cooper sat at his usual table waiting to be served. He hadn't slept much recently and was feeling tired, irritable and not a little scared. He had developed a toothache over the weekend, but it was not just the pain that had disturbed his sleep. There were all sorts of rumours on the Internet and some were linked to Degenesys. Frank Veron had called him on Friday and started asking all sorts of questions about the incident, but Glyn hadn't been much in the mood for talking about it. He suspected that he might be to blame for what had happened and most importantly, for poor Jill's condition, but despite this he had reluctantly agreed to meet Frank this morning at their usual place - the café on Oxford's George Street.

'Hi Glyn, what can I get you?' The pretty waitress had got to know him over the past weeks and they were now on first-name terms.

'Cappuccino please,' he replied, 'and can I have one of those blueberry muffins? 'Oh, and I don't suppose you've got any Paracetomol? I've got a blinding toothache'

'Sure, want a newspaper?'

'No I'm fine – how was your weekend?'

'Wicked!' she replied winking cheekily.

Glyn smiled, wishing he was that young again, and looked out onto the street, which although it was rush hour, was almost devoid of traffic. A scruffy looking man with a mangy dog sat on the opposite side of the road bothering passers-by for their small change. He wasn't getting much joy though by the looks of things. Glyn knew the poor bloke must be freezing but didn't feel much sympathy – he believed people like that usually made their own poor fortune. Most of the people passing obviously shared his views; some shamelessly ignored the traveller's pleas as if he didn't exist; others changed their trajectory so as not to have to make the decision. Glyn wondered where the man had slept last night - it was a cold morning for March, but now the temperature was rising slightly; it had clouded over and it looked like it might even rain.

Glyn thought back to the weekend; he had watched the events in Aylesbury unfold and was astonished by the news of the local evacuation. He didn't have a clue about what was happening, but couldn't help feeling he was in some really serious shit. The only reason he had agreed to meet with the mysterious Frank was in the hope that he might at least learn something about what was going on.

Debbie, the waitress, arrived back at his table with a tray holding his coffee and muffin. 'Enjoy, handsome,' she flirted. 'Call me if you want anything else, anything at all!'

On any other day Glyn would have made a suitably witty response to such a suggestive remark, but he wasn't in the mood and anyway, the girl was at least ten years younger than he was. He had to admit she was fit though, as he admired her slim frame walking across to a table where two old ladies sat gossiping. She wore a white T-shirt beneath her apron, which did not quite reach down to the top of her skirt. Glyn noticed small stars tattooed on the exposed flesh of her lower back; they led downwards, mostly hidden beneath the short skirt. He wondered how many stars there actually were, and more importantly, how far they travelled.

The café was unusually quiet; apart from the two old ladies, the only other customer was a guy in a suit who sat near the door concentrating on the Times crossword and eating a jam donut. The poor man didn't realise that a large blob of jam had squirted onto the collar of his white shirt. Glyn thought he should go over and tell him, but he looked a miserable bastard and probably deserved the embarrassment – let him suffer!

Glyn supped his cappuccino and was amazed at how strong it smelt, like when you first break into the seal of a new tin of instant. It reminded him of the Degenesys reactor room. Then suddenly he felt it – the air seemed charged with invisible energy and Glyn felt his table vibrate slightly. He looked out of the window and was amazed to see a number of pedestrians all looking upwards in the same direction, some were pointing. Intrigued, Glyn rose from his table and made for the café door. The man in the suit and jam-stained shirt looked disdainfully at him as he rushed past, but Glyn paid no heed; he was focused on the commotion outside. Leaving the café, he walked out onto the street and followed the crowd's gaze to where he saw a distant cloud of grey streamers falling gently from the sky.

'It was an airliner!' a young man exclaimed. 'It just disappeared in a flash of red! Must have been a bomb – God, all those people!'

Suddenly there was a scream, Glyn turned to the sound and saw a terrified looking Debbie standing at the café door pointing along the street behind him. He turned and saw the source of her fear. A motorcyclist rode towards them oblivious to the billowing crimson storm that followed at an incredible rate. It was like a Tsunami of red fire that was so bright it burnt the eyes. Glyn was transfixed by the sight and couldn't turn away despite his horror; he watched the inferno overtake the oncoming motorcyclist who catapulted onto the road as his bike disintegrated beneath him. Debbie screamed again and then she fell silent as they were all immersed in a cool crimson holocaust.

Chapter 15

PC Andy Newman looked out of the misted passenger side window of the police Land Rover onto a patchwork of frosted fields and dry-stone walls. The vehicle passed the occasional farm and country house but the landscape here was mostly devoid of inhabited dwellings. Beyond the fields, mist hung over the heather smothered moors and cold, craggy dales.

'Why have I got a bad feeling about this, sir?' Andy asked nervously.

'Well lad, we're going to be first on the scene of the suspected whereabouts of an escaped lunatic - that might have something to do with it I suppose.' The man in the driver's seat's eyes were fixed on the road ahead. 'Don't get excited, the fugitive's probably long gone by now, and if he's not then we'll let your dog, Jake, do the hard work; it's only one man at the end of the day.'

Sergeant Mike Evans was in his late forties and had been in the police force for over twenty years. He didn't normally join the patrols nowadays but this particular morning his shift was at minimum staffing levels. One of his team had been taken out of line to support increased anti-terrorist coverage in York and two other officers had phoned in sick this morning with the flu bug that was supposedly doing the rounds. To cap it all, Andy's usual partner was on light duties having strained his back on Saturday night pulling up an overweight teenager who had got herself stuck in a shopping trolley after drinking the best part of a large bottle of vodka.

There had been several incidents overnight, with a number of youngsters being taken into custody following a fight with some fanatics who had been trawling the pubs, prophesising that the world was about to end. When Andy had checked in, the cells were already full and night shift officers were still queuing with their prisoners to use the fingerprinting and photographic facilities.

The shift had started with the usual thirty-minute briefing session which, this morning had been centred on a psychiatric patient and his escort who had disappeared the day before on a routine transfer between hospitals. They had been told that the missing patient, Arthur Wiseman, was an extremely dangerous individual who should only be approached with extreme caution. The two police officers were not officially part of the manhunt team, which had been established in nearby Middlesbrough, but their patrol fell within the area of the search footprint. As Andy was a trained dog handler the makeshift partnership had received the same briefing as the designated search team just in case of unplanned suspect encounter whilst on duty. As it turned out, the briefing had proved to be more than worthwhile because only an hour into their shift they had received a call asking for assistance investigating a local sighting. An air support unit had spotted a white van fitting the description of the hospital transport vehicle in the courtyard of one of the few large houses close to their current location.

The Land Rover climbed a long gentle hill and as the low-lying mist became clearer Andy spotted the dark blue and yellow Eurocoptor hovering above the road ahead apparently awaiting their arrival and the helicopter pilot made direct radio contact for the first time.

'Red-Kite to Tango-One - we have your visual, over.'

Andy grabbed the mike. 'Yeah, we can see you,' he replied. 'How far's the house, over?'

'It's about half a mile ahead on the left; a large stone built farmhouse, you can't miss it. Turn into the drive just after the outbuildings - it leads to a courtyard at the rear. That's where the van is - we'll follow you in at a distance, over.'

Less than a minute later they saw the farmhouse. Sergeant Evans slowed the van to reduce engine noise and pulled into the drive. As expected, the white van was parked in the courtyard and the sergeant pulled alongside and immediately got out. Andy joined him looking around the deserted paddocks a little nervously.

'You get the dog while I check out the vehicle,' the sergeant ordered.

'Without hesitation, the younger officer opened the Land Rover's rear door and Jake, a large German Shepherd, jumped out. The dog stood silent but alert, awaiting his master's command. Andy attached Jake's lead and followed his senior partner who, having found the van empty was contacting the air support unit.

'Red-Kite come back, this is Tango-one, over!'

'Red-Kite receiving, over!'

'We have a positive ID on the vehicle. Request backup support unit ASAP and building occupancy details, over.'

'Will do! Over!'

'Okay, Red-Kite, we're going in with the dog, keep your eyes peeled for runners, over and out!'

163

The sergeant returned the radio to its holster then unfastened and extended his friction-lock baton. 'It's definitely the right van,' he whispered over his shoulder, 'and there's a whole load of blood in the back. For Christ's sake stay close and be ready to release the dog.'

Together, the police officers crept towards the open double doors of a large conservatory. 'Shit!' Andy muttered as he readied his baton.

Inside the house, Arthur lay in the steaming Jacuzzi bath smiling at the girl hanging by her arms from the radiator pipes. She stared back without expression. Arthur wondered if he should take her again but decided against it; the sex had been good, but not as good as he had expected after all the years of confinement. The first time had been the best, partly because she had still been warm; she might even have still been alive the first time, but he doubted it. The woman, though was another story; he was having much more fun with her...

'Arthur!' Merlin's voice was urgent inside his head. 'Enemies approach, you must flee!'

Sergeant Evans led the way into the house, followed by the young police officer with Jake just in front of him. They entered the conservatory and looked around. There was an open door to their left, which led to the kitchen but there was no sign of anyone in the room. Had they explored further they would have found John Stone, dead on the flagstones with a six-inch knife protruding from his left eye. Instead they passed through a set of double-doors to the hall and immediately noticed a trail of blood leading up the staircase – they followed it in silence. At the top of the stairs Sergeant Evans paused, raised his hand and then pressed his forefinger to his lips; both men listened intently. There was a sound coming from an open door at the end of the hallway – it reminded Andy of the sound his grandfather had made in the final days before emphysema had finally taken him. A regular rasping, gurgling sort of sound that could hardly be described as breathing, but undoubtedly was exactly that. Nervously, the policemen followed the horrible sound and entered the room. What they saw was nothing short of horrific. Lying on the bed, spread-eagled with her limbs zip-tied to the bedposts was what was left of Caroline Stone. Her mutilated body was the result of her captor's new toy – the cavalry sabre that Caroline had removed from the dining room wall to defend herself. Arthur had returned to the kitchen many times through the night to sharpen the blade on the electric knife-sharpener before returning to the bedroom to test its effectiveness. Line after ugly line of gory weals criss-crossed the woman's naked body; her thumbs had been removed and her neck had been opened so that folds of her own flesh flapped in and out of her throat, splattering more blood as she breathed. This was the source of the terrible sound they had followed. Incredibly, not only was the woman still alive but she was conscious and lucid, her manic eyes were fixed on the two policeman as she mouthed three words over and over again.

'Please help me, please help me, please help me…'

Andy retched and turned away but the more senior officer kept his composure and moved towards the woman. He picked up a blood-soaked sheet from the floor and pressed it to the poor woman's neck. Her frantic pleading stopped and her anguish seemed momentarily replaced by anger.

'Bathroom!' She hissed, just before her eyes rolled back and the terrible sound of her breathing finally stopped.

The sergeant paused for a moment, feeling guilty at his relief that this tortured woman was now at peace; then his training kicked in and he turned away. 'Come on, Andy!' He ordered as he strode out of the bedroom and back down the hall. The bathroom was at the other end of the corridor and steam was bellowing from the open door. Andy and Jake followed as instructed.

'Th...that door was closed...' Andy managed to say. 'I'm sure of it!'

Sergeant Evans entered the bathroom and was greeted by the sight of Rebecca's bloated body strapped to the radiator pipes.

'My God!' He uttered as he turned to survey the room. The bath was full with steaming water, which welled, back and forth from one end to the other.

'He was just here!' The sergeant shouted. 'In the bloody bath all the time!'

Then they heard a noise from downstairs; the sound of a chair grating on a flagstone floor.

'The kitchen, lad! Release the dog!'

Andy immediately unclipped the leash. 'Seek, Jake, Seek!'

Jake bounded along the hall and down the stairs, the two policemen following in his wake. By the time the two men were on the stairs the German Shepherd was already out of sight. Then there was a sound of barking, followed by a yelp, then silence. They ran down the stairs and into the kitchen. Jake lay just inside the door or most of him anyway. His decapitated head lay some way in front – it had come to rest beside the body of John Stone. The two men stood in a state of shock neither knowing quite what they should do next. Suddenly their trance was broken by the radio.

'Tango – one, we have a visual, over!'

Sergeant Evans grabbed the radio and started towards the courtyard. 'Where's the bastard now?' he yelled.

'He's entered the stable. Suspect is armed with some sort of sword and… er… seems to be naked! Over.'

The two officers broke out into the courtyard and looked around. The sound of the helicopter hovering above at first drowned out any other noise; then gradually they heard the sound of sirens in the distance. Realising support had arrived, the two men's resolve returned and they both ran towards the stable, batons at the ready.

Suddenly the stable doors swung open and Arthur burst out on the back of Birthday Girl swinging his sword wildly around his head. He took a swipe at the two policemen as he passed, but the sword whistled harmlessly just over their heads. The two men crouched instinctively as they watched the surreal sight of the naked man wielding a sword from the back of the great horse. The scene seemed all the more unreal because of the trail of steam Arthur's body left in its wake as bath water evaporated into the cold air.

'Quick lad, the Land Rover!' Sergeant Evans yelled and they both ran to the police vehicle. By the time they were in pursuit Arthur was already out of sight so they followed the helicopter which was attempting to guide them through the mists and across the frosty fields. Sergeant Evans was back at the wheel and trying to control the Land Rover over the difficult terrain.

'So we're chasing a murderer who thinks he's King Arthur and has just taken an old sword from the residence of a family called "Stone!" Think about it - the press are going to have a bloody field-day.'

Andy ignored his sergeant and was trying to operate the radio but was jostled around so much by the uneven ground that he couldn't do so. However, the helicopter pilot made contact first.

'Lost him in the woods ahead, Tango-one. It's up to you now – I'll gain some height in order to cover the perimeter, over!'

Andy watched as the helicopter swung to its left and upwards with a whine of its engine as it rapidly gained height ahead of them. For a moment he thought he smelt coffee but he suspected it was the aroma of spent aviation fuel, then suddenly the helicopter disappeared in a flash of brilliant red. Andy's eyes were momentarily blinded by its brightness, when they refocused the Land Rover was driving through a cloud of debris falling from above - mainly dust, but larger chunks battered the vehicle as it sped over the uneven ground towards the copse. Then there was another flash, this time brighter still and all around him. PC Andy Newman remembered no more.

Chapter 16

Having reluctantly allowed the journalists to join their party, Matt led them all up the steep, grassy hill to a loose stone wall. Considering that it would offer cover from the icy north wind and presuming that, devoid of any cement or grouting, there would be little in the wall's composition to trigger a reaction, they took shelter under its south face. Then, for what seemed like hours, the five unlikely companions sat with their backs to the wall looking down the slopes, through the remaining patches of mist towards their abandoned vehicles at the heritage centre, maybe half a mile away. Nic sat next to Joe Sumo chatting happily about anything that entered his head, but most of the others were silent. Except Tanya, who seemed to take pleasure in relentlessly taunting Matt for his decision to lead them here.

'So, run me through this one last time,' she said. 'You really believe that your geeky friend over there has somehow predicted a national disaster unforeseen by eminent scientists across the country?'

Matt sighed wearily. 'The eminent scientists are not prepared to stand up and say it, that's all.'

'You're insane, you know that don't you?'

'Maybe I am, we'll just have to wait and see.' Matt gazed at the misty horizon. 'I hope to God you're right.'

The newsreader changed her tone. 'Look Matt,' she said, seriously. 'I know about... your past. Do you think perhaps this whole business...'

'My past has got nothing to do with this,' Matt snapped. 'Let's just drop it okay?'

'Suit yourself,' Tanya said. 'We'll just sit here and wait for Eddie Coleman's hour of revelation.' She leant back against the wall and shut her eyes.

Sitting a few yards away, Nic took a heavy intake of breath. He knew Tanya's volatile temperament better than anyone and he sensed she was close to losing it. The young cameraman turned to Joe Sumo. 'So, what's your take on all this?' He whispered.

'I believe them,' Joe replied simply.

'Hey, who am I to judge?' Nic shrugged. 'I guess you work with these guys – you should know.'

Joe shook his head. 'Our paths crossed only recently,' he said. 'I'm just a museum caretaker.'

'Man, you've got some faith in people,' Nic said, raising his eyebrows.

Joe yawned nonchalantly, stretching his massive frame.

Nic glanced at the man's muscles. 'You don't look like you work in a museum – you should be a bodyguard or something.'

'Once I was a wrestler.' Joe's single eye glistened with pride. 'A long time ago, in Japan, I was high ranking Rikishi in professional stable,' he said.

'A Sumo!' Nic whistled. 'Respect, man! 'Hey, guess what my claim to fame is.'

'You're a cameraman.' Joe muttered.

'No, that's what I am now!' Nic said. 'I used to be famous too, man.'

Joe scrutinised the slender African. 'You wouldn't make a very good wrestler,' he said, smiling. 'What did you do?'

'I once played with the Goldfields!'

'Never heard of them,' Joe said. 'I don't listen much to rock music'

Nic grimaced incredulously at the ex-wrestler. 'They're not a band! The Obuasi Goldfields are the best soccer team in the whole of Ghana, man.' He punched his chest with pride. 'I was their top player two seasons running - and I once scored for my country in the Cup of Nations. That's why I came to England – a talent scout spotted me.'

Joe still didn't seem very impressed. 'And now you're a cameraman.'

'Hey, I was a good footballer, man – you know, tricky and fast!' Nic wriggled his shoulders in demonstration of the fact; then his face dropped. 'But over here the boggy pitches slowed me down and Neanderthal centre backs kicked me off the field.' He shook his head, sadly. 'The crowd didn't take to me; after a few games I hardly ever made the first team.'

'So why stay?'

'My parents idolise me. They were so proud; what could I do? I couldn't go back.'

Joe shook his head again. 'There is no pride like that of a beggar grown rich.'

'Hey, my family were well off, man – they both worked for the Ghana Broadcasting Corporation. I decided to follow their lead, stay here and become a sports journalist, so with the money I'd made from the game I went to college and eighteen months later I passed my NCJT exams. I'm a qualified reporter, man.'

Joe at last looked impressed. 'That's a good story,' he said, nodding thoughtfully. 'The Japanese say that a man who works hard enough can get fire out of a stone.'

Nic smiled at the ex-wrestler, his pride restored. 'I'm not there yet,' he whispered, secretively. 'I'm still just an assistant to Tanya, but at least life's never dull working with *her majesty.*'

Joe glanced at the shivering newsreader who sat scowling at the surrounding hills. 'That I can believe,' he whispered back.

'Hey, Tanya,' Nic called to his senior colleague. 'Tell Joe how I'm gonna be a TV star one day.'

'Yeah, you're a real talent!' she replied grumpily, and then rose stiffly to her feet. 'Come on, Nic - I've had enough of this.' At this, she started to stomp off back down the hill. 'Let's get back into some warm clothes,' she said.

The young cameraman clambered to his feet and shrugged apologetically to Joe before reluctantly following his senior colleague. Matt made as if to challenge them, but then slumped back against the wall, shaking his head in resignation. They had been here for hours and nothing had happened. It seemed Eddie's prediction had been wrong after all.

'Come on,' he mumbled to his friend. 'Let's go back to the car.'

Eddie didn't reply. Instead, he seemed distracted, sniffing the air and staring up at the sky. Then suddenly Matt smelt it – the strong, acrid aroma of coffee on the wind. Immediately, the ground vibrated beneath him and he saw Nic and Tanya both pause in their descent - apparently they too, sensed the change in the air.

Suddenly, a bright flash of crimson silhouetted the two figures; when the flare died, the distant heritage centre was just broken walls and rubble, clouded with dust. The building, their vehicles, everything – had just disintegrated in front of them. There followed a sound, not unlike distant thunder as Matt watched the crimson wave roll on eastward like a ball of lightning. It followed the road, pulsing in intensity as it encountered differing levels of reactive materials and in the sky, low, grey clouds reflected the red wave as if fire somehow raged within them. The pulsating clouds continued to light up the distant sky some while after the initial reaction had passed.

Tanya Fox turned back towards the others with a look of dismay that would have been comical in other circumstances. Matt experienced no pleasure in her bewilderment, just an awful feeling of dread as it dawned on him what this meant; he knew in that instant that their lives had probably been changed for ever. Eddie seemed shocked, as if even he hadn't really believed it could happen. He stood for a moment, mouth agape, staring at the distant ruins. 'It r…reached us,' he stammered. 'Even h…here, it reached us.'

Only Joe Sumo seemed unmoved. 'Red sky in the morning – shepherd's warning,' he muttered, before turning north to climb the hill.

In the Abbey, Mel woke suddenly as sunlight hit her face; she looked towards its source and was amazed to see a small girl standing in the dormitory's arched entrance holding aside the red velvet drape that hung across the opening. The morning sun, low on the horizon shone from behind the girl, casting her shadow far into the ancient building.

'Annie!' A woman's voice shouted from outside. 'Come away from there!'

Everybody woke up then. Hayley spun around from her sleeping position, peering through sleep-blurred eyes. Rupert stood up unsteadily, apparently not remembering his whereabouts at all. Father Peter stirred groggily from beneath his blankets and tried to focus rheumy eyes that were now devoid of his glasses. The girl suddenly disappeared from view as an unseen arm tugged her away and the velvet drape swung back into place; they were once again left in relative darkness.

Mel realised they must have overslept badly, having eventually found sleep at some point in the early hours after what had seemed an impossibly long night spent lying against the cold, uncomfortable stonework. 'What time is it?' she yelled, realising that nobody had the means to answer her question. She hurried across the room, pulled back the drape and looked out on a bright, frosty morning towards a sight that both surprised and alarmed her. The hazy sun was already quite high in the sky suggesting that it was mid-morning at least. According to Eddie, the entropic wave could hit them at any moment and there, right in front of the abbey, stood a huge white camper-van no more than twenty metres from its entrance. Such vehicles were unpopular at the best of times, but today the camper represented no less danger than an unexploded bomb. An overweight man in his late fifties leant against the bonnet, perusing a map and seeming unaware of Mel's presence and the young girl was being marched back towards the camper by a woman presumed to be her grandmother.

'Excuse me?' Mel shouted. 'You can't stay here with that thing!'

Hayley and Rupert joined Mel at the entrance just as the visitors acknowledged her presence for the first time.

'Who are you?' The man asked, obviously surprised at the unexpected appearance of three strangely dressed people in such a deserted location. 'Don't tell me you slept in that ruin last night?'

'Actually we did,' Mel replied. 'But I don't have time to explain now. You have to take that vehicle off the hill and get as far away from it as possible.'

'What are you talking about? We came to have a look around the abbey.'

'My friend,' Rupert said. 'I'm afraid you are going to have to leave - this is private property!'

'No it's not!' The man replied – he was clearly starting to get angry now.

'Come on Graham,' the man's wife shouted. 'Let's just leave – we don't want any trouble.'

'We're not going anywhere, we've as much right to be here as they have. It's a matter of principle!' The man stamped his foot in defiance.

'Please listen,' Mel shouted. 'Get away from the van – it's dangerous! Drive it down to the quarry; you can leave your wife and the child here - when you get back I'll explain everything.'

A look of enlightenment crossed the man's face. 'You're one of those nutters, aren't you?' he said. 'Ranting on about doomsday and terrorist attacks. Leave us...'

Suddenly, without warning, Rupert picked up a stone and threw it at the camper-van.

'Hey! What are you doing?' The man cried. 'That trailer's brand new – don't you dare...'

'Take it off the hill!' Rupert shouted, throwing another stone - this one the size of a small egg; it bounced off the van's front wing with a dull thud.

'Stop it, daddy,' Hayley yelled. 'They haven't done anything wrong.'

'They're going to get us killed!' Rupert shouted, launching another stone at the van's windscreen.

'Stop it!' the man screamed. He was livid now and stood in front of the camper, hands splayed, trying desperately to deflect the trajectory of the missiles. One of Rupert's stones narrowly missed the man's cheek before shattering a headlamp. Realising his defence was a lost cause, the man ran back to the vehicle, jumped into the driver's seat and hurriedly started the engine. The woman and child's pale faces stared out of a side window as the van swung round in a wide arc before making off back down the hill.

Mel gave chase, shouting after them. 'You're in terrible danger, ditch the van and come back to the abbey, please!'

The man leaned out of the window. 'Come back? Are you crazy? You haven't heard the last of this, you bloody lunatics!'

Rupert threw one last stone for luck, but the speeding van was already out of range.

Hayley jumped in front of her father and glared at him. 'Daddy, how could you attack an innocent family like that?'

Rupert shook his red-faced head. 'I...I don't know what came over me; I was just panicking - do you think he'll call the police?'

They all looked down the hill at the retreating vehicle, which was now nearly half a mile away. Then a terrible thing happened - right in front of their eyes the white van suddenly erupted in a flash of crimson light. When the flare subsided, the van could no longer be seen; all that remained on the track was a dark stain covered in debris.

'Holy shit!' Mel said.

'Oh my God.' Hayley groaned. 'What have we done?' She turned to her father who looked horrified.

'I didn't m...mean...' The magistrate stuttered.

Suddenly Mel felt a strange vibration in the ground, a static charge in the air and the unmistakable smell of coffee. 'Oh my God - it's happening!' She yelled. 'Quick, get back to the abbey.'

'Father Peter!' Hayley shouted. 'He's back there alone and he's half blind without his glasses!'

The three of them started to run back up the hill towards the abbey. As they ran they could see more red flashes light up the mist far to the south. Mel realised that's where Matt and Eddie would be.

Hayley suddenly stopped and tears were in her eyes. 'I'm sorry but I have to go back to the trailer,' she said. 'Those people might be hurt and need our help!'

Rupert nodded. 'I'll come with you,' he said, eagerly.

'All right, but for God's sake be careful! I'll take care of Father Peter.'

As father and daughter ran back down the hill, Mel dashed through the ancient arched doorway to see the old priest kneeling before the fire. In his hands he held the golden chalice and it seemed to be glowing with an eerie red light. Father Peter's hands were shaking and he seemed unaware of Mel's arrival. Static filled the air and the ancient building seemed to vibrate with energy. Dust fell from the stone ceiling and Mel wondered if the place was about to collapse.

'Father, are you okay?' she asked. 'It's happening – just as Eddie said it would!'

Father Peter slowly turned towards her. 'It's terrible,' he murmured. 'Devastation everywhere; people are dying… and there's something else…' The old priest's bloodshot eyes glared at her. 'Somewhere out there… someone's laughing…'

Throughout that morning on March 12th, 2020 the entropic wave swept outwards from its epicentre near the town of Aylesbury. The reaction spread across the country like a crimson rash, leaving devastation in its wake. From the skies above, the low clouds pulsed red as flash after flash absorbed the unnatural material of man's desire. The energy of the material's creation was suddenly released back into the environment, but instead of radiating heat, each flash emanated a high frequency wave that surged on, spreading the destruction at a terrifying speed. There were no warnings – whole cities were engulfed in minutes; small inert pockets of countryside escaped the reaction, but still gave passage to the destructive wave like carriers of some fatal disease. Many people died - crushed beneath falling buildings, but most endured the disaster. Confused survivors, dressed only in remnants of their partially disintegrated clothes, now faced an even more terrifying ordeal. Most were caught in the vicinity of the terrible red flashes and their minds were consumed along with their material possessions. They emerged bewildered and with only their animal instincts remaining as a tool to survive their environment - a frightening, dusty world of chaos. Uncontrolled fires ravaged the land - the result of thermal processes now released from the controls of their containment, and there was little in the way of shelter. Most structures contained reactive material so building's roofs collapsed into piles of rubble; and it was very, very cold - the majority of people would not survive the night.

* * * *

Book 2 – The Savage Dawn

"It is not the strongest of the species that survives, nor the most intelligent that survives. It is the one that is the most adaptable to change."

Charles Darwin

Chapter 1

The creature opened its eyes which stung from the billowing black dust and immediately felt the pain emanating from its decaying tooth. Fear gripped it and it slunk deeper into a crevice in the surrounding rubble. Feeling the cold, it looked down at its body as if for the first time and pulled clumsily at the remaining fragments of clothing still clinging to its frame. It was relatively comfortable in the crevice, which was still warm from its previous existence as part of the café's kitchen. Soft material lay on the ground, although even as Glyn Cooper, he would never have recognised the remains of cotton tablecloths that had been stored in a now disintegrated metal locker. Devoid of colour and substance, the cotton had degraded into its original form; a material grown naturally by gradually absorbing energy from the sun and nutrients in the ground, its natural formation immune from the entropic reaction that had obliterated the objects forced into existence by man. All around the creature, other unaffected materials lay amongst the black dust. Rubble from demolished buildings lay everywhere, timber from the roof members were scattered as far as the creature could see, and fragments of leather and natural textiles from interior furnishings lay among the debris. None of the objects meant anything to the creature, but he recognised instinctively the warmth and comfort offered by the soft cotton so he pulled it greedily about his body.

The creature looked out from his new lair onto a terrifyingly unknown world – he had no memory of the things that met his gaze but instinct warned him to be wary of the other creatures that moved amongst the rubble. He also knew to be fearful of the flickering orange light that grew, then faded, then grew again behind a pile of nearby timbers. A strong unnatural smell hurt, almost burnt, his senses – the creature knew nothing of the precious liquid that had powered road vehicles across this very place only a short while ago. Petrol from destroyed cars soaked into the ground having been unaffected by the catastrophe. Along with other fossil fuel products, the energy stored within its chemical composition had been captured in prehistoric times and was not easily released by the sudden entropic reaction.

'Yak, Yak, Yarik,' an unseen, living thing barked from the creature's right, making him shrink back once again into its shelter. Directly in front of the crevice, across the open space that had once been Oxford's George Street, a hairy four-legged animal fed upon a bloody carcass. The canine had no memory of its human masters and instinct told it to feed, so it ripped savagely at pieces of leather, originally designed to protect the motorcyclist from road injury, and gorged upon the corpse's belly.

The creature in the crevice watched excitedly as it spotted another of its own species suddenly appear, crouching behind a nearby wall and apparently stalking the four-legged animal; this creature was skinny and shivering and apparently intended to take a share of the animal's spoils. Then another of its kind – instinctively recognised as female - appeared beside the first. The female was pale and much smaller and the creature in the crevice noticed that five small, pointed shapes decorated this new creature's naked rear as she offered it to the shivering male in front of her. Uninterested, the male shoved her away with a snarl and returned his gaze to the feasting animal.

'Yak, Yak, Yarik,' the female barked and turned away so that she was now facing her hidden observer. Apparently sensing his presence, she slunk towards the crevice, crawling mainly on all fours but rising occasionally into a stumbling walk. Every few strides, the female paused and turned to display her rear, instinctively offering the only gift she had, in return for the protection a male of the species could provide.

The creature with the toothache had little interest in the food that was the source of conflict across the way. His stomach was full from a fried breakfast consumed in another world and topped up by a blueberry muffin eaten less than twenty minutes ago at the café. The female fascinated him though - there was a strange stirring in his groin and a previously unknown need started to develop. The creature's fear gradually abated until this new need became suddenly dominant and, without forethought, he sprang from the crevice, grabbed the female and pulled her back to the warmth of his shelter. The female did not struggle; apparently resigned to the larger male's dominance and once inside the cramped confines of the shelter she immediately turned and raised her rear to display her genitalia to the male. Intuitively, the creature pushed her flat to the ground and entered her cruelly from behind. The pair copulated like the animals they now were, without affection or even very much pleasure; they experienced only a terrible frantic, lustful release.

* * * *

In a land suddenly plunged into savagery, few were left to mourn the collapse of civilisation, but far in the north one man embraced its demise in the belief that an ancient prophecy had just been fulfilled. Despite his pain, Arthur Wiseman knew that his recent escape had been more than just good fortune - at last fate was turning in his favour. After hearing the helicopter explode behind him, he had ridden wet and naked for over a mile, but now his adrenaline was starting to wane and he was beginning to succumb to the freezing temperatures. He was alive, but for how long? He rode on with the cold wind piercing his flesh like a thousand needles until he finally reined in the horse in an attempt to alleviate the agony. At that moment, a familiar voice spoke to him; Merlin's tone was urgent, encouraging Arthur to keep riding – his pursuers were dead, but Arthur had to find shelter if he were to survive.

    Half an hour of misery followed and just as Arthur thought he could go no further, he spotted a building on the horizon. The roof of the farmhouse had collapsed, but one of its stone outbuildings appeared to have survived intact. The surrounding farmland comprised mostly of scrubby grass and heather and was obviously unfit for cultivation, but hardy, black-faced sheep grazed the hills, having built up a natural resistance to the bitter moorland's climate. The shivering man led the horse through the flock towards the building, desperate for shelter and any kind of warmth. The farm looked to be deserted and Arthur sensed that the occupiers lay cold and dead beneath the broken buildings. He knew that it took a brave man to farm these hills and after such a severe winter few lambs would be produced so perhaps the owner had been spared a bleak future.

Arthur kicked in the door of the outbuilding and despite his near-frozen condition, he started to laugh. Apart from their meat, sheep provided another vital source of revenue to the unfortunate farmer, and one that was about to spare Arthur's life. Once again Merlin had saved the day – the wizard had guided Arthur here, probably to the only place in a fifty mile radius that was still intact and, more importantly, was store to at least fifty bundles of white, woollen fleece. Staggered at his good fortune, Arthur took his sword and went to work on one of the bundles.

Over the next hour or so Arthur fashioned himself an outfit by binding together a number of fleeces with leather strops. Finally, satisfied with his work and dressed much warmer, a terrible hunger took him. He turned his attention to the herd outside; the black-faced sheep had clothed him and now they would sustain him.

Arthur relished the chase, slaughtering many of the animals from horseback with his sword and roaring with triumph at every kill.

The next morning, Arthur rode into the smoking ruins of the Yorkshire town with the air of a wild-west gunslinger. He felt invincible with the powerful horse beneath him and the cavalry sabre by his side. His stomach was full and the cold couldn't penetrate the thick woollen fleeces that wrapped his body. The morning was cloudy, but much warmer than yesterday when it had been so cold that he had nearly died in the woods after evading the police. Now warm and replete, Arthur rode into town, the hooves of his mount kicking up black dust as it trotted along what had once been the town's high street. Most buildings had collapsed, leaving uneven structures of fallen masonry and timber amongst the dusty debris that had once been the fabric of local civilisation. Bodies lay among the devastation and some had been mutilated, partially eaten by something - or perhaps someone. Arthur felt many eyes upon him and sensed fear from a multitude of unseen beings. But there was an absence of the more complex emotions that normally radiated from people and he wondered who or what was watching him from amongst the ruins.

    Arthur heard a commotion ahead and shut his mind to the curious telepathy emanating from his surroundings. In the distance, a small mob of near-naked humans were jostling each other in a frenzied attempt to climb a small tree at the roadside. Arthur could just make out two figures perched precariously in its branches. As he came nearer he saw that the objects of the crowd's attention were a man in his thirties and a teenage girl; both were struggling to evade the clawing grasps of their tormentors below. The man was lowest on the tree, crouching on a sturdy limb but a little too close to the ground for comfort. He struck repeatedly at the mass below with what appeared to be a modern walking stick - the type that hill-walkers use. The girl was slightly higher, hugging the tree trunk and kicking downwards at the aggressors with her sturdy boots. They both wore strange orange overalls and they carried rucksacks dangling equipment including grey plastic helmets with head-torches and coils of rope. Despite the fact they were covered in mud, the contrast between them and the horde below was striking. Apart from noticing their clothes were in good condition, Arthur sensed they were intellectually alienated from their attackers. From the terrified couple, whose minds were obviously more psychologically advanced than the creatures below, he sensed a complex array of emotions. As well as terror, more sophisticated feelings of despair, guilt and betrayal emanated from them. The attackers, who were still unaware of Arthur's advance, transmitted only the most primitive of sentiments – hate, lust and anger.

As he approached, Arthur tuned his mind to the aggressors and was amazed at the ease in which he infiltrated their minds. Mentally, he communicated his presence and immediately the clamour ceased; as one, the group turned towards him, mouths agape. He implanted a notion of authority into their collective minds and willed them to abandon their prey and retreat back into the ruins. This they immediately did without exception, lurching ape-like into the shadows. As they moved, their eyes remained fixed on Arthur's, apparently in awe of his commanding presence.

'Everything's changed,' Merlin said inside Arthur's head. 'The world has been cleansed. These creatures are wretched – they need you Arthur!'

Arthur turned his attention back to the couple in the tree. The man was becoming hysterical now that the immediate danger had passed and started gibbering a curious mixture of blasphemy and prayer. Arthur sensed that the girl had much greater inner strength and she demonstrated this by remaining calm and speaking rationally.

'Thanks mister,' she said. 'Those freaks were gonna kill us for sure! Have they escaped from some nut house?'

'Come down, both of you,' Arthur said - his voice smooth and full of compassion.

The girl swung herself down from the tree, followed more gingerly by the now tearful man whose pathetic state was starting to annoy Arthur.

'For fuck's sake stop crying!'

The man snorted in shock and looked quizzically at the man on the horse. Then he started to whimper again and fell to his knees. Arthur turned to the girl and explored her mind; she was strong and at first resisted the intrusion, but he perceived an inner conflict – a desire for salvation, someone to take control.

'Who's your valiant friend?' he asked her.

'My teacher, we're on a field trip!' As she spoke, Arthur detected emotions of guilt, resentment, and shame; she looked embarrassed and he saw bitterness in her bulging eyes. Something was not right about the girl; her head was filled with dark thoughts and undisclosed secrets. But as she looked into Arthur's own strange eyes, he could feel her opening her mind to him. Abandoning all inhibitions, she surrendered her will to her saviour and all of her dark secrets were suddenly exposed. Arthur felt a swell of emotion he had never before experienced in his troubled life. He felt all-powerful, capable of anything and was suddenly aware of his supremacy over his new surroundings.

Unsure of what he intended, Arthur dismounted and approached the girl. Without considering the implications, he handed her the cavalry sabre and willed her to take it; then he turned his head to the man snivelling on his knees in the dust and made an unconscious demand.

The sword struck immediately and the uncompromising way in which the blow was delivered surprised Arthur. He turned back to the girl who looked at him now with complete devotion and smiled. She was no more than seventeen; tall and slim with long dark hair but she was not very pretty; her large blue eyes were striking though, wide and bright and they rolled in a way that reminded Arthur of the inmates at Hareford House.

'Bring me his clothes,' he said to her.

The girl showed no emotion as she undressed the man as he lay dying on the stony ground and she handed the garments to Arthur.

'What's your name?' He asked.

The girl's bulbous eyes flared. 'People call me Collie,' she said, bitterly and angry resentment radiated from her mind.

Arthur caught her thoughts - they called her Collie because they said she howled like a dog. 'Come,' he said. 'We have much to do.'

The girl held out her arm to him and he swung her up onto the horse behind him. Then almost absently, he cast his mind to the creatures in the ruins - a simple command issued with no great effort, but one that they immediately obeyed. Slowly they came, silently lumbering out of the ruins to follow Arthur, instinctively feeling that this superior creature had the power to deliver them from their misery.

Chapter 2

Matt couldn't remember ever being so cold. Dank grey clouds clung to the frosted hills and obscured the horizon. Clumps of coarse, brittle grass danced in the biting winds and crunched under their feet. Feeling small and exposed by the imposing welsh landscape, he was aware that the group was completely at the mercy of the harsh environment. He knew that there was no one to call now if things turned bad - no air ambulance would be dispatched or rescue teams mobilised and Matt had a feeling that things were indeed turning bad. No longer convinced that they were still heading in the right direction, he suspected that they may have veered off track and were in danger of completely losing their bearings. According to the hand-drawn map, a large wind farm would once have stood on the slopes to the west; he imagined the huge structures towering above the rolling hills and dominating the skyline - a stark reminder of mankind's prevalence over such places of desolation. Now, the great turbines must have fallen into dust, back into the very ground that had once supplied the materials of their creation.

Matt had led the group into the bitter hills, confident that he could guide them to the remote abbey. Unfortunately, he hadn't realised how much his orienteering prowess had relied on man-made landmarks - now, as he scanned the horizon, he saw no visible construction from which to navigate. Man's dominance over the land had been a fragile one and now nature once more had the upper hand - they were alone and at its mercy.

They had been walking for several hours and any attempt at conversation had long since ceased. Now, as flurries of snow stung their eyes and obscured their view, the whole party was silent. The icy wind numbed their ears and drowned out all other sounds to such an extent that each member of the party felt isolated, gaining no comfort from the other travellers' company. Matt knew that they could easily freeze to death up here unless they found shelter before nightfall. Their makeshift clothing was inadequate for exposure to these conditions; temperatures would drop further as darkness fell and Matt knew they would not be able to sustain their body heat if exposed to the night frost. Baxter trotted silently by Matt's side as he led the group with Eddie close behind. Nic and Joe followed next with Tanya at the rear, looking more and more dejected as the journey wore on. Matt's sense of direction had abandoned him and the terrible responsibility ate away at his confidence. He paused once again to consult the map, despite the knowledge that these increasingly frequent stops were contributing to the group's growing unease. He was sure that they should have stopped climbing by now, but it seemed that every time they reached the brow of a hill, another rising slope appeared out of the gloom to challenge them.

Matt turned to the party, looking at each of them in turn, trying to assess their mood, their ability to continue. No one spoke or even acknowledged his gaze; they were exhausted and dispirited. He suspected that they had lost all hope of reaching their destination today and each was privately contemplating a night of unbearable discomfort. They should never have embarked on such a lengthy journey. Eddie had said that such a distance was unnecessary as long as they stayed clear of reactive material, but Matt had insisted for reasons that he now realised were selfish – he had wanted to prove something to himself. His irresponsibility meant they were probably all going to freeze to death and Matt decided then, that if they somehow survived this predicament, someone else would have to lead them; he would take a back seat and just look after himself.

'One more climb and we should be able to see the abbey,' he shouted above the wind. 'Then hopefully it'll be down hill all the way.' He knew it was a lie and so did they, but what else could he do – if they stopped here they would certainly die. He turned back to the hill and trudged on upwards with the others wearily following his footsteps. The slope was now becoming steeper and more treacherous; snow had drifted so deep in places that it was not easy to predict the state of the ground below.

Suddenly there was a cry from behind and Matt turned to see Eddie lose his footing, slide to his left and disappear under a drift of snow. Nic was first to react and managed to grab Eddie's hand before he too slid into what appeared to be a large crater concealed by the snow. Both men surfaced and looked around trying to work out what it was they had fallen into. Once disturbed, the snow revealed a deep pit of almost dry, black sludge, which formed a perfectly round crater with almost vertical sides.

'What is it Nic?' Tanya called, apparently concerned enough for her colleague to forget her brooding resentment.

'No idea,' Nic shouted back. 'Bloody death trap though – I can't believe…'

'Wait!' Eddie interrupted, pointing up the hill. 'Wh…what's that?'

Matt followed his gaze – a few hundred metres away, an object resembling an aircraft wing stuck out of the snow like a giant gravestone. He turned north 'Look, there's another one.'

'And over there!' Tanya shouted, pointing west.

As they looked around they could make out several of the strange shapes sprouting from the snow, but obviously alien to the landscape.

'What are they, Eddie?' Matt asked.

'Wind turbines!' Tanya shouted. 'They're wind turbine blades.' She had visited several wind farms during her coverage of the energy crisis.

Matt pulled the hand-made map from his overalls and eagerly studied it. 'We've veered too far east,' he said. If this is the wind farm, we've climbed just about the highest peak around here. If only we knew where north was, we could…'

'To refuse a gift out of pride is foolhardy,' Joe said, holding out a small bundle of cloth.

'What?' Matt walked over to the ex-wrestler. 'What are you saying?'

'You told me you didn't need the compass.'

'Joe, are you telling me you've…?'

'I brought it from the museum as a gift; when you said you didn't need it I thought I'd wait and give it to the lady doctor.' Joe handed the bundle to Matt.

'Joe, you idiot - we've been wandering around these hills and all along you've…' Matt didn't continue; instead he unwrapped the cloth to reveal the small brass-hinged compass. He opened the lid and saw that there was an engraving on its inner face. "*So that you may find me,*' it read. Matt turned until the needle faced north and then re-consulted the map. He pointed northwest. 'See those trees? If I'm right, the abbey's just the other side of them – less than a mile away!'

* * * *

Inside the abbey the four adults huddled around the fire as darkness fell outside. Mel knew that Matt, Eddie and Joe should have arrived hours ago and was growing more and more anxious. She tried to focus her attention on the injured girl who lay sleeping on a bed of velvet drapes against one of the stone walls. Hayley had found the child lying face down on the roadside near the camper-van's wreckage. Her grandparents were both dead; the man's head had been caved in – Rupert said he must have hit a roadside boulder when the van disintegrated and probably died instantly, but the man's wife had still been alive, barely. Rupert had found her bleeding heavily from a stomach wound with no apparent cause and she had died in his arms a few minutes later. Whatever had impaled the woman must have done so before it degenerated, along with the rest of the van.

    'I don't think the girl's badly injured,' Mel whispered. 'She's got some nasty grazes though.'

    'There's something wrong with her,' Hayley said. 'She hasn't spoken a word.'

Rupert stared at the fire – a haunted look in his eyes. 'Her grandparents are out there, just lying in the dirt,' he said. 'The ground's too hard – what could I do?'

'You couldn't do anything more,' Mel said.

'We killed them!' Hayley said. 'We practically chased them off the hill.'

'It's nobody's fault, Hayley,' Mel lied - she too felt guilty, but it was Rupert who had chased the family away.

Suddenly, the child started to groan in discomfort. 'She's waking up,' Mel said.

The four of them crouched around the small, velvet-wrapped girl as she opened her eyes. The child squealed in fear when she saw their staring faces and squirmed as if to escape; Hayley held her gently and shushed reassuringly. The girl eventually stopped struggling but she still looked terrified.

'What's your name, sweetheart?' Hayley asked gently. The child just stared back, her eyes pools of rising panic, so Hayley resumed her shushing sound until the girl calmed down again.

'I don't think she can understand us,' Mel whispered. 'Just like Jill Davies, remember?'

Hayley continued to stroke the girl's head, which seemed to calm her further. 'I think the poor kid's wet herself,' she whispered. 'I should clean her and bathe her wounds. Do we have we anything that will hold water?'

'Here, take the cup,' Father Peter said. 'It's all we have I think.' He started to hand Mel the chalice and then hesitated. 'Be careful with it child, it's very precious.'

Mel took the cup and it seemed to vibrate for a moment as a thousand images flashed through her mind - so rapidly that they made no sense, like a video on super fast-forward. Then the moment passed and she held the cup reverently for a second, before hurrying outside to collect water from the stream. When she returned, Hayley cleaned the child and managed to feed her some baked potato, which the girl at first rejected but then gobbled down greedily once she found the taste. Eventually the child closed her eyes and fell asleep again.

'This must have happened right across the country,' Hayley whispered. 'Do you think there's many like her out there, Mel?'

'Bound to be I suppose, but they won't last long in these temperatures; more importantly, I wonder if there's anybody out there like us - unaffected I mean.'

'Surely we can't be alone,' Rupert said anxiously. 'Good grief, there has to be others.'

'I suppose it depends upon how reactive some materials turned out to be,' Hayley said. 'Eddie guessed that the reaction could degrade clothing, but he wasn't sure whether people's clothes could, by themselves, trigger a reaction. If they could and did, then I guess there's not much hope - how many people wander around naked in the wilderness?'

'Not the sort one wants to meet.' Rupert muttered.

Their thoughts were suddenly interrupted by frantic barking from outside, followed by a distant call for help.

'Baxter!' Rupert exclaimed, rising to his feet.

'Matt!' Mel cried, and she and Hayley raced outside, closely followed by Rupert and Father Peter. As soon as they left the abbey, they saw Baxter bounding towards them; the dog leapt into Rupert's arms, licking his face joyously. Then they saw Eddie and Matt staggering out of the copse, both flanking a young woman, supporting her as if she was injured in some way. Two other men followed them - one small and dark, the other much larger and pale-skinned. They all wore the familiar red-velvet cloaks over Degenesys overalls and by the way they moved were obviously exhausted - fit to drop. Mel and Hayley ran to help the injured woman.

'She's twisted her ankle,' Matt gasped between steaming breaths.

The woman was beautiful; Mel wondered who she was and what she meant to Matt. The stranger was pale and clearly in pain, but even wearing the unusual clothing, she might have graced any catwalk in Europe; her eyes were stunning, her features pure, and when she spoke she did so with a captivating voice.

'Thank you,' Tanya said. 'Bloody pothole ambushed me. God, I need a drink.'

Matt continued to support the newsreader's arm, despite the assistance of both Mel and Hayley.

'Okay, we've got her,' Mel said. 'Hurry inside where it's warmer.'

Eventually they all made it into the abbey and the travellers collapsed in front of the fire. The commotion woke the injured child and she cowered against the wall whimpering unintelligibly. Hayley, noticing her distress, crouched low and cautiously approached her, making the same shushing sounds that had previously calmed the girl; when she was close enough, she gently started to stroke her hair and eventually put her arm around the child's shoulders. At this, to the amazement of the others, the girl started to purr as if she were a cat.

'Who is she?' Matt asked, still breathing heavily from his excursion.

'An unexpected visitor,' Rupert replied. 'Her family are all dead. I… I chased them off…'

'Her mind's blank, like Jill Davies,' Mel said, glancing at Eddie who had previously refused to accept such symptoms could result from exposure to an entropic flash.

'I'm Tanya Fox,' the newsreader interrupted, rubbing her swollen ankle, 'and this is Nic, my assistant.' She nodded towards the young African.

Mel turned to the woman. 'Somehow, I don't think he's your assistant anymore,' she said, forcing a smile. Tanya returned the smile, a little too sweetly.

One by one, the others introduced themselves and recounted each group's experiences since their parting the previous day. Mel didn't mention anything about the cup or the visions that Father Peter had supposedly witnessed; things were emotional enough without paranormal events - real or imagined - adding to the confusion. The old priest said very little throughout and still seemed to be disturbed by what he had witnessed.

Matt explained that Tanya had slipped into one of the foundation craters at the nearby wind farm and had twisted her ankle, but despite this setback they had eventually reached the abbey just as darkness was falling. Matt seemed relieved that the responsibility of leading his companions was relinquished at last, but he looked despondent all the same. Mel knew that she hadn't shown much of a warm welcome on his arrival, but the way he fawned over the arrogant newsreader had annoyed her. Matt had probably forgotten the night at Hayley's house now that there was such a pretty face around.

'Man, I'm starving!' Nic said. 'What's for supper?'

Mel pushed her resentment away and re-stocked the fire so that they could have one more meal of baked vegetables before retiring. That night she slept apart from Matt and was feeling more and more uncomfortable about their relationship. The dormitory was quite crowded now and warmed up considerably as the night wore on. Surprisingly, most of the others slept well on the stone floor, exhaustion playing its part, but Mel couldn't seem to relax and to her, the night seemed very long indeed.

Chapter 3

Beneath the canopy of the ancient woodland it was dark and dank and Matt had an unnerving feeling that he was being watched. The copse comprised mainly of broad-leaved trees, but some conifers were now invading the native forest and a soft bed of pine needles covered the ground between damp patches of wood sorrel and yellow pimpernel. The air was still and the noise his feet made brushing through the woodland plants broke an eerie silence. Matt had chosen to come alone into the copse to collect firewood rather than go with Eddie, Joe and Nic to retrieve the module from the quarry. He had nearly killed them all on the hills yesterday and wanted someone else to take charge for a while - or better still, for good. No one seemed to blame him for his mistake in undertaking such a trek except perhaps Mel who had been strangely distant since his return. He had thought she really liked him, but he had a habit of misreading the signs when it came to women.

    Matt picked up a fallen branch and broke it over his knee before placing it in the velvet drape that was slung from his shoulder. He moved on and could now hear the sound of the stream that ran from the copse towards the abbey. He decided to follow the stream back to their camp rather than try and retrace his passage through the trees. When he reached the bank he looked into the cold water and wondered if there were fish worthy of catching. He had eaten nothing but baked vegetables since the night in the pub two nights ago and he yearned for something more substantial. There was a fishing line in the module and Matt wondered if Eddie and the others had retrieved its contents yet. If so, he might return to the stream this afternoon and try his luck. Perhaps he would ask Mel to come with him; he needed to clear the air and if they were alone he might be able to find out what was bothering her.

Suddenly there was a noise behind him, an unmistakable rustle in the undergrowth. Matt swung around, but there was no sign of its source. Thick brambles lined the stream's bank here and he assumed that something (or someone) was concealed in one of the larger bushes. He moved cautiously towards the nearest bramble and peered into its darkness. All of a sudden a sound chilled his heart; a quiet, guttural growl that Matt sensed was not intended to be a warning. It was a sound born of primal excitement, like that of a predator closing on his prey. Matt backed away, fearing that any sudden movement would cause the unseen creature to launch its attack, but then he turned and bolted as fast as he could along the riverbank. As he ran, the hairs on his neck rose in anticipation that his unseen foe was about to sink teeth or claws into his skin. Matt never looked back and did not stop running until he cleared the wood and was in sight of the abbey. Then at last he turned and was relieved to see that he was not pursued. Feeling foolish, he partly retraced his steps and picked up some of the firewood that he had dropped in his haste, but he did not re-enter the copse. He turned instead and walked down the hill back to the abbey.

Mel was sitting with Father Peter near a fire they had built against the low remains of one of the abbey's outside walls. They had all felt the need to be out in the open after the long dark night. Matt joined them and rubbed his hands in front of the flames to warm them; it was less cold today but it was dull and damp and there was comfort in the fire's warmth.

'Are you all right, my boy? You look like you've just seen a ghost.' The old priest's voice was hoarse from another night of relentless coughing.

'There was something in the woods - an animal I think, gave me a bit of a fright that's all. Where are Tanya and the others?'

Mel glared at him. 'Tanya's inside, apparently she needs to rest her leg if we're ever going to find some proper food,' she said.

'I'm afraid she's not very impressed with our survival skills,' Father Peter explained. 'Mel tried to catch one of the sheep on the hill but she couldn't even get close to the poor beast. It was probably just as well because none of us would know what to do had she caught it.'

'Tanya said I should bash it over the head with a rock!' Mel said, obviously horrified at the thought. 'When she saw our reaction she declared us all wimps and stomped off, which I suppose means that she'd be happy to slaughter one if it wasn't for her swollen ankle.'

'So you're baking potatoes again,' Matt said dejectedly, nodding at the fire.

'Yep,' Mel said, 'I just hope the others get back soon and bring something different to eat.'

'So where's Rupert and Hayley?' Matt asked.

'Both inside,' she replied, 'Rupert's really depressed – he's still blaming himself for what happened to the camper.

Nothing I say seems to make any difference. Hayley's taking care of Amy.' Mel was sure that the girl's name was actually Annie, but their memory of the camper-van incident was vague and Hayley had convinced the others that the child's grandmother had called her Amy when she had dragged her away. The girl, of course, had no view on the matter.

'It's amazing how quickly the child's recovering,' Father Peter said. 'Not least from her wounds; they seem to have healed with uncanny speed.'

'Hayley's really taken to the child,' Mel said. 'She's teaching her the fundamentals of life. Eating with a knife and fork, toiletry - all the basics. She's even taught her a few words. Hayley says she's such a quick learner – a bit like a blank canvas.'

'It's warmer today,' Matt said, looking up at the sky.

The others knew what he was thinking – they had all lain awake trying not to imagine the suffering so many people must have endured before succumbing to the freezing temperatures.

'How many poor souls do you think were affected?' Father Peter asked.

'Well, if it reached us here,' Matt replied. 'You have to assume the whole country was hit; you saw what happened to the camper and I've already seen one building in ruins.'

'People will endure,' Father Peter said.

Mel frowned as if unconvinced. 'Not if most of the survivors are afflicted like Amy.' She said.

'I'm not so sure,' Matt said. 'The girl seems to be recovering well. Look how she's responding to Hayley's attention – she's already learnt to say her name.'

'But that's because we're here to help her. Without the skills developed through life's experiences and the knowledge passed on by others, how will those less fortunate possibly survive?'

'Don't underestimate the power of animal instinct.' Matt suggested.

'Or the power of God,' Father Peter said. 'He will protect others as he has protected us.'

'If they do survive...' Mel started; then she paused, as if reluctant to raise an issue that was concerning her; she drew a breath before continuing. 'If there are a lot of people like Amy out there without anyone to help, who knows what will they become? It's quite possible they'll lack all moral concept – no sense of right or wrong. Who knows how they'll react?'

'You're a behaviourist,' Matt said. 'You should have a better idea than most; what do you think will happen?'

'In theory, their behaviour will be quite predictable,' Mel said, her face betraying the fact that she had already given this much thought. 'You've probably heard of Maslow's hierarchy of needs?'

'Yeah, the triangle,' Matt said. 'I can't remember the detail though.'

'Well, Maslow was an expert in humanistic psychology; he developed a theory of motivation describing the process by which an individual progresses from basic needs, such as food and sex, to the highest needs of what he called self-actualisation. We all come from a world where our basic needs are pretty much fulfilled, so we become obsessed with self-esteem - material desires, status, power - the fulfilment of our greatest human potential. Now it's quite possible that whole communities have suddenly dropped back down the evolutionary ladder to the "basic needs" rung. Food and warmth will be a priority for them – there will be plenty to eat at first,' she said, and then paused, looking at both men in turn, 'and those who survived the night must have found some way to keep warm, so today's temperatures won't be a problem for them. The next basic instinct is to reproduce – they'll be looking to mate, at least until they become hungry, which won't be long now it's getting warmer.'

'And what happens when food gets scarce?' Matt asked.

'Without a moral view on life anything could happen,' Mel's eyes flittered nervously. 'Some could even resort to cannibalism.'

'People might start eating each other?' Matt asked, visibly shuddering at the thought.

'Perhaps,' Father Peter said. 'But you're assuming that all our moral code has been taught to us. That's a very simplistic view – isn't it possible that humanity naturally exists within every man? Goodwill and compassion are also survival needs and they may be deep-routed, not just taught.'

'I expect you're right, Father,' Matt said. 'Let's hope that when we leave this place we'll find everything already getting back normal.'

'Maybe so,' Mel said. 'But we should be careful all the same. If you're wrong and there has been widespread affliction, the survivors might already be forming packs, leaders will develop and primitive rules will quickly emerge. There will undoubtedly be conflict and many more people could get hurt.'

'Then we will need an advantage,' Matt said.
'Hopefully the things in the module will give us that, at least.'

Half a mile away, at the quarry, Eddie slapped his hands on the ceramic module in frustration. 'The m…mechanism must have been corroded by the entropic wave,' he said.

'I thought it was designed to withstand the reaction,' Nic said.

'From the inside, yes, but the m…mechanism is not protected from an external reaction, why should it be? The bloody thing's sealed shut and we have no m…means to open it.'

The three men sat around the module on boulders, each trying to think of a way to retrieve its contents. Nic picked up a small rock; he turned it over and over in his hand. 'Loadstone,' he said absently. 'When I was in Ghana our football team employed a traditional witchdoctor and I remember that he used these to heal our injuries; he said stones like this possess magical qualities and can restore health.' Nic tossed the stone to Eddie.

'It's just m…magnetite,' Eddie said. 'Common iron oxide, that's all.' He tossed it back at the young African. 'Here, keep it, it m…might bring you luck.'

'Hey, let's break it,' Nic said, catching the magnetite.

'Why? It's just m…magnetic rock.'

'Not the stone, man – that thing! Nic pointed at the module before putting the loadstone safely into one of his pockets. 'You say the one at the plant fractured – it can't be that strong.'

Eddie looked doubtful, but Nic insisted they give it a try so Joe Sumo gathered up a rock in his massive arms and staggered over to the unit. He raised the boulder as high as he could and then smashed it down onto the module. It hit with force but the rock didn't even chip the surface. Disillusioned, the three men sat around the module in silence each trying again to think of a solution.

The quarry was actually a borrow pit, a crescent of loose rock cut into the hillside to supply stone for the access roads of the nearby wind farm. The track leading to the ruined abbey ran adjacent to its lowest point and two narrow gravel paths ran from the track, rising up around each ridge of the crescent to the summit of a sheer stone cliff.

'What's in there that's fragile? Nic asked, realising they had just thrown a huge boulder at some of their most precious possessions.

'My glasses for a s...start... and there are some medicine bottles, b...but they're well wrapped and I can't think of anything else to worry about.'

'Then let's try again,' Nic said, pointing upwards. 'From up there!'

They all looked up at the cliff, which towered above the quarry and realised what he meant; they could drop rocks onto the ceramic capsule from height.

Five minutes later Joe and Eddie were at the top. Nic stayed with the module, which they had dragged to a point close to the sheerest, most vertical face of the cliff and wedged rocks underneath its body to maximise the effect of any impact. Luckily there were plenty of large boulders on the cliff top, which was at least fifty feet above the module at this point.

Eddie picked up a hefty rock and shouted a warning to Nic before heaving it over the edge. It missed the module by at least a metre. Joe had a try and also missed.

'Come on, man - remember Pearl Harbour!' Nic shouted.

Joe scowled at the young man below before wrapping his arms around a huge boulder and, heaving himself to his feet, staggered back to the edge to release it. Nic jumped clear as the rock plummeted downwards.

'Direct hit!' Nic yelled as the boulder crashed into the module. 'Hold fire, man! I'll check the damage.'

It was bad news – the module was chipped, but no more. The three men tried to bomb their target several more times but it was to no avail. Eventually they gave up and headed back to the camp, climbing the steep track towards the abbey. Nobody spoke - they were disheartened, tired and hungry. Nic threw stones at random targets along the way and dreamed of being back in his flat, cooking Spaghetti Bolognese - his favourite meal.

Eventually Eddie spoke. 'Not far now – there's the bend where the camper crashed,' he said, pointing ahead.

As before, they circumnavigated the scene of the crash, cutting across the grass rather than passing the place where they knew two bodies still lay.

Nic launched a stone at a crow as it took off from the coarse grass with an ugly raucous call. As the stone landed, he was surprised to see it disturb a number of other crows, which squawked their annoyance as they took flight from a hidden place in the grass. The others were in front and glanced back at the commotion before continuing to trudge onwards and upwards, but Nic wandered over to investigate. 'Hey, come over here,' he shouted.

Eddie was the first to join the young African. Lying at Nic's feet was the carcass of a small sheep.

'Don't touch it Nic,' Eddie advised. 'It's p…probably rotten.'

'No, it's still warm – it can't have been dead long.'

The sheep's eyes were bloody as a result of the crow's attention, but other than that it seemed pretty much intact; that was until Nic turned it over to reveal that the animal's throat had been ripped wide open. 'Jesus! What the bloody hell did that?' He yelled, quickly releasing the animal.

'No idea,' Eddie replied. 'But whatever did, apparently w…wasn't hungry enough to f…finish its meal!'

'But we are!' Joe Sumo growled 'Never look in the mouth of a gift horse.' The huge man stooped, grabbed the animal's hooves and, in one movement, swung the carcass up onto his broad shoulders before starting off back up the hill. The others looked at each other briefly, then Nic shrugged and they both turned to follow their giant friend.

That evening they sat round the fire with full stomachs and speculated on what might have killed the animal. Eddie suggested that the most likely culprit was a large dog of some kind and when Matt relayed his experiences in the copse they all agreed that they should be careful not to be caught in the open on their own.

'Do you think dogs would be affected in the same way that humans are by an entropic flash?' Matt asked.

'No r…reason to think otherwise,' Eddie said, 'except that animals rely less on what they have learnt and m…much more on instinct; they'd find it m…much easier to survive the affliction than their masters.'

'And they'd have no memory of human relationship I suppose,' Rupert said, rubbing Baxter's ears. 'No longer man's best friend I think - not like you boy, eh?'

That night they were all kept awake by Father Peter's coughing, at one point Hayley got up to fetch some water from the stream in the golden cup. Eddie reminded her of their earlier discussion and went with her to collect the water. Outside in the cold air they both felt vulnerable and could have sworn that they were being stalked, but they watched each other's backs and returned without event.

By the early hours, Father Peter's condition had deteriorated so much that he could hardly catch his breath between bouts of coughing. The old priest was feverish and becoming delirious and Mel told the others that she thought he could be developing pneumonia, which might be deadly without proper medicine. They all knew that they must find a way to open the module and retrieve the penicillin that Mel had insisted on stowing there.

As soon as it was light Matt rose and went outside to the stream to drink. He decided that he would go this time and help the others with the module. They had to recover its contents before they could leave the sanctuary of the old abbey and Father Peter needed medicine. The old priest was very dear to him and he would do anything to save the old man's life, even if it meant taking charge again.

Suddenly Nic burst out from the abbey. 'Joe Sumo's gone!' he cried.

'What do you mean gone? Where could he go?'

'He's just gone, man. Do you think he's all right?'

'He's certainly big enough to look after himself. Probably needed to get away from Father Peter's coughing,' Matt suggested. 'I'm sure he'll be back soon.'

Nic was clearly concerned for his new found friend, but Matt managed to convince him that Father Peter was the immediate priority, so Nic reluctantly joined him and Eddie on a second quest to retrieve the ceramic module's contents.

There was a slight breeze as the three men trudged back down the hill once more towards the quarry. Matt noticed that the sheep that normally grazed the hill were nowhere to be seen and he wondered if they had been frightened away by whatever had killed one of their flock yesterday. He pushed the thought from his mind and looked up at the morning sky; the clouds were breaking now to reveal patches of blue and when the sun occasionally shone through, it felt pleasantly warm on their backs. Despite their lack of sleep, they all felt stronger for the previous night's feast and their spirits were higher now that they had left the confines of the dark abbey where the old priest struggled for breath. However, Matt felt a terrible responsibility, knowing that failure to open the module this time might well have fatal consequences.

As the party neared the quarry, they subconsciously slowed their pace - each realising that that they had no real plan as to how they would tackle the problem. Even Eddie had no new ideas, but he told the others that just raining more rocks down was not the answer.

'Hey, the module!' Nic cried. 'Somebody's taken it!'

'What the...' Matt muttered, running to the place where the others had left the module. 'No look, there's a track. It's been dragged away – over there.'

The three men followed the trail across the quarry and up one of the gravel paths that ascended its southern edge.

They discovered the abandoned capsule almost at the top of the cliff with no clue as to how it had arrived there.

'How the hell...' Matt started, but was interrupted by the barking of dogs from beyond the peak of the hill to their left.

'Come on,' Nic yelled, instinctively picking up a few small rocks from the ground as he made off towards the sound.

The others copied him and followed. Over the brow of the hill a few isolated beech trees grew sporadically amongst the coarse grass and they soon recognised the massive frame of Joe Sumo perched unsteadily on the lowest of the tree's bare branches. How he had got up there was a mystery, but why he was there was quite apparent. Barking and growling beneath him, circled a pair of the largest Alsatians Matt had ever seen. As they watched, one of the dogs launched itself at their friend, jumping so incredibly high that Joe had to shuffle his feet to avoid its snarling fangs.

'Help me!' the huge man pleaded. His voice was uncharacteristically high-pitched and he was obviously terrified.

Nic threw a stone at one of the dogs and it caught it hard on its flank. It yelped and retreated, but then turned again to face its new adversaries. Both dogs stared menacingly at the three men and growled deeply as they edged forward with hackles raised. Matt thought back to the day in the woods and guessed that one of these animals had been stalking him then; luckily it must have been fully fed, otherwise he would have been easy meat for such a powerful creature. They both looked hungry now though, and Matt realised that human flesh was once again back on the menu. He threw a stone and it caught the nearest animal square between its eyes. Eddie and Nic slung more stones and just about every missile caught its target. Matt wondered at their incredible good fortune as the two dogs bounded away down the hill; nearly every rock had made its mark. Any other day most would have flown harmlessly wide and the two ferocious animals would have been upon them.

It took them nearly ten minutes to extract their terrified friend from the tree. It turned out that the great Japanese wrestler had suffered from an unnatural fear of dogs since his early childhood.

'What were you doing here alone, Joe?' Nic asked. 'I thought we agreed yesterday that it was dangerous.'

'A dying man cannot just wait for his shroud to be woven. The old priest needs medicine'

Eddie was circling the module. 'Of course!' He said, rubbing his bristly chin. 'You were going to drop it onto the rocks below!'

Matt wandered over to join him and looked down at the quarry. 'Eddie, will it work?' he asked.

'W... well, the total m...mass of the m...module's greater than any of the rocks we've thrown,' Eddie said. 'If it hits a hard target it will carry much more force. I think it m…might just work! Mind you, the s…stuff inside's going to take a battering.'

'We've got no choice – come on Joe, let's finish the job!' Matt said, slapping his giant friend on the back.

Getting the module to the top of the hill took a lot more effort than they expected and they were amazed at how far Joe had managed to drag the thing on his own. Eventually they had it perched precariously on the overhanging edge of the cliff and Nic and Matt went down to prepare its landing place. They made a solid bed from the largest boulders available for it to fall onto, each one carefully shimmed with smaller rocks to minimise the amount it would give on impact. They realised that if they wanted to retrieve the capsule's contents intact they would probably only get one attempt at this, so preparation was all-important. At the top, Eddie shouted instructions to the pair below, whilst Joe Sumo looked around nervously for the return of the dogs. Finally, Matt seemed satisfied with their groundwork and shouted up to the others.

'Ok, we're ready down here,' he yelled, backing away from the target area. 'Let her go, Joe.'

Joe Sumo jammed one of his muscular shoulders against the module and heaved; it teetered on the edge for a moment before toppling slowly into space. Its fall seemed to take an eternity before the module struck the bedrock and the party knew immediately from the sound of the impact that they had been successful. The ceramic capsule broke its back and split in two, its contents spilling out amongst the dust thrown up by the collision. All four men whooped with joy, then danced and hugged each other as if they had just scored the winning goal at a Wembley cup final. For the first time since the disaster something had gone right.

Chapter 4

That night they all slept better knowing that essential possessions from their past life were stacked safely in the inner dormitory. The only items not stored there were the shotgun, which had been propped against the stone wall near the external door, and the water bladders which were now full and surrounded by plastic cups and paper plates. It looked like they were planning a picnic in a war zone.

  The next day, utilising ingredients and utensils recovered from the module, Hayley prepared a mutton broth and Amy helped her attempt to bake bread on a flat stone in the fire. The girl chatted, incoherently most of the time, but uncannily she appeared to understand Hayley's every instruction. It was as if her uncluttered brain could comprehend her mentor's thoughts as well, if not better than her words.

  Father Peter was still feverish but seemed a little improved having already taken his second dose of antibiotics. There had been no sign of the dogs since the episode at the quarry, but Rupert said that he thought he had heard their distant howling in the night and none of them believed that they'd seen the last of the animals. The morning was sunny and the temperature had already risen, suggesting that this would be the warmest day of the year so far. Matt and Mel sat against one of the abbey's ruined walls, taking advantage of the early sun. Rupert, Eddie and Tanya were collecting firewood in the copse and they had taken the gun as a precaution in case the dogs returned. Tanya was walking better now but even so, she would have trouble outrunning a hungry Alsatian.

Nic and Joe were at the river fishing; Matt watched their antics in the distance with amusement – they obviously didn't have a clue what they were doing.

'It's funny how they get on so well,' he said. 'You would never have expected it – they're so different.'

'People are strange,' Mel said. 'I'm surprised that you and Tanya get on so well after all the trouble she caused you.'

'Tanya just takes a bit of getting used to that's all; I think she just likes having her own way.'

'She's very beautiful,' Mel said, glancing sideways at Matt as he watched the unlikely fishermen.'

Suddenly there was a splash, followed by shouts in the distance. 'Hey, big Joe's just fallen in!' Matt laughed, getting up for a better view.

When he sat down again a cloud passed overhead and Mel pulled a blanket over her knees. 'How long do you think we should stay at the abbey?' she asked.

'Not my call.' Matt shrugged. 'Father Peter needs to be fit again and Tanya's injury…'

'I'm sure her leg's not as bad as she's making out.'

Matt looked at her – it wasn't like Mel to be so sullen. 'Are you ok?' He asked.

'I'm all right, I just wish you'd stop taking a back seat all the time; nobody knows what to do in this situation - me included. Eddie's clever, but hasn't got an ounce of common sense! I'm scared that as soon as Tanya's fit, she's going start calling the shots and that worries me.'

'Let her! She can't do any worse than me,' Matt said, plucking at the grass with his fingers.

'I don't trust her, Matt. She only cares about herself and with her ego it won't enter her head that people's lives are at risk here. We need you! Everybody trusts you.'

'Well they shouldn't – anyway, we don't need a leader, just practical decisions born from discussion. Why don't you call a meeting and we'll talk it through.'

'You promise you'll participate?'

'Of course I will – why wouldn't I?'

'Good, I'll get the others together after we've eaten. I'm worried that if we stay at the abbey too long we might regret it. We need to find out what's happening out there.' She got up and strode towards the dormitory, which was now the source of a wonderful smell of cooking.

'I think we need to move on as soon as everybody's fit,' Mel said to the group. They all stared at her, apart from Amy who was preoccupied, playing with Baxter. The old beagle, like the rest of them had developed a curious affection for the child.

'I wouldn't mind a trip into town, Mel' Tanya said, 'but I think the shops might still be closed, don't you?'

Mel ignored the sarcasm. 'We have to find better shelter and some proper food. Have you noticed the sheep have all disappeared?'

'The dogs have scared them off the hill,' Joe said - he would have left right there and then if he had been asked.

'Mel's right,' Matt said. 'We should leave as soon as possible; head to the nearest village and see what we find.'

Tanya raised her eyebrows. 'Whatever,' she said. 'My ankle's not perfect, but I'm in better shape than most of you; I could break camp tomorrow if necessary.'

'No, let's give Father Peter a couple of days,' Mel said. 'In the mean time, we'll plan our route; we've got proper maps now… unless someone has a better idea?'

That night, Father Peter's chest infection seemed to have improved and he slept soundly for the first time in days. He lay in the old dormitory, hugging the bag containing the golden chalice as if he were a small child gaining comfort from a favourite toy. He dreamt that he was standing in a tall stone tower overlooking the ocean. A low evening sun approached the sea's horizon, warming his face as he looked down from unfinished stone battlements onto the rocky knoll below. A tall ship was anchored near the shore and smaller boats were unloading goods at a water gate at the foot of the castle rock. Wagons, pulled by horses, were driven up a ledged path towards the castle between artillery platforms built into the overhanging rock. With him on the tower, two masons chatted as they pulled on the rope of a gin wheel, heaving a sturdy basket of stone upwards from the ground below.

'Bala is a filthy town, without any lodgings fit for gentlemen to lie,' one said. 'I'll not stay there again.'

'Aye, and a dangerous place, best to camp in the castle grounds and suffer the lack of supplies,' replied the other. Both men's tunics were damp with sweat and their hands were callused from many years of such labour. They seemed not to notice Father Peter until he addressed them.

'What is this place?' The priest asked.

The two men stopped heaving the rope and stared at the old man, acknowledging his presence for the first time. Before the men could respond, a clear horn sounded - then another, and there were shouts from the courtyard below. Men on the outer ward pointed north and Father Peter turned to see the source of the commotion. A single horseman rode at speed along the dusty road towards the castle; he wore armour beneath a long red tunic and he carried a white standard, depicting a golden chalice. The knight galloped through the main gate and shouted to those who greeted him.

'They're coming!' He cried as he dismounted. 'They attack Harlech from the east!'

While Father Peter dreamt, the dogs returned. The rest of the party was also asleep and it was very dark in the old dormitory because the fire had almost died for the first time since their arrival. They hadn't stocked it quite as much as on previous nights as it was warmer now and they knew they had the means to easily re-ignite it now that the capsule had been opened.

Suddenly Baxter rose in the darkness and started to growl; it was so out of character for the old beagle that everybody woke as one. Then they heard a terrible howl, so near that it chilled their hearts.

'What is it?' Father Peter gasped. 'What's happening?'

'There's something outside.' Nic whispered, immediately alert.

Matt grabbed the shotgun and lifted the safety. Joe Sumo, fearing the worst, scurried away from the doorway; his single terrified eye shone in the firelight.

'Stoke the fire Joe, and add some wood,' Matt said. 'Let's get some light in here!' He knew the task would take Joe's mind off his fear.

Nic ran into the inner dormitory and returned with an axe from their stock of tools. 'Do you think we should go out?' he asked.

Matt crept to the entrance and carefully pulled the drape aside just far enough so that he could peer outside and poked the barrel of the shotgun through the curtain. The sky was overcast, but the moon lit up the clouds. Patches of mist lay close to the ground and shadows from the swirling clouds swam silently over the grassy mounds. Nothing else moved.

'What can you see?' Nic whispered from within.

'Nothing, I'm going to have a look around.' Matt crept forward with the shotgun. Nic followed as Matt slunk ahead, skirting one of the low ruined walls. Matt gripped the shotgun nervously, conscious that his hands were shaking. He knew that there were so many places amongst the ruins that could be concealing the dogs.

'Don't go too far!' Mel shouted from the abbey.

Matt turned towards the voice. 'Shhh… stay inside!' He called back.

Suddenly there was movement. 'Look out!' Nic yelled.

Matt turned and saw both dogs charging them from behind the end of the wall. Their tails were high as though in good spirit, but Matt knew better – the Alsatians aimed to kill them. He raised the shotgun and pulled one of its triggers but the blast went wide and the dogs were suddenly upon them. Nic's slight build was no match for the bulky animal that hit him and he was immediately bowled over with the dog snarling and lurching at his neck. Matt thrust the shotgun barrel hard into the face of the second Alsatian; it yelped and reeled to one side before crouching, ready to pounce again. Matt fired the gun a second time and the animal whined and bounded ungainly away. Matt turned to Nic, who had both hands round the other dog's throat in a desperate attempt to thwart its ferocious lunges; his hands and face were already bleeding heavily. Matt swung the shotgun like a baseball bat and caught the animal hard on its flank. The dog rolled completely over before righting itself and repeating its attack, but before it reached Nic, Matt struck again, the shotgun this time catching the animal's skull with a sickening thud. The dog immediately fell to the ground stunned - then it slowly got back to its feet and for a moment just stood there glaring at its adversaries. Matt moved towards it, with the gun poised to strike a third time. At this the animal turned and loped slowly off towards the copse with an unsteady gait, its head and tail hanging low.

Matt turned his attention to Nic and helped him to his feet. 'Are you okay?' He asked anxiously.

'Don't know, man - my hands are bleeding,' Nic stared dumbly at his wounds.

'And your head – you've been bitten there as well. Let's get you back to the abbey.'

Nic's injuries were not as bad as they could have been, but he was badly shaken and seemed mildly shocked, not wanting to speak. Hayley cleansed his wounds with water poured into Father Peter's chalice and antiseptic from the module.

'Why are you still using the cup?' Mel asked.

'Superstitious I suppose,' Hayley said. 'I know it's stupid, but I did this with Amy and her wounds healed so quickly.' Mel glanced over at Father Peter and wondered again about the mysterious chalice.

'The dogs are wounded,' Matt said, 'but they're hungry and I think they'll be back when they've recovered. I vote we go after them now and finish it.'

'No!' Mel said. 'You were lucky this time – we've only got one gun and there are two of them - it's not worth the risk.'

Joe Sumo nodded. 'He who hunts two hares often leaves one and loses the other!'

'I think w…we should abandon the abbey as s…soon as it gets light,' Eddie said. 'If they follow, then we'll try and p…pick them off - in the daylight it will be easier.'

Chapter 5

The next day, Matt looked up at the surrounding hills and wondered how much had actually changed following the incredible events of the last week. The party were resting beside a footpath leading down from the hills towards the first proper road that they would encounter on their journey. Along the way they had seen a number of old buildings which, from a distance appeared intact, but upon investigation were found to be uninhabitable. Without exception, the roofs had collapsed and the remaining structures were so unstable that they feared to enter them. Their walls stood precariously; the mortar that had once bound the stonework having now deteriorated into dust.

    The natural landscape seemed unchanged however; the patchwork of green shades was segregated by crumbling stone walls or wooden posts now devoid of interconnecting fence work. Strangely, they had encountered no other humans, living or otherwise, and they wondered what had become of the local inhabitants.

    They had been following a path lined by a series of wooden stakes presumably once supporting barbed wire or other fencing material. Animals grazed all around them as if unaware of the calamity that had affected their masters; numerous sheep roamed the hills and the herds of cattle wandered lazily among the coarser grass. Flocks of birds circled the skies just as they would have done before the disaster. It was difficult to believe that anything significant had happened here, but Matt suspected that the countryside gave a false impression – soon they would realise the full impact of the disaster and he wondered how the others would react if his fears were founded.

Although the landscape appeared mostly unchanged, the travellers most definitely were. All members of the party were considerably leaner now - through exertion and lack of food and most of the men already sported beards. Only Joe Sumo appeared immune – for some reason, he did not seem to grow facial hair, or else he had found a way to shave or pluck his skin, and his massive body seemed as bulky as ever.

Despite his exhaustion, Matt felt that he was regaining the fitness of his youth. He hadn't had alcohol or cigarettes for over a week and he felt clean inside. Aware of his fragile existence in this uncomplicated world, he felt more alive than at any time he could remember.

'Is it me, or does everything seem brighter somehow?' He said to Mel who sat beside him, tightening her bootlaces.

'Maybe,' she said. 'What strikes me is that nothing seems to be shining anymore, apart from the streams. It all seems so natural; you know – unspoilt.'

'I hope the going gets easier once we're on the road, we haven't made much headway today.' Their journey had been laborious to say the least; Amy had to be carried most of the time because she didn't have the footwear that the others now enjoyed - just wraps of sheepskin that they had strapped to her feet and which continually unravelled as she walked. Plus they were encumbered by the possessions recovered from the module. They had taken turns in bearing these items, suspended from a long wooden stake which had to be shouldered by two people at all times. Few could share this burden because Nic's hands were still heavily bandaged from the dog attack, Tanya was struggling with her ankle and Father Peter was still weak from his chest infection. If it hadn't been for Joe Sumo's incredible constitution, they wouldn't have made it as far as they had.

'Come on,' Mel said, 'let's see what's left of the road.'

According to the map, the footpath led to a small village lying on a minor road, which led northwest to the market town of Bala.

Matt and the rest of the party raised themselves wearily from the ground, but Baxter seemed reluctant to move on; the old Beagle hadn't seen so much exercise in many years and was as exhausted as the rest of them.

'Come on old boy!' Rupert coaxed, rubbing the dog's ears lovingly.

'Poor old Baxter,' Hayley said. 'I hadn't really noticed him growing old over the years. He's the probably feeling the toll as much as daddy is.'

Eventually the old beagle raised himself and wagged his tale in gratitude for his master's affection and ambled over to the stream to drink. They had replenished some of their water bags here, hoping the water was fresh, but not really having much choice in the matter.

Nic volunteered to take a turn carrying Amy, thinking he could give her a shoulder ride without having to use his hands, which were now itching beneath the bandages. A sign of healing rather than infection, he hoped.

Matt and Joe lifted the wooden pole suspending their possessions to their shoulders and it seemed heavier than ever.

Even the refilled water bags did not account for this, Matt thought. They might be fitter now, but the lack of decent food was taking its toll on their stamina; he hoped his strength wouldn't give out before his turn as load-bearer was over.

'You okay?' Eddie asked. 'I could h…help on that end if you w…want.'

'No you've only just had your turn,' Matt replied, 'I can manage – you need to regain your strength.'

Suddenly there was a loud pounding noise on the turf from behind them and they felt the soft earth shuddering beneath their feet. Fearing another entropic reaction, Matt turned towards the sound, but there was no crimson fire about to engulf them. Nevertheless, what he saw was equally terrifying - bearing down on him at incredible speed was the dark shape of a huge animal. Matt instinctively fell backwards in anticipation of being trampled, but at the last moment the massive shire horse pulled up within a few feet of him and stamped the ground with its huge feathered hooves. Its large brown eyes stared out nervously from beneath its dark brown mane.

Mel was the first to recover from the fright. 'It's beautiful,' she said, approaching the animal. The great horse backed away slightly as she closed the distance between them, but soothing the animal with her voice, Mel stretched out her arm and gently stroked its muzzle. The creature immediately relaxed and appeared to relish the human contact.

Matt got back to his feet and walked over to them cautiously. 'I thought you said animals would have no memory of their relationship with humans,' he said. 'Why isn't it scared of us?'

'Who knows? Perhaps some sort of instinct tells him that we're no threat; don't forget horses and men have been interacting together for centuries.'

'More likely he w…wasn't caught in a f…flash,' Eddie said. 'He was p…probably grazing up on the hills when the reaction hit and w…was unaffected.'

'We should take him with us,' Mel suggested. 'Maybe he can carry our equipment.'

To their delight, the horse accepted the baggage happily and they even considered letting Amy ride the animal, but decided not to push their luck. They had no reins to lead the horse and they knew it could take off at any time. They guessed that if it did, they could probably recover their possessions, but risking the child was another matter. As they set off again, the great horse seemed content to follow without encouragement and they all felt invigorated by their good fortune. The journey suddenly no longer seemed quite so daunting.

Eddie led the way now, followed by Matt, who carried the shotgun slung over his shoulder and Tanya, who seemed to take every opportunity to stay close to the man who influenced the group. Why this was, Matt had no idea; perhaps she saw him as some sort of threat to her status within the party, or maybe it was something else. Whatever it was he knew that it annoyed Mel, who walked a little way behind flanking the horse on one side with Hayley on the other. Behind them Father Peter walked stiffly with the aid of a stick he had found and Rupert strolled silently alongside Baxter who stopped to sniff at every fence post, presumably hoping for the scent of a fellow canine survivor. Finally, taking up the rear were Nic and Joe Sumo, the latter carrying Amy effortlessly on his ample shoulders. The two unlikely friends chatted happily about their previous lives in two very different counties. The young African seemed fascinated with the ex-wrestler's tales of his Sumo life in Japan, and Joe obviously enjoyed Nic's cheeky banter and frequently boomed with laughter at the young man's humorous observations.

Eventually they came to the road. The path led down a steep incline aside yet another decrepit stone out-building and met the road where it had once crossed the stream via a stone bridge.

'Oh my God!' Rupert said. 'It's as if there's been a war!'

Buildings lined the road but most of their roofs had collapsed and stonework had fallen into the street in many places. A line of telegraph poles were the tallest things left standing and the road itself had broken up into loose aggregate intermixed with the now familiar black dust that was the remnant of man-made construction. The bridge had collapsed into the stream and the stonework served as stepping stones for the party as they crossed it. The horse had no trouble negotiating the obstacles in the water and they set off following the road in an eerie silence as they passed between the crumbling remains of civilisation.

'So now we know,' Matt said. 'It's worse than we feared.'

'But, where is everybody?' Mel whispered. 'The people who lived here can't just have just disappeared.'

'Hello!' Tanya shouted, 'Is anybody out there?' Then she laughed, apparently amused at her companions' anxious faces. 'They've obviously been evacuated,' she said. 'We're probably the only ones stupid enough to…' Suddenly she was hit on the side of her face by a rock. More rocks followed, thrown from somewhere amongst the rubble. Before they could react, rocks were flying at them from all directions and unnatural screams emanated from all around them. They had found their humans after all.

Matt grabbed Tanya and pulled her to her feet and they ran through the bombardment. Rocks struck Rupert and Eddie as they made their escape, but they managed to keep going. The horse reared up and galloped ahead of them, disappearing around a bend in the distance. They kept running until they were out of range of the missiles, then Matt turned and pulled the shotgun from his shoulder, but their adversaries were nowhere to be seen so he continued to follow the party, turning occasionally to check they were not being pursued. The guttural screaming and whooping continued though, until they were out of earshot. Then they stopped - each breathing heavily.

'Jesus, the native's aren't very friendly around here,' Tanya said, wiping away blood from her head.'

'You shouldn't have shouted like that,' Mel said. 'We've got to be more careful.'

'Give it a rest!' Tanya moaned, 'It's me that got hit. How about a bit of sympathy?'

Matt inspected her injury, but it didn't look serious; a large bump was already forming and the skin was broken, but no more.

'Hope it hasn't ruined her good looks!' Mel said to Matt, annoyed at the attention he was giving her. The woman was trouble and she disliked her more with every passing hour.

'Okay let's calm down - nobody's seriously hurt,' Matt said. 'Can anyone see the horse? If we've lost everything we're in deep trouble!'

'He m…made off down the road,' Eddie said. 'If we keep going we'll p…probably come across him.'

Eddie was right; no sooner had they left the remains of the village, they rounded another bend and the horse came trotting back towards them, apparently none the worse for the attack and still carrying their possessions strapped to its back.

'Let's get some distance between us and the village,' Matt suggested, 'then we need to find somewhere to camp for the night.' He realised that, despite his misgivings, he was starting to take control again and he didn't like it. He didn't like it one bit.

They found cover in a rocky outcrop beside a waterfall; the campsite was sheltered from the wind and they built a fire on which they cooked chicken on a spit. Baxter had proved quite adept at hunting small animals despite his age; he had cornered the chicken among the crumbling remains of a farm building they had passed.

'Looks like you were right, Mel' Matt said. 'Those people back there acted like savages.'

'I'm scared Matt. What the Hell are we going to do?'

'Keep going, I suppose,' Matt said. 'But I'm not sure which way we should head.'

'West,' Father Peter wheezed. 'Towards the sea - the coast will offer us sustenance and refuge.'

Matt looked curiously at the old priest, wondering what he knew.

'Hey, man - I love the seaside,' Nic said. 'How far is it?'

Matt consulted the map. 'Fifty or sixty miles as the crow flies, I suppose.'

'West m...makes sense,' Eddie said. 'We'll find s...shelter along the way - there's bound to be a few old buildings s...still intact and we should be able find plenty of food, but we m...may need to hunt for it.'

Tanya smiled sweetly. 'Don't look so... sheepish, Mel. We have a gun now - even you should be able to overcome the odd chicken with that!'

Mel glared at the newsreader. 'I can think of other things I'd rather pot!' she hissed.

'Cut it out, you two,' Matt said. 'We're in enough trouble without bickering at each other. Anyway, I don't think we should use the gun unless it's absolutely necessary; we only have four boxes of cartridges and we don't know when we might really need it.'

'Food's n...not the problem,' Eddie stammered. 'I'm more worried about water. The s...stream at the abbey was clean, but down here, off the hills, it's much more likely to be polluted.'

Joe nodded thoughtfully. 'And when you are thirsty it is too late to dig a well,' he added.

Matt looked up at the gathering clouds. 'Then let's keep to high ground as much as possible,' he said, conscious that he was unintentionally taking charge again. 'We should catch as much rainwater as we can and if we have to drink suspect water, we should boil it. Now, let's settle down and try and get some sleep.'

The next morning, they followed a crumbling road that rose steadily as it approached the mountainous regions of Wales. According to the map, it led to Bala, which nestled in the foothills of the mountains beside a great lake. They had decided that if the town proved to be inhospitable they would join the A4212, a major road, which ran west, through Snowdonia and part way to the coast. It had rained overnight, but the weather brightened as they travelled west and now patches of blue sky brightened their surroundings. Red Kites circled the skies and everyone's spirits rose now that they had less to carry - thanks to Goliath, as Mel had christened the shire horse.

There was little evidence of other people on the road, but they sometimes saw footprints in the damp, sooty substance that covered its surface. On occasion, they felt that they were being watched, but saw no other living humans. They did encounter the occasional body though; the first was that of a fat, naked woman lying face down on a large boulder on the side of the road in what they presumed was a picnic area in the previous life. The body had been mutilated - partially eaten by something. After this first gory discovery they soon learned to avoid others - they could usually tell when they were approaching a corpse because crows and other birds congregated around the area.

Once, when the road passed through a small wooded area, they were amazed to see the most unlikely animals in the trees that overhung the road. Half a dozen golden-brown monkeys shrieked at them as they swung between the branches with their long, spindly limbs and prehensile tails. These coarse-furred creatures had small heads with hairless faces and their hands and feet were black in contrast to their ruddy bodies. Eddie identified them as a species of spider monkey but could offer no explanation as to how they might have got there. 'Perhaps they had escaped from a nearby zoo or wildlife park,' Matt suggested. 'Let's hope that nothing more exotic or dangerous escaped at the same time.'

Nic removed the bandages from his hands to let his wounds breath and Matt was amazed at how well they had already healed. It was lucky they had recovered the antiseptic from the module - dog bites were notorious for carrying infection if untreated.

Nic though, seemed convinced it was due to the power of the loadstone he carried. 'That old witchdoctor knew what he was talking about,' he said, caressing the piece of magnetite from the quarry. 'It's my lucky charm!'

'Better take care of it then,' Matt said, not noticing Mel and Father Peter exchange curious glances.

By the late afternoon they approached Bala, which lay in the Penllyn region of the Snowdonia national park. The town was situated on the shores of the largest natural lake in Wales and they knew that at some point they would have to cross the River Dee, which flowed into it. This would be their first major obstacle in reaching the western coast, but they had no idea how deep or wide the river was, or whether any bridges would still be standing. They were surprised to see that in the distance dark smoke was rising into the air, presumably from somewhere in the town

'Do you think the inhabitants are normal?' Hayley asked. 'Like us, I mean, not like the ones who attacked us in the village.' They all yearned for a return to civilisation and the security that a larger group would offer.

'I can't believe that savages like those in the village could have developed the ability to start a fire,' Rupert said, hopefully.

'Who says it's man-made?' Matt said. 'It could be the aftermath of the recent disaster; the whole place might be gutted.'

Joe Sumo nodded. 'Fire is a powerful slave, but a bad master,' he said. 'We should avoid the town. I have a bad feeling that there is more to fear there than just fire.'

'I agree,' Mel said. 'The town must have been hit, otherwise why the smoke? There has to be survivors in a town that large, but they will almost certainly be afflicted by the reaction. They could have lost any sense of moral code, humans without humanity – that scares me!'

Mel's concerns were justified sooner than she expected; as they rounded a bend in the road, evidence of denser habitation was apparent. Crumbling ruins of buildings on the outskirts of the town were becoming more frequent, but this was not what disturbed them. They noticed for the first time, a row of fence posts lining the road ahead and as they got closer they were horrified to see that each post was adorned at the top by a severed human head.

'Oh, my God!' Hayley cried.

Father Peter made the sign of the cross and clutched at his bag. His hands shook and he muttered a silent prayer under his breath. He had seen this vision before, in his dreams.

The gory sight sickened them all and only Amy seemed unconcerned as she continued to chat away to herself in her strange, broken sentences.

'I don't think we should go any further,' Rupert said. 'What sort of animals would do such a thing?'

'We d...don't have much choice,' Eddie said. 'If we avoid the town by going north, w...we'll be cut off by the river, and if we go s...south we'll have to circumnavigate the lake and it's h...huge.'

'No, Rupert's right,' Matt said, 'I've no appetite to enter the town, certainly not this late in the day. It'll be getting dark soon; let's make an early camp and decide what to do in the morning.'

Not wanting to stay too close to the road (or the town for that matter) the party retraced their steps for a while, before following a footpath southwest into a small wood. Beyond the trees they caught sight of the great lake for the first time and before it, evidence of another smaller road, which ran along its banks. When they reached the road they discovered the remains of a railway line which ran adjacent to it. Remnants of wooden sleepers lay partially buried in the broken flint that served as ballast for the rails which had now disintegrated. They decided to follow the tracks for a while as it easier under foot than the uneven road, which beneath the sooty compound was treacherously unpredictable. If fact, walking the track was so easy that they considered following it all the way to the southern end of the lake, then cutting across country to avoid the town of Bala altogether.

Unsurprisingly Tanya disagreed. 'It might seem easy now, but at some point we've got to head west again and there's no roads shown on the map so far as I can see; fancy climbing those?' She pointed north, across the lake and they all looked at the brooding mountains, their summits obscured now by ominous, rain filled clouds. 'I say we follow the main road through the town.'

'Let's stick to the plan and find somewhere to shelter for the night,' Matt said. 'We'll decide in the morning, depending on the weather.'

It wasn't long before they found what appeared to be the perfect place; ahead of them the steep granite face of the hillside dropped right to the bank of the lake and the road and railway passed through separate tunnels cut into the rocks. Brickwork that had once lined the entrances had fallen to dusty rubble which partially blocked the way in, but beyond the entrance the natural rock walls of the tunnels were sound. Joe Sumo tied Goliath to a nearby tree, using one of the long ropes from the module and unloaded the equipment from his back; then the rest of them negotiated the fallen debris to enter the tunnel nearest to the lake. It was dark and cool inside and a slight breeze blew through from the other end, but the tunnel offered excellent shelter from the impending rain. Eddie and Rupert built a fire amid the entrance rubble, which warmed them despite much of the heat, along with the smoke, being carried away on the breeze. They ate the last of the vegetables, baked once again on the fire and decided that the first priority in the morning would be to replenish their food stocks.

'Another reason for entering the town,' Tanya said. Her apparent dismissal of the savagery that they had witnessed on the main road astonished Matt, but he had to admit that she had a point. They were in no condition to brave the mountains and lacked the equipment to tackle the difficult terrain that lay between them and the coast. Following a major road made a lot of sense.

As soon as darkness fell they slept, wrapped in blankets and huddling close to each other for warmth. It was amazing how intimate their lives had become over the last few days, there being no room in their situation for inhibitions. Personal space was sacrificed for the basic need to keep warm and the close proximity of others offered a strange comfort despite the pockets of friction that had grown within the group recently.

Chapter 6

That night, Father Peter dreamed of the castle again, but this time it was dark and he was alone on the tower. A putrid smell was in the air and as he looked around he noticed that his surroundings had changed. The battlements were decrepit now; the masonry was no longer smooth and finely honed, but worn away as if by centuries of wind and rain. The sky was dark, but the inner ward below him was awash with the light of numerous fires. A great crowd was gathered below and they cheered loudly, shrieking with excitement at what they witnessed.

A young girl's wrists were bound to a wooden stake, which had been driven in the ground. She was naked and screaming as she kicked out with her legs at huge seagulls which paced around her menacingly. Occasionally the gulls would lurch at her feet with their beaks. Others flew above, circling before diving towards her face, pecking savagely at her bloodied flesh. Father Peter was horrified and averted his eyes from the poor child's agony. He scanned the faces in the baying crowd and wondered how they could be enjoying so much, the torment of a fellow human. Nor could he understand why the gulls singled out the girl and were making no attempt to attack any of the onlookers. Some in the crowd were also naked, but most wore animal skins of some kind. Then the priest's eyes settled on an individual who stood out from the rest - the man was seated on a throne and he wore a long fur coat and leather boots. On his head was a spiked German infantry helmet, such as were worn in the first world war and he held a long cavalry sabre across his lap. Beside him sat a girl in her late teens who was also dressed in fine fur and she held the man's hand as she watched the spectacle in front of them.

There was a loud cheer as the bound girl fell amid a chaotic flurry of white flapping creatures – she had given up the fight and was soon to die. Somewhere amid the crowd, drums began to beat in anticipation of the climatic end to the entertainment and the spectators quietened their cheering.

'Stop this! In the name of God - stop this now!' Father Peter implored the commanding figure sitting on the throne. There was no way the man could have heard the plea, but he immediately looked up and met the old priest's gaze.

'Don't worry, your time is near old man – you have what is mine and I will come for it.' The voice, loud in Father Peter's head, spoke with menace and was accompanied by terrible nausea, which caused the priest to fall to the cold stone floor. His head swam and all he could hear was the strange slow drumming from the crowd below.

Father Peter woke suddenly, but the strange drumming continued. He was sweating and felt a dread that was beyond that which could be explained by the dream alone - something was wrong! At first he was unaware of his surroundings, but then he remembered the railway tunnel and the events of the previous day. He sat up and turned towards the tunnel entrance where the fire had diminished to a dull orange glow. Someone was snoring, but otherwise it was silent – the drumming had stopped and he wondered if it had been in his mind all along – a remnant of his nightmare.

All of a sudden a figure stepped into the light, silhouetted by the glowing embers of the fire. 'Matthew?' Father Peter whispered. 'Is that you?' The figure stepped towards him and Father Peter saw to his horror that the man in front of him was naked.

'Someone's here!' He shouted, as the naked man lunged at him swinging something heavy - it struck the priest on the side of his head and he remembered no more.

Matt was suddenly awake. 'What is it?' He shouted, rising from his blankets. A scream! One of the girls, Matt realised – it sounded like Mel.

Suddenly the tunnel was in turmoil; bodies were everywhere, people were shouting and Baxter barked maniacally. Matt recognised the huge shape of Joe Sumo grappling with a tall, but less stocky man who snarled like an animal. Someone grabbed Matt from behind – an arm round his neck pulled him to the ground. Squirming free, he kicked at the intruder who disappeared again into the darkness.

'Matt!' someone shouted. 'Where's the gun?' It was Nic – somewhere to his left.

The gun! What had he done with it? Matt swept his hands over the stony ground in an attempt to find it - or anything that would serve as a weapon. Then he remembered; the rifle was propped up at the tunnel entrance, but it wasn't loaded! He had forgotten to replace the cartridges the night before. They were in a bag – where?

He got to his feet but something heavy hit him on the back of the head and he lurched forward tripping over a soft bulky mass on the ground. A groan – it was Father Peter! Someone kicked Matt in the chest and he rolled sideways, winded now. In his daze he saw people clambering away over the rubble at the tunnel entrance. A rock flew passed his head from that direction and hit the tunnel wall with a crack. Someone was coming at him and Matt braced himself for an attack, but then he saw it was Eddie, and his friend was carrying the gun. 'Eddie, what's happening?'

'Intruders! They've t…taken the girls, Matt – they've got Hayley!'

'Where's Mel?' He asked groggily, his head swimming with pain.

'Gone!' Nic said. 'Amy and Tanya too! Joe followed them into the woods. I don't know where Rupert is – or Father Peter.'

'I'm here!' Rupert shouted out of the darkness. 'Father Peter's been hurt, but he's still alive – breathing anyway.'

'Load the gun Eddie; we have to go after them!'

'W…where are the cartridges? Matt, w…where did you put the bag?' Nic was feeding and stoking the fire and it grew lighter.

'Over there by the wall!' Matt pointed. He joined Rupert who crouched over Father Peter. 'Are you sure he's okay?'

'I think so - he's coming round,' Rupert replied. 'He must have fallen or something.' The old priest was mumbling about seagulls and castles.

'Rupert, you're going to have to stay with him; we've got to help the others.'

The magistrate shook his head frantically. 'What if they come back? You can't leave me here alone!'

'Stay with Baxter; you'll be okay. Look, it's already getting light; they won't return now, I think they've got what they came for.' Matt turned away and grabbed Eddie by the arm dragging him towards the entrance through which Nic had just disappeared, wielding an axe.

Mel regained consciousness to the sound of Tanya shouting; her head hurt badly and she was confused as to where she was. The last thing she remembered was falling asleep in the railway tunnel the night before; now she was lying on a hard floor in the hazy light of morning with her hands and feet bound with tight leather thongs.

'Let us go, you bastards!' Tanya screamed. 'Come back here or I'll rip your fucking heads off!'

Tanya was also bound, but she was kneeling with her hands behind her back and shouting upwards. They were in some sort of rectangular pit; its crumbling, concrete walls were flat and square, about five feet high. They were not alone. Amy lay shivering in the foetal position in one corner, and against the farthest wall, another woman sat silently rocking back and forth holding a small baby to her breast - they were all naked. Suddenly, there was a scream from somewhere outside the pit, followed by whooping from all around them.

'Hayley!' Mel shouted. 'Where are you? Are you okay?'

Another scream – agony this time, rather than fear.

'It's Hayley!' Mel cried. 'What's happening to her?'

'The bastards have taken her,' Tanya snarled. 'They lifted her out by her hair and dragged her off!' The newsreader slumped back down against one of the walls and Mel saw that she was crying.

'It... It's only been a few weeks.' Mel said. 'People are already killing for fun?'

'You don't know that!' Tanya snapped. 'We can't see what's happening up there!'

'You heard the scream! They're hurting Hayley – torturing her or something!'

Suddenly, Tanya seemed to lose control - screaming in frustration, she squirmed against the leather thongs in a berserk frenzy. Mel could see that she was hurting herself, but could do nothing to help. Eventually Tanya calmed down, but tears were streaming down her grazed cheeks and her eyes flared with anger. Breathing in heavy snorts, she glared at Mel as if it were all her fault.

Mel didn't know what to say, so she shuffled over to where Amy was lying.

'Are you okay sweetheart?'

The child did not seem to register the voice; she just stared blankly ahead as if in shock. Mel turned to the other woman; she was obviously terrified, rocking back and forth, clutching the small child. She noticed that the woman had not been tied up as they had and wondered if she could help to free them. Mel made a move towards her, but the woman snarled – a warning not to approach.

'Don't bother,' Tanya growled. 'She's one of them – a savage! She'd probably kill us if she had the chance.'

Mel studied the woman who stared back defiantly - no, she's just protecting her child, she thought. Suddenly there was another scream - this one long and drawn out, ending in a despairing groan. Hayley, or whoever it was - whatever it was, it was over. Mel felt the tears run down her cheeks and wondered who would be next.

It was a misty morning and visibility was poor as the four desperate men entered the town. Joe Sumo had lost the raiding party in the woods; despite his strength, he was not really built for speed, but it was still surprising how their adversaries had outdistanced him so rapidly whilst dragging four prisoners along. Joe reckoned that there had been at least thirty attackers, but only about half a dozen had actually entered the tunnel. They guessed from the direction of their escape that Bala was their destination, so the four travellers followed the footpath back to the road and made towards the town. They decided against a cautious approach because they knew time was against them, so they just marched into town between the lines of heads that had been severed from the necks of unlucky townsfolk.

Despite their bold approach, they were aware that they might be ambushed at any time and Matt held the gun in readiness. This time it was loaded and his pockets were bulging with cartridges. Nic carried the axe and Eddie had picked up a hammer that had been retrieved from the module - Joe however, was unarmed.

The mist gave them some cover, but also concealed any clues to the raider's whereabouts. They had no idea whether the smoke they saw yesterday was still rising - if it hadn't been so misty they could have followed it to its source. Nevertheless, they guessed from the map that the town was small and with the level of destruction they were now witnessing, it shouldn't be too difficult to locate their adversaries. They didn't really have a plan, but figured that the gun would give them the edge if it came to a fight and Joe Sumo was an intimidating figure. The lake was on their left now and the road branched into two at a flat open space, covered in stony soot. There were a few decaying bodies here and numerous magpies pecked at the corpses. They guessed the junction on the edge of town would once have been busy with traffic; maybe the site of a roundabout or traffic lights in the other world.

Bearing left, across the open space, they saw that the bridge into town had indeed collapsed, but the river here, although wide, was quite shallow. They managed to negotiate the crossing without even getting their feet wet, jumping between clumps of fallen masonry. They knew that they were exposed and vulnerable to attack, but their enemies were nowhere to be seen and they entered the main area of town without challenge. It appeared that most of the buildings here had collapsed, but the remaining walls still towered above them. There were lots of places to hide among the ruins and the numerous dark openings amid the chaos intensified their unease. Eddie in particular was getting more and more agitated, turning from one side to the other and fiddled nervously with the clawed hammer he gripped desperately in his right hand.

Then in the distance they heard a scream - faint and to their left. Eddie's face drained of colour, but he said nothing as they picked up the pace, travelling now in the direction of the cry. They followed what was once a smaller road, branching off from the main street, but it was so covered in debris from the damaged buildings that they had to clamber over large pieces of broken stonework, making the going hard and lessening their readiness for any attack. Matt had to shoulder the gun in order to use both hands to scramble over the treacherous terrain. Eventually the rubble cleared and a large open space lay before them, perhaps a car park or market square. The remains of a church stood in the distance to their right, taller than the surrounding buildings; its roof too, had collapsed, but its stone tower remained intact.

They heard another scream from the direction of the lake, followed by the shrieks and whoops of a baying crowd. Matt thought he recognised the voice behind the scream, but he said nothing. He guessed he was not alone in this, because Eddie started to race frantically across the open space towards the sound. The others followed at speed towards the remains of another large structure. This building had totally collapsed and nothing much now stood above head-height, but a maze of low walls covered an area of several hundred square yards and they saw the smoke again, rising through the mists from somewhere beyond the walls. By the time they reached the first wall, the clamorous sounds of other humans was unmistakable. They were very close now and all four men crouched as they skirted silently along the outside of the stonework. When they reached the corner of the building's remains, they paused, reluctant to advance. They were all breathing heavily and Matt realised that his hands were shaking uncontrollably as he gripped the shotgun - he had never been so scared in his entire life. He looked at the others trying to gauge their resolve. Joe's face was grim, but he seemed in control of himself; Nic looked petrified, but he nodded at Matt as if to assure him of his support. Eddie though, was a quivering wreck - bulging eyes, sweating profusely and fidgeting like a child who badly needed the toilet; Matt decided that if it came to a fight, Eddie could not be counted on.

'Let's go.' Matt whispered and he swung around the corner, shotgun poised to fire. Nothing! Another deserted open space with a second wall some twenty metres ahead; smoke was rising from the other side. Between them and the wall there was a large, oval, rubble filled pit, from its size and shape they guessed it might once have been a swimming pool.

'Keep going!' Matt hissed. Staying low, the four men scurried across the debris towards the wall and, as they reached it, they heard shouts of excitement from just the other side. They crouched with their backs to the stonework, breathing heavily. Suddenly there was another scream – anguish and despair – it ended slowly with a morbid finality that only meant one thing - someone had just died in agony on the other side. Matt felt physically sick – they were in a living nightmare – how could this be happening? He couldn't bear any longer, not knowing what was beyond the wall; slowly he raised himself, back sliding against the coarse stonework and, twisting his head, he peered over the brim of the wall.

No sooner had the scream died, than Mel saw heads suddenly appear over the edge of the pit - dirty, unshaven faces, painted white with black lines on their cheeks. They grinned down with eyes fuelled with lust and excitement. Arms reached down to grab her but she squirmed away, out of reach. Two men jumped into the pit and she saw that one of them was naked, his body painted in a similar manner to his face. The other was dressed only in a red velvet poncho - the one that Hayley had been wearing. Both men stank like animals. Grabbing Mel by the hair, they dragged her kicking to where other arms waited to pull her up and out. Behind her, Tanya screamed abuse at their captors but the savages showed no interest in the woman - it was not her turn.

Mel was hauled out of the pit by her hair, the pain an insignificant factor in her state of panic. She was in the hands of heartless savages and they meant to kill her. They dragged her bound, naked body over the rough stone as the shrieking crowd grabbed and kicked at her in frenzied violence. Faces leered close to hers and a scrawny old woman was beating her with something soft and heavy. Horrified, Mel realised it was a human arm - long, slender and pale – Hayleys arm! She was being bludgeoned with one of poor Hayley's arms. Mel started to scream.

Suddenly, there was a gunshot and for a moment, time stood still - the baying crowd silenced and looked around in confusion. One of the savages that had been dragging Mel, stared into her face with a bewildered expression; then, as if in slow motion, fell backwards, his head striking the stony ground with a sickening thwack. The savages backed away from her as if somehow she was the cause of the man's strange demise. There was another shot and the woman holding Hayley's arm swung around full circle and fell to the ground. Shouts now, from her right and the mob scattered at the sight of four men running at them - most took off in the opposite direction, but two large males holding heavy wooden stakes stood their ground. Nic was first to come within range and the men swung their weapons in unison, but Nic ducked their blows and swiped at one of their legs with the axe. One man went down, screaming in pain; the other aimed a second blow at Nic who was now on his back holding the axe in defence, but Joe Sumo hit the standing man with all his weight and they both flew backwards in a heap. Eddie launched himself at the savage with the wounded leg, swinging the hammer repeatedly at his head. The remaining mob regrouped and started to edge closer to the fight, but two more shots rang out and one of the advancing men crumpled to the ground; the others turned and ran to the far wall which they scrambled over in a gibbering frenzy. Joe squeezed the neck of his adversary and twisted it until he heard it crack, then he let him go, the body slumping to the ground. Eddie continued to pulverise the face of his assailant with the hammer, despite the fact that he was already unconscious, probably dead, and Nic had to pull him struggling away.

'Eddie, cool it, man,' he shouted. 'It's over!'

Matt took the axe from Nic and went over to where Mel lay naked, shivering on the ground; her back and arms were grazed and she was crying.

'Are you okay?' He asked, as he cut the leather binding her feet.

'Hayley's dead,' she sobbed. 'They killed her!'

'I know - I'm sorry, we came as soon as we could, but we didn't know where they'd taken you.'

As soon as Mel's hands were free, she pointed over to the pit. 'The others...' she gasped.

Matt tenderly stroked her cheek while Joe covered her with the red poncho that he had retrieved from the dead savage. 'Wait here,' he said.

'Joe, take me away from here, please,' Mel said, as Matt ran over to the pit.

'Thank God!' Tanya cried, 'I thought you were one of them - help us please, we're freezing to death down here.'

'Guys, I need your cloaks!' Matt shouted as he jumped into the pit. He freed Tanya with the axe and wrapped her in his own red cape.

'Who's the girl?' He asked gesturing at the mother and child.

'One of them,' Tanya spat. 'Leave her to die!'

'No!' Mel shouted from above; she was standing over the pit now, staring down at them. 'How dare you!' She shouted through her tears. 'The poor girl's petrified and her baby's freezing to death - leave them and you're no better than those...'

'Savages?' Tanya yelled back. 'In case you don't realise, she's one too! Savage murderers – they killed Hayley! They're not like us you stupid bitch - don't you get it?'

'We can't leave her here…'

'Matt, they're coming back!' Nic shouted. 'We need to go right now.'

Mel heard the shotgun fire. 'Fuck off you b…bastards!' Eddie shrieked, waving the smoking gun above his head.

'Tanya, help Amy out and wrap her up quickly,' Matt said, moving over to where the young woman sat with her child.

She snarled at him with teeth bared like a rabid animal.

Matt backed away. 'Mel, I'm not sure…'

Mel grabbed Nic's coat and climbed into the pit with it. She limped over to the woman and knelt before her.

'You can let me help you or you can stay here and die,' she said, knowing the girl couldn't understand her, but hoping to convey compassion. Suddenly, the girl lunged at Mel, snarling and spitting and grabbing her by the hair. The baby fell to the ground as the mad woman attempted to sink her teeth into Mel's face, but before she could do so, there was another gunshot and the woman's head exploded in a scarlet shower. The woman slumped to the ground, leaving Mel, soaked in her gore and staring in horror at the carnage below her. Mel started to scream when she saw that the baby, now lying in its mother's blood, was already badly decayed – black, putrid holes, instead of eyes stared back at her.

Somehow they made it out of town; the savages made no attempt to follow them but it was a difficult journey all the same. The women were all without shoes and the rocky ground tore at the soles of their feet. Still sobbing, Mel hugged the red drape tightly around herself as she stumbled along over the uneven surface. Tanya's face was stony as she walked – she had said nothing since escaping the pit. Joe carried Amy, who seemed to be recovering from the ordeal now that she was warm and feeling safe again. Eddie trudged behind them all, his face blank and expressionless, eyes staring at the ground.

Nic carried the gun and walked solemnly alongside Matt at the front of the party. 'What are we gonna tell Rupert?' He muttered.

Matt shook his head. 'He just needs to know Hayley's not … not coming back,' he said, almost choking over the words.

'Are you alright, man?' Nic saw that the dirt on Matt's face was stained with tears.

'It was all my fault,' Matt sobbed. '…I forgot to load the fucking gun!'

Chapter 7

Far north of the savagery of Bala, in the shadow of a huge monastery, a young boy tried desperately to ignore the voice that tormented him from within. The voice carried no words, for the boy had no concept of spoken communication - instead, silent images and visual suggestions infiltrated his mind. According to the boy's short memory, the voice had always been there as if part of him - guiding, instructing and prompting his actions, but up until now it had carried generic messages to them all. At first it had told the people to gather together and come to the place from which it spoke; he and the others had instinctively known the direction of the summons and they had moved as one, obeying without question. Cold and scared, they had walked on bleeding feet until weariness overcame them. Then as if a single entity, they halted and huddled together like penguins braving an Antarctic storm. The voice had woken them en masse and they had continued the journey in silence, compelled to obey the telepathic command. When they became hungry, the voice had instructed them again. 'Pick out the weakest,' it said. 'Kill them and feed.'

They travelled like this for several days and many didn't reach their destination; some were set upon for food - others, despite the voice, just gave up and slumped to the ground to die. Those who did survive arrived at the ruined monastery near to death, but even so they had been fearful of the imposing building and were reluctant to enter. The voice had encouraged them; it said not to fear the fires that burned amongst the ruins, but to come closer and be warmed. The boy remembered how the owner of the voice had been standing high up in a pointed stone arch and how he had greeted them with words that they could now hear as well as feel.

'My name is Arthur, son of Uther and I am your saviour, the new king of Britain.' It had said. 'You are most welcome here for we have much to prepare. Many more are coming to join us, but for now you must rest and regain your strength.'

To the boy the man had seemed infinitely superior - radiating power. He remembered looking up in awe at the commanding figure that was so different to the others around him; the man's body had been wrapped in white fur and he held high a shining blade that had flickered in the reflected light of the fires below. The man had looked down upon them with knowing eyes – so unlike the wide, anxious eyes of those around the boy. To them every new vision was frightening and beyond comprehension.

The voice that now tormented the boy was different – it was the same voice, but now it was directed at him alone and its intensity consumed him. The boy knew that those who stared out from the walls of the monastery could also hear the voice, but they understood that it was not meant for them. He could feel the anticipation of the watching mass; they were excited, but did not share his fear. They looked on in the manner of schoolchildren witnessing a large boy torment a smaller child in the playground. They felt no pity for the frightened boy because he was among those who had defied their master. The others knew that to avoid the same fate they must simply obey the rules. Stealing unallocated food was one such rule, and the one most commonly broken. The terrible pain of hunger was sometimes enough to overcome the fear of reproach and the boy had only succumbed to the temptation once, but it was enough for him to be condemned, taken out amongst the trees and strung up by his wrists. The boy was terrified because he understood his fate - he was not the first to suffer this ordeal and he too had looked out onto others who had been punished for similar acts. He knew that at any moment the devil-creature in the woods would come slowly upon him.

Arthur watched the boy from a stone dais in the ruined ambulatory of one of the great Yorkshire Cistercian monasteries. It had once accommodated over two hundred monks and lay brothers but now it was the home of Arthur's people. Much of the huge, cathedral-sized abbey remained intact, including the whole north side plus the greater part of its west front and great fires burned within the shelter of its walls warming the inhabitants who maintained them. Beside Arthur, sat a teenage girl who wore an orange jump suit beneath a woollen fleece, her face was emotionless, but her eyes bulged as she stared maniacally at the spectacle below. However, it was not the girl who interrupted Arthur's thoughts.

'The people need discipline, Arthur,' Merlin said from within. 'There are still those among them that resist your will. Discipline and control, Arthur! You must be ruthless.'

Arthur's attention turned to the people who looked out from the numerous gothic arches of the church - they were his people now and he felt an overwhelming compassion for them.

Most worshipped him and he wallowed in their reverence; he was their king and they rarely questioned his will, even when they suffered. Arthur scanned their minds; there were so many now that it was difficult to distinguish individual thoughts, but any notion of contempt was easy to identify and isolate; any disdain was dealt with swiftly and at the hands of his minions. Their minds were now focussed on the boy who had disregarded his rules and they were excited at the prospect of his punishment. He felt new emotions from them every day as his people developed memories and knowledge, and a myriad of thoughts washed into him, but nothing gave him cause for concern - Merlin was worrying needlessly.

Arthur returned his attention to the boy in the trees, but was suddenly confronted by a singular voice of defiance. However, this time it was not from one of his people. Arthur was stunned by the power of this new presence and by the fact that it seemed to challenge from afar. He turned his head, slowly scanning the horizon, until he faced southwest. Gazing into the distance, Arthur focussed his mind, reaching out beyond the hills.

The boy felt Arthur suddenly release his mind and at last he could focus on his predicament. He looked into the dark woods, scanning for any movement amongst the trees but saw nothing. He glanced up at his hands, which were numb and turning blue - their circulation restricted by the leather bonds which suspended him from the branches above. On his toes, he pushed upwards to release the tension on his wrists hoping he could somehow loosen the straps and pull free, but it was useless. In the last few days he had learnt how a sharp flint could be used to cut through leather, but he realised that in this situation any attempt to escape was futile. The boy looked desperately towards the monastery where he sensed there were others who doubted the master, but they would not dare to challenge his will - the boy knew that he was alone.

Suddenly, he heard the sound: Thud, scrape – thud, scrape, and then a pause before it repeated - the sound of something being dragged through the trees. A moment's silence then: Thud, scrape - thud, scrape; the noise was getting nearer. The boy stared helplessly in the direction of the sound until slowly, out of the darkness, something pale loomed into view.

The injured creature dragged itself towards the boy using the claws of its huge, furry front feet; its soft white coat was bloodied and matted with dirt. The boy smelt the animal almost before he saw it; he started to struggle against his bonds as he watched the terrifying creature slowly, agonisingly, close the distance between them. It paused again, raising its large square head to sniff the air - it could smell the boy's fear-induced sweat. Then it continued towards him, painfully dragging its broken body. Its long furry tail and rear legs slid lifelessly over the fallen leaves behind as the animal approached.

A falling timber had struck the snow leopard when her enclosure had collapsed around her. The pain had been excruciating, but the injury had not hindered her as she escaped into the woods. Food was plentiful and she had hunted rabbits and other small animals in the days that followed. The weather posed no problem either to the big cat whose hundred-pound frame was covered in thick, heavy fur designed for a cold climate. The leopard had roamed for miles seeking a mate that did not exist, but she was happy in her freedom, until over-confidence became her downfall. She had started to stalk sheep on the hills, unsure at first if the larger animals would pose a danger. As she approached the creatures they had run from her, but at first she did not give chase. Eventually though, her predatory instinct took over and she had ran down a large ewe, which was heavy with lamb. She had leaped onto the sheep's back and sunk her fangs into its soft neck. Dragging the sheep's head to the ground, the cat had fallen beneath the heavy animal as it landed. The pain the leopard felt as her damaged spine finally snapped was almost unbearable and to some extent the pain had never left.

    The crippled animal had been starving in the woods when Arthur's people arrived and she had approached the monastery only out of desperation. The people there would have killed the creature for food, had Arthur not intervened. He had protected the leopard, not out of pity - that sentiment did not exist in Arthur's mind and if it had, he would have allowed the animal to die - but the crippled cat fascinated Arthur and he wondered how long it would continue in its to pathetic struggle to survive. He enjoyed the fact that the cat was suffering and that is why he had started to feed it.

As the leopard approached, the boy backed away as far as his bonds would allow, but as soon as the animal was within range, the boy lurched forward and kicked out savagely with one bare foot. The leopard twisted its head to avoid the blow and snarled in pain as much as anger. The spectators in the monastery started to whoop like savages as their excitement grew, free for a while of their master's scrutiny for he was otherwise engaged. The boy kicked again and the leopard instinctively swiped one of her huge paws at the leg; claws tore through the boy's soft flesh and he screamed in pain, but the leopard became unbalanced and collapsed onto her side. Both paused in their agony before the leopard gingerly righted herself again. Another kick, but this time the animal grabbed the leg with both clawed feet and pulled it into her jaws as she collapsed once more to the ground. Despite her pain, the leopard held on and began to drag itself up the leg, climbing the screaming boy's torso using her claws and teeth as anchors until she reached his throat. Fangs sunk into the boy's neck and tightened. Unable to breathe, the boy continued to struggle until unconsciousness ended his suffering. Still clinging to the boy's body, the leopard fed desperately before falling to the ground in agony and despair.

In the monastery a vision slowly materialised in Arthur's mind - sea gulls flying over a castle, tall battlements overlooking the sea and a figure staring out from the top of a stone tower. Arthur knew that he was witnessing another's dream - the old man on the tower was challenging him. The dreaming man was apparently a priest, untouched by the affliction Arthur's own people had suffered, and he carried a golden cup.

    Arthur was heir to the throne of Britain, but he knew this impostor would never accept his sovereignty. He was leading others to the castle and his followers were oblivious of Arthur's right to the throne. They were growing stronger, making plans without Arthur's sanction and he was too far away to intervene. Arthur directed his growing anger at the priest in the tower, but the old man's strength of character surprised him; he was not used to such mental confrontation, even during his long years of imprisonment. What was it that fuelled this frail old man's resolve? What gave him his strength? Then it slowly dawned on him that it was something to do with the chalice that he held - and suddenly everything became clear. The Holy Grail! The legendary artefact that was Arthur's destiny was in the hands of a pretender. Arthur's fury erupted and he lashed out mentally at the man, threatening him - striking him with pure malice. The old man grimaced but stood firm, for he had the cup and it gave him strength. Arthur regained his composure and drilled a single clear message into the man's head.

'Your time is near, old man – you have what is mine and I will come for it.'

That night, Arthur was uneasy despite the comfort of his surroundings. Even the submissive attention of his adopted bride had done little to dispel his concerns. Collie lay beside him now, in a large timber shelter built by his servants to his instructions; it was lined with furs and comfortable bedding and warmed by fires that were routinely fed. Arthur knew that the girl was mentally unbalanced, but she had abandoned herself to him, satisfying his every need. As he lay troubled by his recent vision, she had taken him in her mouth, despite the fact that his body was filthy and he smelt like a pig – apparently unconcerned that he had showed no emotion right up to the final shudder of climax. Arthur liked the girl and appreciated her company but he knew she was unstable and might one day pose a risk. Collie rarely slept, and when she did, she tossed and turned, disturbed by some inner turmoil. Arthur, on the other hand, usually found sleep easily - assured and content in his new found good fortune. But not tonight - tonight he was troubled.

'We must move quickly Arthur,' Merlin said. 'Those who will oppose you are getting organised; if we don't act soon it will be too late.'

Arthur knew it was true - his own people were submissive and obedient, but they frustrated him; they were no more than primitive, disorganised savages and they had to develop skills quickly or they would be useless to him. He was able to guide them - en masse or individually – and he could, to some extent, mentally pass on his own knowledge to them. They were already using tools and building fires, but it was laborious - he was only one man and they were many. They needed a culture that enabled self-development, to feed off each other and evolve – and they needed to do it quickly.

Collie jumped when Arthur spoke to her. 'Tomorrow you must go among the people, find me someone worthy and bring them to me – I need someone to lead them - a commander.'

The girl cowered at the thought, but she knew she had no choice in the matter. The inhabitants of the monastery frightened her – especially the men, who had no shame or self-restraint. She had seen them become aroused in her presence and they would leer at her with insane eyes. Collie felt safe beside Arthur, but the notion of going alone among the others made her shudder and the thought of being close to them conjured up painful memories. Their fear of Arthur was her only comfort – he was her saviour and he would protect her – for now. Her only hope was to keep pleasing him - satisfy his every need - maintain her value. Although only seventeen, she knew how to achieve this – Collie understood men and was very good at meeting their needs and she knew that she had pleased Arthur tonight – distracting him from his obvious stress. It had been her thirtieth blow-job, she realised. Collie always counted because she had promised herself that her hundredth customer would pay with the very object of his pleasure and she would remove his desire for such gratification forever. She hoped it wouldn't be Arthur though, because if it were, she would probably pay herself - with her life. She thought back to the last five years of that short life – blow-jobs one to fifteen had been performed on her stepfather whom she still hated for his violent abuse. Numbers sixteen to twenty-three had been with the husband of a woman whose child she had minded - regularly delivered on the way home in his car. Numbers twenty-four to twenty-six were with three boys from her school who had plied her with cider. The final three had been for the satisfaction of her form teacher, Mr Jackson; the last of which being delivered only two weeks ago in a pothole on the very day that that Arthur had come into her life. Her teacher had instigated their separation from the other members of the field-trip with his usual guile and they had been alone in the cave when the world above them had changed forever. Seventy to go, she thought with morbid satisfaction and with this, her fear abated slightly and she turned to Arthur and smiled.

'Can I take your sword?' She asked.

'Of course,' he replied, nonchalantly. 'But use it sparingly; the people are valuable to us.'

The crowds parted as she walked between the fires and makeshift shacks. The skins of animals were stretched over the wooden frames and a plague of flies buzzed around the meat that hung within them. The stench was terrible and she struggled to control her nausea at the sight of the gory remains that now served as food. Collie knew that the local environment alone could not provide for such a large community, but the evidence of cannibalism still appalled her. Arthur accepted that the weakest were regularly sacrificed for food and he let his people select their own victims. There were frequent fights, mostly over females, which sometimes resulted in fatality so death in the camp was commonplace. The people had already started to communicate in a primitive manner and as she walked among them, grunts and barks carried meaning beyond her comprehension. Collie could feel their emotions though; not to the extent that Arthur could, but she could vaguely perceive mental messages and notions of lust, fear and brooding animosity filled her mind. She wondered whether she was developing her own telepathic ability, but she realised that, more likely, the minds of those around her - now free of mental clutter - were evolving a natural capability to project thoughts and feelings.

Collie was encouraged by their fear, they were wary of the sword that she carried, conscious that it was an implement of death, but also knowing that it belonged to their master, a symbol of his authority. So despite their savage instincts, they shied away as the girl approached.

Some of the people were still naked, but most now wore skins of some kind and many of the men had taken to adorning their bodies with gory trophies of violence. Body parts from small animals were strung from leather necklaces - some of them were even decorated with human fingers. There were very few children now, most had been taken for food and she could see no elderly among the crowd. Natural selection had reduced the population to only the fittest, healthiest and strongest specimens. Collie stopped at very centre of the ruined cathedral and scrutinised the crowd that now surrounded her. They edged closer out of curiosity so she spun around sweeping the sword outwards as a warning not to approach. Most clambered back in fear, so that only the most dominant among them remained at the forefront. A ring of dirty, bearded men now confronted her and she felt even more intimidated, but she had a job to do and somehow retained her composure. She realised that any sign of weakness might be fatal, so she stood tall and met each man's gaze in turn. Her attention was drawn to a large black man holding the heavy thighbone of some large animal. His frame was muscular beneath the skins he wore and he stared back at her with piercing brown eyes. She sensed this man was unafraid, but he seemed to accept her authority and she didn't feel threatened despite his size. The man's confidence impressed her and his composure indicated an intelligence that many of the others lacked - Collie knew that she had found her man.

She approached the man with her sword pointing forward from her outstretched arm. The crowd backed away as she approached, but the man stood his ground until the tip of the sword met his throat. At the touch of the cold metal the man grimaced but stood firm, her eyes held his for a moment and then she spoke.

'Come,' she said, taking his large hand in hers.

The man obeyed without question, somehow understanding her command, and followed her. The grunts and barks returned now as the crowd watched the girl lead the much larger man by the hand towards their master's enclosure.

Inside the shelter, the girl sat to one side as Arthur and the black man faced each other in silent communication. She watched the rapidly changing expressions on their intent faces and wondered how long this would go on. Arthur gestured with his hands but rarely spoke as the two men shared their mute conversation and the girl's boredom was only relieved by the vague images that occasionally leaked her way. Confused visions of horses, weapons and strange constructions infiltrated her mind and she realised that Arthur's new captain was, among other things, receiving a crash course on the technology of warfare. The dark man's intelligent eyes flickered rapidly as he received the information and the wonder on his face reflected his growing enlightenment. The mental intercourse lasted for hours and it was already growing dark by the time Arthur raised his hands and blew out a heavy, exhausted breath. He had finished and the black man raised himself unsteadily to his feet.

'Go now, take what you want and do as you see fit,' Arthur said. 'You are above the law now, but remember my instructions. Return tomorrow and we will continue.'

At this, the man nodded, and this insignificant gesture demonstrated just how far his intellect had advanced in such a short time. Then Arthur's new captain turned and strode out of the shelter.

Chapter 8

Matt trudged along the remains of a road, which meandered through the welsh mountains, heading west. Eddie walked solemnly beside him carrying the gun, which he had insisted on bearing ever since their flight from Bala. They had re-entered the town the previous day, passing through the ruined buildings at pace for they had no appetite for another showdown with the savages that had murdered Hayley. Eddie had slunk through the ruins like an obsessed hunter, taking wild pot-shots at anything that moved. The others had ignored his uncharacteristic aggression despite their limited supply of cartridges, but Matt was worried that his friend might be losing his mind. If a violent streak could surface in Eddie, then what hope for the rest of them? He wondered how long it would be before this new world transformed them all into the same mindless savages that had attacked them.

  They had followed the road west for three days and the whole party was weary and despondent; any enthusiasm they had for the journey had died along with Hayley. Rupert rarely spoke now, except to encourage Baxter to keep up. The depression the ex-magistrate had displayed after the incident with the camper van had returned a hundred-fold at the news of his daughter's death, but Matt suspected the reality of it still hadn't yet sunk in. Mel and Tanya argued constantly and even Joe and Nic seemed subdued. Only Amy appeared unaffected by the events in the town. She sat amidst their possessions, upon Goliath, playing with a little figurine carved out of wood by Joe. Father Peter was the weakest of them all and they had continuously slowed their pace so that he wouldn't be left behind. Whenever they made camp now, they took it in turns to sleep - always leaving someone on guard, but the journey was uneventful and so far they had encountered nobody else on the road. They now avoided habitation wherever possible and no longer sought sheltered places to camp, preferring instead high, open spaces where they would not be easily ambushed. They were seeking such a place now, because the evening was drawing in and some of the travellers were already fit to drop. Matt was still wracked with guilt and blaming himself for Hayley's death. He no longer made any attempt to dictate their movements, leaving Tanya and Mel to dispute every decision, which they did passionately. Their mutual dislike had grown to a new intensity over the last few days and Father Peter often had to intervene when it seemed that their confrontations might even become physical.

'Look, up there!' Nic shouted. 'That might be a good spot to camp.' He pointed to the summit of a small hill a few hundred yards from the road. A ring of standing stones jutted out of the turf like broken teeth.

'It's too close to the road.' Mel said. 'Let's keep going.'

'For Christ's sake, we've not seen anyone for twenty miles,' Tanya said. 'I'm ready to stop and the place looks fine; why don't you give us all a break and drop the paranoia for once.'

'Paranoia? Have you forgotten what happened to Hayley?'

'I'll tell you what,' Tanya said. 'Why don't you carry on and find a better place? The rest of us will camp here and take our chances.'

'Whatever,' Mel said, 'but don't blame me if we all wake with our throats cut.'

Wearily, they climbed the hill and unloaded Goliath between the towering stones. At least the rocks would offer some shelter from the wind.

'I'll take first watch if you want,' Matt said. He was in no mood to sleep despite his fatigue.

'I'll join you,' Tanya said.

'No, I'll do it,' Mel said. 'Somehow I'll think we'll be safer, don't you?'

'Please yourself!' Tanya said, throwing a blanket to the ground beside one of the stones. 'Wake me if the bogeyman comes!'

Soon most of the party were asleep while Mel and Matt, sat facing the road with their backs against one of the standing stones. Mel glanced at Matt as he stared blankly down at the road and gently took his hand. 'I've never seen you look so unhappy,' she said.

There was a long silence and for a while she thought he would not respond. Eventually, Matt spoke to her. 'Did I tell you I had a brother once?' he said.

She stared at his face. 'No I didn't know, what was his name?'

'Aaron,' Matt whispered. 'He died when he was seven.'

She took his hand. 'I'm so sorry, what happened?'

Matt looked into Mel's eyes and saw only compassion. For the first time in his life, he realised he wanted to talk about it.

'It was my eleventh birthday,' he began. 'It was the summer holidays and my parents were both working, so I had to look after Aaron. I was angry because I wanted to be with my friends, but I knew they wouldn't hang out with a seven-year-old, so I took him fishing instead.'

'Did he drown?' Mel whispered, unconsciously squeezing his hand.

Matt just stared blankly ahead, not really hearing the question. 'Aaron kept chattering away, excited about the fishing, but I was just being horrible – telling him he was too noisy and scaring the fish, then one of my friends rode past on his bike.' Matt sniffed a smile as if remembering for the first time. 'His name was Billy Smith; I had invited him to my birthday party but he said he couldn't come – none of them could. I wasn't really that popular back then, you see.'

Somewhere in the distance an owl hooted. Matt stared into the darkness and continued. 'Billy said that some boys from school had found a way into the old mill along the riverbank – there were stories that it was haunted. He asked me if I wanted to come because one of the older boys had cigarettes. I know I shouldn't have gone, but I didn't get asked very often, so I told Aaron to carry on fishing until I returned - he was a good kid and I knew he wouldn't tell mum.' Matt paused for a moment and wiped a tear from his eye. 'I'm sorry,' he said. 'You don't need this crap.'

'Go on, I want to hear.'

'There were six of us in the old mill's basement; it was really creepy, but I think I was the only one who was really scared. We built a camp out of old boxes and smoked cigarettes – I think I lost track of the time. Then one of the older boys built a fire – stupid, I know, but we were only kids. It got out of control so we ran away, leaving the place to burn. I was crapping myself – I knew that if my parents found out…'

'What happened?'

'I ran back to where I left Aaron, but he was gone. The rods were still there, but there was no sign of him. I searched everywhere - the water wasn't that deep, but I was scared he had fallen in. Then I heard sirens over at the mill. I don't know why I ran back, but I just had a feeling…'

'Oh my God - he followed you!'

'When I saw the ambulance I knew it was Aaron; he died from the smoke apparently.'

'Did you tell your parents what happened?'

'The truth came out – it always does. The police took me away for questioning and the press were all over the story. But it was nothing compared to how they reacted when my parents committed suicide a few days later.

'Oh my God! That's terrible.'

'Father Peter looked after me. I don't know what I would have done…'

'It must have been awful; is that why what happened to Hayley has upset you so much?'

'Don't you see,' Matt said. 'That was my fault too!' Tears were now rolling down his cheeks. 'Aaron, my parents, and now Hayley – in a way, I killed them all. Shit, I've even had a hand in destroying the world!'

She leaned over and kissed him. 'You're not responsible.'

'Exactly – I'm not!' He said. 'You're better off without me – I'm a liability.'

'Nonsense, your strength of character holds us… held us together,'

He looked down at their hands. 'I've not been much support recently, have I?'

Mel smiled sadly. 'I thought you were mad at me,' she whispered.

'With you? I thought you were angry with me!'

'Well I'm not - if you must know, I've grown quite fond of you, even if you have been acting like a wimp.'

Matt smiled through his tears and looked into her eyes. 'Here, there's something I've been meaning to give you.' He pulled out a small bundle of cloth from his pocket and handed it to her.

Mel unwrapped the bundle and her eyes widened in disbelief. 'My compass!' She gasped. 'The one from the museum. How…?'

'Joe brought it with him; it saved us in the hills. Open it, there's an inscription inside.'

Mel unclipped the hasp and the lid sprung open. As she read the inscription, it was her eyes that now filled with tears. 'Thank you for coming back for me in Bala' she said. 'You saved my life.'

'I had to,' he mumbled. 'I think I've fallen in love with you.'

Mel smiled through her tears. 'I know,' she said, pulling the blanket over them both.

In the morning they woke to warm sunshine. Nic and Joe were preparing breakfast over a fire.

'Mmm, smells good,' Mel said to them. 'What are you cooking?'

'Chicken and potato broth,' Nic replied. 'Not the classic breakfast, but I figured we needed something hot before we set off.'

Matt got up and examined the standing stones. 'Look here,' he said, pointing at one of them. He hadn't noticed in the gloom of the night before, but the morning light revealed that the rock was decorated with strange graffiti. Mel wandered over, followed by Tanya, rubbing sleep from her eyes.

'They're like primitive cave paintings,' Mel said. 'I wonder who did them.' The pictures depicted horses and men, painted black against the grey granite. One man appeared to be holding a weapon.

'That's a sword.' Matt said.

'I wouldn't get excited,' Tanya said, 'It's probably been there for months - vandals most likely.'

Matt rubbed at one of the painted figures with his thumb; it came away black and sooty. 'It's the stuff from the road – someone's been here recently and they've painted a man with a sword; I wonder what it means?' He looked at Eddie but his friend was sitting gloomily near the fire, showing no interest.

'I guess we'll never know,' Mel said. 'Come on let's eat.'

Over breakfast they studied the map, which was damp and becoming very tatty, close to falling apart. They were nearing another town, probably the last before they reached the coast.

'Trawsfynydd is just over a mile away,' Nic said. 'Should we make a detour?'

'Yes, if we can,' Mel said.

'I don't agree,' Tanya predictably argued. 'What if we miss something?'

'What do you think, Eddie?' Mel was trying to engage the sullen man; she knew he was showing classic signs of disassociation.

'Let's go through the t...town,' he muttered, fingering the shotgun he was cleaning.

'It doesn't matter anymore,' Rupert muttered. 'It's all hopeless.'

'We must head straight for Harlech,' Father Peter said sternly. 'We have to get to the old castle.'

Matt stared curiously at Father Peter; the old priest was in no mood to be denied. 'Harlech it is, then,' he said. 'We bypass the town.'

They set off just as it was clouding over again and followed the road for about half a mile before taking a footpath, south into the hills. According to the map, the path would lead them to a river, which they could follow west to a large lake on the other side of the town.

Matt thought about the Father Peter's suggestion; he guessed that Harlech Castle would still be standing, but doubted it would offer much in the way of comfortable accommodation. It might give them protection though; he knew it was small in comparison to other welsh castles and its walls might be easily defended against intruders.

When they reached the river they stopped to drink, before following the path that ran adjacent to it. Matt walked aside Mel a little ahead of the others.

'You actually made a decision back there,' she said, smiling.

'Actually, I think it was Father Peter who…'

'Don't be modest. With you in charge, we'll get through this. We need you, Matt.'

'Okay, I'll try, but I won't lie to you – I'm scared shitless. Everything's dangerous now, and I think it's going to get worse. Look at the way Eddie reacted in Bala. Father Peter seems to think we can change people, but what if it's us that's changing? We've already had to kill to survive; perhaps human compassion has no place in this world.'

'Father Peter believes God has saved us for a reason,' she said, 'I'm sure he's leading us to something.'

Matt glanced back at the old man who traipsed along some way behind them. 'He's very deep, always has been,' he whispered.

'He knows something we don't, I'm convinced of it,' she said. 'Matt, you're closest to him, why don't you ask him what's on his mind?'

'All right, but I'll have to pick my time. You know what he's like; he won't open up if he doesn't want to.'

They reached the lake and picked up the road on its south bank. Grass and other plants were already sprouting out of the sooty rubble of its surface. Nature was re-establishing itself and soon there would be little remaining evidence of man's long domination over the land. The sun broke through the clouds and Matt suddenly felt his spirits rise; in front of them the road was covered by a vast sea of bluebells. How the plants had established themselves so quickly, he had no idea, but he was taken aback by the incredible beauty of the surroundings. The warm, airy breeze carried with it the wonderful aroma of new life. This was how the world was meant to be, he thought – devoid of the clutter of mankind. He walked along as if in a dream and, in this beautiful lakeside valley, the horrors of Bala now seemed a distant memory.

Suddenly a small man emerged from the trees ahead and crossed the road in front of them; he had shoulder-length black hair in a headband and was dressed in rags. A long, heavy bow was slung over the man's shoulder and he carried a bundle of fruit in his arms.

Eddie raised the shotgun, but Father Peter grabbed the barrel and pulled it gently away. 'Please,' the priest said. 'We cannot start killing innocent people.'

Eddie glared at Father Peter and opened his mouth as if to challenge him, but then thought better of it and released the rifle.

'You'd better take this, my boy,' Father Peter said, handing the gun to Matt.

As the man crossed the road he glanced in their direction and they saw that he was Chinese. He didn't seem at all afraid and showed no sign of aggression; he just ambled off into the opposite trees as if he didn't have a care in the world.

'Should we follow him?' Rupert asked.

'I'm more interested in where he came from,' Tanya said. 'Did you see what he was carrying?'

'Let's take a look,' Matt said. 'Who's coming with me?'

Nobody wanted to stay behind so they all left the road and entered the trees from which the man had emerged. It was relatively dark in the wood and their intrigue soon turned to unease when they smelt the smoke from a fire and heard a hammering noise from ahead.

'Wait here, Matt whispered, 'I'll go ahead and see what's happening. Joe, do you want to come with me?' Matt had found a new resolve, but it didn't stretch to facing unknown foes alone.

The two men crept forward through the trees and eventually looked onto a clearing where the most unlikely sight greeted them. An area of lush green grass stretched out from the wood towards a great lake, which sparkled in the morning sun and, in the centre of the clearing, a single tree supported an impressive timber shelter. One end of a telegraph pole stretched from the tree's lowest bow in the direction of the lake, the other end was planted firmly in the soft turf. The pole supported other posts and branches, which formed a slanted wooden apex and the whole structure was covered in mud and foliage. A similar, smaller shelter stood to one side, supported by a stake in the ground and hanging from a rope stretched between the two structures, various animal skins were drying in the sun.

A lone man in a checked shirt and dungarees was kneeling near a log fire, over which, a skinned rabbit cooked on an A-frame spit. The man was using a mallet to drive a wooden spoke into the hub of an old wagon wheel, which lay on the grass in front of him; he apparently hadn't seen them approach.

To Matt, the idyllic setting could have been the scene from a painting of a different age and he felt his unease immediately evaporate into the sunshine. 'Come on Joe, let's say hello,' he said, striding into the clearing.

As Matt emerged from the trees, the man looked up casually as if expecting visitors, but on registering Matt's strange attire and the shotgun he was holding, he jumped to his feet in surprise. 'What the bejesus… Where the hell did you spring from?' he said, staggering backwards in his astonishment.' Despite the man's shock, his thick Irish accent was unmistakable.

'Just passing through,' Matt said cheerfully. 'You're the first… er… normal person we've met in over a week. You are, aren't you? Normal I mean?'

'Depends what you mean by normal; to everybody else around here, I'm a bit of an anomaly,'

'I'm Matt Campbell and this is Joe Sumo.'

The Irishman laughed out loud when Joe bowed politely to introduce himself. 'Welcome to my humble abode,' he said, offering his hand to Matt. 'My name's Gerry O'Donnell – do you boys want something to eat? I've got plenty.'

'It doesn't look humble to me,' Matt said. 'You should see how we've been living recently.' He looked hungrily at the cooking rabbit. 'We'd love to join you but we're not alone, our friends are back there in the woods – there's nine of us. We're nearly out of food, I don't think…'

'There's plenty for everyone,' the Irishman said cheerfully. 'The more, the merrier, my old mother used to say.'

'Okay then, you're on,' Matt beamed. 'Joe, go and fetch the others.'

As Joe turned back to the woods, Matt surveyed the man's camp. A second wooden-spoked wheel was propped up against a stack of planed timber and various tools were neatly laid out beside it.

'Where the hell did you get all this stuff?' There were hammers, saws, a plane and chisels - all old, but apparently serviceable.

'From the old copper mine,' Gerry said. 'That's where I was when… you know - whatever happened, happened.'

'You're a miner?'

'No,' the Irishman laughed. 'I was visiting - it's a museum, not a working mine. There were others down there when it happened, but they've all gone – went off looking for loved ones.'

'So you stayed here and built all this?'

'Nowhere else to go really - well not easily; I'm from Kilkenny, in Ireland. I thought I'd stay and try an' rebuild this old wagon.'

'This is all very impressive,' Matt said, looking at the shelters.

'It's my trade; I'm a carpenter. Well I was anyway.'

'Looks to me like you're still in business,' Matt said, taking a seat beside the fire. 'How did you light this, you've got matches too?'

The Irishman shook his head, smiling. 'Lighting a fire's not so easy you know.'

'Tell me about it, we never succeeded until we opened the module.'

'I'm sure I don't know what you're talking about. What module?'

'That's another story,' Matt said as the others emerged from the woods. 'I guess we've got lots to talk about over dinner. First, let me introduce my friends.'

And talk they did - right through the afternoon and into the evening and the more they heard about the Irishman's exploits, the more they were amazed at his resourcefulness. He told them that the nearby town was deserted now; the survivors there had died – victims of vicious dogs who had formed a formidable pack within just hours of the disaster.

'It's a very bad place, to be sure,' he said, 'There are bodies everywhere and the smell is terrible.' He explained that food was plentiful though, he had discovered a local market garden where undercover farming techniques had been used to extend the growing season. 'I've got more fruit and veg' in that little shack than I know what to do with. I've taken to trading with a colony of Chinese gentlemen who have taken residence in some caves over there.' He pointed south. 'I don't know who they are because they can't speak a bloody word, but I made them some bows from the yew trees and now they bring me rabbits in exchange for vegetables. Nice little chaps, I'll have to introduce you.'

That night Gerry insisted that Amy slept in his own shelter and he bedded down with the others on the soft turf, near the log fire. For the first time in weeks they felt at ease with their surroundings and they all slept soundly.

In the morning, Gerry cooked them breakfast as he described how easy it was to build a basic shelter. 'Never camp in caves, hollow logs or bushes,' he said. 'Or you'll likely be sharing them with other animals, or at least insects. Trees are good - they offer natural shelter and you can build around them.'

They were all fascinated with the Irishman and even Eddie's mood improved. This idyllic place was apparently having an effect on him too - it was as if he had found a kindred spirit in the creative carpenter who chattered away as he cooked.

They spent the rest of the day at Gerry's camp, basking in the tranquillity of the setting and recovering their strength. Joe and Nic took Amy fishing at the lake and at last Joe caught his first fish. The whole party heard his whoops of joy and looked up to see him gambolling back towards the camp with his trophy held high in one huge hand. Joe's face was beaming with pride as he showed them the small roach he was holding.

'There's not much meat on that Joe,' Matt laughed, but Joe was not put off.

'Ah, the small fish on the hook may yet catch a large one,' he said, before bounding enthusiastically back to his friends at the lake.

'The big fella's a character, to be sure,' Gerry said grinning. 'I wonder what he'll do if he catches anything worth eating?'

'He's a character all right, I don't know how we would have managed without him,' Matt said. 'You wouldn't believe how much he can carry.'

Gerry picked up the wooden mallet. 'He won't need to, if I can fix the wagon.'

'Does that mean you're coming with us?' Mel asked.

'Well, I suppose that depends upon where it is you're going,' Gerry said, crouching beside the broken wheel.

'West, to the coast,' Matt said. 'We're going to check out the castle in Harlech; we figure we'll be safe there.'

'But you're safe here!' Gerry raised both hands and looked around. 'This place has got everything you need, the locals are friendly enough and anyway, I want to finish the wagon. Why don't you all stay here for a while? I'd welcome the company.'

'It'll be getting dark soon, so we'll at least stay tonight,' Matt said. 'Maybe longer if everyone agrees; it'll give us time to build up our strength – the journey through the mountains is going to be tough.'

Chapter 9

That evening they feasted on omelettes with mushrooms and onions from Gerry's store and Matt was glad that they had decided to stay for a while. Just being here, comfortable and well-fed had cheered everybody after the terrible events in Bala, but deep down, he knew that every day that passed was a day lost. Were they really safe here, out in the open? Despite everything, he doubted it.

After they had eaten, Gerry surprised Matt once again by producing a bottle of whiskey and a packet of cigarettes, which he said he had recovered from the mine.

'I've been saving this for a special occasion,' he said. 'It was in one of the cupboards I broke up for timber. There's a few more bottles stashed away and another forty cigarettes.'

'Father Peter is going to love you,' Matt said, studying the whiskey. 'I can't wait to see his face.'

Gerry poured a small tot into eight plastic cups and Matt handed them around.

'Where's Father Peter?' He asked Mel.

'Over by the lake,' she said. 'I think he's praying.'

Matt walked down to the bank and saw the old man sitting on the bough of a fallen tree looking out over the water, which glistened like diamonds in the moonlight. As Matt approached he could hear the priest mumbling to himself and supposed that Mel was right. Not wanting to disturb the old man's prayers, Matt paused some way behind him and sat in the grass, watching from a distance. Something caught the moonlight and Matt realised that Father Peter was holding the golden chalice in front of him; he tried to listen to the priest's words but couldn't make them out at first. Then suddenly, Father Peter's low murmuring grew louder and the voice became agitated. It didn't sound like a prayer - more like he was talking to somebody, challenging them even.

'Father Peter?' Matt said, rising to his feet. 'Are you okay?'

The priest jumped, but didn't turn round; he just continued to gaze out onto the lake and when he spoke his voice shook.

'You shouldn't creep up on an old man like that,' he grumbled. 'You scared me half to death.'

'I've brought you a present,' Matt said, joining the priest. 'I think you'll forgive me when you see what it is.' He sat down beside the old man and noticed the golden cup was now nowhere to be seen, but the priest's bag was in front of him and Matt assumed Father Peter had stashed it away as he had approached. Matt handed him one of the beakers. 'Here, get your lips around that.'

'God bless you, son,' the priest said astonished at the sight of the whiskey. 'Where on earth did this come from?'

'One of Gerry's many treasures,' Matt said. 'I thought you'd be pleased. What are you doing here Father?'

The old priest took a blissful swig from the plastic cup. 'Just contemplating our situation,' he said. 'I still can't get over what happened to that poor girl the other day.'

'I know; Bala was a terrible place, but at least it feels safer here. I'm wondering if we should stay for a while longer

– at least until Gerry rebuilds the wagon; I think he might come with us then.'

'No!' The passion in Father Peter's voice surprised Matt. 'We must not delay; every day that passes brings danger closer. We have to get to the castle as soon as we can!'

'I don't understand,' Matt said. 'What danger? Gerry's convinced there's nothing to threaten us here and we could certainly use the rest.'

The old priest glared at him for a moment, then he seemed to come to a decision; he picked up his bag and took out the golden chalice. 'Take the cup,' he said, handing it to him.

'What?'

'Just do as I say and take hold of the cup.'

From the tone of Father Peter's voice, Matt knew that there was no point in arguing. He held the chalice by its stem and studied it; the surface of its upper body was smooth and unadorned but the large base was fluted and decorated with intricately carved feathers. The stem comprised of two stages separated by golden rims, the largest of which may once have been embellished with small jewels. The cup was heavier than Matt expected and it felt unnaturally cold against his skin. He looked at the night sky reflecting in the polished surface; stars blinked in and out as wisps of clouds momentarily obscured their brilliance and the nearly-full moon's intensity seemed magnified by the golden shell, so bright that it almost dazzled him. Then, just as Matt was about to question again the purpose of the ritual, the reflected moon suddenly turned a deep crimson and he became drawn into the vision, transfixed by the pulsating red glow as it misted over and gradually faded. The cup's surface was black now, as if absorbing all light like a celestial black hole. It was as if he were staring into an endless void of emptiness which threatened to draw him in, sucking at his soul. Matt closed his eyes and in his mind he saw a world of swirling mist. Gradually, pin-pricks of fire materialised behind the haze and as their intensity grew, Matt realised that the fires were moving nearer, bobbing towards him through the mist. Figures now came into sight, hideous humans carrying flaming torches, hundreds of them emerging out of the vapour like an army sent from Hell. More and more creatures materialised and seemed to pass through him, their dark, menacing eyes staring out from grim painted faces. Then among the horde, Matt saw a tall, scarred man riding a great horse. As the man approached, the masses gave way, separating out until only the mounted figure stood before him. The scarred man wore a spiked helmet and held a long sword which, pointed threateningly towards Matt as the man reined the horse to a standstill and sat motionless staring down at him with dead, shark-like eyes. Matt was terrified, but he continued to grip the golden chalice. The scarred man's stare mesmerised him and commanded his attention until all else around him faded.

'You have what is mine and I am coming for it,' the rider snarled, suddenly swinging the sword in a wide arc around his head and towards Matt's throat.

Matt screamed, dropping the cup to the ground and the spell was immediately broken. Trembling, he turned to the priest and opened his mouth as if to speak but no words would come; his throat was constricted in fear.

'Now you understand.' The old priest said. 'Something evil manifests itself and it intends to destroy us all. We must prepare ourselves before it is too late.'

The next morning Matt looked out one last time onto the lake, hoping he wouldn't regret his decision to split the party, but he knew now that Father Peter had to leave immediately. Holding the chalice had convinced him that they were all in peril, but the scarred man's malevolence was undoubtedly focussed on the priest and the strange artefact he carried. Matt had no idea whether the vision had portrayed current events, or were some strange premonition of the future, but he had no doubt that the scarred man was real and that he intended to seek out and destroy the priest, along with any who followed him.

They had all argued long into the night, their emotions fuelled by the first alcohol they had consumed in weeks and most of the others could see no sense in moving on before the wagon was built. The journey west through the mountains would be difficult enough, but without the horse they would have to revert to shouldering their possessions over the rough terrain. However, Matt knew it made no sense to separate Goliath from the wagon. He didn't mention the strange vision because he knew that they were already struggling to come to terms with their predicament. Supernatural premonitions of a force plotting to destroy them would probably send them over the edge, but Matt had to get them to a place of sanctuary and prepare for the conflict that he believed would surely now one day come. Matt intended to lead his party due west, crossing the mountains with only the bare minimum of equipment needed to establish themselves at the castle. The plan was that the others would follow them later with Goliath pulling the wagon, taking the longer but less arduous journey along the ruined roads which meandered through the hilly terrain to the south.

    Eddie was still fuelled with anger from the events at Bala and was itching to move on, but Rupert's depression at the loss of his daughter had deepened and he had no appetite for the journey. Mel suggested that spending time in such a tranquil setting might help Rupert to come to terms with their loss, so it was decided that he should stay with Gerry at the lakeside camp along with his old beagle. Amy also would stay, despite her pleading to go with them. Matt knew she was too young for such an arduous trek and was not well equipped for the journey. He judged the rest of the party fit to travel, apart from Father Peter who had no choice but to go with them. Matt somehow knew that the frail old priest was their talisman; both he and the chalice were fundamental in their quest to survive and bring civilisation back to their lives. That meant he must be protected from both the natural and perhaps even the supernatural, which now seemed to be making an appearance in the ruined world; Father Peter would have to brave the mountains on foot.

Matt helped Joe to strap a large duffel bag to the same pole that had previously carried their equipment. The bag, which had been recovered from the mine, had the word RES-Q printed in bold letters on its red canvas and had once contained ropes and fall-arrest equipment used for caving emergencies, but now it was full of food and water. Gerry had also provided them with three rucksacks, which meant that they could share their burden more evenly and that their hands would be free to help them negotiate the treacherous terrain that they expected to encounter. They added two more ropes to the one that had been recovered from the module and stashed one in each of the rucksacks. Matt slung the gun over his shoulder, but the remaining tools, cooking utensils, blankets and clothes were distributed evenly in the three rucksacks. This meant that they could take it in turns, three of them carrying a rucksack and two bearing the pole. Father Peter would only be asked to carry his own small bag containing his personal possessions. When Matt was satisfied that the duffel bag was secure, he asked Joe if he would help him bear the heavy pole on the first leg of the journey.

'The heaviest burdens always go to the mule,' Joe laughed. 'Give me the heavy end.'

Matt thought back to the night in the museum when he had been so intimidated by the ex-wrestler's massive frame. This gentle giant had saved them on so many occasions since, that they now took his unassuming nature for granted. Joe never complained or questioned any decision, even when things went wrong; he just got on with it, obeying their requests, quietly supporting them and giving them the confidence to carry on.

'Joe, do you think I'm doing the right thing?' Matt asked. 'Leaving the others behind, I mean?'

Joe looked at him with his one good eye and frowned. 'If you desire the comfort of others you must prepare for the sorrow of parting.'

Matt smiled. 'Thanks Joe; I don't know what I'd have done without you.'

Joe looked shocked. 'You are my friend,' he said. 'A friend is sometimes as good as a brother.'

The six travellers said their goodbyes. Gerry gave Matt one of his precious packets of cigarettes for the journey and then walked over to Father Peter; in his hand he carried something wrapped in a piece of sackcloth. He handed the package to the priest.

'This was also in the mine,' he said. 'I have no use for it, but something tells me you might.'

Father Peter unwrapped the package and his eyes widened. It was an old leather-bound journal with a small pencil pushed into its spine.

'I'm afraid the first few pages have been written on,' Gerry said,' but you can always tear them out, I suppose.'

Father Peter stared lovingly at the book. 'God bless you, my son,' he whispered.

Matt had known the old priest for many years and he couldn't remember ever seeing him so moved. How the mysterious Irishman had known that Father Peter had been yearning for something more substantial to write with was beyond him.

Finally, with mixed feelings, the party set off into the trees to begin their long trek to the western coast; Matt took one last look back at those he was leaving behind and wondered if he would ever see them again.

Chapter 10

That day the travellers made very little progress humping their possessions over the difficult terrain and Matt estimated that, at their current rate, it would take them at least four days to reach the coast. Although there were numerous lakes and streams to refill their water bags, they were concerned that contamination was to blame for the stomach cramps they had all been experiencing over the past few days, so Mel had insisted that in future they should boil all water before drinking. This was time-consuming and slowed them considerably, but the main concern was their lack of food. Wildlife and grazing animals were scarce at the higher altitude and Matt worried that their meagre rations might not last them the journey.

    They climbed steadily throughout the day, but the mountain peaks seemed as distant as ever, their snow-clad ridges ominous obstacles in their path. The skies had remained clear so far, but beyond the mountains, brooding dark clouds obscured the highest peaks and it had grown very cold again. This barren wilderness was so far removed from the beautiful lakeside valley, that the last few days now seemed no more than a dream. It was as if the valley, along with the enigmatic Irishman who had taken abode there, were somehow immune from the savagery of the world around them. Matt wondered if pure chance had led them there or whether some other force was at play. The magical place had certainly saved them at a time of their greatest need and had delivered them from their despair, but now back in the mountains, they were vulnerable again and all their fears returned.

That night they slept in the open, sheltering amongst large boulders beside a lively stream that cascaded down the mountain in a series of frothy waterfalls. It was the coldest that Matt had felt since the fateful night he had guided the others through the snow towards the old abbey, but this time he had Father Peter in tow and the old man was already tiring. The priest was coughing again and Matt feared that his chest infection was returning, realising that if the old man fell ill up here he would never survive the journey.

In the early hours of the morning it started to rain and without decent shelter or waterproofs their clothing soon became saturated. Nic managed to light a fire and its heat gave them some comfort as they huddled together in a desperate attempt to keep warm, but it was a miserable night and nobody slept. As soon as it was light again they set off, chilled to the bone, but hoping the efforts of the climb would generate body heat and relieve their discomfort. It was not to be though; the wind picked up as they climbed and the rain drove relentlessly into their faces. After only a few miles they were all exhausted and so cold that they could barely move. Father Peter struggled on, bravely gripping his stick in one hand and the old golden cup in the other. How the frail old priest battled on against the elements was miraculous; it was as if the relic he held gave him inner strength, but his face was grim and Matt realised that he would not sustain these conditions for much longer. If the rain stopped they might stand a chance - if not, hypothermia was inevitable and they would certainly perish.

Together, they dragged themselves forwards, the driving rain obscuring their vision until finally they reached a low ridge and for the first time the ground levelled out making the going somewhat easier, but their energy was all but spent and before long Father Peter fell to his knees in exhaustion. Matt lowered his end of the pole to the ground and staggered over to the priest.

'We can't stop here in the open Father,' he said. 'We'll freeze to death if we give up now. 'The old man just shook his head, too exhausted to even reply.

'What are we going to do?' Mel said. 'I don't think we can go on much further, Father Peter's completely worn out.'

'His spirit is strong, but his flesh is weak,' Joe said. 'Let me bear him.'

So they laboured on with Joe Sumo carrying Father Peter on his back and Nic helping Matt lug the heavy baggage pole across the hill, but Matt knew it was futile; soon they would succumb to fatigue and their journey would be over. The rain continued to fall as they stumbled forwards in their misery; no longer talking, they trudged desperately onwards. Eventually Matt dropped his end of the pole to the ground and bent over in an attempt to regain his breath.

'It's no good,' he gasped. 'I can't carry it any more.'

'We have to turn back,' Tanya said.

'Even if we did, we wouldn't make it now,' Mel said. 'Not in these conditions.'

'At least we'd be going downhill,' Tanya argued, slinging her rucksack petulantly to the ground.

Nic lowered his end of the pole and wiping the rain from his eyes he scanned the horizon. 'Hey, over there!' He shouted above the wind. 'Is that a building?'

They all looked in the direction he was pointing and saw that he was right; at the foot of a distant incline, perhaps half a mile away, they could just make out the walls of a ruined structure. Beyond it, the mountains loomed grey amidst the billowing clouds.

'Come on,' Matt cried. 'One last effort and we might be able to reach it.'

They staggered on with Joe still bearing Father Peter, who grasped the golden chalice in one frozen hand while the others helped to drag the pole through the muddy grass down the hill towards the ruined building. Eventually, they reached its stone walls and lowered their burdens to the ground. Why anyone had built a house out here in the wilderness none of them could guess, but they hoped that it would offer some kind of shelter from the freezing rain. They clambered over the low broken walls and what they found amidst the rubble exceeded their wildest expectations. Partially obscured by fallen timber beams, they saw granite steps leading down into a dark cellar, which had somehow survived the devastation. Wearily, they dragged themselves inside the shelter and collapsed in exhaustion onto the cold stone floor. One end of the cellar had partially collapsed, but a substantial area remained intact and in complete shelter from the elements.

'We have to build a fire,' Matt said through chattering teeth. 'Over there, near the steps.'

Nic, who had become an expert in the art of fire-making, was shaking so much that he just couldn't manage the task, so Joe volunteered to work under his instructions. The big man arranged rubble in a small circle at the foot of the stairs and carefully placed valuable kindling from one of the rucksacks within the surround. Mel found some dusty sacking material, which she tore into strips and pushed in amongst the tinder wood with her frozen fingers. As soon as she was finished Joe tried to strike a match, but its head just crumbled away as he dragged it along the matchbox edge.

'They're damp,' he said, drawing out another one.

There were only about ten matches left in the box and without fire to warm them, they would not be able to dry their clothes. They all knew that their lives depended on the remaining matches and they watched desperately as the next one flared dimly and immediately died.

'Wait, try this,' Mel said, rummaging through her rucksack and retrieving a small glass bottle. 'It's alcohol based – antiseptic from the module.' She dribbled a small amount onto the dry sackcloth and Joe tried again, but the next match crumbled without even a spark.

'Matches! Why didn't you think to pack a bloody cigarette lighter?' Tanya said, glaring at Mel. 'It doesn't take a genius to…'

The next match flared briefly and just as it was about to die, a pale blue flame sprung from the sacking; Joe blew gently at it and it suddenly flared into life. Over the next few minutes they anxiously nurtured the fragile flame as if it were a new-born child, feeding it gently until it grew to a point that the tinder wood turned black and eventually licked into fire. Gradually they added larger pieces of timber gathered from the ruined cellar floor and soon the fire was roaring and its blissful heat radiated out to embrace their freezing bodies.

All afternoon and the following evening, the heavy rain continued as they nibbled at their meagre rations and discussed their predicament.

'We should definitely go back,' Tanya said, 'and wait for the weather to improve.'

'I think she's right, man,' Nic said to Matt. 'We have enough food for another day at best; more than enough to get us back to the lake, but we'll run out if we try and reach the coast.'

'Father Peter's too weak to walk anywhere; we all are,' Mel said. 'If only we had Goliath.'

'He who travels on horseback knows not the toll of those on foot,' Jo Sumo said grimly.

'We can't go back to the lake,' Matt said. 'We're not safe there.'

'Why do you keep s…saying that,' Eddie said. 'It's the only place I've felt s…safe in weeks.'

'What do you think, Father?' Matt asked. 'Do you think we can reach the coast?'

Father Peter shook his head wearily. 'We have to try.' He turned to the others. 'Matthew is right, we can't go back.'

'Why not?' Tanya argued. 'What's the point in killing ourselves in a quest to reach some dingy old castle that might not even be there anymore? If you want to commit suicide that's up to you, but as soon as the rain stops Nic and I are returning to the lake – the rest of you can decide for yourself.'

'You don't own Nic, you know,' Mel said. 'I don't know who you think you are, but...'

'I'm a survivor!' Tanya shouted her down. 'Nic knows it – that's why he'll follow me.'

They all looked at the young African who squirmed uncomfortably under their scrutiny. 'Tanya's got a point, guys,' he said eventually. 'But I don't think we should split up, why don't we vote on it?'

'Good idea,' Tanya said. 'Well, I'm for returning as soon as the rain stops. Nic, are you with me?'

'I guess so,' Nic said.

'Joe?' Tanya said. 'You know I'm right - will you come with us?' The big man glanced at Nic and nodded reluctantly.

'But we must go on,' the old priest wheezed. 'I'll go alone if I have to.'

Tanya glared at Matt. 'Don't you realise the crazy old fool's going to get us all killed,' she said.

'You don't understand...' Matt said. He paused before continuing: 'Okay, give me the cup, Father.' The priest returned his gaze with uncertainty. 'Please Father; they have a right to know.'

Reluctantly, Father Peter pulled the golden chalice from his bag and handed it reverently to Matt who placed it on the stone floor at the centre of the group.

'So now we're having a séance,' Tanya said. 'Why don't we...'

'Shut up and touch the cup,' Matt snapped. 'All of you.'

Silently, the six travellers each placed a finger on the chalice's rim, stared into its surface and waited.

The next morning they ate breakfast as they stared out gloomily at the relentless rain.

'We can't go out again until it stops,' Matt said. 'Our only chance is to keep dry.'

'What about the food?' Nic asked. 'If we delay any longer it'll run out long before we reach the coast, what are we going to eat then?'

'God will provide,' Father Peter said.

Tanya looked sceptical but didn't argue; she hadn't disclosed what the chalice had shown her the previous evening, but whatever it was it had apparently changed her mind about turning back. The previous night seemed like a dream now and Matt remembered little of the events in the dark cellar. He recalled focussing on the cup, watching the flames of the fire reflecting in its surface and hearing only the hypnotic dripping of water from the dank cellar's ceiling onto the stone floor below and the crackling of the burning timbers on the fire. Had he fallen asleep and dreamed the vivid images? Or had the dark, smoky atmosphere and their state of exhaustion invoked some sort of mass hallucination? Whatever had induced his state of mind, he knew that the others had shared the strange images. Their dreams that night had all been different, but there had been a common theme - horrific premonitions implanted presumably by the golden cup. Joe said he saw people nailed to wooden crosses by a baying crowd; Nic described a horde attacking a settlement of frightened men, women and children with cruel weapons and Mel had imagined a vast army of screaming savages running towards her out of the sun. However, they had all shared one common image - that of a dark man, scarred and menacing, bearing a gleaming sword and he had relayed a common message to each of them. A warning that he was coming for the priest and that he would reclaim what was rightfully his - the golden chalice.

'We should leave that thing behind, man,' Nic said. 'If the dark dude wants the cup, why not ditch it?'

'Because it's important,' Matt said. 'There's a power within it that seems to be getting more potent every day – we need it with us. I'm not sure why - I just know it.'

'And because our adversary needs it, or thinks he does,' Father Peter added. 'If we leave it here, he'll find it and it will feed him – he's cruel, we cannot let him take it!'

'Arthur…' Tanya said quietly. 'He calls himself Arthur and he thinks he's some sort of king. He's delusional - he wants…' She paused, seeking words that would not come - her face suddenly twisted with revulsion. 'Never mind, the freak's insane.'

'Perhaps, but he's also very dangerous,' Father Peter said. 'He is gathering people to him, and they are vulnerable to his evil intent. His influence is a disease that must not spread and the golden chalice has a part to play - for good or ill - to prevent it. I've seen it in my dreams. You must help me with this, even if… even if it ends in our ruin.'

'That's why we have to get to the castle,' Matt said. 'Father Peter thinks that the chalice and the castle are somehow connected. Perhaps it wasn't Eddie that led us into Wales – maybe the cup is guiding us, influencing our minds.' Matt knew he sounded insane, but his personal visions had finally convinced him that something mystical was summoning them to the castle. He had never visited this part of Wales before, but last night he had seen the fortress in his own dreams. A vision of the distant past, gleaming towers rising proudly from a rocky outcrop, its seaward side defended by sheer cliffs and surrounded on the others by a deep ditch. In his dream, royal flags flew from the castle's battlements and a seemingly impregnable gatehouse faced inland towards the hills, where a vast siege army camped and waited for nightfall. Inside the castle chapel, a captain of the guard knelt before a throne surrounded by clerics dressed in red and blue robes. A young king sat upon the throne, a silver band around his head, his pale face looked down towards the captain and he had spoken words that Matt could not understand. In one hand, the king had held a sword. In the other...he had gripped the golden chalice.

That afternoon the rain finally stopped and the clouds parted to reveal patches of blue sky. The party emerged from the smoky cellar and the fresh mountain air invigorated them enough to continue on their quest to reach the western coast. Father Peter had regained enough strength to walk unaided and they all felt renewed appetite for the journey. The afternoon breeze still chilled them, but with their clothes now dry it was refreshing rather than biting as it had been the day before. But they were hungry and the food they carried - mainly vegetables and fruit, lacked the fat and protein that their energy-sapped bodies yearned.

      They set off following the valley, which according to their tatty map would lead them through a low pass between the two mountain peaks, which dominated the skyline ahead. They followed a stony path adjacent to a small river, which ran down the valley from a pine forest nestling between the mountains ahead. A single buzzard circled the skies above them and high up to their left they could see goats grazing on the steep hillside. They considered a detour to try and take down one of the animals with the shotgun, but the climb would only exhaust them further. The chances of getting close enough to the creatures without any cover was unlikely, so they gave up the idea and continued due west towards the forest. At one point they disturbed a mountain hare, which bolted out from right beneath their feet and bounded off across the grassland. By the time Matt had readied the gun the hare was out of sight and they realised that they had missed out on the rare opportunity of a meat supper. From then on Nic led the party, carrying the gun loaded and with the safety off just in case a similar opportunity materialised.

    When they reached the forest they continued to follow the river upstream between the towering evergreens. A flock of crossbills were feeding on the seeds of pine cones high up in the tree tops and an occasional grey squirrel shimmied through the foliage, but always out of range of their gun. A few weeks ago Matt wouldn't have entertained eating such creatures, but now the thought of roasted squirrel meat made him salivate.

    The river branched and they continued west, following what now became a tiny, moss-lined stream cut deep into the forest floor. Realising that the stream would probably disappear completely before they travelled much further, they refilled their water bags ready for boiling at their next campsite. The evening was drawing in and they would soon need to find a sheltered place in which to spend the night.

Matt traipsed on through the dense conifers at the rear of the party watching Father Peter trudging ahead, trying to gauge his energy levels. They had to cover as much ground as possible before nightfall, because tomorrow they would probably run out of food and from then on they would all be running on empty.

Suddenly Matt flinched at the crack of the shotgun from up ahead and he hurried forward, overtaking the old priest to enter a clearing in the trees where he saw Nic crouching on the grass, re-loading the gun.

'What was it Nic?' He asked. 'What's happened?'

'Bloody deer!' Nic said excitedly. 'Right in front of me as I came out of the trees. Great big thing with antlers and everything – it was just looking at me, man - I don't know which of us was the most surprised.'

'Did you h…hit it?' Eddie asked.

'Think so – it ran off that way, back into the trees but I think it's hurt by the way it moved.'

'Joe, stay here with the others and try to light a fire,' Matt said. 'I'll go with Nic and see if we can find it.' The two men crept off through the trees in the direction that the animal had fled. Nic went first, moving as silently as possible through the undergrowth and Matt followed in his trail.

'Look, I was right, man,' Nic whispered. 'There's blood here, it's definitely injured. Come on.'

After a few hundred yards, the ground became boggy and Matt paused, listening for movement, but all was silent and the deer was nowhere to be seen. 'We'll probably never find it now,' he hissed. 'It could be anywhere and it's getting dark – we should head back before…'

Suddenly the animal burst out of the undergrowth to their right and sprang across their path. Just before it disappeared again, the deer's front legs buckled and it crashed to the ground before rolling over and righting itself. Nic fired again but the shot went wide as the animal limped off once more into the trees. Both men ran after the injured animal, their exhaustion now forgotten in the excitement of the chase. As they crashed through the dense foliage, they caught glimpses of the deer, which twisted and turned in its attempt to escape them. Just when they thought they had lost the animal, they burst into another clearing to see the injured deer kneeling unsteadily on its front legs breathing heavily; it stared at them out of the darkness with wide, frightened eyes. Both men stood motionless for a moment as they returned the stricken animal's gaze. The creature was incredibly large, at least four foot tall at the shoulders, with a reddish-brown coat and short, beige tail. It lifted its powerful head until its antlers almost touched its bloodied flank and it bellowed. As the powerful roar echoed through the forest, Nic raised the shotgun, fired and the animal crashed lifelessly to the ground.

'Poor thing,' Nic said. 'It didn't deserve to die like that.'

'We have to eat, Nic. You might just have saved our lives. Do you think we can drag it back to the others? It looks heavy.'

'I reckon we could... if we knew which way to go.'

Matt suddenly realised that they had lost all sense of direction in the chase and he looked around at the surrounding trees, which were now rapidly falling into darkness.

'Jesus, we're lost,' he said. 'What do we do now?'

They were reluctant to abandon the animal, but they had left their possessions with the others. They had no tools with which to butcher the animal, no means to light a fire and didn't even have any water to drink.

'I think it's this way,' Nic said, shouldering the gun. 'Let's go before we lose the light completely.'

Together, the two men started to drag the carcass by the antlers, in the direction Nic had suggested. As they went they shouted to the others, but they heard no reply. They were tired and hungry, but staying put wasn't an option; the boggy ground was no place to camp for the night and without fire, they would probably freeze. In silence, they dragged the animal through the trees, not even sure they were heading in the right direction and before long they could no longer see more than a few feet in front of them.

Slowly it dawned on Matt that they were in serious trouble. 'Fire the gun again,' he said. 'The others must be able to hear it; they can't be that far away.'

'I've only two cartridges left, man - do you have any?'

Matt shook his head. 'In the rucksack – I left it behind.'

Nic raised the gun's barrel and pulled the trigger; the blast echoed out through the trees and the silence that followed was stifling. The two men sat on the warm body of the deer and waited.

'Should I try again?' Nic asked.

'Wait a while; it might be our last chance.'

The darkness engulfed them as they shivered under the dripping trees. Matt couldn't feel his feet, which were soaking wet from the chase through the boggy terrain. 'I'm sorry, Nic; we should never have charged off like that.'

'We did what we had to do; the others need to eat. Why do you keep blaming yourself, man?'

'Because I feel responsible; for some reason, everyone looks to me, but I don't deserve their trust. I'm no leader, never have been.'

'We've survived so far; you've kept us together, despite everything that's happened. We all trust you, even Tanya in her own way.'

'Thanks Nic, I appreciate it, but this time I might have finally blown it. Fire the gun again – we'll soon find out.'

Nic loaded the last cartridge and shot the gun upwards, into the trees. Branches and leaves fell about them and then the silence returned; they were alone and helpless, waiting for a miracle.

Back to back, they leaned on each other, sitting on the carcass as the cold penetrated their bodies, chilling them to the bone. Matt felt himself drifting off into an uneasy sleep and his mind wandered deliriously. He dreamt of the scarred man's army again and saw dark shapes crouched over many furnaces dug into the ground. They were working metal, creating vicious looking weapons amid the flames. Matt realised, other than the possessions they had recovered from the module, they had not seen metal for many weeks and wondered how these creatures had sourced the raw materials and more importantly how such primitive intellects had suddenly mastered the art of the blacksmith.

Matt's head nodded forward and he almost fell face-down into the sodden earth, but he jerked upright again, his consciousness returning momentarily along with the freezing pain that racked his body. He opened his eyes and wondered why he could still smell the furnace smoke from his dream. Then he saw a flickering in the trees, an orange flame bobbing through the undergrowth.

'Help,' he shouted. 'Is someone there?' Then out of the trees he saw the huge frame of Joe Sumo, lumbering out of the shadows carrying a flaming torch.

'He who hunts when it's freezing is a noble man,' Joe said, 'or more likely a fool!'

Despite the cold, Matt laughed; the unlikely Japanese philosopher had saved them once again.

That night they slept with empty stomachs, but in the comfort of a roaring fire. They camped among the trees in the clearing that Nic had first spotted the deer. The rain held off and despite their hunger, they enjoyed a relatively comfortable night, but as soon as it was light they butchered the animal and roasted its meat. For Matt, the mouth-watering aroma was almost too much to bear; given half a chance he would have eaten the animal raw, but he waited along with the others as the venison's dripping fat splattered onto the fire. Joe had single-handedly carried the heavy carcass through the forest as he led his two friends back to where the Mel and the others waited beside the fire that had been started with their penultimate match. On their return, Mel had run to Matt, wrapping her arms around him and holding him tight. Her tiny body, warm from the fire, had felt wonderful and he knew then, that he was really in love for the first time in his life.

After eating the most delicious meal that any of them could remember, they set off again, invigorated by the rest and with their stomachs full for the first time since leaving the lakeside valley. They emerged from the other side of the forest and were greeted by blue skies and warm sunshine as they headed west between the towering peaks of Snowdonia's mountains.

'It's so beautiful here,' Matt said to Joe, who walked beside him. 'But it's daunting as well; we're so alone in this ruined world - insignificant somehow.'

'Kuni yaburete, sanga ari!' Joe replied, holding up his hands and turning full circle as he admired the snow-clad peaks. 'The land is not ruined – look, there are still mountains and rivers!'

Chapter 11

Two days later, Matt looked down through the morning mist, from an old wartime pillbox. The squat shelter had been built into the cliffs as part of a network of coastal defences that had been hastily constructed during the Second World War to prevent an anticipated German invasion. The concrete front of the old shelter had collapsed, leaving a large opening overlooking the sea. The opening was overhung by a stout, timber boom that had once been used as a hoist. A thick rope ran through a solid steel staple embedded in the boom, one end coiled at their feet – the other swayed below them in the morning breeze. Despite the collapsed frontage, the building's stone roof remained intact and had sheltered the party from what would be the last overnight frost of the year.

The previous night they had staggered down out of the mountains in near darkness and had nearly plummeted over the cliff edge. It was pure luck that Nic had spotted the entrance to the pillbox among the cliff-top rocks and they had stumbled down its worn, stone steps, through a short tunnel, into the darkness of its shelter. The place had smelt of urine, but it was surprisingly spacious inside and they had collapsed to its stone floor, grateful for the refuge after days of exposure in the mountains. They had not even been able to muster the energy to make a fire and Matt had woken cold and stiff, to discover for the first time, the panoramic view that the shelter offered.

The small town of Harlech was directly below him, smoke rising from hidden places amid the ruins, but from this elevated spot he could see no evidence of the people who made the fires. The great castle stood behind the town, separating it from the silver sea beyond. Black-headed gulls soared between ancient stone towers, which rose from a rugged promontory of granite into the misty sky. It was a sight of serenity, which threatened to deceive; Matt knew that any place of habitation was dangerous now and they would have to be careful when they approached the town.

The boy crouched low as the six strangers descended the cliff path, heading towards the town. He waited until they disappeared behind a rocky outcrop before running back to warn the others.

It was early morning and most of the townsfolk were still asleep as he scampered between the ramshackle shelters built amongst the ruined buildings of Harlech. He headed for Tank's shelter which was one of those nearest to the castle and he knew better than to cry out and risk disturbing Big'un - the cruel, bald giant of a man who now resided there. Flustered chickens squawked between the boy's feet as he ran through the cluttered streets and into the timber-roofed tunnel, which led to Tank's sleeping chamber. Ryan was the only surviving child in the town and he knew that his precarious existence depended upon the valuable knowledge that he alone held. But he also knew that one false move and he would meet the same end as the other children who had all died at the hands of Big'un who now dominated the place, tyrannising those who lived in the shadow of the castle.

Two months ago, Ryan had scrambled, bloodied and bruised, from the wreckage of the light aircraft, which his father had attempted to land on a disused runway a few miles to the south. Something had happened to the world below them during the long flight from Reykjavik and his previous life now seemed nothing more than a distant dream.

The bewildered boy had bandaged his own wounds using the survival kit from the plane and wandered, in a state of shock, along the coast seeking help. But on reaching the town it was the inhabitants, not he, who needed saving. He had found the sixty or so survivors, most of whom were naked and near to freezing, crawling amongst the ruined buildings in dazed confusion and, not knowing what else to do, he went among them, helping the wounded as best he could. Because of his size, most of the bewildered townsfolk hadn't feared him as he coaxed them into sheltered areas and lit fires to warm them. The survival pack had contained everything from toilet paper to insect repellents, but the waterproof matches had, more than anything, helped them survive that first terrible night in the ruined town.

He crawled into Tank's low shelter; no longer noticing the smell that he had grown accustomed to over the weeks. He had taught these people so much in that time but personal hygiene did not seem to interest them and he had now given up on encouraging them to clean their own bodies.

At first he was blinded by the relative darkness of the shelter, but he could hear Tank snoring on the straw bedding that lined the shelter's floor. Dust, thrown up by the boy's feet swirled in the spears of light which filtered through gaps in the low timber roof. The makeshift ceiling comprised of old floorboards laid across the low stone walls which were all that remained of the original building.

    The boy paused, recovering his breath as his eyes adjusted to the darkness. He was reluctant to wake the bearded man, knowing that the mental sickness that afflicted the local people had initially left them with no compassion for their fellow humans. They had been easily irritated and apt to strike out without warning at the mildest provocation, but the boy and the townsfolk had gradually developed a relationship born of the skills that he brought to them and they tolerated him for it. It was easier now that they could talk - not that they were capable of meaningful discussion yet, but they were at last using the words he had taught them and some were even stringing coherent sentences together. The boy was surprised at how receptive they were to his tuition, but he guessed that it had something to do with their apparent capability to perceive the thoughts of others. Ryan had heard stories about blind people experiencing sensory enhancement and he wondered if the affliction had somehow awakened a previously dormant ability in their brains. Whatever it was, it had enabled the townsfolk to develop practical and social skills so quickly that the savage culture he had at first witnessed had now been transformed into a primitive society where personal relationships were already developing. The boy had even grown close to some of the townsfolk. Tank was his favourite, for he had been the first to demonstrate humour - the first to actually laugh at the boy's imitation of the Big'un as he mimicked the ape-like gait of the colossus in the castle. Tank was a large man himself and had adopted leadership of the townsfolk before the Big'un had arrived. But the huge, bald man had one day appeared among the ruins of the town. Nobody saw him arrive and where he came from the boy had no idea. One day he was just standing there, naked and wielding a weapon that cast immeasurable fear into the others. The boy recognised the implement as an old wall tie from some demolished building, a four-foot metal bar ending in a heavy iron cross, but the others saw it as something mystical - powerful and beyond their comprehension. That very first day, the Big'un had killed Drake, a much smaller man whose curiosity had been his downfall; Drake had approached the giant man, naively thinking that the fragile culture of collaboration that the townsfolk had developed would automatically be adopted by the naked stranger. Instead, the brute had patiently watched the smaller man approach him, before nonchalantly wielding the weapon with devastating effect. Swinging the heavy wall-tie once around his head and striking Drake with such force that one leg of the cross embedded itself in the side of his skull, taking the smaller man right of his feet and killing him instantly. At this, the others had retreated back into their shelters and allowed the stranger to take their food and other valued possessions, including the two emergency space blankets retrieved from the survival pack. Big'un, as Ryan called him, had taken refuge in the castle, not seeming to fear the structure as the others had done, and only came out to plunder more food or the occasional child. They all feared Big'un - none more so than the boy who seemed to be a subject of fascination for the brute. Big'un would sometimes stalk him through the ruins, following without haste as the boy scampered desperately away to hide among the debris. Big'un never put much effort into the chase, but it seemed to amuse him in some strange way. The others never intervened, accepting the giant's superiority and in awe of his powerful appearance, but they also sensed that there was something different about him, for his mind was closed and they could not feel his thoughts. They would nervously watch the giant retreat back into the castle, his huge body now wrapped in the silver blankets and carrying, on his shoulder, the fearful weapon that had killed Drake and they would breathe a collective sigh of relief when he disappeared once more into the intimidating fortress.

'Tank?' the boy whispered nervously, but the snoring man didn't stir. He wondered what Tank's real name had been before the war, or whatever else had caused the terrible devastation. Ryan had named each of the townsfolk and they all now responded to their adopted titles, some even using the names to address each other.

Ryan placed his hand on the sleeping man's hairy shoulder and gently shook him. 'Tank, wake up!'

Tank jumped up with a start and banged his head on the heavy floorboards above, causing more dust to shower the room. Instinctively, he swiped out an arm, striking the boy on the side of his face and knocking him to the ground. Then, rubbing his head he growled at the boy who had woken him. 'Ryan,' he snarled, 'Tank sleeping!'

'I didn't want to wake you but someone's coming.'

Tank frowned, slowly deciphering the words in his mind. 'Big'un?' he asked, fear suddenly in his eyes.

'No - strangers,' the boy said. 'Out of the mountains.'

Another pause, then as if suddenly comprehending the boy's message, Tank scrambled through the tunnel and out onto the debris-strewn street. The boy followed as the bearded man ran wildly about, throwing pieces of concrete shrapnel at the other shelters and shouting unintelligibly, to wake the others.

Matt dropped his rucksack and surveyed the ruined buildings. Everywhere he looked there was evidence of recent habitation; the narrow roads were littered with animal bones and human excrement, a fire still smouldered amidst the nearby rubble and primitive shelters lined the street - dark openings under timbers lain across crumbling walls. The ruined structures were higher here than in the previous towns they had explored; most of the stone-built buildings were older and although most roofs had collapsed, sturdy walls still stood high in many places, casting dark shadows over the broken town. The castle loomed ominously in the distance seemingly untouched by the recent disaster, but the town itself appeared deserted.

'There are people here,' Joe Sumo said. 'I can feel them, but they're scared of us.'

Matt nodded and handed the shotgun to Nic before clambering up onto the roof of one of the shelters. 'Hello, is anybody here?' He shouted, but only the sound of seagulls broke the following silence.

'Let's explore the castle,' Tanya said. 'This place give me the creeps.'

'Okay, but stay close together,' Matt said. 'Joe's right - we're not alone here; people are watching us.' Feelings of animosity, fear and curiosity emanated from the unseen host and he felt ravaged by the onslaught of emotions that infiltrated his mind.

They walked on towards the castle and Matt tried to visualise how the town might have looked before the disaster. He imagined narrow streets lined with contrasting grey and white stone walls, window boxes bursting with spring flowers and slate roofs sprouting tall chimney stacks. He visualised crowded side streets with colourful canopies over gift shop windows, quaint pubs and busy cafés. Where was everybody? The small town's population must have been over a thousand, plus tourists attracted by the famous castle. Where were the bodies? More importantly, where were the survivors?

Ahead the castle, seated on a rugged promontory, now loomed high above them and Matt wondered which direction would offer them the easiest access into the fortress.

'Stop, that's Bigun's castle!' A boy's voice called from above.

Matt swung round, scanning the high walls, searching for the source.

'There,' Father Peter said, pointing. 'By the pillar.'

The boy was standing high on one of the walls, his head nervously poking round the side of a column of stone bricks. 'What do you want?' He shouted.

'Refuge and sanctuary – just like everybody else!' Father Peter replied. 'Who are you? Why don't you come down and talk to us properly?'

'The castle's taken – Big'un lives there - he'll kill you if you go there.'

'Come down,' Mel shouted to the boy. 'Are you alone here?'

Suddenly a large bearded man climbed up beside the boy. 'This is Tank,' the boy said.

'Tank!' The man confirmed, banging his left shoulder with his right fist. In his left hand he held a heavy wooden stake.

Slowly, others came to stand around the ruined walls above them. Maybe fifty or sixty people - mainly men and a few young women, but no children other than the boy. Most wore dirty rags, but some were wrapped in animal furs or sheepskin; the boy was dressed in dirty jeans, sweatshirt and trainers. These were the first proper clothes any of them had seen since Gerry O'Donnell had appeared in his dungarees having emerged, unscathed by the disaster, from an underground mine. Matt wondered what story the boy had to tell, for he could clearly speak and, like the mysterious Irishman, seemed mentally unaffected by the recent catastrophe.

The dishevelled people looked down on them and Matt thought his brain would burst from the intensity of their primitive, mental scrutiny. Their unified mindset was transparent; he and the others were unwelcome here, but the townsfolk feared them too much to chase them away.

'Go away,' the boy shouted. 'Before something bad happens.'

'Look, son,' Matt started. 'We've just crossed the mountains…'

A murmuring in the crowd and the formation of a new collective thought interrupted Matt's plea - a telepathic incantation gradually infiltrated his mind – one, which gradually formed substance and became verbal. The mass above began to chant, quietly at first but the amplitude increased steadily: 'Big'un! Big'un! Big'un!...' and some of the crowd were now looking in the direction of the castle.

'Give me the gun, Nic,' Matt said. 'I think we've got a visitor.'

Mel, Tanya, Eddie and Father Peter backed away and took cover behind a mound of fallen masonry, leaving Matt, Nic and Joe to face the unseen object of the crowd's attention. They all stared down the street in the direction of the castle; a myriad of plants had already established themselves amongst the timber and stone debris of the devastated town. The surreal landscape and the overshadowing backdrop of the medieval fortress made their surroundings feel almost alien, like a scene from a strange fantasy world.

The atmosphere was almost unbearable as the three men waited for the unknown adversary to appear and the crowd above them quietened in anticipation of the confrontation. Matt was reminded of their fateful sortie into Bala when the same feeling of dread had engulfed him before attempting to rescue Hayley and the others from the savages that had taken residence there. Despite the presence of his comrades, Matt was reliving the lonely feelings of the eleven-year-old boy whom, long ago, had just discovered his parent's bloated corpses.

The fearsome creature that eventually lumbered into view barely resembled a human being and only added to the surreal setting before them. Pale and naked beneath a large silver cloak, the huge man was devoid of hair and had a mongoloid appearance. He lurched forward in an ambling gait with one shoulder dropping below the other as he held the steel shaft of the heavy wall tie in his massive, hairless hands.

On he came, close enough now for them to make out bloodshot eyes glaring menacingly from beneath his prominent forehead. Matt knew the creature intended to kill them from the intensity of its gaze; he lifted the gun, planning to fire the first shot over the creature's head. If it kept coming, he knew he would have to shoot the creature dead.

'Shoot it, man,' Nic said. 'The thing's a fucking monster.'

The creature was less than twenty feet away now but Matt waited a few more seconds, before slowly squeezing one of the two triggers. Nothing happened - the mechanism resisted the pressure of his trembling finger. Frantically, Matt checked the safety, but it was in the off position. In a state of panic, he lowering the gun to aim now at the advancing giant and pulled hard on both triggers simultaneously, but his fingers met an irresistible mechanical force.

'The mechanism's jammed!' he shouted to the others. They should have checked the gun before coming down the hill into town, but it was too late now.

The creature accelerated as if sensing its sudden advantage and started to swing its fearsome weapon. Matt instinctively backed away as the monster came at him, but his heel caught on something and he fell backwards, striking his skull on the uneven ground. His head swam as he watched the massive creature bearing down on him, the great metal wall-tie sweeping an arc towards his face.

Matt closed his eyes in anticipation of the terrible blow, but it never came because Joe Sumo hit the monster in its midriff with a shoulder charge, unbalancing it and diverting the trajectory of the wall-tie. The iron cross narrowly missed

Matt's head, one of its spikes digging deep into the damaged road.

Nic grabbed the shotgun and clambered up onto one of the nearby shelters, trying to free off the trigger mechanism as Matt groggily dragged himself away through the dirt.

Joe Sumo and the creature faced each other now. In a display of super-human strength, the bald giant recovered his weapon by dragging it plough-like through the road's surface. Joe Sumo circled the creature, which growled ominously as it turned slowly on the spot, following the ex-wrestler's position and ignoring all others.

Even Joe Sumo's massive frame was overshadowed by the creature's bulk and the slightly-built Nic, having given up on the gun, thought better than to enter the affray. This fight was way beyond him, so he helped to drag Matt to safety and picked up a heavy rock in readiness to throw, hoping that he might at least be able to distract the creature at a crucial time.

The bald giant lifted the heavy wall tie off the ground and held it horizontally between his massive body and that of his circling adversary. Joe Sumo's one good eye stared intently at the creature, waiting for it to make a move. The circling continued until the colossus suddenly pushed out its right hand, jabbing the crossed head of the wall tie towards Joe's face. Joe Sumo ducked, narrowly avoiding the blow, but stumbled slightly as he did so. The creature, sensing Joe's imbalance, kicked out with one of its huge scarred feet and caught the ex-wrestler in the ribs, knocking him to the ground. The creature charged, swinging the wall tie through the air and down onto the prone man. Joe twisted away but the weapon crashed onto the wrestler's forearm, pinning it to the ground between two prongs of its cross-shaped head. Had his arm suffered a direct hit, it would certainly have been broken, but instead, it was trapped by the embedded weapon. Joe kicked at the shaft of the wall-tie and the monster almost lost his grip on the weapon as the force tugged him sideways. Joe got to his knees and, using his free arm, pulled the head of the cross out of the ground and rolled away just in time to avoid another kick aimed this time at his face. Joe Sumo scrambled to his feet as the creature recovered his weapon and the cautious circling recommenced. Joe suddenly crouched, grabbing a handful of the sooty dust from the road's surface. He intended to throw it into the giant's eyes - it was an old trick, but somehow he thought the creature wouldn't have seen it before. Just before he made his move, the giant charged, swinging the weapon as he came. Joe ducked under the wall tie as it arced towards him and he punched the creature hard in the groin. The giant immediately dropped the weapon and doubled over in pain. As he went down, Joe kneed him in the face and blood splattered outwards as the giant's head was thrown backwards, his nose split in two. The deformed man roared and charged again, this time grabbing Joe Sumo by the throat with both his hands. Joe grabbed the giant's wrists and tried to pull them apart, but the creature's strength was incredible and the ex-wrestler started to feel his consciousness slip away. He kicked out desperately aiming for the creature's groin again, but only struck a muscular thigh causing no real damage. Suddenly, the giant was stunned by a rock, thrown from somewhere behind and his grip momentarily loosened. Joe took advantage, thrusting both arms upwards in a wedge, forcing the giant's own massive arms apart. The creature lost its grip, but grabbed

Joe by the wrists and pulled him towards its grotesque, snarling face; crooked teeth threatened to bite into Joe's throat. Joe Sumo tilted his head backwards, exposing his bruised windpipe to the lurching fangs, but at the last moment he tensed his neck muscles and head-butted the giant, hard between the eyes. The creature fell backwards, hitting the ground and throwing up a huge cloud of black dust as it lay stunned for a moment amongst the debris.

When the dust cleared, the monster looked up at the sight of Joe Sumo holding aloft the great wall tie, ready to bring it down on the now defenceless giant. The creature slowly dragged itself backwards through the dirt, realising that it was now completely at the mercy of its aggressor. Joe followed, weapon poised to strike, as the creature continued to back away, until someone suddenly jumped between them.

'Don't kill him, Joe,' Mel pleaded. 'It's not his fault! Let the poor thing go.'

Joe looked uncertain; every instinct urged him to finish his enemy while he still could. The prone giant looked up into Mel's face, seemingly not able to comprehend why she had intervened. The creature's eyes were now devoid of the malevolence that had focussed on his enemy, they stared at Mel with bewildered uncertainty as if remembering something long forgotten from its past. Suddenly, the giant spun its huge frame around and scrambled off over the debris. Joe gave chase, shouting after the creature and Nic followed, throwing rocks at the retreating giant until it passed beyond the last of the buildings and out of town.

Matt, still groggy from the blow to his head, joined his friends and watched the giant drag itself up the very path that they had descended only an hour ago. At one point, the huge creature stopped and turned back to face them for a moment, before continuing dejectedly up the hill.

'What the hell was that thing?' Nic asked. 'Some sort of overgrown retard?' His keen eyes followed the creatures retreat. 'You should have killed it, man!'

'No, Mel's right.' Joe said. 'We should not condemn one whose fortune is unknown.'

'He was probably disadvantaged in his previous life,' Mel said. 'But here and now, with such physical strength, he was a king for a while - and he even lived in a castle.'

The three men turned back towards the town and saw that the people on the walls had now descended and were rapidly approaching Father Peter and the others.

'Quick, something's happening,' Matt shouted, running back towards the group.

The townsfolk parted to let them pass and Matt could sense that the crowd's animosity had been replaced by emotions of wonderment that couldn't be explained purely by the giant's demise; the people were enthralled by something else. Awe-struck faces, now devoid of fear, gazed in wonder at the old priest and the object he held in his hand.

'It just started to glow!' Tanya said. 'You could see it through the bag!'

'It must have something to do with the castle,' Father Peter said as he stared incredulously at the glowing chalice. Bright, crimson waves radiated from the cup's polished surface and golden flames seemed to dance within its bowl with mesmerising effect.

Walking slowly, as though in a trance, the boy moved towards the chalice with both hands held before him as if to embrace the light. 'This is what the dark king seeks,' he murmured.

Standing upon a huge stump of masonry - one of two, which rose out of the castle's eastern ditch, Matt shielded his eyes from the morning sun as he looked up at the gatehouse entrance. A pair of solid stone turrets flanked the gate, their foundations seamlessly fused to a sheer apron of smooth stone above the rock-cut edge of the grassy ditch. The gatehouse stood at least twenty-five feet above the moat, which was never meant to be water-filled, designed instead to act as a physical obstacle to hostile forces and provide a deterrent to advancing siege towers. Two hundred years ago, the mound on which they stood had been the base of one of the supports for a stone bridge, which had once spanned the ditch. More recently the ruined mounds had supported a wooden staircase allowing visitors access to the main entrance. Timber from the collapsed staircase now lay haphazardly below them in the damp grass.

'Did anyone bring a ladder?' Tanya asked.

'Big'un used to climb up there,' Ryan said, pointing to their left. He alone among the townsfolk had been brave enough to accompany the seven travellers to the castle walls. The others seemed to have an inherent fear of the intimidating structure and refused to approach beyond the buildings of the ruined town. The boy pointed to the low wall of the outer ward, which skirted the main castle walls. At one point its partial collapse had formed a rocky outcrop rising out of the ditch up to the low battlements.

'I can climb that,' Nic said, dropping his rucksack and removing one of the ropes. The young African was the most agile of the group and within moments had clambered up into the outer ward. Having scaled the wall, Nic secured one end of the rope and tossed it over the side for the others to pull themselves up by the same route.

Joe went first, knowing that if the rope held him, it would certainly support the others. Then between them, Joe and Nic pulled Father Peter up onto the wall, followed by Mel, Tanya, Eddie and finally Matt. They looked down at the boy who had remained in the ditch.

'Are you coming, or what?' Mel shouted down to him. Ryan looked back towards the town for a moment, and then scampered up the steep slope to join them. The outer ward apparently circled the whole castle ending at each side-wall of the gatehouse, but offered no access to the gate itself.

'Let's see if there's a back door,' Matt said, making his way around the battlements, towards the enormous, round southeast tower. As they circumnavigated the tower they saw that the ground below them dropped away sharply until they were looking down over a sheer cliff. Far below, a long path of innumerable steps meandered down the cliff from the outer ward towards the sea. The stairs were defended at regular intervals by artillery platforms cut into the rock-face above the pathway. A huge inner wall ran along the southern edge of the castle and housed four large windows, which looked out towards the sea. In the centre of the wall they found what they were looking for; a small entrance cut into the stone at ground level, giving access to what was once the castle's great hall. At last they were inside the ancient fortress and like excited children they split up to explore.

    Father Peter sat with the boy in the warm sunshine on a low wall of the inner courtyard and watched Tanya disappear up a set of wide, stone steps into the gatehouse. Joe and Nic climbed a narrow staircase up towards the battlements and Mel and Matt entered the dark doorway of the southeast tower. Father Peter studied his surroundings; all that remained of the inner buildings - the halls, chapels, kitchens and dwelling areas - were low walls and stone floors. The rest of the courtyard was laid to grass - now overgrown, with stone mosaic pathways running in every direction. The only intact structures were the towers and gatehouse guardrooms, but despite the inhospitable surroundings, Father Peter felt at ease for the first time in weeks. He had visited this place so many times in his dreams that the stone walls and tall towers seemed familiar and somehow comforting. He knew that this place was important, that he and the others were meant to be here and that for the time being they were safe. The old priest opened his bag and peered into where the golden cup still throbbed with crimson light as though it too, sensed the significance of the place. As if some dormant power in the ancient building had been waiting for something to release it.

    The boy sat next to the priest, his eyes transfixed on the bag he held. 'Are you a wizard?' The boy asked.

    'I'm afraid not,' Father Peter laughed. 'Though, with this beard, I suppose I am starting to bear a resemblance to Gandalf?'

The boy looked at him curiously. 'You look a bit like Dumbledore,' he said.

Father Peter smiled, then scrutinised the boy. 'What did you say, back there, about a dark king?' he asked him.

'They all dream about the king,' the boy replied absently, still staring at the bag. 'Before I got here many people had already left to find him. He has a great sword and an army – but they needn't have gone,' the boy looked at the old priest as if coming out of a trance. 'Because he's coming here… to the castle… He's coming to take the magic cup.'

* * * *

Book 3 – The Siege of Harlech

"He that is kind is free, though he is a slave; he that is evil is a slave, though he be a king."
                                                    Saint Augustine

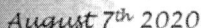

August 7th 2020
It was foolish of us to have ridiculed the concept of evil when it was so evident in every aspect of modern life. Now that civilisation is lost, evil's physical manifestation pursues us with malevolent intent. None of us sought this conflict, but undoubtedly it will come to pass for we have all foreseen it.
Unchallenged now, the dark king invades our dreams and each day his physical form and those of his minions grow nearer. Very soon he will make his attempt.
We will endeavour to defend this ancient place, but tall towers will offer no great defence against an enemy who can infiltrate our minds.

As far as our adversary is concerned Harlech Castle is a fortress without walls and we are at his mercy.

Our only hope lies in the courage and fortitude of the virtuous men and women who reside within.
Father Peter

Chapter 1

The creature that was once Glyn Cooper was now called Yarik. He looked up at the full moon anchored just above the treetops. The large pale disc fascinated the creature because he never saw it move. It always did so when he wasn't watching, sometimes high and small, sometimes low and frighteningly large - like tonight. And it was not always as plump as it was now, presumably having gorged itself on its tiny, bright kindred that surrounded it; sometimes its innumerable shimmering prey evaded it and it went hungry, so hungry that it almost faded away. And sometimes when it grew lighter, it too was hunted, hiding with its smaller kindred as its more powerful brother roamed the sky. Yarik had seen the pale disc grow bloated twice now; he remembered how cold he had been the first time he had stared up in awe at the fearful sight.

    Yarik tightened the leather wraps around his ankles and tucked the sharp flint inside the soft leggings. He still wore skins, despite the warmer weather, because they protected against injury; one of his companions had been bitten by a dog and the wound was festering and swollen, slowing the party down. The flint he concealed was Yarik's most precious possession, for with it he could skin the animals he caught. Plus, it could be used as a weapon in close combat and, most importantly, he believed that it had the power to make fire. Yarik had seen this with his own eyes once and he was determined that one day he would master the art himself. To make fire was a valuable skill; the bitten man was the only one of his group who could do so. But he used wood instead of flint and how he did it nobody knew, because he wouldn't let the others watch in case they stole his power.

There were only five of them left - two females and two other males; the injured man was sleeping uneasily near a fire of his own making. The other male, a tall gangling creature, was lying with one of the females, the one with pointed shapes on her rump. Yarik had been with this particular female for as long as he could remember and it was from her strange bark that he had taken his name, but he shared her now with the others. The second female was not wanted in the same way because she looked and smelt bad, but she was a very good hunter. Many others had fallen on the dark road that they had followed north towards the calling; some they had eaten, others they had left to the black and white birds that inevitably followed them. They would have abandoned the injured man long ago, had he not possessed his incredible talent; but even so, now it was warmer it was perhaps only a matter of time.

Suddenly, Yarik's head was inundated with confused messages - warnings from the others and he received a terrifying vision of strange men on the backs of hill-beasts – instantly, he knew they were under attack. He jumped to his feet and spun round to see five men on horses riding hard towards them out of the darkness. He didn't know at first whether man or hill-beast was in control of the attack because his mind had never before conceived such collaboration, but then he realised that the humans were in command, because their thoughts were the most dominant. The riders were a fearsome sight; each wore furs, seemingly tailored to their bodies, which in itself seemed incredible, and they carried dark, heavy-looking weapons made from a material which Yarik had never before seen. The riders' heads and faces were devoid of the hair that was normal on a man and their foreheads bore a deep, black scar like an inverted "V". As the horsemen reined in their animals and paced around the group, Yarik noticed that around each of their necks hung a human jawbone on a leather thong.

'Come with us,' one of the riders shouted and they all understood the command despite the unfamiliar words.

Yarik's party followed without dispute, knowing that the calling had led them here for a purpose, and whatever would befall them now was surely their destiny. They were nearing the end of their journey for these riders were undoubtedly emissaries of the dark king who had so long ago summoned them.

It soon became apparent that the injured man could not keep up, so one of the riders cut him down cruelly with his weapon and left him crippled on the ground to die. Yarik followed the horsemen for several miles before the landscape started to change; the trees that lined the wide road gradually gave way to broken buildings and before long, trails of dark smoke could be seen drifting into the moonlit sky ahead. Yarik's mood lifted as it always did when he saw evidence of fire because he associated it with his own survival; he also assumed it meant their journey would soon be over and he would at last be able to rest.

They approached two stone columns flanked by two more men of the rider's ilk; both shaven with marked foreheads, but instead of the short blunt swords of the riders, these men carried spears with crudely made, barbed metal heads. The two guards silently acknowledged the riders as they passed between the stone columns. They were guided along a path between ramshackle shelters and a few small fires with dark figures huddled around them. At one point, they passed a group of men working around a particularly intense fire, which was lined with stones and embedded in the ground. The fire shone white in the darkness as one of the men pumped on a skin bladder, while the others pulled glowing implements, one by one, from the flames and quenched them in a small, water-filled ditch.

    Soon they came to an immense wall of rubble, piled so high that its top was obscured in the smoky darkness; Yarik could hear men above them, presumably on top of the great wall. The riders dismounted and two of them led the horses away; another man appeared and grabbed the two females, pulling them off in a different direction. Yarik was one of the two remaining prisoners and felt increasingly uneasy as his captors pushed him and the lanky male through a small tunnel that ran through the wall. They both emerged in a brightly-lit area surrounded on all sides by the great wall of rubble, which ran in an oval around a flat grassy arena. Yarik could now see a mass of people on the wall, their faces lit by the many fires which burned among the debris. In front of him, sitting of the grass were around forty other men such as he, bearded, naked or in rags. These were obviously other refugees who had been summoned here by the dark king. Yarik walked over, sat down among them and waited.

Arthur looked down onto the arena from his place on the wall of rubble that had been formed by the fallen structure of the stadium building. He sat next to his female and was surrounded by elite warriors as he watched two more immigrants emerge from the tunnel below. Arthur was back in control after narrowly avoiding catastrophe on their long march south. He realised now that a large army could not easily be sustained even when they sometimes fed upon themselves, and his starving people had been close to rebellion before they reached this place. As usual Merlin had guided him – a hierarchy of control was required and his people needed to be culled. His army should grow to no more than a few thousand – more than this and people would grow hungry and mutinous; with such numbers, Arthur found it increasingly difficult to bend their minds to his will. Quality, rather than quantity, would bring him the dominion he desired and history had proven that physical quality could only be achieved by natural selection.

Even Arthur was surprised at how successful this strategy had been; in less than two months he had developed a culture where his people were well fed and obedient. A process whereby they developed quickly the skills they were assigned and a command structure in which his warriors were well drilled and disciplined. The risk of rebellion was now a thing of the past. The scene below him now was the first stage of the selection process and one, which also served to entertain him and his devoted people.

'There are sufficient numbers now, Arthur,' Merlin said to him. 'Why don't you start proceedings?'

Arthur counted the newcomers, making the number forty-four; this was more than enough for the contest, so he made a silent command to his captain.

Yarik watched the tall, black warrior clamber down the side of the wall and then up onto a tall crumbling concrete platform overlooking the arena. On his head and covering his shoulders, he wore the skin of a snow leopard, which flowed down behind him like a cloak. The great cat's pale fur shone in the firelight and all those on the pitch below looked up in veneration at the imposing figure. In one hand the captain held a crudely forged, metal blade and in his other, a drawstring leather bag.

'Welcome to you all on behalf of the King,' he cried, sweeping his weapon high above his head. The crowd on the wall cheered enthusiastically, but those on the pitch remained silent in their fear. The captain turned and pointed his blade towards where his king sat, and on cue Arthur rose to rapturous applause.

When the noise subsided, Arthur addressed them. 'Some of you will win my favour tonight and be rewarded,' he shouted. 'Others will serve me in different ways, but you should all feel great honour knowing that you have played a part in your king's destiny.' More cheers as Arthur sat down again and allowed his captain to continue.

'Know now that I am the King's Captain,' he cried. 'Bar the king himself, I am the most powerful man in all these lands.' The crowd cheered again and he waited once more for the applause to abate.

'Once I was no different to any of you - alone and without honour.' He held his sword aloft. 'Without this blade I was weak,' he shouted. When the cheers subsided again, he pointed at his forehead. 'And without this mark, I was alone…'

Yarik saw that his head bore the same mark as the horsemen that had taken them.

'But without this…' the captain roared, grabbing at the human jawbone hanging from his neck. 'Without this… I am dead!' At this, he pulled open the bag and threw the contents down to the frightened people below.

Yarik looked around him as the twenty jawbones rained down into the crowd. A huge beast of a man next to him looked perplexed, as did many of the others, but Yarik immediately knew what this meant and dived onto the ground to recover as many of the human bones as he could grab. Others soon cottoned on and jumped into the affray, but Yarik rose triumphantly, clutching three of the jawbones to his chest. Somebody punched him in the face, ripped one of them from his grasp and made off at pace, towards the other end of the arena. People were running in all directions now, some were grappling with each other for their share of the spoils. In amongst them, the huge man who had been next to Yarik grabbed frantically at anybody who ran past carrying a prize but, although he looked extremely strong, he was not as quick as most of the others and his lunges fell mainly to fresh air. Yarik made a decision and held out one of his two jawbones to the brute who immediately ran over and grabbed it. Yarik's mind was hit with pathetic gratitude and he ushered his new-found ally to the shelter of one of the walls where both men watched the turmoil slowly subside.

The king's captain, still clutching his own gory necklace, shouted down to them one last time. 'At sunrise, this token will be your key to salvation and glory,' he said, before turning away and disappearing back into the darkness.

At ground level a new dynamic was forming as pockets of jawbone winners were creating alliances to help each other repel the attacks of desperate individuals, but occasionally one of the more powerful raiders would come away victorious, leaving the defending group suddenly squabbling violently amongst themselves again. Gradually a status quo emerged, where the more powerful men tended to hold the prizes and grouped together, leaving the empty-handed unfortunates to scheme amongst themselves. Yarik was nowhere near as powerful as many of the others, but as he had hoped, his indomitable partner was a significant deterrent to potential aggressors. So far they had been left alone, but Yarik knew that it was going to be a very long night.

* * * *

The following day, Yarik queued with nineteen others in the bright morning sunshine. The previous night had been an ordeal of unrelenting violence and now, more than anything he needed to sleep. But Yarik felt elated all the same. He knew that he had survived the night against the odds and was now experiencing previously undiscovered emotions - a sense of pride in himself and an alliance for those around him who had also emerged victorious from the arena. A mutual respect had been formed among the new jawbone possessors and a sense of camaraderie was already developing in the group as they jostled forward to receive their prize.

In the daylight, Yarik realised for the first time the extent of the king's encampment. A vast flat area surrounded the arena and a sea of primitive shelters and small, smoking fires stretched as far as the eye could see. The only other structure between the arena and the distant collapsed buildings was a large stone circular platform, perhaps twenty feet across and slightly raised from the ground; a neat ring of stones separated the platform from the main dwelling area. They had been told that the area beyond the circle was out of bounds to them, as was the walled compound behind the arena where the women dwelt, preparing food and clothing and tending the king's horses. Yarik wondered how the two females he had arrived with had fared in their new environment and if he would ever see them again.

A few rows ahead, Yarik could see that his powerful combat partner from the previous night had at last reached the front of the queue and was being handed a weapon; he watched enviously as the man was led away, back towards the arena. A few minutes later Yarik was handed his own heavy, black blade which still steamed from its recent quenching. He was also given a rock and was shown how to sharpen the blade, instantly understanding the technique due to the strange mental connection, which they all now shared. Yarik followed the others back to the arena wall where roasting meat awaited them.

After they had eaten, Yarik and the others were led back through the tunnel into the arena again, but this time they were accompanied by one of their captors. A tall shaven-headed guard dressed in fur and bearing, as all of the guards did, the mark of Arthur's people on his forehead. Inside the arena, Yarik was surprised to see that those who had failed to obtain a precious jawbone were still there, sitting huddled together, frightened and hungry upon the grass. However, this sorry mob had now also been joined by a number of dishevelled looking females. Yarik immediately recognised two of the dejected crowd from his original party – the unattractive female and the gangly male - the female with stars was nowhere to be seen. Yarik stared at the pathetic faces of his ex-companions and felt no pity for them. He could sense their misery and he despised them for it, Yarik had fought to prove his worth and had been victorious, but these people were weak and had no place in the king's company.

The guard held out his weapon towards Yarik's group with both hands and proudly pointed out its sharpened edge and where the handle had been bound with leather.

'Without this blade I am weak,' he shouted, repeating the words of his captain. 'No better than these retched creatures, who lack the valour of those who honour their king.' Walking over to the frightened mass, the guard grabbed one of the females by her matted hair and pulled her, struggling to the forefront.

'But with this blade, I am strong,' the guard shouted, and still grasping the female's hair, he brought his weapon down, striking her viciously on the knee. The female screamed as her near-severed leg gave way beneath her and she fell to the ground, blood oozing from the ugly wound. Still pulling on her hair, the guard dragged the screaming female onto her back before swinging the weapon a second time, bringing it down hard onto her exposed throat. The screaming stopped abruptly as the female's head lolled unnaturally to one side as her neck separated to her spine. As a crimson geyser erupted from the gory opening, the female jerked in sudden spasm and died. Wiping a bloody mess from the blade of his weapon, the guard returned his gaze to the new recruits; his eyes glared at them maniacally as he pointed at the other group. 'Show me,' he shouted.

Yarik and the other new recruits brandished their weapons and charged.

High up on the arena walls, Arthur sat beside his captain and watched the massacre unfold. He hoped that he might spot a talented individual; someone whose natural ability in combat might take him all the way to becoming one of the king's elite knights. He knew it was unlikely though, their victims were unarmed and helpless; this was just a taste of the challenges that the recruits would have to face if they were to progress. To be branded with the mark of Pendragon they would each have to stand alone on the great stone table and defeat another who already bore the mark. Only those that survived Arthur's table three times were promoted to the king's elite and declared immune from further challenge. Once selected, the special ones were dressed in the finest clothes and trained by the captain himself in warfare and horsemanship.

'These newcomers are special,' Arthur said to his captain as, below them, the guard led his recruits back out of the arena. 'They have travelled furthest and are therefore the most perceptive. To have heard me from so far away is impressive; we should find a place for them. What are our current numbers?'

'We have two hundred elite, but many have yet to master their horse,' the black warrior answered. 'But that number should double in the next week as many are now close to advancing from the table. We have at least a thousand bearing the mark of Pendragon and a few hundred more, like these, who now carry weapons. But we are running out of iron and steel for newcomers; many of the foraging parties are picking up disease in the city and fewer are returning now with forgeable metals.'

Below them, a group of women entered the arena carrying sturdy poles and set to work recovering the bodies. They too, were well trained and had been instructed that nothing should go to waste.

'It is enough,' Arthur said. 'Soon we must break camp and move on – our enemies are also gaining numbers and might one day rise against us - we must strike them down before they grow strong.' Arthur gazed southwest into the darkness, '…and we must destroy the priest before he poisons people's minds.'

Chapter 2

Matt looked down onto the courtyard from the battlements of the castle's northeast tower and tried to remain calm, but he could sense Mel's eyes boring into his back as he pretended to survey the building works below. The well near the chapel had already been restored and one of the western towers was now habitable. Both seaward towers had latrine chutes burrowed deep into the rock so that seawater could wash away any waste thrown into them. However, the southern tower's chute had apparently collapsed and cold air billowed up it, transforming the whole tower into a vertical wind tunnel. They would have to seal the chute if that tower was to be made hospitable.

The newly-built stone and timber shelters, now running along the castle's north wall, were luxurious in comparison to what they had grown used to on their long journey to Harlech. Two lower walls - the remains of the castle chapel - ran parallel from the great north wall into the courtyard. Large wooden sleepers, recovered from the town, now spanned these new structures and any gaps were sealed with clay from the beach. At the front of this communal building, stone blocks were stacked shoulder height to form a new south-facing wall with a single opening in the centre. Summer was approaching, so the upper part of the block wall was left open to allow smoke to escape from fires that were built every night to illuminate the building's interior. Ten smaller lean-to shelters ran along the remainder of the northern wall from the communal building to the castle well. The lean-to shelters were temporary sleeping quarters – Nic, Joe and Eddie each had their own private shelter and Matt and Mel shared one, having now declared themselves a couple. Father Peter and Ryan had taken residence in the upper of two habitable rooms in the northwest tower and the old priest spent many hours deep in thought, staring out to sea from its single stone-arched window. The boy seemed in awe of the priest with the mysterious golden cup and now rarely left his side. Father Peter never seemed to tire of the boy's endless questions and would let Ryan sit with him at a makeshift desk, helping the priest record his memoirs, which he now captured in the old journal recovered from the mine. Tanya slept alone in the tower's lower room; she was becoming more and more withdrawn, isolated from the rest of the group and clearly despising the relationship that was developing between Matt and Mel.

    Seven of the lean-to shelters remained unoccupied and no more would be built unless the townsfolk could be persuaded to sleep within the confines of the castle. The people of Harlech were still wary of the newcomers and were hard to engage with, but the compassion they showed for each other was sometimes endearing to watch. Culturally, they were so far removed from the savages of Bala that it gave everyone hope for the future. The arrival of one small boy, at a time when their minds were at their most receptive, had triggered a seed of humanity in the primitive townsfolk; a humanity which seemed to be evolving with every passing day. Perhaps, in the small town of Harlech, the re-civilisation of the world had begun.

    Ryan's story, from the plane crash through to their arrival, had captivated them all, but Mel, more than anyone had been fascinated by his account of how the town's social structure had developed. It gave her hope that similar social evolution might be occurring elsewhere - perhaps influenced by others who had survived with their memories intact. Despite this comforting thought, she also knew that such privileged pockets, if they did exist, would be very much in the minority. Many other cultures would develop and most would be savage and cruel, born only of the survival need. Human social behaviour was complex; where the overall population normalised, if it ever did, would depend on many variables, but history told her that conflict was bound to play a major part in establishing the norm. Protecting and educating the people here was a critical first step in what she knew would now become her own personal crusade. It had to be, for she now had a greater need than anyone for the re-emergence of a compassionate society; a need that, until today, none of the others had been aware of.

  Mel now spent the majority of her spare time amongst the townsfolk and was astounded by their language development. Impossible as it seemed, they were all now speaking quite fluently and it occurred to her that it must have something to do with the strange telepathy that they all seemed to possess. She had suggested to Matt that the boy's arrival had allowed the people to somehow absorb the language from his very mind because he tended to think in words rather than just concepts. It's quite possible, she had explained, that without such influence, speech might never have developed at all. Instead, the townsfolk's telepathy might have evolved to a new level. Matt had no reason to doubt her theory – nothing would surprise him anymore - or at least, that's what he thought until a moment ago when Mel had broken her news.

'When...?' he asked, trying to conceal his emerging panic.

Mel sensed his tension. 'When did? Or when will?' she snapped, obviously feeling let down by his reaction.

'Er...When will? I suppose,' Matt answered, taking a deep breath and turning at last towards her.

'In the New Year, I expect.' She looked into his eyes. 'Well, what are you thinking?'

'That it's going to be cold,' Matt said, 'and that there'll be nobody to help if something goes wrong.'

At this, her annoyance faded and was replaced by something colder. 'I'm scared, Matt - more than you can imagine.' She bit her lip, determined not to cry. 'Please tell me it's going to be alright.'

Matt put his arms around her, pulling her close as he stared over her shoulder, towards the eastern hills. 'Don't worry,' he said quietly. 'We'll be okay.' But the tone in his voice betrayed his true feelings; the thought of becoming a father would have filled Matt with dread at the best of times, but here and now the responsibility seemed enormous. 'Have you told any of the others?' he asked.

'Are you kidding? Who do you think I'm going to tell? Tanya? God, she's going to love this!'

'Perhaps, you're mistaken,' he said, a glimmer of hope momentarily brightening his eyes. 'How can you be sure, without...?'

'For Christ's sake Matt, I'm pregnant! We're having a baby! There's no mistake, get used to it!' She pushed him away and turned back to the fire they were supposed to be building.

    The two of them were on the battlements, because Nic had sworn he had spotted a sail on the horizon earlier that morning. They all knew how unlikely it was, but Ryan was so excited at the prospect that, to appease him, Mel had persuaded Matt to help her light a signal beacon right at the top of one of the towers. He now suspected she had an ulterior motive in getting him up here alone – she had wanted to break the news to him in private.

    Feeling guilty about the way he had reacted, but not knowing how to make amends, Matt turned to the south-facing wall of the castle and tried to visualise how the permanent buildings would fit in amongst the remaining ruined walls. They would have to start building soon because they had to be finished before winter - especially now, he thought. So much time had been spent rebuilding the wooden platform at the gatehouse that the interior construction, apart from the temporary buildings, had so far been neglected. But at least they now had an access-way strong enough to support the transportation of heavy building materials recovered from the town. Piles had already been amassed adjacent to the southeast tower, the townsfolk had helped them to stack hundreds of stone bricks against the castle wall there and an even larger mound of timber – sleepers, planks and boards were piled high under the shelter of the tower itself. An untidy mass of leather, cotton and other natural textiles, stuffed in an alcove in the south wall, just behind a mound of what was the most valuable material of all – old scrap metal that had survived the entropic reaction. Somewhere amongst this pile lay the heavy wall-tie that had once been the possession of the castle's previous resident.

Matt gazed out at the sparkling ocean and wondered what events were unfolding beyond the hazy horizon. Once more, an overpowering feeling of insignificance engulfed him; they were just vulnerable specs in a seemingly infinite world of chaos and destruction. What were the chances that any of them would survive the winter? Looking out across the empty sea, he wondered if it really mattered anyway. Then he looked down at Mel, her dirty, blistered hands working at the fire and realised that actually it did; she was going to have his baby and there was no hiding from it. He was responsible for them and whatever it took, they had to survive – it was up to him to make sure of it.

'Come on,' he said, kneeling down to help her. 'Let's get this thing going.'

She looked up at him and smiled, but behind the smile Matt could see there were tears just waiting for an excuse to fall.

'Hey, I'm gonna be a dad!' he said, laughing. 'Bloody Hell! Hasn't the world suffered enough?'

Once the fire was alight, Matt suggested that they stay up in the tower for a while. He lit one of his precious cigarettes in its flames and together, they peered over the battlements to watch the activities below. They saw Joe Sumo and Tank clumsily manhandling a large telegraph pole over the access platform into the gatehouse; behind them followed a trail of laughing townsfolk, each carrying valuable flotsam from the town. Mel giggled at the sight and Matt sensed her anxieties diminish, but he felt no such relief. Time was against them - if his recent dreams were anything to go by, they had to fortify the castle as a matter of urgency.

'Matt look!' Mel shouted suddenly, pointing up at the eastern road.

Bounding down the hill was the unmistakable sight of Rupert's old Beagle and following behind was a horse drawn wagon and a line of people walking erect and each carrying a sturdy longbow.

'Rupert!' Matt gasped. 'Thank God!'

'Look, I can see Amy in the wagon with Gerry O'Donnell,' Mel said, excitedly. '… and there's Rupert! But who are those people following them?'

Matt shielded his eyes from the sun. 'I don't know,' he said, 'but they look Chinese.'

* * * *

Matt swigged from the whiskey bottle and passed it back to Gerry O'Donnell. The two of them were sitting with Mel in the open courtyard, breathing the clean night air and relishing the party atmosphere that was developing within the castle walls. Most of the others were inside the communal building, preparing what was promising to be a quite a feast. The travellers had arrived hungry and low on rations, but among their supplies they brought with them the remaining bottles of whiskey and two more packs of the cigarettes that had been recovered from the mine. Nic and Joe were roasting a small pig on a spit over a fire and the night was so calm that despite the building's open frontage, it was getting quite smoky inside. The castle was well stocked with food now; the town's ruins had offered up all sorts of unexpected delights; a large amount of rice and dried pasta had been found unspoilt, and they had recovered salt, pepper and other spices from the demolished buildings. Fresh meat though, still had to be hunted and vegetables were now getting scarce. However, with the help of the townsfolk they had now started to round up livestock and fence them in, plus the crops in the fields were growing fast and would soon be harvested. Chickens roamed freely inside the castle and fresh eggs now featured in what was becoming a surprisingly healthy diet for the castle's inhabitants.

The three of them had come outside for some fresh air, but the aroma emanating from the building was still wonderful and the effect of the whiskey was already contributing to a cheerful atmosphere.

'It's weird how they don't speak,' Matt said, looking at the six Chinese men who sat in a circle in front of the main shelter.

'They don't need to,' Gerry laughed. 'Because they know what each other's thinking. Sometimes, if you concentrate, you can tell what's on their minds. It's like the whole world's gone quieter somehow and if you listen hard enough you can hear a little bit more than you could before.'

'How did you persuade them to come?' Mel asked.

'It was unexpected, to be sure, and very strange.' Gerry said. 'On the day we were leaving they just turned up, each carrying a bow as if they were expecting trouble. I think they came to protect us, but I have no idea what from - we've seen nothing on the road.'

'Perhaps they've been dreaming too,' Matt muttered.

The Irishman looked at him quizzically. 'Dreaming?'

'Everyone's dreaming about a man in the north,' Mel said. 'Sounds stupid I know, but people say he's building an army and heading here, to Harlech.'

'There are other dreams as well,' Matt said. 'The castle for instance – I've dreamt about this place loads; past events I guess, but sometimes I'm sure I've seen glimpses of the future – especially when I've been holding the…' He trailed off, feeling uncomfortable.

'When you've been holding that old chalice?' Gerry nodded. 'It seems to me that the cup is playing tricks on your mind.'

'No, the chalice is wonderful,' Mel said. 'Even more so now that we're at the castle. Just touch it and you get zapped with something – it's one hell of a sensation - images flash through your brain so quickly you can't take them in. I don't know, it… it's a bit like a computer zip file I suppose, because at night, when you're asleep, it sort of deciphers itself and then you start to dream.'

'And it's so vivid,' Matt added, leaning forward. 'Frightening at times, but also kind of addictive.' He felt embarrassed admitting the fact. 'We're all using it every night now, can't seem to sleep otherwise.'

'Can't you now?' The Irishman tapped the whiskey bottle. 'Well, if you don't mind I think I'll be sticking to this.'

Eddie wandered over towards them, his gangling frame silhouetted by the fires. 'Grubs up,' he said. 'You'd better w…wake Father Peter - Joe's started to carve the m…meat.'

They all ate together, in the communal building, the six Chinese sat huddled in one corner; Gerry sat nearby, whispering to Ryan and Amy who both kept erupting with giggles at whatever he was telling them. The rest of them were seated in two small arcs facing each other and chatting; Rupert though, hardly spoke and Matt could see that the poor man was still deeply depressed at the loss of his daughter.

'Those Chinese lads are quite r…remarkable,' Eddie whispered, nodding in their direction and as he did so, all six of them glanced over. 'According to Gerry, every one of them can s…spear a chicken at fifty yards!'

After they had eaten, they cracked another bottle of whiskey and Gerry surprised them all yet again, by producing a small wooden whistle from his tunic. 'Fancy a sing-song anybody?' His slurred, Irish accent was stronger than ever. 'I fashioned this out of a willow branch.'

Without invitation he entered into a rendition of Molly Malone and before long, most of them were singing along. This was much to the amusement of the Chinese party who obviously thought the singers had lost their minds. Even Tank did his best to join in, mimicking their words with amusing inaccuracy, but only Father Peter knew more than the first verse and after the fifth tuneless chorus of "Alive, alive O!" Gerry grew impatient and moved on to play something different - this time, a quite impressive version of 'Whiskey in the Jar.' At this, Joe and Nic jumped up to perform an impromptu Irish jig, with Baxter, howling excitedly and leaping around them. Everyone joined in the chorus, repeatedly booming out "Whack for the daddy O," until eventually the whiskey in the jar, not to mention that in the bottle, finally came to an end and they all collapsed, laughing onto the floor.

There was a silent pause before Nic spoke. 'Let's get the cup,' he said, looking to Father Peter for approval.

Matt saw the concern on the old priest's face. Father Peter had tried to dissuade the others from overexploiting the powers of the chalice, but over the weeks the ritual of passing the cup before retiring had become a habit within the group. Matt knew that the things it showed them were sometimes disturbing and the nightmares they suffered affected them all. Tanya in particular, was becoming more and more withdrawn and Matt suspected that the things she saw troubled her more than most, but for some reason they all constantly craved to hold the cup and feel its energy.

Reluctantly the old priest reached for his bag as an uncomfortable silence filled the shelter. Those who were familiar to the ritual felt suddenly awkward sharing it with the newcomers in the camp, but they all watched in silent anticipation as the priest carefully unwrapped and exposed the chalice. Those who didn't know what to expect gasped as the cup started to pulse with light in the priest's grip.

Father Peter closed his eyes for a moment before handing the cup to Mel whom, on receiving it, visibly shuddered as if she had been shot with adrenaline. The next in line was Tanya who grimaced as she received the artefact; she held it in trembling hands for several moments before hurriedly passing it on. Eddie grasped the chalice and he grinned insanely as he clutched the cup to his chest. Then it was Matt's turn - as soon as his fingers touched the cool metal stem his mind was engulfed with a strobe of images, which blinded him with their vivid intensity. The sensation soon subsided and Matt offering the cup to Gerry O'Donnell. The

Irishman smiled, but shook his head, holding up the empty whisky bottle. Matt smiled back and turned to the second oldest man present.

'You've held it before Rupert,' he said. 'But it's much more intense now, you want to try it?'

The ex-magistrate held out a shaking hand and gingerly grasped the cup's golden stem. He jumped as if the metal was charged with electricity and his face paled, tears welling in his eyes as he hurriedly handed the cup back to Matt. Matt guessed what the old man had visualised. They had never told Rupert the horrific details of the terrible night in Bala and Matt didn't envy the poor man's dreams tonight.

And so the cup passed between them - to some the sensation was familiar and strangely comforting, to others it was new and frightening, but none were unmoved by the experience. That night they dreamed, among other things, of the scarred man in the north. While they slept, no one saw Rupert enter the northwest tower and climb its dark narrow staircase towards the battlements above.

Matt woke to the cries of gulls and distant barking and noticed that shards of light were already penetrating the lean-to's ceiling. The sun was already rising above the castle's eastern wall and he realised they had overslept. He turned over and as the sunlight caught his eye he recognised, for the first time in months, a headache born of too much alcohol. Beside him, Mel yawned before drowsily rolling over and snuggling up against his naked body. Her smooth, warm skin felt so good against him that his mind was consumed with sudden desire, but he knew it was late and others might already be milling around outside, so he pushed such thoughts from his mind and kissed her instead on the forehead. 'Good morning, beautiful,' he said, cheerfully.

'What time is it?' Mel groaned, clenching her fists and arching her back. Dangling between her breasts, the small brass compass glinted in the morning sun - a symbol of their commitment to each other. She stretched her naked body with such unintentional seduction that Matt forced himself to look away.

'It's late,' he said, turning his mind to the day ahead; now that Gerry was here the Irishman could supervise the fortification of the castle. Matt knew that the man's building skills would be invaluable and, for once, Matt could take a back seat, or even take a day off to explore the coastline beyond the castle.

'What's Baxter barking at?' Mel said, suddenly discovering her own minor hangover.

'He's out on the beach chasing gulls by the sound of it,' Matt said, kneeling to dress.

'Well, I wish he'd bloody shut up – I've got a headache.'

'Must be all that whiskey you were drinking.'

'Cheek! I had one cup - I'm pregnant remember!'

'I guess there'll be a few hangovers this morning – no one's used to alcohol anymore ' Matt said. 'Did you hear Tanya screaming last night?'

'Serves her right, she always has a bad night after holding the cup; I don't know why she does it. What about you, what did you dream of?'

'The usual,' Matt said. 'I think he's getting closer.'

'I know, I thought it might take him years to find us, but he already knows where we are.'

'And he recognises us,' Matt said. 'Somehow he even knows my name; probably he knows all of us. Why do you suppose he hates us so much?'

'I think he's scared of us – well, Father Peter mostly, and he wants the cup. He'll kill us all if he gets the chance - I'm really worried about the baby, Matt.'

'Father Peter's convinced that there's a force here that protects us more than the castle walls ever could, but even if he's right we should start preparing for a possible attack. If my dreams are anything to go by, this Arthur, as Tanya calls him, has amassed an army of hundreds, if not thousands. I'm not sure what we can do to stop them, but Gerry has agreed to help secure the castle. There are plenty of pairs of hands now, so I was wondering - how do you fancy a ride along the beach instead?'

'We can't, Matt; we moan at Tanya for not helping enough - she'd have a field day if we skive off.'

'Who said anything about skiving? We need to understand the lay of the land - from which direction an attack might come, that sort of thing.' Matt stroked his chin and grinned. 'Look, if you're not up for it, I could always ask…'

'Don't you dare, you bastard!' She grabbed him in a headlock and pulled him back down. Don't even think about leaving me grafting, while you and the wicked witch head off into the sunshine together.'

She knelt over him now, astride his body with her hands on her hips and pushing her breasts out indignantly. In the filtered sunlight, her pale body looked wonderful, but anxiety suddenly overwhelmed Matt again. He lay there for a moment, listening to Baxter's distant barking and feared for his new found happiness. Everything seemed so fragile now and the thought of losing Mel and what she was now carrying was unbearable.

'What *is* wrong with that bloody dog?' Mel said again.

'I don't know and I don't care. Come on, let's try and sneak away before we get roped into something.' Matt finished dressing and peered out from the shelter, squinting in the bright morning sunshine. The courtyard was deserted except for the odd hen pecking at the loose pathways. Damn, I should have followed my instincts, he thought lustily. But it was too late; Mel was already dressed. 'Come on, let's find Goliath,' he whispered, then he grabbed her hand and led her across the courtyard towards the gatehouse.

The gatehouse was deserted too, but they could see some of the townsfolk milling around the ruined buildings of Harlech. Matt ducked into a storeroom and returned, carrying one of the rucksacks and the shotgun. The gun was always clean and loaded now – nobody would make that mistake again.

'Where is everybody?' Mel asked.

'Don't know, but don't knock it. Come on, let's head north; no one's been in that direction yet and I'm sure that's the way the enemy will come.'

The fall to the sea at the northern end of the castle was not as steep as the rocky outcrops to the south and they were easily able to lead Goliath down between the rocks set in the grassy slopes that ran down to the beach. As they descended, they heard a shout and looked back towards the castle. Matt saw two figures up on the northwest tower and others looking out seaward from the battlements of the outer ward.

'That explains it,' he said. 'Another boat sighting! This time some other poor bastard can light the signal fire.'

'But there's nothing out there,' Mel said, scanning the ocean.

'Really? You surprise me!' Matt laughed. 'You know what Nic's like, I'm sure he's just winding us up.'

'Well I wish he wouldn't – he keeps getting Ryan's hopes up. It's not fair on the poor kid.'

'Come on; let's go before they spot us.'

Together they rode Goliath along the dunes with rolling waves crashing onto the beach to their left. It was a beautiful day and they might have been any normal young couple without a care in the world. The world was not the same though; subtle changes reminded them all the time. Only natural landmarks shaped the horizon now and the man-made structures they did encounter were already becoming overgrown with vegetation including the roads and footpaths. It was so quiet now, with just the sounds of gulls and the breaking waves - the sky seemed so blue and the air so fresh that it was as if they were on a different planet.

They rode for several miles before stopping to rest on an elevated grassy dune that offered a good view in all directions. Ahead of them the sand gave way to clay and beyond the mouth of a river they could just make out the ruins of a large town. To the east, a flat plain lay between them and the distant foothills that were the start of the Snowdonian Mountains. The whole area appeared deserted and they could see no smoke above the town. A mile or so back they thought they caught sight of people, high up to their right near what looked like a cave cut into the hillside, but the figures had disappeared so quickly that neither of them was sure that they had ever actually been there.

'I just know the attack will come from the north,' Matt said, pointing to the town. 'Arthur will never bring his army over the mountains, so they'll either come through that town and along the beach, or from further inland along the railway that runs right into Harlech.'

Mel pulled some rice cakes from the rucksack and handed one to Matt.

'It's funny isn't it?' She said. 'Somewhere out there there's a guy called Arthur, claiming to be the king of Britain and he's on a quest for a holy chalice. It's all a bit of a coincidence, don't you think?'

'Yeah, a coincidence of his making! The man's probably some nut infatuated with the legend and that's why he's so obsessed with us and the cup.'

'I'm not so sure. The world's changed, Matt; nothing makes sense now, strange things are happening to us all the time and we're not even shocked anymore. Think about it: telepathic people, visions, glowing cups – who knows? Perhaps this guy really is King Arthur!'

'Mel, the story is just a myth, created at a time when people still believed in magical swords. There is no magic Mel, only science – we just don't understand some things yet, that's all.'

'Perhaps there's no difference between magic and the science we don't understand. What if the legend of King Arthur isn't just a story from the past? Who says it's not an ancient prophecy of things to come? After all, even you now admit to seeing visions of the future.'

'Then I'll be Sir Lancelot,' Matt grinned, pulling her towards him, 'and you can be my Guinevere - come here and I'll impale you on my weapon.'

'Get off,' she said, pushing him away. 'Your weapon's caused enough trouble already; anyway Guinevere was Arthur's girl, not Lancelot's.' Her laughter fell away at the thought. 'It is just the cup he wants, isn't it, Matt?'

'Don't worry, if he's lusting after anyone, it'll be Tanya, not you – she's more the classic princess!'

'Bastard!' she said, grabbing him in another neck-lock. 'You'll pay for that remark!' They rolled over in the sand and Matt kissed her. Then they made love, high up on the dunes, in the sunshine and in full view of absolutely nobody.

By the time Mel and Matt returned to the castle the sun was large and low over the sea. They had returned by a different route, first heading inland until they found the crumbling, overgrown road and then they followed its direct route back into Harlech. They met no other people along the way but a small pack of scrawny dogs approached them near an old church in a tiny village a mile or so north of Harlech. Matt had killed one of the dogs with the shotgun and the others had scurried off into the undergrowth behind a broken graveyard. The church itself seemed intact and Matt made a mental note that it would be worth exploring when they had more time.

As they approached from the north, the castle was an impressive sight; its western wall shone in the late afternoon sun and its towers rose like majestic chess pieces from a giant board of craggy bedrock. To their left, fields of maize swayed in the warm breeze and swirls of grey smoke drifted up into the blue sky from both the town and from within the castle walls.

'I wonder how the building's going.' Matt said as they entered the gatehouse, but from the look of the empty courtyard there was very little activity. They walked across to the communal shelter where a fire burned; presumably a meal was cooking because it was neither cold nor very dark yet. They were right; as they entered the building, they saw a chicken roasting on the fire. Eddie and Father Peter sat either side of a huge oak table, each on the end of a sturdy bench; they both turned to Matt as he entered but neither spoke. Matt immediately realised that something was wrong.

'Nice table,' Matt said, wondering what the problem was. 'Looks like Gerry's handiwork.'

'Yes, h…he's out with Tank now, rebuilding the collapsed section of the outer w…wall.'

'Sit down boy,' Father Peter said. 'We've had quite a bad day.'

'Where is everyone?' Mel asked, anxiously.

'Ryan's taken young Amy to show her round the town,' Father Peter said. 'I think he's taken quite a shine to the girl. Oh, and Joe and Nic have gone hunting with the Chinese archers.' The old priest tried to sound upbeat but his eyes looked sad and tired.

'What's wrong Father?' Matt asked gently.

'Where the hell, w…were you?' Eddie sounded upset. 'What do you mean by going off like that, w…without telling anyone?

'I'm sorry, Eddie; just tell us what's happened?'

Father Peter rose stiffly from his seat. 'I'm afraid it's Rupert,' he said. 'We found him on the rocks this morning - or rather Baxter did. It would seem that the poor man must have jumped from the battlements.'

Chapter 3

The next morning Nic and Joe returned from their hunting trip, each carrying a small piglet. They had left the Chinese archers stalking the wild herd that roamed the woods above Harlech. The creatures bore no resemblance to the lumbering livestock that may once have grown fat in the pigsties of local breeders. The entropic disaster had wiped any agricultural domestication from their minds and the animals had now reverted to the basic instincts of their feral ancestors. Consequently, the larger animals were formidable foes - strong and fast, with powerful jaws and strong, sharp teeth and the primitive arrows did not easily penetrate their tough hides. Despite the inherent dangers, the two friends had been invigorated by the chase and it had helped them overcome the grief they felt following the discovery of Rupert's body on the rocks.

The growing population was not so easy to feed anymore and providing enough meat for them all was a demanding task. Survivors from the surrounding villages had started to arrive at Harlech - their primitive intellects apparently drawn like moths to the sanguine light radiating from the communal mind set of the townsfolk. Sheep were now confined to the lower hills and chickens were numerous within both the town and the castle, but their numbers had to be conserved for the onset of winter so wild animals were hunted whenever possible. Pork was now the favoured choice of the vast majority of the Harlech population because it cooked so well on an open fire.

When the two men reached the gatehouse they saw Gerry and Tank still working beneath the access platform. 'Hey Gerry!' Nic shouted. 'I thought the platform was all finished.'

'Pretty much, young fella,' Gerry shouted back. 'Just a few minor changes that Eddie came up with – a little surprise just in case the gate's not as strong as we think.'

Nic looked at huge oak doors, which now hung open on their original metal hinges and thought they looked impregnable. The doors comprised of roof members, strengthened and bolted together by thick steel bars and angle-iron; all ancient scrap recovered from the town's ruins.

'Looks pretty solid to me, man,' Nic said, intrigued as to the nature of the modifications, but knowing that further questioning might result in being roped into help, so he followed Joe into the gatehouse to dump the carcass in the storeroom. Nic continued on into the courtyard – he wanted to tell Matt that the hunters had spotted Big'un still lurking around in the woods. He ducked through the arched doorway in the west wall, which had now been fitted with a sturdy timber door and saw Matt on the outer-ward, hanging precariously over the edge of the wall re-pointing the stonework with clay from the beach.

'Careful, you don't end up on the rocks, dude…' Nic shouted, then he remembered Rupert and quickly changed the subject. 'Hey, guess what we're having for supper?'

Matt looked up, his face grimy and stained with sweat. 'Er… pig again?'

'Well yes, but its fresh pig!' Nic added cheerfully. 'Cheer up man, it's a beautiful day,' he grinned as he watched

Ryan and Amy emerge from the sea and run across the beach below them.

'Yeah, a beautiful day for swimming and hunting,' Matt grumbled. 'Some of us are bloody working though. Pass that clay over here would you?' Matt pointing at a bucket just out of his reach.

'Hunting's not as easy as you think. Those boars have got big teeth man, and all we have are Stone Age weapons; we could really use something more state of the art.'

'Eddie's already on the case; he's in the southeast tower working on the forge. He says the forced draft from the waste chute there is an ideal oxygen source for a furnace. He wants to make a kiln, too – for ceramics.'

'Seems we're getting real civilised,' Nic beamed. 'I might go and see if I can…' Suddenly he was distracted by something on the beach and his smile immediately faded.

'Nic, are you alright?'

'Something's wrong with the kids!' he said, and for the first time Matt heard the faint cries from below.

Matt scrambled to his feet and peered over the battlements, Ryan was sprinting towards the castle, followed by Amy, who stumbled momentarily in the sand, picked herself up and continued to chase frantically after her friend. Both children were shouting incoherently.

'What is it?' Matt called down to them. 'What's wrong?' Then, faintly on the afternoon breeze, he caught the Ryan's words.

'Boat!' The boy yelled. 'There's a boat coming!'

Matt looked up and scanned the horizon; suddenly he saw a distant sail, dirty white against the deep azure ocean.

Damn, he thought. There was no time to light a fire! 'Quick, get the shotgun!' he shouted.

Nic ran off through the arched doorway and disappeared into the courtyard. As he went, Matt heard him calling excitedly to the others.

The boat was maybe half a mile away and travelling north; it had already passed the castle and was now heading away from them. Matt waved his arms and shouted, but he knew that it was hopeless - the boat was too far away for anyone to see him, let alone hear his cries.

All of a sudden, Mel was at his side. 'Nic says there's a boat,' she gasped. 'Where is it?'

'Over there,' Matt pointed. 'Where the Hell is Nic?'

'Dunno, but Joe's gone to the tower to light a fire.'

Matt could hardly make out the sail now – they were going to be too late! Then Nic came crashing through the door; in his haste he stumbled to the ground and the shotgun slid along the grass towards Matt who grabbed it, checked it was loaded and rose the barrel. He fired into the sky and the gunshot echoed around the cliffs – they all watched the distant, diminishing sail.

'Fire again,' Nic said desperately.

'No, we can't afford the cartridges,' Matt said. 'If they didn't hear that, they…'

'Look, it's turning,' Mel said quietly. Then louder 'See, they're turning round!'

'It's coming back,' Nic confirmed, then he grabbed Mel and they both started jumping around, holding on to each other in their excitement.

Matt stared at the boat, urging it closer. 'Come on Joe,' he whispered to himself as he glanced up at the northwest tower. Suddenly there was smoke. 'Yes!' He shouted, punching the air. 'Quick, let's get down to the beach.'

* * * *

The dinghy bobbed over the breaking waves as it approached the shore and they could see two men on board; one holding the rudder and one frantically pulling down the dirty sail from a cross-member fastened to a makeshift mast and supported by thin ropes. The inflatable boat looked in good condition, but it was obviously not intended for sailing; having no keel, it pitched alarmingly in what was only a light wind.

At least twenty people lined the beach as they waited for the boat to land, including Baxter who was barking enthusiastically for the first time since finding his master's body on the beach. A few of the more curious townsfolk shuffled around nervously some way from the shoreline; they had learned so much recently, but the concept of floating transport was still beyond them.

In the front of the dinghy, one of the men finally managed to stow the sail and grabbing a rope, he jumped into the water. Striding through the waves, he pulled the boat towards the beach until the other man tossed another rope towards Nic, who caught it expertly and started pulling the dinghy onto the sand.

Matt stepped forward to greet the men who both wore dark trousers, sturdy boots and dirty, white sleeveless shirts.

'Andy Rainford,' the first man said, offering his hand.

Matt guessed the stranger was in his late forties; he was well built with cropped hair and was cleanly shaven. Both men carried side arms, holstered at their belts. Matt studied the men's shirt and noticed their shoulders were endorsed with badges, black with four yellow bands.

The man noticed his glance. 'Er, Captain Andy Rainford, Royal Navy,' he added. 'This is Warrant Officer, Jim Price.' The other man, who was younger and less well built, stepped forward and also shook hands.

'Welcome to Harlech,' Matt said. 'Boy, are we glad to see you?'

A few hours later, the communal building was developing a party atmosphere for the second time that week, but Matt and Mel sat alone with the senior officer on the grass of the outer ward gazing out to sea.

The captain explained that they were survivors of HMS Sabre, a fleet submarine that they had abandoned in two hundred metres of water a mile off the Irish coast. He told them that they had scuppered the vessel after receiving orders for an emergency shutdown of the pressurised water reactor and to wait to be recovered.

'Apparently there was some sort of national emergency,' he said. 'All nuclear reactors were being shut down until the situation could be recovered.'

'So how did you get out?' Mel asked.

'There was a rescue submersible in the area - an "LR5"; it makes a watertight seal onto the submarine's escape hatch,' he explained. 'We were the last fifteen to be recovered, but during transfer something happened and we lost contact with the host vessel. It was against procedures to surface without active communications, so we waited for more than an hour while we decompressed and then the battery power supplies started to fail.'

The captain paused; Matt could see that telling the story was distressing him. 'There was nothing there, was there?' he said. 'When you eventually surfaced I mean.'

'Just debris in the water... and bodies – a hundred men died; drowned probably, while we were waiting below.'

They all sat for a while in silence, looking out onto the ocean, and Matt thought of all the people he had seen killed over the last few months.

Eventually, the captain turned to face him. 'What happened?' he asked. 'Did we miss a war or something?'

Matt told him their story, well most of it. In the presence of a Captain of the Royal Navy he decided not to mention some of the mysterious things they had grown to accept recently, not least the visions they were experiencing and he left out any reference to Father Peter's cup.

'Why the castle?' The captain asked. 'No offence, but it's not exactly luxurious, is it?

'We're safe here,' Mel said indignantly. 'You may not have noticed, but there are some pretty unfriendly people around nowadays.'

'Yeah, sorry – I know there are. I forget sometimes – we've been fortunate, that's all.'

'You haven't had any trouble?' Matt asked incredulously.

'Of course - early on, but not since we crossed The Straits. We've made a settlement on Anglesey; the population there is pretty sparse and it's isolated from the mainland. The survivors tend to be most hostile in densely populated areas, especially the towns; I dread to think what the cities are like.'

'Don't tell me on Anglesey the natives are all friendly,' Matt said.

'No, they'd resorted to savagery just like everyone else; we had a huge fight in Bangor and a lot of people died. We've had a few scraps on the island as well, but we're on top of it now, I think. We've only explored part of the island and there may be thousands of others still out there, but we've got some decent weapons.' He tapped his pistol. 'Six Brownings and an assault rifle, but we don't tend to trust that because it keeps jamming on us.'

'All we've got is an old shotgun,' Matt said, 'and I'm afraid we're down to our last twenty cartridges - that's why we're holed up here, in the castle. Rumour has it the savages are getting organised out there, some even say there's an army moving south, headed up by a lunatic who claims he's the new king.'

'Have you built shelters on the island?' Mel asked. 'We've just started to construct something more substantial for the winter.'

'We have built some, but most of us have taken up in an old stately home. The roof's collapsed, but two floors are intact and the building's in quite good nick, well by today's standards, anyway.'

'We haven't found too many places left standing,' Matt said, 'apart from ancient buildings like this.'

'The stately home's fairly old, but quite a lot of other buildings survived. We've got some refugees from Cumbria who say their farms were completely unaffected by the disaster. According to them, there's a little valley up there undamaged and with everything just sitting there - buildings, even a few cars all intact and just abandoned!'

'Then, what happened?' Mel asked in disbelief. 'Why did they leave?'

'Sellafield happened,' the captain said. 'The old nuclear plant must have gone up; some of the survivors are really sick, and so are some of their horses. They drove their whole herd south to avoid the fallout; lucky for us really, horses are valuable now.'

'How many of you are there?' Matt asked.

'Our little community's up to about a hundred and fifty, but a lot were – you know – afflicted by the disaster. Apart from my crew, the only unaffected survivors are two co-pilots from the LR5, the farming families from Cumbria and three lads who were caving on the island. That's fifty-nine of us who can remember the way things were. All the others have relied on us to teach them how to survive, but it's already hard to tell the difference. They pick things up so quickly, they can all talk now and every man Jack of them can already ride better than I can.'

'What if this army really does exist?' Matt asked. 'Do you think you're safe from them?'

The captain shrugged. 'On Anglesey, we've got nearly a hundred fit men who can fight if necessary and we've got a few modern weapons so we can probably defend ourselves. I can't believe such primitive minds would be able to organise themselves well enough to trouble us and even if they did, they've got to get across the Menai Straits and the bridges are down.'

'You must have somehow got across,' Mel said.

'At the narrowest point it's just a few hundred metres wide, but it's only possible to cross when the powerful currents abate between the tides, that's about an hour, twice a day. The water's like a millpond then, and you can cross, but only in the summer. Soon we'll be completely cut off from the mainland and the island will be inaccessible until the spring; hopefully by then, we'll have the island's population under control and after that, nobody will be strong enough to bother us.'

Gerry came to let them know the food was nearly ready. 'Come on you lot,' he said. 'The grub's up and you're missing all the shenanigans.' So they all stood up and followed the Irishman back into the courtyard where, once again, the wonderful aroma of roasted pork waited to greet them.

Just before they joined the others, Matt paused and turned to the captain. 'So why the boat?' he asked.' Where have you been?'

'Looking for people like you to rescue!' the captain said. 'Nobody's safe on the mainland. We've come to take you to Anglesey.'

'But we can't,' Matt said. 'We have to stay here…'

Gerry, who was just behind them, placed his hand on Matt's shoulder. 'Don't be too hasty, fella,' he said. 'That young seaman's been telling me some tales; it seems they're all living the life of Riley over there and if you're thinking any of us would choose to stay in this old stone coffin, then I'm afraid you're not the full shilling. Gerry O'Donnell, for one, will be going with them.'

Matt made as if to argue, but the Irishman shook his head. 'Mark my words young fella,' his face unusually stern. 'If the others have got any sense, I'll not be going alone.'

Chapter 4

Yarik clung desperately to the neck of the hill-beast as it bolted down the slope towards the trees. The creature – a horse, the others called it – had gone berserk after being jabbed in its flank by a sharp weapon. The guard responsible was a bad tempered brute who obviously begrudged having to teach the newcomers horse-craft, but Yarik knew that this particular act of provocation had been driven by a more sinister motive. Yarik had been singled out from the moment he and the guard had been paired together for combat at the Round Table. Tomorrow would be Yarik's first test at the stone plinth where individual warriors fought to the death. Victory would bring him promotion to the King's Elite Guard and he would be branded with the mark of Pendragon, but Yarik knew that such a victory was unlikely. His opponent already bore the mark, having twice emerged victorious from the table and knowing that a third victory would bring the guard immunity from future challenges. For all his cunning, Yarik knew he was no match for the more powerful man, and his opponent must have known it too, but this didn't stop the guard abusing his authority by attempting to injure Yarik at every opportunity, just to gain an advantage in the arena.

  Despite the fact that he was the smallest of the surviving newcomers, the guard had paired Yarik with the largest and worst tempered of all the horses. He had been ordered to try and mount the fearsome stallion, which had towered over him, stamping the ground belligerently. It had taken several days of painful tumbles before the animal had eventually tolerated bearing the weight of Yarik's battered body, but even then he had very little control over the creature. Eventually though, slowly and surely, Yarik had managed to earn the stallion's respect despite the constant acts of cruel intimidation by the devious guard. Unfortunately, all control was now lost again as the frightened animal plummeted towards the woods.

Yarik could hear the guard laughing behind him as his horse careered down the slope. He knew he had a choice to make - try and regain control of the animal, or jump off before they reached the wood. He knew from experience that bailing out was the safest option, because to be thrown amongst the trees could be lethal, but falling at speed anywhere was risky and incurring even a minor injury ahead of tomorrow's trial might have fatal consequences.

Yarik stared down at the ground which seemed so far away as it rushed past in a blur of green and yellow then, looking up at the fast approaching trees, he made his decision. Letting go of the animal's neck, he kicked himself away and curled into a ball. His back hit the ground first and he felt something crack as he rolled, skidding in excruciating pain across the soft grass towards the wood. He came to rest, stunned and winded, among tall, coarse weeds near the roots of a large beech tree.

Fighting the spasm that was preventing him from drawing much-needed oxygen into his lungs, Yarik saw his mount's thudding hooves disappear into the woods. Gradually he managed to gasp his first shallow breaths of air - so precious, despite being tainted by the rank-smelling foliage around him. As he recovered his composure, it came to him that something about the putrid smell was familiar. A memory of the past perhaps, or maybe just animal instinct, but something was focusing his attention on the tall coarse weeds with their large trumpet-like flowers and prickly spores.

Gingerly, Yarik got to his knees and curiously sniffed one of the flowers but the pain in his side reminded him of his dilemma - another injury and another advantage to his adversary. He turned and faced the laughing guard who now rode towards him. Other novices sat on their horses in the distance, presumably grateful that they were not subject to the same level of abuse that their stricken comrade had to endure. As his tormentor approached, Yarik realised the hopelessness of his situation; the grotesque face beneath the guard's shaven head sneered at his pathetic rival. The Mark of Pendragon, burnt into the man's forehead was testimony to his superiority; the muscles bulging beneath his tailored furs made him look invincible. Suddenly, without really knowing why, Yarik plucked several of the prickly spores from the rancid smelling plant and quickly stuffed them into his tunic. Then the grinning guard promptly kicked him in the side and laughed at the agony it caused. Not wishing to display further weakness, Yarik rose defiantly to his feet and stood tall and proud, despite his suffering.

'I'm afraid you've lost your horse,' the guard smirked. 'Come on, my little friend – you can ride with me. Can't have you sneaking away before we meet at the table tomorrow or I might have to face someone worthy of my blade.' He laughed again as he held out his hand and pulled Yarik painfully up onto the horse behind him.

Sitting so close behind the powerful guard emphasised to Yarik, the difference in their physiques. His eyes were level with his adversary's thick grimy neck and the man's shoulders seemed immense in comparison to his own. Yarik looked down at the water bag bouncing against the guard's muscular thigh and realised that he stood no chance against this brute. Then a painful scratching against his chest reminded him of the prickly spores he had collected. Pulling them from his tunic he squashed one with his thumbs and immediately remembered where he had seen them before. These were the plants that some of his party had eaten on their long journey north. He remembered how they had all fallen sick - feverish and disoriented and suffering excruciating stomach pains, they had grown so weak that they could hardly stand. Yarik and the other healthy refugees had left them to die and he had never seen the foul smelling plants again - until today. Yarik stared at the damp furry seeds oozing from the husk – these plants make men sick, he realised - so weak they can hardly stand! Suddenly an idea formed in his mind and he quickly pulled the notion back into his head, mindful that the guard might read his thoughts. Carefully he pulled the water bag nearer, removed the wooden stopper and dropped in the seeds.

Arthur climbed up the steps of the arena wall towards a dark, star-filled sky. He wanted to be alone with Merlin so that they could confer in private. Recently the nights had been very warm and Arthur's shelter stifled him so he regularly climbed up onto the wall where the night air helped to clear his mind. He took his seat and looked out at the hundreds of small fires burning below. The fires were essential to light the encampment and they also served to deter the scavenging creatures that seemed to be growing in numbers with every day that passed. Rats were prevalent in the cities but they were now spreading to the outskirts and were attracted by the encampment. The guard dogs caught some vermin in the woods but many more made it through into the camp and wherever they scavenged, disease followed.

The numerous fires were a measure of Arthur's growing army – they were close to two thousand now, despite some falling to disease. Two thousand was the optimum number that could be sustained as a mobile unit – and they were all prime specimens, selected from only the strongest survivors of the human race. The selection process he had introduced was designed to cull any weakness that existed within their ranks. All that remained now was to complete the training, but it was taking longer than Arthur had expected and he was growing impatient.

'We are short of horses,' Merlin said from within. 'So many have been killed for food here.'

'If only half can ride we may as well all march,' Arthur growled, 'and we shall have wasted weeks of preparation.'

'Send the horsemen first then,' Merlin suggested. 'The rest can follow – if they are needed.'

'No, splitting the army will only encourage rebellion; my influence will be weakened. Anyway, I want our enemies to despair at the sight of the force I have mustered; I want them to throw themselves down before me and to beg for my mercy. When they see my army, they will acknowledge my sovereignty and if they don't worship me, I will put them to death.'

'How will you do that, Arthur?' Merlin whispered inside his head. 'How will you punish them? ...You could crucify them I suppose – don't you think crucifixion would a suitable demise for those who plotted against you?'

A smile crept across Arthur's face; he knew that Merlin sometimes used him to satisfy his own desires, but he cared not. 'I suppose crucifixion would be a fitting end,' he said. 'How ironic it would be for that self-righteous old priest to be nailed to the very cross he worships.' The thought brought new motivation to Arthur and he stood up, shouting for his captain. Almost immediately, the black warrior appeared out of the shadows below and bounded up the steps.

'Tomorrow will be the last of the Round Table trials,' Arthur announced. 'At the next moon we will march south, taking only the horses necessary for reconnaissance. The same applies to the women, take only those essential to our needs, the others can be sacrificed; any soldiers not bearing the mark of Pendragon by the time we leave should also be destroyed.'

The captain bowed, turned and without speaking, made off down the stairs. Arthur felt immediately relieved - he knew it would be a long march and it might take them a number of weeks to reach the castle, but the decision had at last been made. His army was finally heading south to claim the golden chalice – his knights were going to war!

Suddenly, Arthur sensed another mental presence and he immediately looked southwest, into the darkness where someone had just penetrated his thoughts. The presence he felt was from afar - it was not the priest this time, but one of the females, the skinny one. The woman was familiar to Arthur and he despised her because he knew she was a doctor of the mind. Her sort put labels on people: borderline, manic, neurotic, schizophrenic, psychotic, psychopathic – they would label anybody they couldn't understand. They thought themselves superior to those they categorised, but they were wrong - the human brain was far more complex than they realised. They had once labelled Arthur, believing that they understood his psyche, but his mind was far beyond their comprehension. He knew, because he had often visited the dark recesses of the minds of others. Only Arthur truly understood the intricate workings of the insane because he had so often delved into their brains. He had also delved into the minds of those deemed to be sane, including the very doctors who treated him and what he had sometimes seen there, hidden and constrained by some subconscious morality, had occasionally shocked even Arthur.

    Now, once again, he was connected to the mind of one of those who would presume to judge him and he knew she was unaware of his presence. Arthur had perceived the woman's thoughts the moment she had peered into the golden chalice - his chalice! He controlled his fury and focused on the woman – there were people with her; their numbers were growing and they were building, strengthening and preparing defences. There were newcomers – two men with a boat and guns; people around her were laughing but despite this, the woman was afraid of something – what was she scared of? Arthur delved deeper, tracing the tendrils of her fear and then suddenly he found its source – she was fearful for her unborn child! And so she should be, Arthur thought, for I am coming to ruin the party. Suddenly the woman sensed his menace and was aware of his intrusion for the first time. Arthur felt her fears intensify just before she managed to close her mind to him. Another presence now – a man this time. This one's mind represented everything Arthur hated about the world - a man who worshiped technology and grieved its demise. In other circumstances, Arthur might have feared this man for he had the capability to compromise his plans, but the man was weak and lacked the strength of character to challenge him; just a weak-willed coward who would one day grovel at the king's feet. Before Arthur could probe further, the cup was passed on again - another man, young and unafraid filled his mind, but this mind was immature and naïve – nothing for Arthur to fear. Then another - physically powerful, but lacking the wit to present a threat. Arthur glimpsed into each of their minds and gained snippets of information from each one. He learned their numbers, their fears and their ambitions; he sensed pockets of conflict and uncertainty among them that perhaps, if the opportunity arose, could be used to undermine their unity. Another man took the cup now, and Arthur immediately recognised the mind of their reluctant leader and smiled. This was more interesting - Arthur had enjoyed the mental connections he had previously shared with this mind because the man had mental insecurities and was haunted by his past. Arthur liked to probe this troubled mind, searching the darkest places for painful, sleeping memories to poke awake, but for some reason, just lately this had been much harder to achieve. Somehow the man had found a new resolve and the means to close the door on his past. Arthur knew that this one, without his demons, could become dangerous, so he made a mental note to seek him out early and mitigate the risk. Then the man was gone and Arthur was connected with another woman. This one's mind was complicated but in a way, easier to understand. This was because Arthur knew she shared many of his own values and for that reason he sometimes allowed her access to his own thoughts. He would open his mind so that she could share his passion, experience his power and be in awe of him. He knew that she had grown to both yearn and dread the connection and that she sometimes teetered on the edge of insanity when he spoke to her, teasing and playing with her emotions. Arthur knew that she could not feel his torment now, but soon she would experience it in dreams that would twist her unconscious mind and feed her obsessions. He sensed that one of the woman's many obsessions was Arthur himself – and that particular obsession was growing.

Many minds entered his own that night and then retreated again unconsciously troubled by the experience, but the one that Arthur craved the most did not materialise. The priest rarely took the cup nowadays because he knew how exposed he had become. The old man had the strength of mind to actually converse with Arthur and to read his thoughts, but in doing so he paid a terrible price because the things the priest saw filled him with doubt. The old man was fragile and so was his faith; Arthur knew that given the opportunity, he had the power to destroy them both. The priest knew it too.

* * * *

The two naked men stood facing each other on opposite sides of the circular granite plinth; a platform that had once been the base of a statue of a sporting legend from the football field. All that now remained of the statue was its bronze anchor - a thick, round staple embedded in the centre of the plinth. Threaded through the staple now, was a thick, frayed rope, the ends of which were tied to the right ankle of each contestant. Surrounding the plinth, hundreds of men and women jostled for positions that might offer a better view of the impending duel. The beat of a slow, dull drum from somewhere behind the crowd added to the atmosphere of the occasion, which served as rare entertainment for the pleasure-deprived population of Arthur's encampment. The majority of the crowd knew what it meant to stand on Arthur's round table and face another warrior in deadly combat, but those watching had all emerged victorious from the contest and so revered the very concept of the event.

The combatant with his back to the sun had the advantage of unimpaired vision and was by far the largest and most powerful of the two men. The muscular warrior was shaven headed, a human jawbone hung from a leather thong around his neck and he bore the mark of Pendragon on his wide forehead. In his right hand he gripped a heavy, wooden-bodied mace, with seventeen metal spikes bound by iron supports protruding from its head. Whilst the mace had been created recently - its spikes having been hammered into shape at a nearby forge - in his left hand, the man held an evil looking remnant from the past. A primitive hay-baling instrument - a wooden-handled hook that he had found among the rubble and had painstakingly re-sharpened into a wicked point.

The smaller man had only a single weapon, preferring to utilise his other hand to bear a thin, buckled metal plate to serve as a primitive shield. His weapon was also forged at the local fires and was more akin to a sword than a club. A metal bar had been hammered flat to form a blade that splayed wide at its end so that it was shaped like a pelican's beak. A number of fjord-like cracks had formed under the hammer giving the sharpened blade a serrated edge and its handle was grooved and wrapped in leather to improve the grip.

Yarik stared at his adversary, looking for a sign of weakness. The huge man looked ill and was sweating profusely, but he was still standing and staring back with accusing eyes as if he somehow knew that his opponent had caused his sickness. The man's stomach heaved and he gagged, spewing vomit onto the blood-stained granite floor just as the drumming stopped and a horn sounded to signal the start of the contest. The crowd cheered at the sound and Yarik started to circle the perimeter of the arena, brandishing his strange sword in front of him. His opponent recovered from his nausea and also started to circle, maintaining their distance apart. Suddenly he kicked his right leg backwards, pulling on the rope and unbalancing Yarik so that he fell to one knee. The larger man screamed a battle cry and charged; the crowd yelled with him as he bore down on the smaller man and swung the spiked mace towards his head. Yarik rolled over, narrowly avoiding the blow and slashed his weapon at the guard's legs catching his right thigh with the tip of the blade. Yarik had drawn first blood, but it was little more than a scratch and did not seem to hinder the larger man as he turned and swung again at Yarik's skull. This time, Yarik deflected the blow with his shield, but the force nearly broke his arm. He tried to clamber to his feet but his legs had become entangled with the rope and he stumbled. The baling hook caught him in the shoulder and the evil-looking implement dragged him painfully backwards.

Pulling free and spinning towards his foe, Yarik thrust his weapon at the guard's stomach and it drew blood, but again the wound was not deep enough to cause serious damage. His blade was designed for slashing, not stabbing and the blow did no more than to cause his opponent to retreat. Yarik finally got to his feet, but he was bleeding badly from his punctured shoulder. He tried to raise the metal plate in readiness for the next attack, but it was too painful, so he threw the shield to the ground and also backed away from the fight. The two men stood apart, evaluating each other's damage as the crowd roared encouragement to attack. Both men were bleeding, but only Yarik's wound was serious enough to affect the fight. The larger man must have realised this because he started to grin, but the taunting smile was interrupted as he suddenly heaved again, bile rising to into his mouth. His stomach was empty from a long night of vomiting, but he still retched uncontrollably and doubled up from the pain in his abdomen.

Yarik saw his opportunity and charged, swinging his weapon hard at his distracted opponent and this time the blade did its job. It cut deep into the guard's right bicep, severing its tendons and rendering the arm useless - the man screamed in agony and the spiked mace clattered to the granite floor. The crowd roared their approval as the larger man fell to his knees, weakened more from his poison than from his wounds; his head lolled back and his eyes rolled backwards in their sockets. Yarik took one step forward and swung his sword with every ounce of his remaining strength. The heavy weapon met the guard's exposed throat and rendered both flesh and bone with the sickening thud of a butcher's cleaver. The partially decapitated head toppled backwards and slowly slid down the back of the still-standing guard, peeling a long strip of skin away from his spine as it descended. The crowd fell silent as the massive warrior slumped to the ground in an expanding pool of blood. Then they cheered wildly, partly for the one who had just joined their ranks, but also each in memory of their own cruel victories. Savagery was their only value now, and victory in battle was all that mattered.

Chapter 5

Yarik looked on nervously as the two sweating men worked the fire. The forge was dug into the ground, lined with stones and filled with burning coals. The flames pulsed orange to white, orange to white, in synch with a regular "foarr-whoaring" sound. A tunnel of air fed the flames from below, driven by leather bellows, furiously pumped by a heavily built man. The other blacksmith stabbed the glowing embers with a leather-handled iron bar, the end of which, glowed cherry red. Embedded in the coals, the V-shaped end of the branding iron sat waiting to burn the Mark of Pendragon into Yarik's skin.

    Up until now, the initiation process to become one of the King's Elite Knights had been one of unprecedented indulgence for Yarik who had never before experienced such exquisite and gratifying pleasure. It had started from the moment he was offered his choice in females; at least thirty young women had been presented to him and they were all prime specimens selected by the King himself. These were the breeding stock for a flawless race of warriors that would one day become an invincible army, serving Arthur into his old age. Of all the females Yarik could have selected, something drew him to a familiar figure – he chose the young woman with stars on her rump - the mate who had accompanied him on his journey north. The female's joy at being chosen was unmistakable and Yarik wondered at the strange emotional bond that had formed between them. The female was one of the non-speakers, but she was attentive and well drilled in the initiation process because she had already been chosen on two previous occasions. Yarik understood that his mate would serve at least three other men, but at least they were reunited. The female fed and bathed Yarik; then shaved his head and face using a special blade that she had personally honed over many days. Then they mated before she was finally led away to be returned to the females camp.

Such brief pleasures were unsurpassed in Yarik's short memory but now, staring into the glowing embers, he did not feel quite so comfortable. A small crowd had gathered to witness the final stage in the initiation process and as the blacksmith drew the glowing branding iron from the forge, Yarik perceived painful memories emanating from their minds.

The larger of the two blacksmiths abandoned the bellows and stood behind Yarik, grabbing him forcefully and pinning his arms to his sides. The other advanced with the iron, grinning as he came. Yarik grimaced as he felt the heat radiating from the inverted 'V', which glowed through smoke as it neared his forehead.

'Wait!' The shouted command suddenly halted the proceedings.

The hefty blacksmith immediately released Yarik who turned to see the crowd parting as a band of soldiers approached. Amid the troop strode the king himself, dressed in fine furs and wearing the spiked metal helmet, which served as his crown. The king was flanked by a dozen of his favourite knights, including the Captain of the Guard whose dark skin contrasted with the pale, leopard skin cloak he wore. Arthur held aloft his shining sabre, which seemed so elegant in comparison to Yarik's primitive weapon and the king's dark venomous eyes drilled into him.

'What is your name?' Arthur asked.

Yarik felt his mind ravaged and fought to repel the violation. 'They call me Yarik,' he said.

'I am told your victory, at the table today, was an unexpected one.'

'I used the skills I have been taught,' Yarik said.

'Liar!' The king snarled and Yarik's head suddenly exploded with pain; he sank to his knees.

'Do you think I'm oblivious to your devious ways?' Arthur continued. 'I can see your mind, just as I can see the minds of all my people. You poisoned one of my knights, letting him die in his own vomit while you bask in undeserved glory.'

Yarik hung his head in submission and waited for the king to reap his punishment. Arthur raised his sword high above his head and swung it down towards Yarik's neck but the blow never struck; instead, the blade stopped in mid-air.

'But I admire an inventive mind,' the king said. 'So long as its owner can be trusted.' He slowly lifted Yarik's chin with the blade of his sword until their eyes met. 'Can you be trusted, Yarik?'

Yarik squirmed under the king's scrutiny but finally managed to reply. 'With your life,' he said.

Arthur's mental intrusion delved deeper into Yarik, probing for thoughts of deception. 'We'll see!' Arthur finally said, before slamming the hilt of his sword against the side of the kneeling man's head; Yarik slumped to the ground in an unconscious heap.

Yarik woke to the sound of a growling dog. He was lying on his side in soft earth amongst trees and he was not alone. In his arms, lying in the foetal position and sleeping peacefully was his mate - the female with the stars. Yarik was parched, desperate for water and his head thumped; he drifted in and out of consciousness for a while before his mind focused on the sound of the dog. He lifted himself onto one elbow and looked towards the sound. It was late in the day and the light was fading but he could make out the dark shape of one of the camp's guard dogs no more than fifteen feet away. As soon as he moved the growling intensified, but Yarik realised that the animal must be tethered to one of the trees – it was one of the many dogs that guarded the perimeter forest. The animals helped to keep out the rats and deterred predators, but their main purpose was to raise the alarm in the unlikely event that intruders should enter the forest.

The girl stirred and sat up groggily and he saw that she was naked – then he realised they both were. He quickly felt his neck for the human jawbone but it was gone; without it Yarik no longer held any status in the king's army. Suddenly the girl became aware of the growling and started to panic, but Yarik calmed her, sending her a mental image of the rope restraining the animal and she relaxed. Yarik turned towards the encampment – half a mile away he could see the fires burning and he felt a sudden longing to be among them again, with his people. Then he saw something silhouetted by the distant fires - twenty feet away, his own sword was embedded in the earth, the blade's unusual shape unmistakable even in the poor light. There was something else with the sword -

hanging around its hilt was the precious jawbone that he had earned on his very first night in Arthur's camp.

Gingerly, Yarik got to his feet and for the first time he noticed that one of his ankles was tethered to a rope; it brought back memories of his combat at the Round Table. He knelt and attempted to free himself, but the knot was tight and sealed with tar. The girl was tied up in a similar manner and both their ropes trailed across the forest floor towards where the hungry dog salivated over their scent. Yarik realised that this was his punishment - they had been left in the forest to die of thirst, or face the dog in the hope that they could untie the other ends of their ropes. Yarik motioned the girl to stay still and he crept forward towards the animal. The growling intensified before erupting into frenzied barks. The huge animal lunged at him but fell just short, restrained by an unseen leash. The dog was thickset with a wide head and huge jaws; it was the largest of its kind that Yarik had ever seen – he knew that to face it naked and unarmed would be suicide, but then he remembered his sword. If he could just reach his weapon he might stand a chance, but then it dawned on him – if he could retrieve the sword he could use it to cut the rope, he didn't have to face the animal at all.

Crawling across the dirt, towards the blade, he passed his mate who sat with her arms around her knees watching him. He crawled another yard before the rope attached to his ankle grew taut. Turning round, he tugged at it and it gave some slack, but he saw his mate fall to her side and she cried out. He returned to check on her but she was unhurt and he wondered if their ropes were tangled. He tried again and this time he made it a little closer to the sword before the rope restrained him. He gave it another tug, but once again the girl was dragged suddenly towards the dog. Then at last he understood their predicament; there was only one rope! Attaching him to his mate, it was looped around something at the tree, a low branch probably. He could probably reach the sword, but in doing so he would drag his mate towards the tree and into the jaws of the waiting animal.

Yarik stared into the darkness towards the unseen, growling animal - there had to be a way. Perhaps he could gain enough rope to reach the sword without pulling his mate into the animal's reach. How could he find out? If he tried to drag her towards the animal she would struggle against him and there was a danger he would pull her too far. How far was too far? That was the question. He crawled back past his mate, towards the dog; the nearer he got, the more frenzied the animal became. He was just a few feet away now and growls turned to furious barking and as he moved nearer still, the animal lurched recklessly at him, still restrained by the unseen rope. Against his every instinct, Yarik crept even nearer until he could feel the animal's putrid breath on his face as it barked. The dog was going berserk now, but still Yarik edged closer, ignoring the spittle spraying his face - if the dog's leash snapped or even slackened, Yarik was finished. Deafened by the animal's furious onslaught, Yarik picked up a stone and thought about striking the dog, but he knew such a small rock would only anger the creature more. He looked around for a heavier weapon, but the ground had been stripped of anything that he might have used. Beyond the dog though, there were many potential weapons – scattered over the ground were human bones – scraps from Arthur's Round Table.

Yarik forced himself to turn his back on the rabid animal and tried to gauge the distance between him and his mate and whether he had earned enough slack for her to reach the weapon. She stared at him, petrified, hugging her knees and rocking back and forth. Yarik forced an image of his sword at the girl hoping that he could persuade her to try and retrieve it, but he could feel the turmoil in her mind and knew she would not respond. Yarik couldn't concentrate with the furious racket a few inches behind him, so he decided to move away from the ravenous creature and return to his mate. Before he did so, he drew a line in the earth with the stone. It marked their zone of safety from the animal.

It took Yarik a long time to pacify the female and by the time he had managed it, the dog too had grown quiet. He held his mate for what seemed like hours, trying to think of a way to retrieve his weapon without putting either of them at risk. If he could get to it quick enough, he might be able to run back and slay the animal before it killed the girl, but to do so he would have to persuade her to run at the animal and he knew that would be impossible. He had to do something, though - Yarik had been thirsty many times, but he had never before needed water so desperately. His dehydrated body had lost a lot of blood from the shoulder wound and was growing weaker by the minute. He knew that the longer he waited, the less chance he would have against the animal.

After what seemed like an eternity, the dog eventually quietened and Yarik assumed it had fallen asleep. He waited a while longer then he gently roused the girl and put his fingers to her mouth, mentally imploring her to stay silent. Then he took her hand and cautiously moved forwards again, beckoning her to follow. At first she resisted, shaking her head fearfully, but he calmed her and sent her another mental message - trust me, it said.

Inch by inch they crept forward in perfect silence, a skill they had developed on their long and dangerous journey north together. Yarik knew that if the dog woke now and resumed its deafening assault on them he would not be able to encourage his mate to close the gap further, but the animal was nowhere to be seen - it was either preoccupied or more likely, still asleep. Eventually, incredibly, they reached the line he had drawn without attracting the animal's attention and Yarik turned to the girl. He had to persuade her to stay here while he returned to the weapon. He touched her cheek with the back of his hand and smiled at her - she returned the smile, but her eyes were wide with fear. Yarik knew that any little thing could send her into blind panic, so he pointed at the line in the earth and gave a mental image of safety, he looked into her eyes and saw that she understood. Yarik didn't know why she couldn't speak - many never did, but it was nothing to do with a lack of intelligence - possibly it was even the opposite, he thought.

Yarik took hold of the girl's ankle and gently moved her foot towards the line. Then he made a chopping movement with his hand – keep your foot here but don't let it cross the line he tried to explain. She nodded, seemingly understanding the instruction. He took the rope and coiled the slack near her leg, then he held up both hands, palms towards her and started to move away. Immediately her eyes widened again and she shook her head. Yarik paused and put his fingers to her lips and then made the same gesture with his hands, this time mentally assuring her that he wouldn't leave her for long. He backed away again and this time she remained composed, although he could tell from her face that she was still petrified. Guiltily, he crept away into the darkness.

    Yarik crawled forward knowing that a single sound might rouse the dog from its slumber. Mouth agape to reduce the sound of his heavy breathing, he edged toward the vague silhouette of his sword. The weapon was only a few feet away when he felt the rope tightening behind him. Yarik pulled no further in case he panicked the female. Instead, he lay flat on his stomach and stretched his body towards the weapon until his fingers were just inches away from the blade. He wriggled his body forward, knowing that the rope was tensioning behind him and must now be disturbing the girl. His fingertips touched the cold metal and he squirmed forward another inch. Pinching the blade between his fingers he tried to work it loose from the earth, but suddenly there was a tug at his leg and he lost an inch; the female was resisting him, pulling her leg back from the line. He gently, pulled forward again, but the girl was fighting him now. He shouldn't have drawn the line; it was only making her panic. It was now or never - he tugged at the rope and lunged at his sword, grabbing the blade between his fingers, but the girl yelped and tugged him back again. Yarik lay still, sweat stinging his eyes, and listened - silence at first, then slowly he heard the low growl of the dog; immediately, he felt another tug on his leg as the girl attempted to put distance between her and the waking animal. Yarik held firm, knowing this was their only chance, but the rope pulled harder and he had to use all of his strength to maintain his ground. Suddenly frantic barking ensued, the girl started to scream and

Yarik knew the dog had seen her; he lurched at the sword, knocking it over and he nearly had it in his grasp, but was pulled back once more by his anxious mate. Again he lunged, but again the rope prevented him from reaching the sword; the girl's terror-fuelled strength was amazing. A manic turmoil of screams and barks filled the air as the rope suddenly went slack and he knew that the dog had the girl; it had grabbed her ankle and was now dragging her along the ground. Yarik jumped up, grabbed the sword and ran back towards his mate; the girl's screams of terror turned to those of agony, and the dog's barks became muffled growls as teeth sunk into her soft flesh. Yarik raised the weapon and charged towards the savage sound, roaring in fury as he went, but on seeing the carnage the cry died on his lips and he stopped short, falling to his knees in despair. He was too late, the beast had already opened the girl's throat and her eyes stared out lifelessly as the hungry animal gorged upon her.

Arthur looked down upon the kneeling man. 'So you chose to return,' he said, quietly. Yarik looked up at the king but said nothing; the last of his resolve and all emotion had died along with his mate and he cared now, nothing for himself. Weak from his wounds and numb from shock, he would have accepted, or even welcomed, a fatal blow from the king's sword.

'You have proven your loyalty,' the king smiled. 'By sacrificing your mate and returning to me, you have confirmed your allegiance. I am your life now; forget any dreams you may have had for now you are mine and I will do with you as I wish. Have no regret, for you have earned high regard – your victory at the table demonstrated cunning and now you have proved your loyalty. I have been seeking someone like you, Yarik, someone I can trust to carry out a very important task.' Arthur pulled a ladle from a steaming cauldron of broth and handed it to Yarik who took it gratefully and wolfed down the food. 'I am told you can ride,' the king continued. 'Unfortunately many others cannot, so my army now has to march against an enemy who by the time we arrive will be well prepared. Something has to be done to undermine their confidence, Yarik – do you understand?'

Yarik nodded; he would have thrust his head into the fire if so commanded.

'You have sacrificed your female and now I will trust you with my own; she too, is loyal to me and very cunning. At first light you will travel south together – you are to ride ahead of my army and infiltrate the enemy. Use your guile to gain their confidence and learn their plans; you are to hinder their preparations and instil fear in their people. If you are careful they will not suspect you, for you do not yet bear the mark. Do you understand?'

'I will do as you command,' Yarik mumbled.

'One more thing - there is one among them that I would see… especially disadvantaged. You must seek out an old man – a decrepit old priest who is their talisman.' Arthur looked to the south and his eyes flared. 'Take your poison, Yarik… and feed it to the priest.'

Chapter 6

Matt sat with Eddie on the warm sand watching Ryan and Amy splashing about in the sea. Waves surged past the children towards the beach where Captain Rainford and the Warrant Officer were checking the boat. Weather permitting, the two submariners planned to leave soon and it still hadn't been fully decided whom, along with Gerry, should go with them to Anglesey.

'Those two kids would be first on the boat if I had my way,' Matt said. 'But Ryan's refusing to leave and I doubt Amy will want to go without him.'

Eddie shrugged his shoulders and wiped sweat from his brow. It was one of the hottest days so far and the two men were taking a break from the sweltering work that continued in and around the castle walls. Joe was working at the forge that Eddie had constructed within the southwest tower and Gerry was supervising the erection of new courtyard buildings. Matt and Eddie continued to work on improving the castles defences; shoring up crumbling walls, strengthening gates and devising contraptions to hinder an advancing foe. This morning they were digging a trench in the clay that lay below the main access path, which ran up from the beach towards the castle, but it was much harder work than they had envisaged and they were shattered. They planned to embed sharp wooden stakes within the trench, concealing them with skins pegged across the opening and covered with soft sand, but the sun had hardened the ground's surface and digging down to the softer clay was proving difficult with the rusty old spades from Gerry's mine.

'Where's F...Father Peter?' Eddie said. 'Perhaps he could talk some s...sense into Ryan.'

'He's up in the fields with Mel and Baxter. I think he's worried we're all going to leave him here alone. You'd think he'd trust us after what we've been through.' Eddie shuffled his feet and looked uncomfortable. 'Is something wrong?' Matt asked him.

Eddie was astounded at the question. 'For Christ's sake Matt, Rupert w...wasn't the only one who cared for Hayley, you know!'

'Sorry, I didn't mean...'

Eddie put his face in his hands. 'No, it's m...me,' he mumbled. 'My head's still pretty m...messed up – you know, the violence of it. I not s...sure I can stomach any more of that s...sort of thing.'

Matt stared at his friend, but Eddie's grubby fingers concealed his eyes. 'What are you trying to say Eddie?'

'I'm not a f...fighter, Matt; none of us are really.' Eddie pulled his hands from his face and wiped sweat from the back of his neck. 'Waiting here for some lunatic with a sword and an army that we've got no chance against doesn't m...make much s...sense to me.' He gestured at the boat. 'Not now that we've got an alternative,' he added.

Matt glared at him. 'Don't tell me you're thinking of leaving Harlech - after all we've achieved?'

Eddie's face flushed. 'You know I love building all this s...stuff, but all the time I'm trying not to think about why we're doing it – to hold out against an army of s...savages! I've never been one for confrontation, Matt. At school the little kids used to make fun of my s...stammer, the older ones used to beat me up and I never once s...stood up for myself. You see, deep down I'm just a coward; always have been – always will be! I'm no good to you here, and I've got n...nothing to be here for – n...not any more. If I go to Anglesey, I could help them rebuild – it's what I'm good at and it might make me feel... I don't know – whole again.'

'What about Father Peter and the cup? That must mean something.'

'Yeah, it m...means I hardly ever sleep now – when I'm not dreaming of Hayley's m...mutilation, I'm seeing even worse things - things that m...might happen to me if I stay here. The old chalice an incredible thing but it can't help us - the whole world's turned r...rotten and all the cup does is show us just how rotten it is.' Eddie was growing more and more agitated as he spoke and suddenly rose to his feet. 'The truth's horrible and I don't w...want to see it anymore; it terrifies me and if I don't s...stop looking it's going to drive me insane.'

'For Christ's sake, Eddie. You can't leave, we need you here.'

Eddie turned away, 'I'm s...sorry,' he mumbled and walked back towards the castle.

That night, Matt's fidgeting was disturbing Mel who lay beside him in their shelter.

'What's wrong, Matt? It's hard enough trying to sleep in this heat without you tossing and turning all night.'

'If we sleep, we'll only dream of him,' Matt replied. 'That's all we ever do – sooner or later it's going to drive us crazy; look at Tanya, she spends all of her time working night shifts at the forge just to escape her nightmares.'

'At least she's finally contributing something,' Mel said.

'There's something wrong with her,' Matt said. 'Her eyes give me the creeps.'

Previously, that evening, their ritual of passing the golden chalice had taken place as normal and as usual, Tanya had slunk into the room to participate. She sat silently to one side; her once beautiful face gaunt and sallow through lack of sleep. For the past week she had spent every day cooped up alone in her room, emerging only at night for the ritual of the chalice, before skulking off to toil in the southwest tower. It was as if churning out iron arrowheads in preparation for the inevitable battle was her way of retaining some control over the one who tormented her sleep.

'What is it Matt? It's not like you to be so negative,' Mel said. 'Something's wrong isn't it?'

Matt sat up and rivulets of sweat ran down his sunburnt chest. 'Eddie's decided to leave with the others,' he said.

'Oh, is that it?' Mel stroked the hairs on his arm. 'I thought he might - he's not really been enthusiastic about this place - or anything really - since Hayley died. Plus he's really scared - we all are, but Eddie knows he nearly lost his mind in Bala and he's petrified of losing control again. You can see his point – he'd be better off in Anglesey until things have been sorted out.'

'I know, but it's not just Eddie.' Matt looked into her eyes. 'I've been thinking about you and the baby.'

'What?'

'Mel, you can't stay either; it's just not safe. I'm sorry, but I think you should go too.'

'No! I can't leave you - I won't!'

He took her shoulders and kissed her between the eyes. 'Mel, we've got to think of the child; when it's over, I'll come and find you. I promise!'

'But… I…' Mel shook her head and started to cry.

The next morning Matt, Joe and Nic stood on the beach with Baxter, watching the boat rise and fall with the incoming waves. A warm breeze was blowing from the south and Captain Rainford had decided that it was perfect conditions to make the journey. Those leaving were already on the boat – Mel and Amy huddled together sobbing - neither wanting to go, but deep down each knew it was for the best. Ryan had adamantly refused to leave and had not been seen since the day before; presumably he was hiding somewhere in the ruined town as he had done many times when evading the monster who had lived in the castle before their arrival. Eddie sat in the rear of the dinghy beside Gerry, who seemed to be the only one not saddened by their departure, but Eddie avoided Matt's eyes as the boat bobbed in the water.

Eventually, the two naval officers finished loading the dinghy and pushed it out over a wave; they jumped aboard and heaved up the makeshift sail, which immediately caught the wind and started to pull the boat out to sea.

'Goodbye my friends,' Gerry shouted from the dinghy. 'May we all be alive and healthy the next time we meet.'

Joe and Nic waved enthusiastically as Baxter barked his farewells, but Matt just stared sadly at Mel who returned his gaze through tearful eyes. 'Remember the compass,' he mouthed, as they slowly drifted apart.

To Matt the following weeks were just a blur; he worked every day on the buildings inside the castle with a party of men from the town; it was slow work without Gerry and Eddie to guide him, but eventually the structures took shape. The new stone buildings lining the castle's interior walls were similar in construction to the communal building, but these shelters were fully enclosed and incorporated individual fireplaces and chimneys. Each had its own cooking range and a primitive toilet that would have to be emptied daily. The walls were lined with small alcoves designed to hold candles recovered from the town. To supplement these, Ryan and Father Peter had made their own, using tallow from rendered pork fat; the resulting products were foul smelling, but impressively effective. Each shelter had its own furniture, mostly antiques discovered in the ruins, but in Gerry's absence, Nic had proved to be a competent carpenter and had produced a few home-made tables, benches and beds by himself. The old lean-tos were left standing in case of emergency, but were now uninhabited as Matt and the others moved into the newer buildings. People were still drifting into Harlech from the surrounding villages and some of the townsfolk had finally taken residence inside the castle walls.

Matt missed Mel terribly and without being able to share his accomplishments with her, there seemed little point in working so hard, and all the time a shadow hung over him. The spectre of Arthur, the dark king remained, and Matt knew from his dreams that his army drew ever nearer. Arthur was coming, Matt was sure now, and the madman had only one purpose - to massacre them all.

Joe and Tanya continued to take shifts at the forge and kiln and a daily stream of pots, vessels and tools were produced from the town's raw materials. Scrap metal was honed into weapons in readiness for the forthcoming attack. The Chinese continued to hunt every day, but now their arrows bore metal heads and they were much more successful in bringing down larger animals to feed the town. Matt had persuaded them to replicate their bows so that the townsfolk could arm themselves with projectile weapons and so be much more effective in defending the castle from attack. Every day, in the courtyard, at least fifty men practised archery now, aiming at animal-skin targets stretched over wooden frames. Hundreds of arrows were being produced daily and stockpiled on the battlements, plus heavy rocks had been hauled up on gin wheels in readiness to throw down upon potential assailants. The castle was secure and in the event of a siege, could support the whole town… for as long as food and water supplies held out.

'I guess we're as ready as we'll ever be,' Matt said. He and Joe sat with Father Peter, opposite Nic and Tank at the communal building's main table discussing the day's progress. It was still very warm but now the air had turned humid and the evening was muggy and uncomfortable.

'There's over a hundred men in Harlech, now,' Nic said, 'Most are pretty handy and can be armed quickly. If the dark dude shows up now, I think we'll kick his arse!'

'We should only use force to defend ourselves.' Father Peter said. 'Those who come to fight us have been corrupted by evil, but deep down they are no different from anyone here.'

'Do you think he'll have more men than us?' Nic asked.

'I expect so,' Matt replied. 'Maybe two or three times our number. It's difficult to tell from the dreams, but hopefully they'll be disorganised and we have the advantage of the castle.'

Tank looked up when Matt mentioned his dreams. 'Now it's time?' He asked, hopefully. As one of the few townsfolk who now shared the ritual of the chalice, Tank, like all the others, counted the hours until he could hold it again.

Father Peter looked dubious, but rose from the table to retrieve the artefact from his bag. Right on cue, as though she sensed the cup's appearance, Tanya moved quietly into the room and sat at the table,'

'I've gotta say sweetheart,' Nic said to her. 'You're really not looking so good lately.'

'What's it to you?' She spat.

'Are you okay, Tanya?' Matt said. 'Are you getting sick?'

'Yeah, I'm sick of this shit hole, I'm sick of this bloody weather and I'm sick of you whining on, so give me a break and pass me the fucking cup.'

That night, as soon as Matt fell asleep he dreamed of Mel. She was back in the castle again and her surroundings were dank and quiet, but in the distance the sound of fighting was unmistakable. Heavy boots and the clash of steel - yells of victory and screams of agony – a far off noise of chaos and death. Mel was looking down at the pale face of Father Peter and she was crying; the old priest was laid flat on a low table and he was close to death, Matt knew that when the old man died, all hope would pass away with him. Then another vision filled his dreams – he was high up now, on the dark cliffs above Harlech; the moon and stars failed to penetrate the low swirling clouds but a flash of lightning momentarily illuminated the area. Standing on the cliff edge, suddenly revealed by the light, was Arthur, self-proclaimed king of England. He held both hands high towards the sky as thunder crashed around him. In his right hand he pointed his sword to the sky as if daring the lightning to strike again and he laughed. It was the maniacal laugh of victory, for in his left hand, the king held the golden chalice and it glowed sickly red. Corrupted by its bearer, it pulsed now in phase with Arthur's own evil heart.

Matt jumped up from his bedding in a feverish sweat; he looked around the room, unsure for a moment of his surroundings. Slowly his panic waned and he realised that it had only been a dream, but it was a dream implanted by the golden cup - a prediction of the future. Arthur would be victorious, the dark king would claim the chalice and all would be lost.

* * * *

Yarik watched the girl wade out of the lake; beads of water formed on her olive skin and ran down her naked body. Her breasts were full and firm and her nipples stood proud, chilled by the cool water despite the warm sunshine. She sauntered towards him until she stood just a few inches from his own body and he felt as if he would explode.

'Mmm, is my new friend feeling horny?' She teased, her strange green eyes staring into his own. 'Go on, have a feel if you want.' She ran her hand over her own body - from her shoulder, down over her breast and flat stomach until it came to rest between her legs. 'I'm all wet,' she whispered, 'Are you sure you don't want to feel?'

Yarik backed away.

'I know you're scared of him.' She taunted, suddenly angry. 'You're right to be because I am his queen and he adores me - he would rip your fucking head off if you so much as touched me and you know it.' She laughed and her eyes bulged insanely. She moved forward again and stroked his face. 'It doesn't stop you thinking about it though, does it?'

Yarik turned away, but she jumped in front of him and arched her back provocatively, hands on hips and thrusting her breasts towards him. 'Remember, every time such an idea enter your lecherous head - he knows! He sees your every thought and when we return, he'll remember.' She stood aside, allowing him to pass. 'So Arthur thinks he can trust you, does he?' She said. 'Maybe he can – we'll see.'

It was the third day of their journey and Yarik knew they were nearing their destination; Arthur had guided them here, infiltrating their minds and influencing them from afar. The king monitored their progress and was aware of their every thought, but his presence was fading now as the distance between them increased. The female's taunting showed no signs of abating though, and she was probably right – even now, if Yarik so much as touched her he would be condemned and she relished every moment of his torment. Yarik could read the female's mind and he could see she was aware of his desires and took to feeding them at every opportunity, but he also knew that, for some reason, she despised him for it, just as she despised any man who dared to look at her.

Yarik mounted his horse and set off, momentarily glancing back at the girl. 'Come,' he said. 'Not far now.'

'Wait for me, you freak,' she snarled, dressing quickly and gathering her possessions as he disappeared into the trees.

Soon their horses were alongside each other and she glared across at him, studying his face. 'They'll see straight through you, you know,' she said. 'Arthur says these people are like me and can remember the old ways. That means they're intelligent and angry at what they've become and I'm told they're cruel, burning their enemies alive. You're going into their camp as a spy and you don't have the wit to deceive them. I pity you - you haven't got a chance.'

Yarik heeled his horse and trotted away from his tormentor, but suddenly a huge boar erupted from the nearby undergrowth and the horse reared up. Yarik fought to control his mount, but lost his balance and crashed to the ground, striking his head and momentarily losing consciousness. When he came to, he looked up at the point of an arrow, only inches away from his face. His eyes focused on the archer who stared down without emotion as he stretched his bow; others archers quickly joined the first, all aiming their arrows at the prone man. They were all similar in stature - small but muscular, with headbands over long straight hair and not one of them spoke.

'Stop!' Another man appeared; this one was young, with much darker skin and he carried a spear instead of a bow.

'Who the hell are you, man?' He asked, pushing the archers away.

Yarik slowly got to his feet. 'My name is Yarik,' he said, proudly.

The girl suddenly rode forward, emerging from the trees 'And mine's Collie' she said. 'And who the fuck are you?'

* * * *

Somewhere on the island of Anglesey, Mel sat cross-legged on the grass facing thirty smiling children. 'Five little speckled frogs, sat on a leafy log…' they sang at the top of their voices, each child copying Mel's animated gestures as they did so. In the distance the great mansion stood defiant, despite its fallen chimneys and partially collapsed roof. It had been Mel's home for nearly a month now and she had to admit that, in comparison to the castle, the old house was a wonderful place to live. She even had her own room, with a beautiful arched window still containing some of its original glass panes in an ancient wooden frame, but Mel missed Matt terribly and wondered if Tanya was up to her old tricks now that she was out of the way. She worried about Father Peter's health and whether Nic and Joe were okay; she hoped that Ryan wasn't too sad without Amy and she prayed that Baxter was safe and sound. If only there was some way to contact them – she never thought she'd miss her mobile phone, but being separated from her friends made her terribly lonely and she would have given anything to call them. People here were very friendly and she no longer had the constant feeling of impending doom as she had at Harlech, but she belonged with Matt and deep down she wished she had never left.

There were over a hundred residents in the old house and a similar number dwelt in shelters within its grounds, but she hadn't really grown close to any of them. Andy Rainford's men made regular expeditions into the island and occasionally to the mainland, seeking out towns and villages in a landscape now reclaimed by nature, overgrown and unrecognisable from its previous existence. Wherever they went, they brought back refugees and sometimes traded with friendly communities. But these were few and far between; particularly on the mainland and without their guns they would not have returned from many of their sorties. Reluctantly, the riders had killed hundreds of people on the island - gangs too committed to savagery to be reunited with civilised ways, but now it seemed the island was a relatively safe place to live. Primitive communities existed in fragile coexistence; local tribes with heathen ideals and barbaric ways squabbled and traded with each other, but most were approachable with care, and they had all learnt to respect firearms.

Anglesey, in its isolation, was the perfect place to establish a civilised community and Mel knew that the best way to achieve this was through the children. Her self-appointed mission was to teach future generations the benefit of human compassion and whenever she could, she travelled the island with Rainford's men, spending time with children from the towns and villages they visited. Most were receptive and welcomed her efforts, but some were more fixed in their ways; the mutes in particular, were less welcoming. Over the months, those who couldn't speak (or perhaps felt no desire to) had tended to form their own isolated groups within communities and were far less approachable.

Today she was teaching local children in the grounds of the house, because most of Rainford's men were exploring the mainland to the east. They had heard of terrible developments in the more densely populated areas, so they planned to ride as far as Chester or Wrexham on a mission to understand what was happening in the larger towns. Captain Rainford was worried that if the stories were true then their peaceful existence on Anglesey might not be as secure as they first believed.

Mel smiled at Amy who sat among the children. '…One jumped into the pool, where it was nice and cool…' she sang cheerfully, but Mel knew the girl was also missing someone she had grown to love.

The garden was beautiful despite the overgrown lawn. Behind the children, dragonflies hovered over a small lake with a rockery island; standing on the island was the statue of a young man gazing sadly at the water. It depicted Narcissus who it is said had fallen in love with his own reflection, and being unable to fulfil his unrequited love had pined away and died. Mel thought she knew exactly how he felt.

Beyond the pool, horses grazed. Most of the animals had been driven south from Cumbria to escape the nuclear fallout from the Sellafield power plant there. Many more were with Captain Rainford's expedition on the mainland. Mel and Eddie often rode the horses when they weren't working, but Gerry preferred to concentrate on his own private project; renovating an old boat he had discovered at the harbour.

'...Four little speckled frogs, sat on...' Suddenly the children became distracted by something behind her and she turned to see two riders galloping towards them at speed - it was Captain Rainford and Eddie. Mel rose to her feet as they approached.

'Off you go children; it's time for a break,' she said, clapping her hands. 'Stay away from the lake,' she shouted after them as they ran off to play in the long grass. The two men dismounted and left the horses free to roam.

'I didn't expect you to return so soon,' Mel said, concerned by the look on the two men's faces. 'You said you'd be gone for at least another week.'

'Mel,' Eddie said. 'S...Sit down; Andy's got s...some news.'

'What is it?' Mel stared anxiously at the Captain. 'Tell me what's wrong.'

'Your story about an army heading to Harlech,' Andy said. 'It's true – we've seen them. They're about forty miles east of here, north of the mountains and heading towards the coast.'

'Oh my God! How many are there?'

The captain's face was grim. 'You thought there might be hundreds? Well, we counted over two thousand, and they're all armed. You should have seen them, Mel, so many - so organised - it was terrifying.'

'Two thousand? Harlech hasn't got a chance against such a force!' She turned to Eddie. 'Please, we've got to help them.'

'Help them?' Eddie looked horrified. 'Two thousand s...soldiers between us and Harlech? What the Hell can we do?'

'Ride to them!' Mel said, turning to the captain. 'Andy, your men, you've got to help.'

Andy shook his head. 'It would be suicide. We'd help if we could, but I'm afraid your friends have made their choice; they knew the risks - that's why they sent you here.'

'But they're not expecting so many,' Mel implored. 'Eddie, please?'

'Eddie looked petrified. 'S...sorry, there's nothing we can do Mel, I wish there was, honestly.'

'Then we've got to at least warn them somehow!' Mel pleaded. 'One or two of us could ride south, get there first.'

'Even if you could outdistance them, you'd be trapped,' Andy said, holding her shoulders. 'Matt wouldn't want you to do that and you know it.'

'No!' Mel slapped the captain's chest in frustration. 'We have to warn them; they might be able to get away, hide in the mountains or something.' Mel was starting to panic. 'If you won't help, then I'll go by myself.'

'Don't be ridiculous...' Eddie started, but the captain interrupted by raising his hand.

'Perhaps we could...' he said, frowning up at the sky.

'What... what can we do?' Mel asked.

'If we had a bit of wind, we could take the boat and maybe beat them to Harlech.' The Captain scanned the horizon. 'This weather's about to break so the wind might pick up, I wonder which way it will blow?'

'It's too dangerous,' Eddie said, clearly horrified at the idea.

'Not if we stay offshore,' Mel said eagerly. 'We'll only land if we have time and it's safe to do so.'

'I suppose we could take the rifle,' the captain suggested. 'Fire a shot to get their attention; we could warn them without even going ashore, then take off again holding up somewhere down the coast until the wind changes.'

'I'm s…sorry Mel, we can't do it - it's too risky.'

Mel glared at Eddie, shaking her head in disbelief. 'I thought Matt was your friend.'

Eddie looked down at his feet. 'I'm s…sorry,' he murmured.

'Don't worry Eddie, it's probably best you stay here,' the captain said. 'I'll go with Mel - you can be in charge until my men return - can you do that?'

Eddie nodded. 'Thanks,' he said quietly, and meant it.

Chapter 7

'Order the men to make camp on the beach, but keep things quiet and light no fires until nightfall,' Arthur instructed his captain. 'I want to see the castle before it gets dark.' Arthur's horse turned a full circle before galloping off towards the eastern hills where low brooding clouds clung to the cliff tops.

There was a distant rumble of thunder as he rode into the trees and up into the foothills of the Snowdonian Mountains. Arthur climbed steadily, his horse stumbled on some of the steeper slopes, but he soon reached an elevated clearing high above the beach. Arthur paused to look down at the vast army stretching along the coastline and a surge of excitement ran through him. He had dreamt of this moment for so long - the time when he would rise up against those who had wrongfully imprisoned him so many years ago.

'Look at them, Arthur,' Merlin whispered inside his head. 'All that lies between your army and victory are the crumbling walls of a ruined castle and the rabble of vagrants who abide there.'

'We will attack at first light,'

Merlin laughed. 'It is not like you to be impatient, Arthur. Perhaps we should be more cautious; our enemy is weak, but they have had time to organise themselves. Who knows, they may prove to be more troublesome than you think? Don't forget, you haven't even seen the castle yet.'

Arthur had spent many years of his imprisonment studying medieval warfare strategies and knew that throughout history, much larger forces than his had been decimated by a well-defended fortress, but even so, he couldn't help feeling inspired by the scale the army below. He forced himself to turn away from the impressive sight and set off again, riding around the peninsular. He followed a raised path, which led around the foot of a sheer cliff; on his right a steep grassy slope led down to the rocky sand hills below. The wind suddenly flapped Arthur's long hair into his eyes and he sensed that a storm was brewing. He brushed his hair aside, just as Harlech Castle's formidable towers came into view from behind the rock face.

'Finally!' Arthur gasped as he reined in his horse and stared in awe at the impregnable walls and crumbling battlements. Studying the symmetry of the architectural masterpiece before him, he immediately started to formulate an offensive plan. He knew that feudal castles such as this could be easily breached with mobile cannon but of course he did not yet have the advantage of gunpowder. The medieval equivalent was the trebuchet - a catapult, which could launch missiles large enough to damage even these great walls but, while it was not beyond his capability to construct one locally, he immediately decided against it. Arthur admired the castle and had no desire to damage it; his goal was simply to penetrate its walls and once inside, destroy every one of its smug inhabitants. However, he could see that the castle defences were well designed and positioning siege towers would prove almost impossible. The main gatehouse would be a weak point, but it could easily be defended from above, so focusing on the main gate alone, would be suicide. The outer walls did not seem particularly high and a large and determined infantry force with the aid of grappling irons could quickly scale them, but even if the outer ward could be taken, the main inner walls were far too tall to be climbed in the same manner. However, there would almost certainly be inner gates, which would be vulnerable to a battering ram, and once inside, irrespective of losses, his well-trained knights would soon overcome the defenceless inhabitants.

'Now what do you say, Arthur?' Merlin asked.

'The castle looks strong, but its inhabitants are weak. I still say we should launch an early attack - victory should be ours by the end of the day.'

'If archers defend the battlements you will suffer many losses,' Merlin said. 'Why not be patient, implement a siege and savour the situation for a while. The most effective weapon is demoralisation and you have sufficient numbers to surround the castle. Intimidate your enemy for a while, maybe they will grow hungry and discouraged to the point of surrender.'

'As usual, you speak with wisdom,' Arthur said. 'Our enemy can stew in their despair; then when they finally open the gates and plead for mercy, I will take them one by one and crucify them on this very hill.' Arthur pushed the delicious thought from his mind and returned to the problem at hand. He studied the hills, looking for a suitable vantage point from which he could watch his siege unfold, and immediately caught sight of the old pillbox high in the cliffs above the town. It was perfect, from there he would be able to see the beach where his army camped and it also overlooked both the town and the castle; from there he would witness his destiny unfold. Satisfied, Arthur spurred his horse and galloped back towards the beach just as the first spots of rain began to fall.

Yarik sat among the ruined walls of Harlech as thunder rumbled in the heavens above. A large fire illuminated the frightened faces of those who sat in a circle around him.

'The dark king is coming,' he whispered, 'and the king's army is invincible. I know because I have seen them.' Yarik sensed the crowd's terror as he fuelled their fears with stories of impending doom. 'Those in the castle care only for themselves and when the time comes, they will betray you. The gates will be closed and you will be left alone to face the enemy.'

'No! The strangers will defend us.' A young man suddenly stood among the townsfolk. 'There is a priest among them whose God has the power to protect us,' he said.

Yarik shook his head. 'To them we are no better than dogs,' he said. 'Do you think they will ever accept you as one of their own?'

'What should we do?' someone asked.

Yarik laughed. 'There's nothing you can do,' he said. 'It's too late - accept your fate and die protecting your masters; that is your role.'

'No!' The young man argued. 'The priest's cup will save us – it has magic.'

'The cup is for the king!' Yarik shouted. 'He will claim it and then he will kill you all. Hide in the mountains if you wish, but he will find you and you will all suffer for renouncing him.'

'Perhaps we should go to him,' someone suggested. 'Beg for the king's mercy.'

Yarik laughed again. 'Better to take your own life now, than suffer his vengeance. I'm afraid you are already dead, my friend.'

* * * *

In the darkness, Captain Rainford struggled to retrieve the sail as the boat lurched in the wind and nearly capsized. The inflatable tender, which had been recovered from the submarine rescue vessel, had been fitted out with a makeshift mast tethered by mooring eyes at the front and rear of the craft. However, although it featured a deep, inflatable keel for strength and stability, it was never designed for sailing, particularly in these conditions.

'Row into the waves,' he shouted to Mel who now fought the boat with a single oar; the other had been lost overboard soon after the storm broke. Rain lashed against her face as she steered the boat into the next swell and the dinghy rose high into the air before crashing down again with such force that she was thrown onto its reinforced deck. She looked up at the captain as he finally unfurled the sail and the boat steadied at last. All day they had been floundering on a sea with a surface like a millpond. There hadn't even been enough air to fill the sail so in an attempt to reach Harlech before the enemy they had rowed until exhausted. Then, just as they had been about to admit defeat, there had been a sudden breeze. Unfortunately it turned out to be the first breath of an approaching storm and the wind was now at a level where it threatened to overturn them.

'It's blowing us inland,' the captain shouted. 'Pass me the oar.'

Mel had lost all sense of direction and looked out into the darkness, hoping to find her bearings. Lightning flashed and the Captain's grim face was momentarily illuminated as he struggled to maintain their distance from shore, but it was hopeless.

'For God's sake keep an eye out for rocks,' he yelled. 'We're going ashore. Get the gun - we may overturn when the waves start to break.'

Mel grabbed the nine-millimetre pistol from the boat's locker and held it tight as she stared nervously into the darkness. Suddenly there was another flash of lightning and she screamed at what it revealed - momentarily, she saw hundreds of grotesque figures standing on a beach less than a hundred yards away, their hideous pale faces staring out towards her as she drifted towards them. She fired the gun blindly into the darkness as thunder crashed around her.

'What is it?' The Captain shouted.

'They're waiting for us,' she screamed. 'On the beach just there.'

'Where? I can't see anything. Are you sure?'

'I'm telling you… Oh my God, look - there's hundreds of them.'

'Quick, give me the…' the Captain started, but an arrow flew out of the darkness and pierced his throat; he fell backwards into the water.

Mel screamed again and overwhelmed by panic, she jumped out of the boat and frantically tried to swim away, but something grabbed her ankle and pulled her backwards as waves crashed over her. More hands found her body and dragged her roughly from the water onto the beach, as she coughed and spluttered seawater from her lungs. Grinning faces peered down at her as she struggled to free herself, but someone kicked her hard in her side and she was left winded. She lay still in the sand as her captors released her, backing away and forming a circle around her, then one of them stepped forward, raising an axe above his head and she closed her eyes anticipating the blow.

'Stop!' A voice of authority came out of the darkness and a large man dressed in white fur stepped forward carrying a flaming torch. 'Don't kill her yet, she might be useful. Tie her up and in the morning we'll take her to the king; he'll know what to do with her.'

Arthur stood on the stone floor of the pillbox and watched the boat drift closer to his waiting soldiers with every new flash of lightning. A roll of fur bedding was piled against the rear wall and he had been provided with plenty of food to last the night, but both were as yet untouched. Eating and sleeping could wait as he watched the events unfold below him. When he saw the woman finally captured, he turned his attention to the town where he could see people milling around between buildings illuminated by numerous fires. He scanned their minds, but they seemed oblivious of their impending doom. He cared not for these people; they were not his enemy, just poor souls influenced by the manipulating minds of those within the castle. None the less, they would all be put to death for their mistake. Long ago, Arthur had called from afar and none of these people had heard his summons, else they had chosen to ignore it - soon they would regret that choice.

Arthur knew that his spies were in the town and he could feel their presence, but he did not make contact for they had already provided much information about the castle's defences. Arthur was more interested in his adversaries inside the castle itself. He reached out for their sleeping minds, searching first for the girl he liked to torment. She was asleep, but her dreams were already troubled and he listened to her thoughts for a while as she tossed and turned in her bed. Then he spoke to her.

'When the time is right, you must come to me,' Arthur said quietly. 'Crown me as your king and perhaps I will spare you; I may even suffer you as my queen for a while.' Then the mind was lost to him and Arthur knew that the terrified girl had woken. He turned his thoughts to their pathetic leader and found him dreaming about the one who had just been taken from the boat, but as much as he would have enjoyed it, Arthur refrained from showing him her current plight. Instead he probed into the dark corners of the man's brain and resurrected memories of his long dead sibling.

'Your brother wants to know why you let him die,' Arthur goaded. 'His charred corpse still strives to understand why you abandoned him that day.' Matt's unconscious mind made a feeble attempt to repel the invasion but Arthur was too strong and continued to torment his victim. 'Soon, everyone around you is going to suffer, just as your poor little brother did so long ago… and once again, you will be to blame. You selfishly hold them here against their will, even though you knew I was coming. Now it's too late,' Arthur jibed. 'You should have fled with your cowardly friend…' the connection was suddenly lost as Matt's waking mind closed on him.

'I hope I'm not disturbing their sleep, Merlin. That would be inconsiderate of me, seeing as they have such an important day tomorrow!' But the wizard was elsewhere and did not respond. Who's next? Arthur thought. Not the priest, not yet anyway - it was too soon for that confrontation. Maybe he could reach the coward and find out where he was hiding – yes that would be very useful. Arthur focused his mind and searched the night for Eddie Coleman's unique thought patterns and the ease with which he located the man made him wonder if his powers might be growing. Arthur probed the coward's mind but this time his victim was awake so almost immediately the intrusion was repelled. However, the brief connection was interesting to say the least. The man was evidently far away from the castle and Arthur could not see his surroundings because it was dark, but he could tell that the man was in trouble – the snivelling coward was apparently drowning somewhere in cold, dark water. Wild emotions were running through the man's panicking mind – beneath his fear there was a deep and terrible guilt, but as powerful as this feeling was, there was an even stronger emotion, and one which was so out of character that Arthur was strangely unnerved. The intense hatred radiating out from the man surprised Arthur, who somehow knew that much of it was aimed at him.

Eddie had read somewhere that the best way to swim with a horse is simply to slide off it and hold onto the mane, allowing you to float along next to the animal. In reality, it had not been that easy. Firstly, it was dark and Eddie hadn't even been able to see the far bank. He had known that it had to be a least three hundred metres away and he wasn't sure he could actually swim that far, but the campfires in the distance had given him confidence. Captain Rainford's men were not stupid enough to attempt the crossing at night and were obviously waiting for daylight before returning back across the Menai Straits into Anglesey. The second problem was that, although it was low tide and the current had stabilised, the wind was rising and it the water was already choppy. To make matters worse, thunder was in the air and it had started to rain.

Eddie had ridden the horse down the muddy bank into the water - at first he had thought it might prove to be shallow enough to ride right across, but it had not been the case. Soon the water had been up to the horse's neck and that was when the trouble began. The horse hadn't started to swim, but instead it lurched forward, kicking the substrate with its hind legs. This caused a lot of turbulence and Eddie lost his grip on the slippery animal and he went under. Now a flailing hoof caught his knee and he spun around in the inky darkness and swallowed salty water. After what seemed like an eternity he surfaced, gasping for breath and Eddie realised that after all these months he had finally lost his glasses; a week ago he would have been distraught at the discovery, but now he didn't even care - what the hell – he could still see… just!

Somehow Eddie was now in front of the horse, either that, or it had turned completely around; in any case, the animal was now lunging towards him. Knowing that the horse's commotion was likely to send him under again, Eddie started to swim away from the animal in what he hoped was the direction of the opposite bank. Eddie was already out of breath and his knee hurt from where he had been kicked; he suddenly realised that he had no chance of reaching the other shore. He swam desperately on, but had lost all sense of direction in the darkness and now the horse was nowhere to be seen. Treading water, he tried to spot the campfires, but he was either too low in the water, or he had drifted out of sight. Desperately, he swam blindly on until his energy was finally spent and he went under again. This time, he didn't surface in time and breathed the first liquid breath of a drowning man; the experience was strangely soporific and Eddie drifted into an euphoric acceptance of his own death. At last he would be unburdened of his shame and his guilt would be replaced by peaceful serenity. Eddie embraced the drowsy relief he was experiencing, but just as his consciousness faded, he became aware of an alien presence inside his head. The dark king was back, trying to infiltrate his mind and probe his dying thoughts. How dare he intrude at such a time! Eddie felt anger well up inside him; he forcibly repelled the intrusion and the effort refocused his consciousness. Suddenly a dark shape brushed past him – it was the horse. Reaching out, Eddie grabbed at the animal but couldn't get purchase on its slippery flank. He tried again and this time his fingers closed around the horse's tail and he was pulled forward through the water; the momentum caused him to rise and he eventually broke through the surface. His first attempted breath sent him into a spasm of coughing, but finally he recovered enough to pull much needed air into his lungs. The horse was swimming properly now that it was in deep water and its movements were smoother. Eddie managed to pull himself forward until he once again gripped the horse's mane. Letting the animal do the work, Eddie focused on regaining his composure, but he still wondered if the horse was swimming in the right direction. Then he saw trees in front of them and realising the animal was nearing dry land, with the last of his strength he pulled himself onto the horse's back just before it lurched out of the water and clambered up the muddy bank. Eddie clung desperately to the horse's neck as it shook the water from its body then, looking around, he realised that they had climbed ashore some distance south of the submariners' camp.

'Come on, boy,' he spluttered, encouraging the horse. He had developed a new-found respect for the animal. Horse and rider wearily dripped their way along the mud flats until they reached the camp. Eddie saw that the men were grouped around a dozen campfires and at first they seemed unaware of his approach, but suddenly a stern voice challenged him.

'Stop! Who goes there?' A man with a pistol stepped from out of the shadows and before Eddie could stammer a response, the camp was in turmoil - within seconds a hundred men surrounded him.

'Eddie, what are you doing here?' Jim Price, the warrant officer strode forward. 'Don't tell me you've just swum across the straits in the dark?'

'I h…had to get to you before the tide turned,' he said. 'I needed to catch you this s…side of the water in case…' Eddie started to cough again.

'What's the problem, Eddie? Why are you here?'

'The Captain's gone with Mel to warn the people of Harlech about the army but I wouldn't go with them,' he looked imploringly at the warrant officer. 'How could I do that?' There was a crash of thunder and rain started to fall again. Eddie looked around at the men's weary faces and he could see that they had been in a fight. These people were risking their lives so that he and others could lead a peaceful existence on the island.

'What's wrong with me?' He said to them. 'I've lost everything I ever loved because I'm too s...scared to stand up for myself. I'm still s...scared - in fact I'm bloody petrified, but I realise now that I don't actually have anything else to lose.' Eddie's eyes filled with tears at the memory of Hayley being ripped apart in Bala.

'All of a sudden I'm bloody angry!' He shouted at the men. 'And do you know what? I'm no longer going to stand around pretending that horrible things aren't happening in the world. There's a madman out there - right now he's focused on Harlech, but s...sooner or later his attention will turn to Anglesey.'

The crowd murmured as if the very same thing had been on their minds; Eddie noticed that one or two of them were nodding.

'I don't care if it's the last thing I do,' he continued without a single stammer. 'I'm not going to be afraid anymore – I'm going to go and stand with my friends and if by doing so, just one evil bastard pays, then perhaps it will have been worth it!'

One or two shouts of approval rang out from the crowd, but Jim Price held up his hand. 'Eddie, calm down...' the warrant officer started, but Eddie was on a roll and wouldn't be interrupted.

'I'm not going to beg for you to come with me, but just think about it,' he shouted at the men. 'I didn't take my chance when it came and now it's too late! The same thing might happen to you if you don't act now. Your captain is out there helping my friend because I was too scared to go! If he dies, then it's my fault - but you'll be guilty as well unless you ride with me!' Eddie looked straight at the warrant officer. 'You've got to help me,' he demanded.

    The man smiled. 'Rousing speech Eddie,' he said, nodding in admiration. 'Real Henry the Fifth stuff - I didn't know you had it in you!' Another lightning flash illuminated the warrant officer's rain-drenched face. 'You needn't have bothered though,' he said. 'We would have gone anyway. The Captain knew it; that's why he tried to persuade your friends to leave before we got dragged into the fight. The bastard's always trying to keep us out of trouble. Come on – dry yourself off while we prepare the horses.'

Chapter 8

'Matt, wake up! Come on, man - wake up! We've got ourselves a serious problem!'

'What is it?' Matt was suddenly awake and looking up at Nic's wide eyes.

'There's only a bloody army sleeping on our beach!'

'What? How many?' Matt jumped up, pulling on his clothes.

'You don't want to know, man – trust me!'

'Shit! Get everyone inside the castle now. Where are the Chinese? Don't say they're out hunting.'

'No, they seemed to know what was happening before I did – they're up on the towers keeping watch.'

'They don't speak, Nic! Get someone there who can tell us what's going on.'

Nic nodded. 'I'll send Ryan up with them,' he said, ducking out of the shelter.

An hour later Matt stood on the battlements, counting the people entering the gatehouse; less than a hundred so far, all carrying their meagre possessions and whatever food they could manage. Matt wondered why there were so few. He had expected at least half as many more would seek sanctuary in the castle, but even so, he wondered how long the food would last. There was a time when he knew everyone in the town, but now he only recognised those who practised archery in the castle. Mel would have known them all, he realised; she would have spent time among them, getting to understand them and learning their strengths. Suddenly Matt missed her more than ever.

As the townsfolk entered the castle, those trained were each handed a bow from a stockpile in one of the gatehouse storerooms. The archers were led up onto the battlements in case of a sudden attack, but everyone else was left milling around the courtyard in confusion. Suddenly Matt recognised a face in the crowd. 'Glyn Cooper?' He whispered in disbelief. The man walking across the access platform with a young dark-haired girl looked just like a colleague from the Degenesys plant. Thinner perhaps and with an untidily cropped beard that made him look a bit older, but the resemblance was uncanny. How could it be? How could Glyn be here, in Harlech?

'Hey!' Matt shouted down to the man, but he couldn't be heard above the noise of the crowd below, so he turned and hurried down the uneven steps to the courtyard and pushed his way out, through the crowd. Briefly, he caught sight of his old friend, but lost him again as people jostled out of the gatehouse. Suddenly the man was there, standing right in front of him and there was no mistake - it was definitely Glyn. He was wearing a beige deer-hide tunic and he carried a strange weapon with curved serrated blade. The man looked like he'd been in the wars - every inch of bare flesh was covered in scars, but he looked healthy enough - as did the girl who was with him.

'Hey Glyn, it's me,' Matt said. 'Matt Campbell.'

The surprised man just stared back as if searching Matt's mind for an explanation as to why he was being singled out. The girl looked equally bemused, but she reacted differently, suddenly turning away and disappearing into the crowd. Matt felt the mental intrusion and realised that Glyn must have been afflicted like most of those around him – he couldn't remember him.

'Who are you?' Yarik asked.

'I...I used to know you,' Matt said. 'Before any of this happened, we were friends. We both lived a long way away – how did you get here?'

The man scrutinised Matt. 'A lot of grass has passed beneath my feet and I've seen a lot of things on my travels, but I've never met you,' Yarik said. 'You've made a mistake, my friend.' He turned away and followed after the girl.

When all of the townsfolk were inside the castle, the gatehouse was cleared of people, but the gates were not closed yet. Joe and Tank manned the gatehouse allowing any stragglers to enter, but had been instructed to close them at the first sight of the enemy. Matt and Father Peter stood on the battlements under gloomy thunderous clouds, waiting for the inevitable. All around the castle walls, people watched nervously for the first sign of attack.

'Why don't they come?' Matt asked. 'I can't bear this tension.'

'They will, soon enough,' Father Peter said calmly.

'Perhaps we should go out to them Father - try to negotiate or something.'

'An honourable thought, but it would be futile. I think we should wait for them to come to us.'

'We need to know what Arthur's planning.'

'Yes, we do,' the old priest murmured, then he looked up into the hills towards the old pillbox. 'Keep your eyes peeled, my boy – there is something I have to do.' Moving away, Father Peter ducked into an arched opening, which led to a steep spiral stone staircase. He descended the stairs and emerged into the crowded courtyard where people were now grouped around numerous fires. Others were erecting temporary shelters, readying food and busily preparing for the expected siege. Father Peter carefully dodged between them, heading for the northwest tower. He bumped into a young girl, who stared at him with curious bulbous eyes. The priest was sure he recognised the girl from somewhere but just couldn't quite place her. They scrutinised each other for a moment before the girl smiled sweetly and turned away. There was something about the smile that unnerved the priest, but he pushed it from his mind and entered the dark tower. When he reached his room, he closed the door behind him and walked around a small table to kneel beside his makeshift bed. He pulled the table aside, careful not to spill precious water from the clay jug that was there and reached under the wooden frame of the bed to pull out his bag. He sat on the bed holding the golden chalice in both hands, staring at the pulsating crimson light that radiated from its surface. Father Peter hadn't held the cup for some weeks now, choosing not to face his adversary until it was absolutely necessary, but at last the time had come when he should show himself once more. Slowly and quietly, he recited the Lord's Prayer before lying down on the bed and closing his eyes.

Collie's gaze followed the priest, but she waited for a while before following him. Scanning the battlements to check she was not being watched, she darted into the darkness of tower's door and silently climbed the stairs. There was a doorway to her left and she crept into a dark room. As she waited for her eyes to grow accustomed to the gloom, she became aware that she was not alone – someone was sleeping here, if you could call it sleeping. Assuming that it was the old priest, she crept forward towards the makeshift bed. The woman lying there was the most beautiful person she had ever seen, but she was obviously troubled. Her long brown hair was matted and her face was damp with sweat and she tossed around the bed as if an invisible assailant was wrestling with her. Collie stood there in the darkness and watched the woman grimace and writhe in her sleep - suddenly the sleeping woman started to mumble.

'Leave me alone…I'm not your queen… I cannot come to you… don't hurt me… help me Matt, please…'

Collie knew that one called Matt was the enemy's leader, but why was this woman ranting about being a queen? Was she dreaming about Arthur? The woman in the bed became even more agitated and her ramblings grew louder. Worried that somebody might come to investigate the noise, Collie ducked back out of the doorway and continued up the stone steps until she reached another door; opening it she slunk into a second room, this one lit by an arched window.

When Collie eventually emerged again from the tower, Yarik grabbed her arm and pulled her roughly into the darkness of a stone archway. 'Where have you been,' he demanded.

'Having fun,' she said, holding up a small leather pouch.

'That's mine!' Yarik grabbed the pouch and opened it. Inside, only one of the jimsonweed spores remained. 'What have you done with them?' He asked.

'Just doing as we were told,' she said, pushing past him.

'Where are you going?' Yarik shouted after her.

'Can't you hear him?' She turned back, her bulbous eyes mocking him. 'He's calling us back.' Collie disappeared back into the busy courtyard, leaving Yarik with his thoughts. The notion of re-joining Arthur's ranks repelled him, but if Collie returned now without him, what trouble would she make? Yarik knew they had both been sent to disrupt the enemy's plans, but he was now filled with uncertainty. The man in the castle had claimed to know him – Yarik would have expected such a trick from what he had heard about these people, but there was something about the stranger that intrigued him. The man's head had been full of incredible memories. In comparison, Yarik's own mind was devoid of anything but the recent past. He thought back to the time when he had first seen his mate amid the fires and devastation of the great city. That fateful moment, when fear of his surroundings had so rapidly turned to lust, had become his first real memory. Now he had many more - he recalled the horrifying details of his journey north, driven by a summons inside his head – cold, hungry and stopping only to feed on the weak that travelled with him. He remembered being among Arthur's people, fighting for survival in an environment of savage competition, and he recalled how he had sacrificed his own mate for the pleasure of Arthur, his supposed king. Yarik often dreamed of that moment, waking in a state of panic and suppressing the anger that boiled up inside him before the others would sense it. Yarik's dreams were confused and misleading, but his memories were real and crystal clear. Some were precious, like the quiet, peaceful times he had spent with the female, but most were horrifying and unpleasant to recall. What he had seen in the stranger's mind lacked the clarity of his own memories for it came from the cluttered mind of one who remembered an entire life. He had seen a chaotic mixture of flashbacks bouncing around the man's head and most of the images that came to him were beyond his comprehension, but amid the confused memories he had witnessed something inconceivable. People interacting with each other in a way he had never believed possible - human relationships based on friendship and trust. These concepts weren't present in Yarik's own short memory, but that was not all that bewildered him – he had seen a vision of himself in the man's memory. A different version of him who was called Glyn Cooper and who shared compassion with other humans. He also sensed from the man's mind that a bond had once existed between the two of them, but not like the bond he had formed with his mate. A connection that was less passionate, but fulfilling none the less - it was the feeling of friendship with another man.

Nic re-joined Matt on the gatehouse battlements, having posted Ryan as lookout on the northeast tower. Thunder crashed around them as rain lashed down from a dismal sky. 'I've brought you a bow, man – I know you can't shoot straight but I figure even you can't miss if there's as many as we think.'

'Thanks Nic, I appreciate the vote of confidence. Where is everybody?'

'I saw Father Peter going back to his room; he's probably praying or maybe…'

'Wouldn't surprise me - he went off on a mission.'

'Joe's still at the gate, with Tank. Ryan's on the tower and can you believe Tanya's asleep?'

Matt looked out towards the meadow where the horses were sheltering under trees to avoid the rain. 'Can't blame her - this waiting is killing everyone; even the horses are spooked.'

Nic looked concerned. 'Maybe we should have brought them inside, man.'

'Goliath's tethered in the courtyard, but there's no room for any more and we could be holed up here for some time.' Matt looked back at the horses and worried again about their food supplies; perhaps Nic's idea wasn't so bad after all.

Suddenly there was a shout from below and a young girl burst out of the gatehouse and ran across the access platform away from the castle. Nic immediately raised his bow and prepared to fire, but Matt stopped him.

'Who is she?' He asked.

'One of the travellers we found in the forest, I think; she was with some guy all covered in scars.'

'I saw her in the courtyard; she was with someone I knew from the past, but he didn't recognise me. Why do you think she's running away?'

'Domestic I expect; you know what women are like. We gonna let her go?'

'We can't really stop her if she wants out. Who knows? She's probably making the best move of her life.'

'Don't say that, man!' Nic said. 'I thought this castle was gonna protect us.'

Matt slapped him on the shoulder. 'Yeah, of course it will,' he said. 'We'll be fine.' Just then there was a shout from above and they looked up to see Ryan pointing along the road from the castle. Matt followed his gaze and saw six riders approaching.

'You spoke too soon, man,' Nic said.

Two tall men rode in front of four others who held long, feathered, spear-like weapons; they carried the spears vertically as if they were banners. The four warriors in the rear wore leather and fur; their foreheads were branded with an inverted 'V' and they each wore around their neck a bleached-white, human jawbone. These men were frightening enough, but the two who rode in front sent a chill of fear into everybody who witnessed their approach. The large black man on the left, wore a head-dress made from a big-cat; its white fur coat ran down over his dark shoulders to form a long cloak ending with the rear legs of the animal dangling each side of his mount. The black warrior rode forward carrying a wicked looking spiked-mace in his right hand. The man on the right was not as tall, but he was even more intimidating - malice radiated from him as he rode towards them. He too was dressed in fur robes, but on his head he wore a spiked German helmet and a finely-made curved sword hung at his side. All on the castle walls were silent as the six riders approached and Matt stared in awe at the man who had for so long been a figment of his most terrible nightmares.

Chapter 9

Arthur looked up at the gatehouse battlements just as lightning ripped the night apart. He rode forward onto the timber access ramp, leaving his captain and the four other riders behind him. Thunder crashed as though from within the very castle itself and Arthur laughed out loud at the pale, nervous faces staring down.

'Where is the priest?' He shouted into the rain.

A terrible silence followed, broken only by the clatter of hooves on timber as Arthur's horse fidgeted on the wooden platform. Behind the gate, Yarik stood with a dozen frightened men, having been rallied to the gatehouse by the mountainous man they called Joe Sumo. Yarik was spared the vision of malevolence that stood just beyond the solid timbers, but he knew all too well who challenged them. All but Joe had cringed at the sound of the rider's approach, but even he jumped when Arthur shouted again.

'I am Arthur, the new King of Britain! Who here, has the wit to confer with me?'

On the battlements, Matt felt the eyes of his companions fall upon him and he wondered again how he had assumed their leadership. Reluctantly, he stepped forward, placing trembling hands on the warm, wet stonework and he leant forward to meet Arthur's gaze. Immediately, Matt felt the man's powerful mind focus upon him and all hope left him. This madman had tormented him from hundreds of miles away; now, up close, the intensity of his power was crushing. Matt dragged his gaze from Arthur's menacing eyes, staring instead at his own scarred fingers, which gripped the stone battlements. For a moment he felt less intimidated, but he knew the terrible scrutiny remained fixed upon him. Drawing in a deep, humid breath, he steadied himself before answering in a voice that rang surprisingly clear in the damp night air.

'I speak for the people of Harlech,' he shouted. 'Why have you come here?'

Arthur laughed again. 'You speak for no one but yourself, boy killer. Why would these people trust you?' He waved the back of his hand in a gesture of dismissal. 'Go - bring me the priest.'

'You speak to me or no one!' Matt shouted back. 'What do you want?'

Arthur scanned the faces on the castle wall. 'You know why I'm here! Deliver to me the Holy Grail and some of you may be spared.'

'The cup is ours – why should we give it to you?'

Arthur drew his sword and pointed it at Matt. 'I have two thousand reasons on the beach, you fool. I do not come to parley!'

Nic stepped forwards beside Matt and pointed the shotgun barrel downward towards Arthur. A dozen archers followed his example and aimed their arrows at the man below. 'We have no wish to fight with you,' Matt shouted, 'but we will defend ourselves if necessary. Leave us alone and take your thugs with you.'

'Thugs?' Arthur yelled. 'These loyal knights are liberating the people of Britain. The anarchic world for which you pine has gone forever; my knights have a mission to bring order back to these lands.'

This time it was Matt who laughed. 'Go back to wherever it was you came from or we will shoot you where you stand.' In a show of contempt, he started to turn away, but was stopped in his tracks as Arthur shouted again.

'Come back, you insolent fool. How dare you turn your back on your king?'

It was as if his brain exploded inside his head and he suddenly found himself back at the wall facing his adversary again. He felt an uncontrollable urge to climb up onto the ramparts and jump to his death. Struggling to control his actions Matt managed to growl through gritted teeth - 'Shoot him!' The pain in his head immediately subsided as Arthur turned his mind to those who threatened him with their bows.

Arthur snarled, swinging his sword around his head and the defender's weapons fell from their hands; the shotgun and a dozen bows clattered to the flagstones at their feet. 'Do not defy me!' He snarled. 'Open the gates now, I command you!'

Suddenly, a small rock struck the flank of Arthur's horse and it reared up on its hind legs. A lesser horseman would have fallen off the platform into the grassy moat below, but Arthur just managed to retain control. His livid face stared up to locate the source of the missile and immediately caught sight of a small boy on the high tower to his right. Arthur drilled into Ryan's mind and the boy and the madman locked eyes, but incredibly it was Arthur who first averted his gaze.

'Sit in this decrepit tomb then,' he growled. 'I care not. Soon I will come and take what is mine.' Arthur beckoned for his captain and the large, black warrior urged his horse forward onto the platform to join his master. 'While you await your doom, here's a trinket to help you sleep.' On Arthur's command, the captain slung a small ball of tightly bundled cloth up onto the battlements where it fell at Matt's feet. Then, as suddenly as they had arrived, the six men turned their horses and galloped off into the darkness. Matt crouched to retrieve the object and stared at the ball of grimy cloth, tied with a tight leather thong.

'What is it?' Nic asked.

Matt felt a growing apprehension as he unwrapped the bundle, but his trepidation failed to prepare him for what it contained. Nestling in his hand was the old brass compass from the museum; the compass that he had given Mel with the promise that he would never leave her again.

Unaware that her lost compass was causing such despair, Mel lay in agony on the cold stone floor of the old pillbox looking up into the crazed face of a young girl. She had the same desperate look as the teenage suicide victims Mel had treated back in Oxford. The dark smudges under her captor's eyes suggested that she had not slept properly in weeks; her gaunt, tired face was not dissimilar to Tanya's, but this girl was far less beautiful and the manic look in her swollen eyes seemed more embedded somehow.

'Why have you done this to me?' Mel sobbed and even the slight movement of speaking caused excruciating pain in her hands. Both of her arms were stretched out wide, spread-eagled and fastened to an old railway sleeper. She looked sideways at one of them; her slender arm lay bare against the timber, bound loosely at the elbow by a loop of rope and beyond it, her hand was nailed to the sleeper. The rusting spike that impaled her palm was shaped like a small tent peg and she felt its rough edges grating against her bones. A scarlet rivulet ran down her forearm to congeal in the bloodied rope at her elbow.

The girl skipped to the cliff-top opening and pulled playfully at a rope, which was threaded through the brass ring of the old wooden lifting-boom projecting out above her head into the darkness. 'You think it hurts now?' She sniggered. 'As soon as it's light, he'll have you swinging out on this in full view of your friends.' The girl giggled, screwing her face up at the thought of it. The other end of the rope was tied to the centre of the sleeper behind Mel's neck, ready to hoist her up and hang her from the boom over the cliff edge where she would be supported presumably, by only the nails in her hands.

Mel tried to ignore the pain, focusing instead on the girl's skinny frame and she noticed that her stomach bulged beneath her tunic. 'You're pregnant,' she gasped.

'What's it to you?' Collie scowled. The night-sky flashed behind her and a sudden downpour splattered the stone floor at her feet. 'All you need to know is that I'm here to keep an eye on you until Arthur returns.'

'Is he the father?'

'Why the hell are you so interested in me?' Collie snarled.

Mel recoiled at the fury in the girl's eyes and almost passed out at the agony it caused. When she looked again, the girl's murderous face was only inches from her own and she was pressing a knife to her throat.

Anger suddenly replaced Mel's pain. 'Either kill me or let me go, you lunatic!'

Collie laughed and returned the knife to its hiding place. 'No, I don't think that would be a good idea - Arthur's not the most tolerant guy. I'm to be his queen, but even so, I don't really want to be pissing him off.' The girl wandered back to the opening and looked down towards the castle.

'Can you at least tell me what's happening?' Mel pleaded.

'Not good news I'm afraid. I've been down there with your friends and I have to say, morale's not good. They all know they're going to get slaughtered.'

'You've been inside the castle?' Mel said, suddenly alert. 'Did you see Matt - the one who's…in charge?'

'Yeah, I saw him – is he your man?' She asked, returning Mel's gaze. 'I can't say I was that impressed.'

'How was he? Did he seem okay?'

'Oh he's fine,' Collie said, and a curious look came into her eyes. 'He's with a brown-haired girl now; from what I saw, she never leaves his side…' Collie bent down so that her face was again, only inches away from Mel's. '…Even when they sleep!'

'He's with Tanya? I don't believe you!'

'Yeah, that's her name – a bit spooky; but she's a real babe – I'm not surprised he's fucking her.'

Just then, the gloomy pillbox darkened further as a shadow fell across the entrance and Mel felt Arthur's presence even before she saw him. Ignoring the two women, he stomped across the pillbox to look out onto the castle, his sopping wet clothes leaving a trail of water across the stone floor. He stood steaming in the night air, a puddle slowly forming around his feet as he glared down at the fortress. Mel had not yet seen the man's face but she could feel his fury as he gazed into the darkness. Slowly, Arthur turned and faced her and she saw that his eyes were burning coals of wrath.

Father Peter's mind drifted as he wallowed in a feverish slumber. Church bells rang in the distance and the sweet smell of bonfires brought warm memories of long summer days spent playing with his childhood friends. In his dream, he opened his eyes to see dark birds circling above tall city walls. Slowly he became aware of the dark presence, patiently awaiting his attention. Below him, the cobbled square was empty apart from one man - Arthur was grinning up at him, wearing a dark robe and holding a flaming torch. Arthur spat on the stone steps which rose up to the small dais on which Father Peter now sat with his wrists tethered to brass rings embedded in the stone blocks behind him. One of his bound hands gripped the golden chalice.

'Give it up, blasphemer and denounce your sins.'

'It is not meant for you,' Father Peter groaned.

'Oh, but it is,' the scarred man replied. 'It is my destiny to wield the Holy Grail.' Stepping forward, Arthur pushed the torch into the faggots that were stacked at the base of the stone dais and flames immediately sprung upwards and began to lick at the old priest's feet. Father Peter felt Arthur inside his head. 'You are dying, old man – I can feel the poison in your brain – don't you see it's over?'

The old priest guessed Arthur was telling the truth – he could almost feel the millions of tiny blood vessels leaking toxins into his brain and the tissues swelling within his skull. The rising pressure stemmed the flow of blood so that its cells could not flush the accumulation of toxins that were slowly killing him. In Father Peter's delirium, the flames grew higher and engulfed his legs; his flesh was burning, but strangely he felt no pain.

'I may die, but you will never be king,' he gasped. 'Already your people doubt you. When you entrapped them, they were vulnerable and naïve, but now they have questions that you cannot answer. There is humanity buried in them and soon it will surface and spread, then you will be exposed as the impostor you are - a parasite that thrives on the despair of others.'

'Don't you see, old man?' Arthur laughed. 'The castle is falling – I am already victorious!'

Father Peter looked up at the chalice and through the rising flames he could see the cup pulsing with crimson light. Suddenly, he caught sight of a boy's face reflected in its surface. He had glimpsed this vision many times before - the boy's face was kindly with strange amber eyes. In his dream, the old priest looked down at Arthur and smiled. 'Events are unfolding that you cannot perceive,' he said. 'Another will be born to the throne you desire – a true king will rise out of Harlech and you will be forgotten.' Suddenly, Father Peter felt the intensity of Arthur's fury tear through his swollen brain and it seemed his blood was boiling in his veins; somehow though, he managed to maintain his assault on his mental intruder. 'Your people are turning – already one of your spies has chosen to defy you'.

Father Peter felt sudden relief and the presence was gone, but agony still wracked the old man's body until his poisoned mind slid into a feverish, dreamless void.

Tanya woke from another torturous nightmare; her head span as she raised herself groggily from her bed and wondered how long she could go on like this. Father Peter was mumbling incoherently in the room above and she felt an uncharacteristic pang of sympathy for the old man; it was obviously his turn to be tormented by the one who called himself Arthur.

    She shuffled over to the door and listened to the old man's murmurings. It was the first time she had heard the priest disturbed in such a way and it was almost comforting to know that she was not the only one who suffered. Curiously, she climbed the stairs and immediately the muttering stopped; thinking she had woken the priest she was about to retreat, but just then Father Peter let out a long snoring sigh. He was still asleep, but it seemed his interrogation had ended for now. Tanya crept into the room and over to Father Peter's bed; she felt incredible heat radiating from the sleeping man's body and she realised he was sick. It crossed her mind to call someone, but then a reflection of light caught her eye - there was something shining in the old priest's arms. With trembling hands, she reached to grasp the stem of the golden chalice and gently pulled it free of his sweltering grip.

Despite the circumstances, Yarik was sleeping peacefully for the first time in his short and painful memory, but his serenity ended when Arthur viscously grabbed his mind.
    'Why are you still with the enemy?' He demanded.
    Stunned by the assault, Yarik was amazed at the ease with which Arthur stole into his mind. He realised then, that as

long as Arthur lived he would never be at peace, not even when he slept. Anger swelled inside him and for the first time, he answered back. 'Leave me alone! These people aren't our enemy; I've seen their minds. They're scared, but they mean us no harm; why should we destroy them?'

Suddenly pain erupted inside his head as Arthur's fury ravaged his brain. 'Die with them then, you traitorous fool!'

The agony grew until Yarik felt his heart faltering in his chest, then suddenly the pain disappeared. Somebody had stumbled over him, waking him and causing the terrible connection to break. He saw the woman who had kicked him shuffle across the courtyard, seemingly oblivious to the sleeping bodies beneath her feet. As if in a trance, the woman stumbled over grumbling people, carrying something that glinted in her hands. Yarik watched the woman enter the southwest tower and disappear through a doorway, which glowed with the warm, orange light of fire. Scared to go back to sleep, Yarik considered following the girl, but then he heard the sound of distant horns. It was a familiar sound and one that filled him with dread. Arthur's army was readying for attack.

Mel opened her eyes and grimaced at her aching hands as she surveyed the pillbox's interior. She saw the deranged girl sleeping on a pile of bedding in the opposite corner. Arthur was still looking out towards the castle, but now he seemed to be arguing with himself.

'I know what I said, but things have changed.' A pause...

'You are wrong, I have to act now – I can feel my own people doubting me, they see my caution as indecisiveness;

every minute that passes I lose the confidence of my soldiers and all the time the enemy is mocking me.'

Mel watched in terrible fascination as the enraged man quibbled with some unseen presence.

'What do I care?' He said. 'We will still see victory and we can train others. I will not be humiliated, Merlin. We will strike now and we will strike hard!' Arthur turned northwards and raised his hands to the sky; his frame was suddenly illuminated and thunder shook the pillbox. It was almost as if he had commanded the lightning to strike, but Mel knew it was an illusion - even Arthur couldn't control the weather. A demand had been issued none-the-less; a silent command not aimed at the storm, but at the vast army on the beach. Almost immediately Mel heard the sound of horns blown from below. She looked to the castle and from where she lay she could just make out one of the highest towers. God help them, she thought.

The terrible horde rose as one in answer to the silent command. Captains blew their horns and soldiers grabbed their weapons. Orders were barked from every direction, as men stamped out fires and formed preordained ranks in the torrential rain.

On the castle battlements, Matt heard the sound and shouted to alert the others. 'They're coming!' he cried. 'Man the walls!'

Nic was suddenly at his side carrying the shotgun. 'So much for giving us a night off,' he said.

'I guess we've pissed him off more than I thought,' Matt said, but he wondered if Father Peter had somehow forced the enemy's hand. 'Nic, find Ryan and tell him to go to Father Peter and stay with him, then check Joe's got the gate covered and everyone with a bow is on the battlements. Anybody without a weapon must keep the others stocked with arrows.'

'What about me – what should I do?'

'Take the gun and get the Chinese archers to the west wall to guard the inner gate - apart from the main gatehouse, that's where we're weakest. I'll stay here with these men and defend the gatehouse from above.'

Nic ran off and Matt looked around at the twenty or so people manning the eastern battlements and he hardly recognised any of them. They all looked to him with frightened faces and Matt wondered how it had come to this. He shivered and felt for the small brass compass at his neck. I should say something, he thought – rally the troops, stir them up and give them hope. But what was the point – their situation was hopeless. Suddenly Matt felt a hand on his shoulder and turned to see a face from his past. 'Glyn!' he said.

'Yarik,' the man corrected. He looked at the other men on the wall and then down at his feet as if ashamed. 'I have come to tell you the truth,' he said.

'What - that the enemy sent you here?' Matt said. 'That you're one of them?'

'You...you knew that I was a spy?'

'Not at first, but there was something in your eyes; you never were any good at keeping secrets.'

Yarik looked up at Matt and tried to read his mind. 'What was I like... before...?' He asked.

Despite their predicament, Matt laughed. 'To be honest, you were a pain in the arse,' he said. 'Too ambitious for your own good.' His laughter died and turned to a compassionate smile. 'But we had many a beer together.' He nodded thoughtfully. 'You were a good guy, righteous even - always standing up for your friends; that sort of thing.'

Yarik stared out into the darkness. 'I have done some very bad things – betrayed people who trusted me - I've even killed…' His voice faltered. 'I deserve to die,' he said.

'We've all done bad things,' Matt said. 'If Father Peter were here, he'd tell you that God forgives all.'

'Your priest can help me?' Yarik asked – his desperate eyes fixed on Matt.

Before Matt could answer, somebody on the northeast tower shouted a warning and pointed to the town. Matt turned and saw the horde advancing through the ruins - there seemed so many. Then there were more shouts behind, coming from the west wall – the castle was surrounded.

'I suggest we start by saving ourselves, Matt said. 'Will you fight with us?'

Yarik nodded grimly. 'Until death!' he said.

Matt turned to the others who defended the wall. 'Do not be scared,' he shouted. 'We've all prepared for this - the castle's strong and so are we if we stick together.' Despite his words, a number of anxious archers unleashed their arrows, which whistled harmlessly into the ruined town.

Yarik turned angrily to them and shouted. 'Save your arrows until you can see the Mark of Pendragon!' He cast a mental image at the defenders and they immediately understood his command.

The words meant nothing to Matt, but he suddenly sensed a new resolve in the men on the battlements and he felt a glimmer of hope. Here was one who knew the enemy they faced and yet was prepared to stand against it - perhaps they had a chance after all.

Suddenly, the advancing foes charged, yelling and clashing weapons as they ran.

'Men of Harlech,' Matt shouted. 'Defend your land!' A great cheer ran along the ramparts as the defenders moved to the walls, stretched their bowstrings and fired.

Chapter 10

Tanya entered the tower basement and closed the door leaving the shouts and blaring horns behind her. Inside the tower, the furnace glowed with latent heat, having been abandoned when Joe was called to guard the gate. Its fires now lay dormant, awaiting the oxygen, which would bring them back to life. The heat in the tower was stifling with the door closed, but Tanya wanted to be alone; she looked into the cup's polished surface and the warm pulsing glow could not be attributed to the fire's reflection – she knew it came from within the metal itself.

Have I really come here to destroy it? She wondered; her face screwed as she tried desperately to focus her mind. She swept freshly cast pottery from a workbench and placed the golden chalice carefully on its wooden surface. Turning to her left, she pulled a damper plate out of a slot in the wooden ducting that ran from the sealed-off waste shaft. Immediately the furnace roared into life as a column of air billowed up the shaft, through the clay-sealed ducting and up through the smouldering charcoal. Moving back to the bench, she scraped out the steel crucible as Joe had taught her and, holding it in a pair of tongs, lowered it carefully into the furnace and onto a steel grate just above the burning charcoal. Her face burned with radiated heat and she smelt the hairs on her arms scorching as she became momentarily mesmerised by the flames.

Why am I doing this? She thought, but deep down she knew that she had subconsciously planned the moment for months. She lifted the wooden cover from the flask to reveal black, tightly packed sand and looked around the cluttered benches. Instinctively, she picked up a large, freshly fired clay bowl and pressed its rim deep into the firm, oily sand. Outside the tower, the shouting had intensified, but within its basement Tanya was oblivious to the first throws of a vicious battle. She stared at the golden chalice and for a moment caught her own reflection in its surface. She had been pretty once, but the face looking back at her was ugly, its beauty ravaged by her nightly torment. The person staring back at her looked insane.

As she grasped the stem of the chalice, the pulsing, crimson light returned to its surface and her reflection was swallowed by it. As if in a trance, she carried the cup to the furnace and lowered it into the crucible - as soon as it touched the hot surface it melted into delicious metallic soup. She had expected some dramatic occurrence at the cup's demise – a flare of energy or a great crash of thunder - something at least to signal an end to its magic. But there was nothing to mark the event other than the sweet smell of smoke from the molten metal. Gripping the crucible in the specially forged tongs, she lifted it out of the furnace and over to the sand-filled flask. Carefully she inverted the crucible and poured the molten liquid into the mould she had made with the rim of the bowl. Her hands were shaking though, and a small drop of metal splashed onto the bench, immediately solidifying into a star of gold. Cursing her clumsiness, she steadied herself and tried again, this time carefully filling the mould with the liquid. The volume was perfect and the circle of gold formed a convex rim as the molten metal almost overflowed the mould and then, as suddenly as it had melted, it solidified.

Tanya stared at the golden circle for what may have been minutes or hours, wondering what the consequences of her actions would be. She felt as if she had committed a deadly sin and had betrayed everyone, not least the one who visited her in her sleep. Then she thought of the corrupt face that had stared back at her from the cup's surface and she remembered everything she had lost.

'Fuck it!' She said, taking the tongs and scooping the golden band out of the sand. She waved it in the air for a minute before touching it gingerly - she was surprised at how quickly it had cooled. Holding it now in her hand she viewed a perfectly formed circle of gold – it started to pulse again and she realised the magic was still within it.

'You asked for a crown,' she whispered. 'I wonder what you're going to make of this?'

A volley of arrows rained down on the advancing enemy, but very few found their mark. A number of darts pierced exposed flesh and a few attackers fell to the ground, but most of the men wore thick, leather garments, which at this distance were adequate protection from the primitive missiles fired from the castle.

Matt watched the hideous creatures draw closer; every man's head was shaven and to Matt, who had grown accustomed to long hair and beards, the attackers looked inhuman. Human jawbones and other gory embellishments hung from the attacker's necks and each bore the same inverted V burnt into their forehead. It soon became apparent that, what had at first appeared to be a disorganised rabble charging at them, was actually a number of ordered ranks, each with a different objective. The first wave, on reaching the low ruined wall of the closest town building, dropped behind it as successive waves vaulted over them and continued the assault. Those who continued, split into groups. One frenzied band yelled and swung axes about their heads as they charged onto the gatehouse platform and attacked the timber gates with their weapons. Another group, wielding grappling irons on ropes, split into two and poured into the grassy moat in both directions. In the distance, lumbering out of the ruins at a much slower pace, twenty or so large men huddled together carrying a heavy object. Behind them all, well out of range of the archers, a thousand warriors emerged from the ruins and stood with torches, shouting encouragement at the advancing mob.

Matt peered out into the gloom and tried to make out what heavy burden the smaller group was carrying when suddenly an arrow whistled over the battlements and clattered into the wall behind. More arrows followed and one of the defenders took a direct hit in the shoulder falling backwards with a groan. Matt saw that the group crouching behind the low wall had sprung up and loosed a volley of missiles at the castle walls. They stooped again and another rank rose behind them and fired another volley up into the battlements. Matt ducked down and sat with his back against the ramparts. How had he been so gullible to assume that Arthur's army would be an unruly disorganised pack? At that moment his hope finally evaporated and he realised they would never be able to repel the attack.

Just then, Yarik sprung up and grabbed the bow from the stricken defender and fired an arrow down into the moat. 'Man the walls,' he shouted. 'Shoot the men at the gate!' At this, some of the frightened defenders joined him and sent a volley of missiles vertically down, into the hacking mob. Screams echoed up from below as some of the arrows found their mark and the horrible sound encouraged everyone to re-man the walls and resume the defence.

Suddenly, Ryan sprang through an archway and almost took an arrow in the face. 'Get down!' Matt screamed at him.

Ryan, ducked and crouched beside Matt, his face was pallid and his whole body shook. 'It's Father Peter,' he said. 'I think he's dying!'

At the western wall, cheers rang out from the defenders as the first ranks of the attack fell into the hidden trench and were impaled on the spiked stakes that had been embedded in the clay below. Only the Chinese archers remained impassive as screams of agony reached the castle; they stood motionless, bows held at their sides as they stared, grim-faced at the advancing army. Nic cheered with the others, but his elation soon disappeared when he saw the enemy's vast numbers pour over their injured comrades and charge up the cliff path towards the castle. Every attacker carried a flaming torch and the string of lights bobbing up the cliff-side made for a surreal scene in the darkness. There was nothing the defenders could do as the horde advanced and it seemed to take forever before the first ranks of the attack disappeared behind the lower walls of the outer ward. Suddenly, a hundred grappling irons flew over the wall, thudded into the grass and tore grooves in the turf as they were pulled tight to clank against the ancient stonework.

Nic levelled the shotgun; the archers followed his lead and raised their bows. Another eternity passed before the wall sprouted heads and dark bodies started to clamber over. The shotgun fired and arrows whistled through the darkness; many of the assailants fell backwards but others scaled the wall and ran towards the main wall of the castle, directly below the defenders. Wave after wave followed, and although many of the attackers fell to arrows, the outer ward was soon heaving with their adversaries and some were now firing back.

The mass below were sitting targets for the Chinese archers who fired volley after volley down into the defenceless mass, but for every man that fell it seemed that two others took their place. Nic wondered if the growing pile of carcasses would eventually serve as a means for the enemy to scale the walls. Suddenly, the man standing next to him took an arrow in the throat and fell in a heap at his feet. Nic crouched next to the gurgling man and wondered what he could do to help. The injured man clutched at his wound and stared imploringly at Nic for a moment, before starting to convulse in hideous spasms of death. Everyone on the walls ceased their defence, turning instead to witness the shocking sight as the man slowly fell still and died. Horrified, Nic jumped up and fired both barrels of the gun at the attackers below and two of the enemy fell. Then he realised there was a method in the madness below; men were running from the wall carrying timber and stacking it against the inner gate and then returning to be fed more from the men below. Torches were thrown beneath the timbers and flames quickly grew in intensity until a fire raged against the wooden gate.

Nic turned and shouted a warning to those in the courtyard. 'They're trying to burn their way in! Collect water and douse the gate.' Frightened faces stared up at him, and a few ran off towards the well. Nic clambered down the stairs to help; he knew if the gate failed, they were finished.

'Come on - hurry!' Ryan pleaded as Matt followed him up the spiral stairs of the northwest tower. As they entered Father Peter's room, Matt could smell the putrid odour of death in the air. The old priest was lying on his bed, soaked in sweat and the heat radiating from him was unreal. Baxter sat in the corner of the room and on seeing Matt started to whine, as if pleading with him to help the old man.

Matt put his hand to Father Peter's brow and was shocked at the intensity of the fever. 'How long has he been like this?'

'I don't know,' Ryan said. 'I only found him a little while ago.'

Suddenly the old man's eyes opened and looked up at Matt.

'The cup's gone!' he wheezed. 'She's taken it!'

"What?' Matt said, the reality slowly dawning on him. 'Ryan, where's Tanya?'

'Last time I saw her, she was going back to the furnaces.'

'Get him some water,' Matt said. 'I have to go, but I'll send someone to help.' He ran down the narrow stone steps and back into the courtyard. It was chaos; people were running everywhere and some were throwing buckets of water at the western gate. He pushed through the crowds there, towards the southwest corner; when he reached the tower he saw that the door was closed. It was always left open because of the heat inside - he pushed at it but it wouldn't budge. He kicked at the timbers and realised that something had been propped against it from the others side. He kicked again, harder this time and, as the door burst inwards, a wave of heat engulfed his face. Inside, the furnace was roaring out of control; the waste shaft's wooden covers had been broken away and wind howled up into the basement. The whole tower formed a massive chimney as a column of hot air roared up the broken staircase, through ancient halls and out onto the tower battlements. Matt looked around; broken clay pots lay amongst fragments of timber and dozens of arrowheads were scattered across the floor. The workbench had been swept clear except for an upturned crucible and the timber flask in which arrowheads were cast. Matt looked at the flask and noticed the remains of a circular indentation in the dark sand. He picked up the crucible and felt that it was still hot – something had been cast here recently.

'Tanya!' Matt shouted up the ruined staircase, but he knew she could not have gone that way. He moved across to the waste shaft and peered down into the vertical stone tunnel. Wind howled up past his face, carrying with it the pungent smell of the sea. He saw light at the bottom of the shaft - the rope that Eddie had used to clear debris from the chute had been re-lowered into it and was flapping around in the updraft.

'Tanya!' Matt yelled again, this time downwards, against the wind. Had she squeezed her way down the shaft? It was possible, there was nothing to her anymore - but why leave the castle? It was suicide. Then suddenly it made sense - she had lowered herself down the shaft to go to Arthur, but what had she done with the cup? He swung around and stared in horror at the crucible - surely she couldn't have?

Something next to the vessel caught Matt's eye and he ran back to the bench where a splash of metal glinted on its surface. Touching it gingerly with his forefinger, he found it to be quite cool so he picked it up and examined it. A seven-pointed star with three small holes in its body; its symmetry reminded Matt of a snowflake. As he studied the fragment, it started to pulse with a dull red light - it was so beautiful that he almost forgot his predicament. Untying the compass from around his neck, he threaded the leather lace through one of the holes in the star, then retied it again so that the two precious tokens hung together. As soon as the pulsing metal touched his chest it reminded him of holding the chalice - immediately he knew what he had to do.

Tanya scrambled free of the tunnel, emerging from a small craggy fissure in the rocks. To her right she saw a column of torches winding up the shallow steps of the western precipice towards the castle. Concealed by darkness, she slunk away to her left, across the rock-pools and up onto the grassy banks of the castle's southern ditch. She looked up through the rain at the ramparts of the outer ward, which were high above the ground at this point and consequently were not under attack. However, she could hear the cries of battle from above and she realised the enemy had already breached the outer walls of the castle. Skirting the south wall, she reached the eastern tower and looked north towards the gatehouse. The area between the castle and the town was swarming with the enemy; a large mob was attacking the main gate with axes and the eastern ditch was awash with men swinging grappling hooks and attempting to scale the outer walls. Keeping to the southern edge of the ruined town, Tanya slunk through the rubble towards the eastern cliffs, which now loomed out of the darkness. When she reached the steeper terrain, she was forced to turn west. Reluctantly she approached the ruined town, which was now crawling with the enemy like a rotting carcass consumed by maggots. Her heart pounded as she slunk towards the baying crowd, but they were so engrossed in the battle that they seemed not to notice as she weaved silently among them towards the steep eastern road. The rain stung her face as she staggered up the overgrown track into the cliffs from where she knew Arthur surveyed the battle.

The road was empty - or so she thought, but as she climbed into the darkness she was suddenly grabbed from behind and thrown roughly to the ground. Standing over her were two large men, grinning down with broken teeth. She tried to wriggle away backwards, but one of them grabbed her ankle and dragged her back. The other leered at her and dropped his leather wrap so that he stood naked except for the human jawbone adorning his neck. A terrible smell wafted towards her as the naked man lurched at her, grabbing her tunic and ripping it open. The golden ring clattered to the ground, but the man was so fixated on her exposed breast that he seemed not to notice. Tanya reached out, grabbed the gold band and thrust it upwards, into his face - the man recoiled when he saw the crown burst suddenly into crimson life.

'It's for him, you freaks!' Tanya screamed at the two men, who now looked uncertain and backed away.

'That's it - fuck off before he reads your filthy minds and fries your brains.' She scrambled to her feet and backed away from the men who had now been joined by several others attracted by the strange glowing band. The mob followed at a distance as she clambered up the cliff road, until she reached the path, which branched away towards the old pillbox. The men did not pursue her further for they knew too well who inhabited the old shelter.

Tanya reached the entrance of the wartime pillbox and stared down the stone steps into darkness. She could feel Arthur's presence - a terrible amplification of the persona that had so often occupied her mind. A feeling of dread washed through her and she almost turned away.

'Come to me,' a voice said, and Tanya was unsure whether the words came from the darkness below or had been conceived in her own head. The command was not to be denied though, and she stepped down into the dark staircase. As she entered the shelter, another voice cried out from her right, this one weak and desperate.

'Tanya,' the voice said. 'Please help me.'

Tanya turned to see Mel, spread-eagled on the stone floor. She was tied – no - she was nailed to a wooden sleeper and Mel's face screwed in agony as she squirmed desperately to attract Tanya's attention.

'So at last you have come.' Arthur said, and Tanya turned to the man silhouetted by the pillbox opening. She stared at the face, which had tormented her dreams for so long and she knew then that she and this man had long shared a common destiny, but Arthur's eyes did not meet hers - instead they were fixed on the glowing band she carried.

'What is that?' Arthur purred, as if suddenly hypnotised by the pulsing metal.

'It is for you,' Tanya replied. 'If you are to be our king, then you need a crown - I made it for you!' Arthur smiled and the hairs on Tanya's neck bristled despite the warmth.

'You shall be my queen then – for a while.' Arthur moved towards her, his eyes glowed with anticipation. 'Give it to me!'

Suddenly there were footsteps behind her and Tanya realised there was another presence in the room.

'No!' Collie screamed as she charged out of the shadows brandishing a knife.

Tanya spun around and managed to grab the girl's wrists before falling under the weight of her assault; she lay wrestling for her life as the golden ring rolled across the flagstone towards Arthur's feet. Tanya was on her back, staring up at the bulging eyes of a lunatic whose uncanny strength forced the knife ever closer towards her throat. Both hands shaking desperately to hold the blade away, Tanya looked to Arthur for salvation, but he ignored her plight and just picked up the metallic band. Tanya screamed as she felt the knife part the soft flesh of her neck and her dying eyes watched the smiling man turn away to gaze down at the battlefield. The last thing she ever saw was Arthur, slowly and reverently, placing the chalice crown upon his head.

Chapter 11

The gate shuddered in its frame as another heavy blow crashed into the splintering timbers. The battering of the gate was deafening and Joe knew it was only a matter of time before the whole thing caved in and they would be exposed. He looked at Tank's grim face as he propped another wooden sleeper against the timber and Joe could see that the big man was up for a fight. A little while ago, Yarik had descended from the battlements to warn them that something had been brought onto the platform to attack the gate. Now, on the other side, the enemy wielded what Yarik had described as a great weapon - the size of a man, but made from a material that glinted in the firelight like no other he had seen. Joe wondered again how the stranger knew so much about the enemy. Yarik was not a large man, but he had a steely look - whatever his history, Joe was glad of his company at this desperate time. Three other men also defended the gate; their wide eyes flitted around as they fidgeted and fingered their weapons nervously; these men knew that in a few minutes hell would be upon them and Joe doubted that they would hold their ground for long.

'When the gate breaks,' Joe said, tapping the heavy hammer he held, 'our only chance is to destroy the access platform on the other side. There are two wooden stakes built into the structure on either side; if we can knock them free, the platform will collapse under its own weight.' Eddie's foresight in installing the self-destruct mechanism into the timber construction might still save the day, but first they had to somehow force their way through their assailants to reach the triggers. He and Tank had been chosen to man the gates for that very reason; they were the two largest men in Harlech and if they failed to reach the stakes then it would be all over for those left inside the castle.

Another terrible impact rattled the timbers and a flash of bronze appeared though a splintered fissure. For the first time, Joe saw hideous faces through the gap - shaven heads and crazed eyes bobbed into view as, between rams, axe blades now rained into the ever-enlarging fracture.

'Tank, you know what we have to do?' Joe said.

The bearded man nodded and held out his hand in a gesture of friendship. Joe took it and the strange look in Tank's eyes suggested that he was not so much afraid, as confused.

'Why do they hate us so much?' Tank asked

Joe shook his head. 'They say it is the curse of man to be forever in conflict,' he said sadly. Suddenly a shadow loomed over them and Joe turned to see Matt astride Goliath and he was holding the shotgun.

'Tanya's taken the cup and I have to go after her,' he shouted. 'You're going to have to open the gate.'

Joe Sumo eyed Matt's shotgun. 'Sometimes the best defence is to attack,' he said. 'But there are many enemies beyond the gate - the gun alone will not protect you.'

'But Goliath might,' Matt said, slapping the animal's muscular flank. 'Father Peter's sick and needs help - whatever happens, you have to protect him; do you understand?'

Joe nodded. 'I will try,' he said as another crash sent wooden splinters flying into the gatehouse. 'They also say that fortune favours the brave,' he shouted. 'Are you ready?'

'As I'll ever be,' Matt replied, levelling the shotgun.

Yarik, who registered Matt's thoughts more than his words, shot a mental command at the three anxious men by his side. Nervously, they raised their bows as Joe strode over to the gate. He swung the mighty hammer, looping it upwards where it struck the main timber cross-member and the doors suddenly imploded. Men tumbled inwards and their battering ram - the barrel of an ancient cannon - clanked heavily onto the flagstones. Other startled faces stared in at them for a moment and then the enemy charged. The defending archers released their arrows wildly before dropping their bows and running away. Matt fired both barrels into the attacking mob and immediately re-loaded as he kicked at the horse's flanks. Joe, Tank and Yarik, who alone stood firm against the onslaught, parted as Goliath charged forward, brushing the enemy aside as if riding through a field of corn and spilling enemies into the moat. Joe and Tank followed up behind, swinging their weapons at those left standing in Goliath's wake, while Yarik savagely attacked the stricken cannon bearers, hacking at them mercilessly with his strange serrated sword. Joe heard the shotgun fire again as Matt disappeared behind a crowd of adversaries who were now regrouping in numbers. Joe pushed forward into them, parrying their blows, and focusing on one thing – the trigger mechanism. Then, through the crowd, he caught sight of it - surging forward, he swung the hammer again and the wooden stake flew from its housing and into the air like a javelin. Joe felt the timber structure shift beneath his feet as he was forced back into the gatehouse by the advancing horde. He knew it was up to Tank now to dislodge the other stake to finally collapse the platform.

The enemy poured into the gatehouse and a vicious battle ensued. Joe used all of his wrestling skills and superior weight to take out many of the attackers and Yarik spun like a demon, expertly slicing his weapon through his opponents' limbs, but Joe knew that the vast numbers now pushing towards the gatehouse would soon overwhelm them. He looked up and saw Tank fall under a mass of assailants onto the wooden platform. A blade swung at Joe's head and he ducked under it, countering with a punch into his attacker's face. He tried to charge forward to help Tank, but there were just too many bodies forcing him back.

'Tank's down - help him!' He shouted.

Yarik, being more nimble than Joe, had more success. He dodged the blows of two assailants and forced his way out onto the platform, but as he did so, Tank burst up out of the mass of bodies like a killer whale performing a theme park stunt. Yet more men spilled from the platform and Joe could now see Tank's muscles bulge as he tugged at the timber stake, but numerous arrows had pierced the great man and he was already weakening. Suddenly Yarik was there with him, both men frantically heaving at the wooden trigger as the enemy tried to take them down.

Joe lost sight of the struggle as he fell again under the weight of his adversaries. For a moment all seemed to be lost, but then he heard a terrific crash as the access platform collapsed into the moat, along with Yarik, Tank and dozens of the enemy. Those that had already reached the gatehouse immediately faltered - behind them, where moments ago their comrades had stood, a chasm had suddenly appeared and they were trapped. With renewed vigour, Joe jumped up with a roar and charged at the bewildered foe forcing them as one over the edge into the moat below. Cheers rang out from those in the courtyard, but they were cut short as a volley of arrows whistled past Joe's face and cut into the crowd behind. Joe retreated from the gatehouse just before the enemy, who had already regrouped on the other side of the moat, fired a second volley.

'Take cover and use your bows to defend the gate,' Joe shouted. Then he turned and ran into the courtyard only to see that the opposite gate was already in flames and about to collapse. People were throwing water at the timber in a desperate attempt to quench the fire. Nic was among them, but Joe could see that their efforts were in vain.

'Nic!' Joe shouted and his friend left the gate and ran to him, sweat pouring from his face.

'Joe, we're fucked, man! There are thousands of the bastards. What are we gonna do?'

'Abandon the gate! Get the people up onto the walls where they'll at least have a chance. Then follow me; we've got to help Father Peter before it's too late.'

Oblivious to the battle, Father Peter swam in a sea of delirious visions; images of horrifying events, scenes of historic martyrdom mixed with surreal visions of the future all flowed through his confused and feverish mind. In his current dream, three clerics peered intently at a prisoner before them; she was a girl of about nineteen years.

'Who are you, child?' One of the clerics demanded. 'Where are you from?'

'My name is Jehanne, as you well know,' the girl responded indignantly. 'My parents are farmers from Domrémy.' The girl grimaced at the memory. 'My mother is called Isobelle and my father is Jacques D'Arc. Neither are involved in this affair.'

'Why does a farm girl carry a sword?' growled another of the clerics.

'It was a gift,' the girl answered innocently.

'Is it not true that you stole it from the chapel of Saint Catherine de Fierbois,' demanded the third cleric.

The girl took a breath and raised her eyes towards heaven. 'The sword was sent to earth by God and his angels led me to it.'

'So you just found it?' The first cleric asked.

The girl sighed. 'It was under the earth, hidden behind the altar, not deeply buried,' she replied. 'The sword was rusty and upon it were five crosses; when the priests of the church rubbed it, the rust fell off at once without effort.'

The three clerics looked to each other and shuffled uncomfortably in their seats. 'You have the impudence to claim that the sword's existence was revealed to you by divine voices?'

'Well, I found it, didn't I?' she replied.

'And tell us… what blessings have you since invoked upon on the weapon?'

'Don't you understand? God has blessed the sword!' She said. 'It needs no blessing from me.'

'So, you have never prayed that the sword might bring you fortune?'

'Never, there was no need!'

'Where is the Sword of Fierbois now, witch?' The second cleric demanded. 'It was not with you when you were taken!'

The girl's eyes blazed. 'What became of the holy sword is of no concern. You will never possess the weapon!'

Suddenly the vision faded and another dream replaced it. Father Peter was now in a dark tunnel filled with cobwebs. The walls of the tunnel were smoothly tiled, but grimed with age and lined with tattered posters. Some of them were advertising West End theatre shows, and other London events. In the distance, Father Peter could just make out that one of the posters depicted a great sword, such as the one the girl prisoner had described. He started to move forward through the tunnel to read the words upon the poster, but suddenly a man appeared in front of him wearing a crown of gold, which pulsed with a red light.

'Why are we here, old man?' Arthur asked him.

Father Peter looked around the dark tunnel and rats ran over his feet. Suddenly he knew. 'Because in this dismal, decrepit place, lies all of our destinies.'

'I am your destiny,' Arthur snapped, 'and your people's too, for now I wear the chalice crown and the battle for Harlech is already won.'

'You're wrong,' Father Peter said calmly. 'One day, the true king will stand in this place, and he will discover the secret of the sword.'

'You fool! This is just an illusion created by your poisoned brain. If this place holds a secret, then it will die with you!' Arthur closed his eyes and the golden band burst into brilliant crimson light. In his dream, Father Peter collapsed to his knees in agony.

Matt crouched low, hugging Goliath's neck as the horse careered through the hostile mob. Vicious weapons hacked at them as they surged through the horde, but Goliath's ferocious charge was irresistible and their attackers bounced off them as they went. The castle was far behind them now and they were entering the fields to the north of the town. The lush meadows where Goliath once grazed peacefully were now awash with enemies who thrust flaming torches at the charging horse. The cliffs loomed out of the darkness ahead and Matt thought they might actually make it through the enemy ranks, but Goliath slowed as the heaving mass at last started to overwhelm him. The great horse gradually ground to a halt, stamping his feathered hooves and circling in an attempt to evade the onslaught of heavy blows. Matt fell from Goliath's back as the horse reared up in panic and the attacking horde momentarily parted to avoid the animal's flailing hooves. Goliath saw his chance and leapt through the gap, charging back in the direction of the castle. The enemy let the horse make its frenzied escape, focusing instead on its dismounted rider.

Matt looked up at countless snarling faces and knew that he had only moments to live. He could feel the collective mind of his enemy relishing the prospect of his demise. Garish faces sneered down at him as he pointed the shotgun towards the advancing mob. He pulled the trigger and one painted face exploded in a fountain of blood as a deafening gunshot filled the night. The surprised mob backed away and stood in a circle as the dead man fell in a heap beside their prey. Matt could feel their uncertainty - they had no knowledge of guns and were in awe of the magic they had just witnessed. It was short-lived though, for the creatures were driven by something they feared more; it was as if they were a single organism with a common aim of destruction. Death and violence in Arthur's camp was a daily occurrence and this was no different, they had scant value for life and had been trained only to kill. Matt felt their violent lust return and he knew that his remaining shells would not be enough to deter his enemies. One barrel was still loaded, and his pocket held the last two cartridges that had been recovered from the module so long ago. Possibly the last two shotgun cells in the whole country, he thought. Not that it mattered, for Matt knew he would never get the chance to reload.

    Matt felt his enemy charge even before he saw them move, and fired a last desperate shot into the crowd. He never saw how many of his enemies fell because the rest were upon him before the echoes of the blast had left his ears. Knowing this was the end Matt fell into a foetal position and lay helpless as the violent pack descended upon him.

Ryan sat cross-legged at the foot of Father Peter's bed. On his knees, he held the bible that the priest had carried unfalteringly on the long journey across the mountains. He opened the old book somewhere in the middle and began to read to the dying man. Baxter lay curled up nearby, silently watching the boy with sad, soulful eyes.

    'Blessed is he that considers the poor,' Ryan read. 'The Lord will deliver him in times of trouble.' The boy didn't really know if the words were appropriate, but somehow he felt the sound might reach into Father Peter's unconsciousness and reassure the old man. 'The Lord will preserve him, and keep him alive; and he shall be blessed upon the earth; and thou wilt not deliver him unto the will of his enemies...'

Suddenly Baxter started to whine and there was the sound of heavy footsteps on the stone stairs - Nic charged into the room, closely followed by Joe Sumo. Ryan immediately burst into tears. 'Father Peter's dying,' he cried. 'I can feel him slipping away.'

Nic moved quickly to the bed and felt the old man's brow. 'He's burning up, man,' he said, looking at Joe.

'Fear is the fever of death,' Joe said grimly. 'I think the dark one is inside him.'

'Please do something,' Ryan pleaded.

'I am no doctor,' Joe Sumo said, retreating to the end of the bed.

'Keep reading,' Nic told Ryan, pulling something from his tunic.

Ryan continued: 'The Lord will strengthen him upon the bed of languishing; thou wilt make all his bed in his sickness.' As he read, Nic poured water into a bowl and dipped his loadstone into it.

'I don't know if this is gonna help,' Nic said, 'but I've seen a man with a torn hamstring get up and score a goal after a spot of African voodoo.' He started to run the wet stone over Father Peter's burning body and began to chant words that he hadn't heard since leaving Ghana. 'The dark be lightened...' he said, running the stone from the old priest's forehead down over his chest. Dipping the stone again, he ran the stone down

475

one of Father Peter's arms. '…the harsh be softened, the rank be sweetened…'

Ryan continued to read from the bible. '…Lord be merciful unto me: heal my soul; for I have sinned against thee….'

'…By the power of the stone and by the power of the water…' Nic chanted, running the stone down Father Peter's other arm.

Suddenly Baxter started to bark and there was a commotion from down below.

'The enemy is upon us,' Joe shouted, darting from the bedside and grabbing the heavy hammer. 'Stay with the priest. I'll try and hold them off.'

Chapter 12

Eddie felt as if a cold hand had just grabbed his heart. Once, as a boy, he had fallen asleep at a family barbecue with a half-eaten hotdog in his hand. He remembered waking up on the warm grass, and looking down to see his hand completely obscured by a thousand teeming ants. He remembered how he had danced and shrieked in insane panic, oblivious to his amused onlookers as he attempted to shake the insects from his arm. The town below him now, reminded him of how his hand had looked that day; Harlech was also teeming with creatures, but the invaders were far more dangerous than ants.

Warrant Officer Jim Price reined in his horse beside Eddie's and unholstered his automatic pistol. 'Just as well we've got the guns,' he said, studying the chaos below them.

Eddie watched the warrant officer's thumb un-cock the pistol's safety-catch and was surprised by the man's composure. They were about to lead a cavalry against an enemy that outnumbered them twenty to one. Surely no amount of military training could prepare you for that, but Eddie remembered that a hundred horsemen rode behind them and these guys had seen a lot of action over the last few months. This was just more of the same, he supposed, but on a larger scale.

In contrast to the warrant officer's apparent composure, Eddie was petrified. Fear was not exactly an alien emotion to the engineer who, in the past, had suffered panic attacks merely at the thought of presenting a team brief to his staff. But the dread he currently felt was different; it was deeper and had more substance somehow. He knew that he was most likely going to ride to his death today, but he felt no panic as he might once have done. This was not a fear of the unknown - this was for real, which made it controllable somehow, possibly even useful. And underlying the dread, was a far deeper emotion – unspent anger and a desperate desire for revenge.

'Take this,' Jim Price said, handing Eddie the Browning. 'You know how to use it?'

'It's a single action, semi-automatic pistol with a thirteen round magazine capacity,' Eddie replied and, scared as he was, his voice was steady - devoid of his familiar stutter. 'I know guns and their components, but I've never fired a pistol. So it's probably best if you keep it.'

The warrant officer winked at him. 'I'm pretty handy with a bow now and I can't use both - go on, take it.'

Eddie reached out a trembling hand and took the pistol; the last time he held a gun was when he had lost control of himself in Bala. He remembered going berserk in revenge of Hayley and how insanely satisfying it had felt killing those responsible for her death.

'By the way, you've got fourteen rounds, not thirteen - there's one already in the chamber.' The navy officer passed Eddie a handful of spare shells. 'And here's a few more in case you get a chance to reload.'

Eddie examined the gun briefly and his technical mind immediately understood how the magazine was replenished. 'Okay, what's our strategy?'

'Well, we know from experience that our guns will evoke panic - the enemy usually retreats from gunfire, but so far we've never faced more than a hundred or so. There must be a couple of thousand down there and we've only five pistols and the assault rifle between us, so our chances aren't good.'

Eddie studied the scene below, trying to estimate the number of men in the fields. 'Look how the enemy are split,' he said. 'Half are attacking the castle's western wall from the beach. If we charge the ranks to the east and can reach the town we'll have less than a thousand enemies caught between us and the castle - they'll all be in the open, without cover.'

'That's assuming we can get there,' the warrant officer said. He scanned the clamouring mass and a figure among them caught his eye. 'Hey, there's a rider down there!'

Eddie peered into the commotion and saw the unmistakable frame of Goliath rearing up amidst the enemy, but he couldn't make out any rider. The sight of the horse in trouble though, was enough to spur him into action. He looked up at the swirling dark clouds. 'This is for you Hayley,' he whispered and without further thought, the once timid engineer let out a cry that would have struck fear into the boldest warrior. As he screamed, he spurred his horse and set off at a gallop towards the enemy horde.

'Come on men, let's go!' Jim Price yelled, following Eddie's lead and within seconds, nearly a hundred horsemen were charging down the slopes towards the battle.

Arthur felt Tanya's mind slipping away into nothingness as she died. It was a shame, for the woman had brought him a mighty gift and probably deserved better, but there were more important things to think about – for example, her killer still brandished the bloodied knife and was distracting him from the battle.

'I am your queen!' The insane girl shrieked at him. 'This bitch has done nothing for you.'

Arthur knew the girl was dangerous and that her insanity had reached a point of no return. Turning back to face the conflict below, he nonchalantly stabbed the girl with his mind, implanting a notion that sent her screaming from the pillbox. He probably should have killed her, but something told him that one-day she might still play a part in his plans. Relieved of the distraction at last, he turned his mind to the priest.

Arthur soon found the poisoned man's rambling mind drifting in and out of dreams that were of little importance. The priest was dreaming of holy martyrs with blessed swords and his delirious brain was oblivious to the intrusion. Arthur was happy to remain hidden inside the old man's head for a while; only when the priest was drawing his last breaths and dreaming his last dreams, would Arthur reveal himself and display his new found power. Arthur had waited a long time for this moment and the old man's final despair would be so satisfying, but the thought was suddenly lost when the priest's mind entered a new and strange environment that for some reason unnerved Arthur. The dying priest was dreaming of a cold dark place – a tunnel full of rats, but it was not the animals that made Arthur anxious; there was something else here - something dangerous that must not be unleashed and unless Arthur did something, the damn priest was about to discover it.

In the priest's dream, Arthur suddenly revealed himself; he stepped out in front of the old man, blocking his way. 'Why are we here, old man?' Arthur asked him.

The priest's mind was filled with notions of salvation and of a world reunited with humanity. The idea abhorred Arthur - a return to the weak ideals of their previous lives was not what this world needed; it needed strong leadership – it needed Arthur. 'I am your destiny,' Arthur snapped, 'and your people's too, for now I wear the chalice crown and the battle for Harlech is already won.'

Unbelievably, the insolent priest tried to challenge Arthur - daring to dispute his destiny. Anger rising within him, Arthur closed his eyes and focused the power that surged into his head from the golden band around it. He felt energy swell within his mind until he could hardly contain it, then he unleashed its full force directly at the priest. The intensity of the onslaught was such that he thought the priest could never survive the attack, but incredibly, when the energy surge subsided, the old man was still there – weak, but still alive. Then voices came to Arthur - a distant incantation.

'…The Lord will strengthen him upon the bed of languishing…' someone chanted.

'…The dark be lightened, the harsh be softened, the rank be sweetened…' spoke another.

'What's happening?' Arthur silently screamed, but the only answer was the sound of gunshots. Gunshots from the battle below! Arthur released the delirious mind and turned his focus once more to the conscious world. He stared down at the battlefield in dismay - below him, out of nowhere, a hundred riders were galloping through his army towards the town -

gunfire rang out and his men were already giving way to the onslaught. One horseman was distinguishable from the others and not just because he rode ahead of the rest. Arthur perceived his mind and immediately recognised the rider although he had never met him before. Once again he was surprised by the intensity of the man's hatred. It was the gangling coward! How could this man, of all people, be leading such an assault against him?

Just then Merlin spoke to Arthur, urging calm. 'It matters not,' the voice said. 'For now you wear the chalice crown - none can stand against you!'

Arthur unclenched his fists and drew a deep breath. 'Stand firm you fools!' He bellowed into the darkness and, although nobody below could hear the words, his soldiers received the order as clearly as if it had been shouted in their faces.

Matt curled on the ground waiting to die, but for some reason the fatal blow never came; instead his semiconscious mind registered the sound of gunshots and thundering hooves. Someone tripped over him and a body crashed to the damp ground beside him; the prone man's face stared at him with lifeless eyes and Matt saw that part of his skull was missing. Others scrambled over him as Matt grabbed the shotgun and started to drag himself through the panicking mob. Inch by inch, he crawled through flaying limbs and falling bodies towards the rocks that lay at the foot of the eastern cliffs. At last he reached the shelter of the rocks and turned to survey the chaos. Horsemen galloped through the savage horde shooting indiscriminately as they went. It was still too dark to make out who these strangers might be, but whoever they were Matt knew that they had just saved his life. Arthur's men were in complete disarray at the sudden onslaught. Men were running in all directions trying to avoid the armed horsemen and at first it looked as if the riders might reach the town, but then something incredible happened. The panicking mob as if a single entity suddenly stopped in their tracks and turned to face the horsemen. It was as if the movement was a well-drilled military tactic to draw the horsemen in and trap them. Hundreds of men now stood firm against the mounted attackers. The horses became unsettled and the momentum of the charge was immediately lost. Roles were quickly reversed and the riders and were now the subject of attack; desperately they drew together and tried to defend an elevated circle of grassland as the hostile mob regrouped. Baying for blood, the enemy edged towards the horsemen, but they moved cautiously, obviously still wary of the guns.

Matt crouched behind a low ridge and reloaded the shotgun with the last of the cartridges. Hoping he could distract the enemy long enough for the horsemen to regain the initiative, his finger closed on the first trigger as he targeted a huge beast wielding an axe. Suddenly there was a scream from above and despite the clamour of the battle, Matt immediately recognised the voice. 'Mel!' He gasped, looking up at the towering cliff. The scream had come from the old pillbox and Matt could tell from its tone that she was in terrible pain. Mel needed help, but how could he get to her? The overgrown road, which led to the summit, was far to his right and to reach it on foot through so many enemies would be impossible.

Not knowing what else he could do, Matt shouldered the shotgun and started to climb.

Yarik felt a terrible guilt as he stared up from the moat at the enemy pouring into the gatehouse. He knew that he had been one of them once, but now he couldn't understand why they were attacking the helpless inhabitants of this town. For what purpose should these people suffer? He knew that their master was behind the violence, but they were all guilty - himself included, for he had killed many innocent people and had even eaten their flesh. Yarik had witnessed compassion for the first time in this place, and the sudden insight that it brought came at a price. He knew then that if he would ever be able to live with the atrocities he had delivered, he would have to make amends.

The enemy was stacking timber from the demolished platform against the moat wall, using the precarious ramp to gain access. The gatehouse was no longer manned, but a few of the townsfolk, led by the Chinese archers, still attempted to defend the castle from the upper battlements. Yarik had learnt enough about warfare to know that their plight was hopeless. Now that the walls were breached, it was only a matter of time before the defenders were overpowered and taken prisoner, and he understood enough about Arthur's regime to know that to be captured would not be a pleasant experience.

Yarik had so far been ignored by the attacking mob, but it would be getting light before long and he knew they would turn their attention to him as soon as the battle was won. He had to get away from this place - but how? A heavy wooden beam lay across his legs, pinning him to the ground and he lay helplessly trapped at the bottom of the grassy moat. Scattered timber and broken bodies lay all around him and he scanned the debris for something that might be of help. Some distance away he spotted Tank's mutilated body - the huge man's head lay at an unnatural angle and his eyes stared lifelessly into the rain. Lying near to him was a discarded grappling hook; Yarik's eyes followed the rope's meandering route through the grass and saw that it disappeared beneath the painted corpse of a semi-naked warrior only a few meters away. The grass was long there and it was quite possible that that the rope continued to run this side of the body, perhaps even close enough for him to reach. Yarik grabbed a long piece of timber that lay nearby and pushed one end through an area of grass where he thought the end of the rope might be concealed, then he scooped it upwards in the hope of revealing it. Nothing! He tried again in a different area, but to no avail. On his fifth attempt the rope end flicked up into sight and Yarik felt a glimmer of hope - now that he knew the rope's location, he might be able to retrieve it. He managed to scoop the rope up again and this time it slid down the timber until it was close enough to reach. He grabbed the rope and started to pull it taut - if the grappling iron dug into the ground he might get enough purchase to pull himself free. Unfortunately, as he tugged, the iron hooks slid hopelessly over grass. Yarik continued to pull until the grappling iron snagged the body of the painted man and even then it still did not grip. Instead, pulling on the rope just dragged the mutilated body towards him. Eventually, rope, hook and painted body all lay in a heap by his side. Deciding on another tactic, Yarik untied the grappling hook and started to hack at the piece of timber that trapped his legs, but it made so much noise that he risked attracting unwelcome attention to himself.

Suddenly something was coming at him over the ridge of the moat. He spun around to see a great horse career into the ditch. When it reached the castle wall, it reared up snorting in fear - the poor animal's flanks were bleeding badly and it was in a state of panic. Yarik recognised the beast from his time in the castle; he thought its name was Goliath. He no longer feared horses, having gained an affinity for the animals during his training at Arthur's camp. He called to the horse, trying to calm it, but the animal continued to circle around, wide eyed and stamping its hooves. Yarik persevered and eventually the horse noticed him and quietened.

As if Goliath sensed Yarik's predicament, he nervously approached the prone man and lowered his huge head. Speaking words of comfort, Yarik carefully tied the rope into a loop and gently slid it over the horse's neck. Then he pushed the animal away, slapping the grass with his hands. Goliath instinctively knew what was expected of him and backed away, tensioning the rope, and inch by painful inch Yarik felt himself pulled from beneath the timber beam that trapped him.

To Mel it seemed like she had lain on her back for an eternity. Moving any part of her body transformed the dull throb in her hands into a crescendo of pain. So, not even wishing to turn her head, she had watched Tanya's murder through the corners of her eyes. Weakened through loss of blood and exhausted by her pain, she drifting in and out of consciousness, waiting for death to take her. She wondered what was happening below the cliffs and whether Matt and the others were still alive.

Suddenly her hands flared with agony and she was dragged violently across the floor by the wooden sleeper's nails. Her scream filled the pillbox and her eyes sprang open to see Arthur heaving on the other end of the rope, which now ran taut, through the lifting boom's eye and back across the shelter to where it was tied to the sleeper. Arthur was using the lifting boom to drag her across the stone floor towards the opening.

'Please stop,' she shrieked. 'Don't pull it again. Please I beg you.'

Arthur let go of the rope and walked across to her, smiling. 'I know it's painful,' he said. 'But we don't have much time – the battle is nearly over and morning is approaching.'

Mel looked up over her head towards the opening and saw that the thunderclouds were breaking to reveal a pink morning sky. The sun was rising somewhere behind the snowdonian mountains and, although darkness still prevailed in the shadow of the cliffs, the shade would soon give way to the creeping edge of dawn.

'Your stuttering friend has just arrived and he's brought guests with him. Unfortunately, they won't be here for long and it would be really sad if they didn't get to see you.'

Mel suddenly realised Arthur's intentions - all along he had been waiting for daylight so that those in the castle could witness her crucifixion. He wanted them to see her nailed to the sleeper, hanging from the pillbox's lifting boom in the knowledge that they would all eventually suffer the same fate. She knew then, just by looking at the madman's face that, one by one, he would take the people of Harlech until his sadistic hunger was eventually satisfied, then he would move on to the next community that displeased him.

Arthur retrieved his end of the rope and heaved – Mel screamed in agony again as she was dragged another foot across the floor. Still lying on her back, she craned her neck to see when the next painful lunge would come. When it did, she pushed her legs in synch with the movement to try and take the strain from her wounded hands.

'That's better,' Arthur said. 'It's much easier when you co-operate.'

'Please stop,' she wept. 'I'll do anything, just don't hurt me anymore.'

'We're nearly there,' Arthur said sympathetically. 'Do you think you could stand up as I take the weight of the timber? I'm sure it won't hurt so much that way.'

Mel strained her neck, and peered backwards through tearful eyes at the inverted sight of her captor readying to heave again. Then suddenly, silhouetted by the dawn light, she saw a figure rise behind him. She couldn't believe her eyes – standing in the pillbox opening was… Matt!

Arthur immediately sensed the intruder behind him. Casually, he dropped the rope and slowly drew the cavalry sabre from its sheath.

Matt stood with his back to the hundred-foot drop and watched Arthur gradually turn to face him. He tried not to be distracted by the scene of carnage behind the man with the glowing crown. Tanya's corpse was illuminated by sunlight, which now streamed down the entrance steps from the cliff top above, but the pool of blood surrounding the body was nothing compared to the gory trail left by the wooden sleeper that Arthur had been dragging towards the entrance. Someone was lying behind the sleeper - it was too dark to make out the identity of the bloodied victim, but somehow Matt guessed it must be Mel. Pushing the horrible thought from his mind, he focused on his adversary and raised the shotgun ready to fire. However, when he saw the smiling face of his nightmares, he was suddenly filled with doubt.

'Welcome,' Arthur said. 'I'm so glad you came; now you can help me with my burden.'

'Matt?' The weak, almost drowsy voice came from behind the sleeper and his fears were confirmed - it was Mel! Furiously, Matt went to squeeze both triggers, but immediately his hands started to twist the gun barrel up towards his own face. Trembling with the exertion of wrestling his own limbs, Matt was soon staring down the barrel of the gun.

'Go on - do it for your brother,' Arthur said. 'You know you deserve it.'

The crown on Arthur's head pulsed even brighter as Matt felt an overwhelming urge to finally end it all, but all of a sudden it was countered by a warm sensation at his chest. Tendrils of soothing heat penetrated his heart and snaked into his blood stream. As the calming sensation coursed through his body, Matt saw Arthur glance down at the golden pendant hanging from his neck.

'What's that?' Arthur demanded, glaring at the glowing star.

Suddenly free of his opponent's mental control, Matt levelled the shotgun and fired both barrels. Arthur's sword spun backwards out of a hand which exploded in scarlet spray.

Arthur looked down at the bloody mess and stooped to retrieve one of his fingers from the stone floor. When he stood up, he was no longer smiling - instead, his thunderous eyes bore into Matt and the shotgun suddenly flew from his hands, clattered once on the stonework before bouncing out over the cliff edge.

'Take the rope!' Arthur demanded, and this time there was no denying the command. Matt reached down with trembling arms and gathered up the end hanging from the lifting boom's eye. He waited for Arthur's next instruction in the horrifying knowledge that the other end was still attached to the wooden sleeper on which Mel was cruelly impaled.

Arthur's fury filled Matt's head. 'Two birds with one stone, I think!' The madman snarled.

Unable to control his actions, Matt started to coil the rope round his own neck. Then, under the glaring intensity of his adversary, he stepped backwards into nothingness. Just as he toppled into space, Matt thought he saw a massive figure fill the pillbox's entrance.

Chapter 13

Joe Sumo charged down the spiral stairs of the northwest tower and piled into the advancing foe. Bodies tumbled backwards down the stone steps and he stood there brandishing the heavy hammer, daring them to re-ascend. At first they hesitated; the stairs were only wide enough for two men to climb at a time and the massive frame that filled the staircase above them was a daunting sight. Then from somewhere behind the attackers a command bellowed and it was immediately apparent that the men on the stairs feared the owner of the voice more than the man in front of them. Two of the enemy charged, but Joe managed to beat them back with the hammer, his superior size and elevated position giving him the advantage. Baxter was barking frantically at the top of the stairs and behind him Ryan and Nic's incantations still emanated from the room above.

    The enemy re-grouped and shuffled their ranks until two large men holding pikes took the advanced position. Again they charged, this time with their weapons brandished in front of them. Joe swung the hammer and broke one of the pikes against the stone wall, but the second weapon pierced his shoulder and he fell backwards onto the cold, stone steps. One of the attackers stood over Joe and tried to force the pike deeper into his body; the other retrieved the broken spearhead and made to thrust it into Joe's stomach. Suddenly Baxter leapt over the prone man and launched himself at his adversaries. Taken by surprise, they were distracted long enough to allow Joe to regain his footing. Baxter bit hard into one of the attacker's hands before being thrown backwards. The dog's back struck the edge of a stone step and he yelped with pain before bounding back up the stairs in retreat.

Joe was bleeding heavily from his shoulder and had lost the hammer, but he stood strong, ready to hold ground against a third attack. Two more pike-men took the lead position and charged; this time Joe grabbed the shafts of both weapons and used his incredible strength to force the men once more back down the staircase. But more bodies pushed upwards in support and Joe, still holding the two weapons, was forced upwards again. This time Joe knew he was in serious trouble; he couldn't let go of the pikes or he would be overpowered, but with neither hand available to gain purchase on the surrounding stonework, he was unable to repel so many attackers. The staircase scrummage was slowly forced upwards until Joe desperately defended the doorway to Father Peter's room. Suddenly, an arrow flew from between Joe's legs and pierced the thigh of one of the pike-men. He fell to the ground and Joe at last had a hand free. Taking the single remaining pike in both hands, he pushed with all his might until his nearest attackers tumbled backwards. Nic fired another arrow - his last, and once again the enemy was forced to retreat.

Suddenly, there was terrible roar from down below and Joe saw some of his attackers being pulled backwards. Clambering through and over them was a huge black man wearing the coat of a large white cat - the animal's head served as a head dress, fangs snarling silently from above the dark warrior's branded forehead. The black man bellowed like an enraged bull as he charged up the stairs wielding a large two-handed sword. Joe knew that if the man reached the open room the enemy would flood in behind him and all would be lost. So, as if diving into a swimming pool, the massive wrestler hurled himself down the stairs towards the charging warrior. The two men's heads cracked together and they fell in a heap onto the cold steps. Joe landed awkwardly and the black man recovered from the collision first. He leapt onto Joe and holding the blade of his sword sideways in both hands, he forced it downward onto the ex-wrestler's throat. Joe also grabbed the sword in both hands and a battle of strength ensued. Joe was the heavier of the two men but the black warrior was taller, leaner and bound with muscles; he also had gravity on his side. Joe's injured shoulder flared with pain as he fought a losing battle to repel the descending sword. He looked up into the snarling face of his adversary as he felt the blade of the weapon press against his neck. He couldn't draw breath as his windpipe slowly collapsed beneath the force and Joe Sumo's eyes rolled back in their sockets.

Mel had witnessed some horrific scenes recently, but none had prepared her for the terrible sight of Matt stepping backwards into space with a noose around his neck. Her howl of despair turned to one of agony as the rope suddenly broke Matt's fall and the momentum dragged her and the wooden sleeper right to the edge of the pillbox opening. Only her weight, and that of the sleeper, anchored the rope, preventing it from running through the boom's eye, allowing Matt's body to plummet to the rocks below. Mel lay there in torturous pain, staring up into Arthur's smiling face as the madman watched Matt spinning and slowly choking to death on the rope noose below him. Then suddenly, she noticed another shadow and realised that someone else was in the pillbox with them. She wondered if the girl with the knife had returned, but she couldn't see the intruder from where she lay. Even if some hero planned to liberate her from her torture, she knew they would never succeed. Arthur would sense the new presence and when he did, he would simply take control of their will and force them to do whatever his sick mind desired.

Arthur continued to laugh at the sight of Matt spinning below him and seemed unaware the intrusion. Mel wondered if she had been mistaken about the unseen presence and strained her neck to scan the interior of the pillbox. A hideous figure stepped into view and a huge distorted face on massive, stooped shoulders studied her. 'Big'un!' Mel gasped, realising that this was the creature they had ousted from the castle - the one that she had begged Joe not to kill.

For a moment, recognition flashed in the creature's Mongoloid eyes as if remembering her previous compassion. It turned away from her to focus instead on the back of the laughing madman. Big'un's deformed face broke into a crooked-toothed smile as he caught sight of the glowing band of gold on Arthur's head.

Mel still couldn't understand why Arthur could not sense this intrusion and she wondered if the creature's damaged brain was somehow impervious to Arthur's telepathic powers.

Arthur was not oblivious to Mel's thoughts though, and through her, immediately sensed his danger. Choking on his laughter, he span around to face the creature and Mel saw horror in his eyes as he took in the sight of the huge, deformed man towering over him. The golden band pulsed in crimson intensity as Arthur attempted to penetrate the flawed mind of the creature, but it seemed that his powers were ineffective against this monster. One huge, pale slab of a hand reached out towards the chalice crown and Arthur stepped backwards away from the brute. Suddenly his arms were flailing around as he teetered precariously on the edge of the pillbox's opening. Arthur desperately grabbed the outstretched arm just as it plucked the golden band from his head.

'Nooooo!' Arthur screamed in terror as Big'un attempted to shake him free.

Mel felt Arthur's panic and mentally shared his horror as he plummeted downwards towards the rocks below. Big'un turned, smiling crookedly at his new-found prize and casually lumbered away towards the now sunlit stairs.

Ryan cowered behind the bed desperately gripping Father Peter's hand as Nic frantically searched the room for something that might serve as a weapon. Smashing the flimsy bedside table that was his own amateur attempt at carpentry, he took one of its heavy legs and charged down the stairs to protect his friend. The black warrior had pinned Joe to the steps and was forcing the blade of his sword down onto his throat. The two bulky men completely blocked the narrow staircase, preventing the enemy below from climbing any further. Nic could see that Joe was losing consciousness, so he swung the table leg like a baseball bat and smashed it into the face of his assailant. The black man's nose split open like a ripe plum and he fell backwards onto the men below spilling them back down the steps. Nic pulled the sword from across Joe's neck and tried to revive his friend, but before he could do so the black man roared with fury and remounted his attack. As the warrior charged, Nic instinctively swivelled the heavy sword and rammed its hilt into the steps. The attacking man saw it too late - his momentum drove him onto the weapon, impaling his chest and piercing his heart. Arthur's great captain emitted a furious, gurgling roar before slumping lifelessly to the ground. Everyone stood motionless, staring at the fallen warrior. Then Joe started to groan and the sound spurred the remaining attackers into action. They advanced again, snarling as they clambered over Joe's stricken body towards Nic who retreated, weaponless once more. Suddenly a spear of morning light penetrated the stairwell through one of the narrow stone windows. As it illuminated the advancing men's faces, their snarling expressions suddenly turned to confusion. They looked like the victims of a stage hypnotist who had suddenly snapped his fingers at the end of his act. Nic watched their bewildered expressions change to fear and they dropped their weapons and ran, jostling each other back down the steps.

'Nic, come quick!' Ryan shouted from above. 'It's Father Peter – he's waking up!'

* * * *

Eddie had never felt so alive as he galloped through the enemy horde, mercilessly shooting down anyone who dared to stand against him. Arthur's army was in disarray and most fled the onslaught, but those brave enough to face the attack fell beneath the horses' hooves, or to bullets from the riders' guns. Eddie roared as he charged ahead of the others and for the first time in his life he felt invincible. Their intention was to retake the town and use the cover of its ruined buildings to launch an attack on the enemy caught between them and the castle. However, the way things were working out, Eddie wondered if they should perhaps stay on the horses and continue to create mayhem among the enemy ranks.

A stocky brute of a man, swinging a spiked mace, stood directly in Eddie's path. Aiming the pistol as he rode towards the indomitable figure, Eddie waited until they were just a few yards apart before pulling the trigger. The bullet entered the man's head at the tip of his strange brand, the brute collapsed in a heap and the horse rode over him.

Eddie searched for another victim, but all of a sudden the enemy seemed to mass in front of him. Fleeing men turned as one and formed ordered ranks with their weapons raised high against him. It was as if he suddenly faced a completely different foe and Eddie knew that to ride blindly into the spears would be suicide. His horse reared up, nearly dismounting him and suddenly an arrow pierced Eddie's calf. Grimacing with pain, he turned around, anxiously seeking support.

'Make for that hill!' One of the other riders shouted and Eddie galloped after the man in the direction of the cliffs. Soon most of the horsemen were congregated on an elevated area of ground, busy reloading their guns or replenishing their arrows. All around them the enemy ranks crept forwards. Soon, they were surrounded by nearly a thousand warriors, all bristling with weapons and intent on murder. The riders had to dismount as a volley of arrows flew into their ranks and they quickly formed a circle to return the enemy fire from over their horses' backs.

Eddie fired into the advancing pack without targeting any particular enemy; the attacking masses were so dense now that it was impossible to miss, but he soon ran out of bullets. Gunshots eventually subsided and the opposing forces started to exchange volleys of arrows, each man replenishing their missiles from those on the ground. All the time, the enemy continued to creep forward until Eddie could see the murderous look in each of their eyes.

So this is where it ends, he thought and it struck him that he wasn't even scared. Soon he would be with Hayley again in the knowledge that he had done his best to avenge her from the savages that now inhabited the world. 'Come on you bastards!' He shouted, flinging his useless pistol at the enemy. He watched the spinning gun as it followed a slow, graceful arc; suddenly a shaft of dawn light glinted from its surface and at the same time a terrible scream rang out from behind him. Eddie turned in the new morning light, just in time to see Arthur's body crash into the rocks at the foot of the cliffs.

The enemy seemed to falter as if for the first time uncertain of their goal. The alien will that had driven them here was no more and their well-drilled ranks reverted to a disordered frenzy. Immediately some turned and tried to escape through the mass, but others started to fight among themselves and Eddie found himself in a sea of broiling chaos. Suddenly there was a rider among them - Eddie didn't recognise the man, but the horse was unmistakable. It was the same animal that had borne their possessions on the long trek across Wales - the stranger in the enemy midst was riding Goliath.

'The dark king is dead!' Yarik cried. 'Go now, for the battle has ended. Find whatever peace you can in this world for at last you are free men.'

Slowly, incredibly, the crowd simply dispersed - some formed groups and slunk away towards the beach, others hurried off in the direction of the mountains. To Eddie, this once hostile army now looked more like a crowd of exhausted partygoers leaving some humungous dance festival, but even then he wondered how long these vulnerable people would remain leaderless. How long before they returned with a larger force, better weapons and an even more insane leader?

Mel grimaced as the sleeper scraped another inch closer to the edge of the pillbox opening. The weight of Matt was slowly pulling her towards the precipice and she knew that she would soon fall to join him in an agonising seesaw of death, both hanging by the rope suspended from the lifting boom's eye. Making a decision, she took a deep breath before slowly, agonisingly, drawing her hand off the nail that impaled it. The pain was so intense that she thought she would pass out, but eventually it pulled free and a geyser of blood erupted from her palm. She dragged her arm through the loop of cloth that bound her elbow to the sleeper and, as she did so, the timber twisted away almost dragging her over the cliff. She ripped her other hand from its nail just before the timber beam slid out over the side. Mel grabbed the cloth from the ground and pressed it to her wounds, desperately fighting to remain conscious.

Staggering to the edge, she peered down to see that Matt was still spinning on the noose around his neck, his weight counteracted by the massive sleeper, spinning beside him. Somehow, he had managed to get both of his hands up high enough to grasp the rope above his head and was desperately trying to support his weight to prevent strangulation. His face had already turned blue though and one by one, his fingers lost their grip on the rope and his arms fell limply to his sides.

'Matt!' She screamed and her mutilated hands reached out to grab the rope suspending the sleeper. Urgently, she heaved it downwards and the pain was almost unbearable, but the heavy timber acted as a counterweight and, as the rope ran through the boom's eye, Matt was hoisted upwards towards her. Again she pulled, nearly toppling as she did so, but she regained her footing and heaved one more time before Matt was suddenly level with her. She grabbed his arm and pulled him into the pillbox; the lifting boom swung inwards as she did so, lowering him onto the ground. Quickly, Mel untied the rope from around Matt's neck and she could see straight away that he wasn't breathing. Feeling his wrist with slippery red fingers, she thought she detected a weak pulse.

'Don't die on me now, you bastard!' She said, lowering her mouth onto his and blowing life-giving air into his lungs. She paused and breathed again, tears falling now onto Matt's face. 'You can't die,' she cried. 'I love you!'

Suddenly Matt coughed and dragged a painful breath of his own, through his damaged windpipe. He looked up at Mel's tearful face and smiled. 'I know,' he croaked.

Matt stood on the beach and watched the boat slide through the glistening waters towards the beach. The sun was shining and it was very warm, but the thunderstorm had marked the end of the oppressive humidity and had replaced it with a freshness that made him feel good to be alive.

'You okay?' He croaked to Mel; his damaged throat still made it hard to speak.

'I'm fine,' she smiled at him, holding up her bandaged hands in evidence.

Yarik led Goliath over to them and glanced at the approaching boat. 'I'm going to leave now,' he said. 'Before the others arrive.'

'Nonsense!' Mel said. 'They'll want to meet you - without you, none of us would even be here.'

Yarik shook his head. 'Without me and my kind, many more of your people would have survived. I'm sorry, but I don't belong here.'

'Where will you go?' Matt asked.

'There are a lot of frightening people about now,' Yarik said, gazing at the hills. 'Trained warriors without a leader are dangerous. I have to find them and teach them what I have learned here otherwise all of this will happen again. If I can, I will lead them north, away from here.'

Matt nodded, knowing it to be true. He offered Yarik his fist in a gesture of camaraderie, just as he had done once before in very different circumstances. Yarik looked puzzled for a moment before he perceived Matt's mind and returned the gesture. As their knuckles met Matt said. 'A long time ago

I joked that you were a hero, but now you should know that you truly are. There must be something we can do to help,'

Yarik looked embarrassed. 'There is one thing,' he said, glancing up at Goliath.

Matt grinned. 'Take him,' he said. 'Looks like he's made his own mind up anyway.'

Yarik nodded once and leapt up onto Goliath's back. 'Perhaps we'll meet again,' he said.

'It's a small world,' Matt said, wondering at the amazing circumstances that had brought the two men together.

Matt held one of Mel's bandaged hands as they watched Yarik ride off towards the mountains and guessed that he would never see the extraordinary warrior or his brave horse again. When the rider was out of sight, Matt turned to see Nic and Joe wading into the warm water to greet the boat, with Baxter splashing around them, barking with his usual excitement. Father Peter and Eddie stood either side of Ryan at the water's edge holding the boy's hands as he fidgeted excitedly.

'Ryan's missed Amy so much,' Mel said, laying her head on Matt's shoulder. 'It's so sweet.'

'The boy's amazing – there's something very special about him – you should have seen how he stood up to Arthur.'

'And he saved Father Peter's life,' Mel said.

'I know,' Matt said. 'But, I reckon the old priest's tougher than we thought.'

'He's certainly made a remarkable recovery, but he hasn't said much about his ordeal. Have you spoken to him, Matt?'

'Not really, but he says he finally understands what he must do. He's as mysterious as ever I'm afraid.'

The boat was nearly at the beach now and they could see Gerry O'Donnell at the wheel. 'Top o' the mornin' to you,' the Irishman shouted from the craft. 'The navy boys say you've had a bit of excitement here. I can't say I'm sorry to have missed it.'

Eddie didn't want to get his injured leg wet so he joined Matt and Mel while Nic and Joe struggled to pull the boat as close to the shore as they could. Unlike the dinghy on which Gerry had left Harlech, the one he now captained was a far more impressive vessel and it sat lower in the water.

'Nice wheels, man,' Nic shouted to the Irishman. 'Where did you get the boat?'

'I've kept myself busy while you've been up to your shenanigans,' Gerry laughed. 'I won't lie to you, she's not all my own work, but she took some rebuilding, to be sure.'

Suddenly Amy jumped from the boat with a splash and ran to Ryan, flinging her arms around him. The boy looked embarrassed, but the sparkle in his eyes was plain to see. Together the two of them ran off along the sand with Baxter at their heels, chattering as if they had never been apart.

'Come ashore,' Matt shouted to Gerry. 'I feel another party coming on.'

Gerry looked uncharacteristically self-conscious for a moment. 'I'm afraid we're not stopping,' he said. 'I only came to drop Amy off, and to pick up any passengers.'

'Where are you going?' Mel asked anxiously.

'Ireland,' he said. 'Something's been calling me back for quite a while now. I reckon I'm needed there.'

Father Peter turned and walked towards Matt. 'Give this to the boy,' he said, handing his ledger to Matt, 'and tell him to keep on top of it; one day it will be very important.'

'What do you mean?' Matt said. 'Why don't you give it to him yourself?' Despite his words the reality was slowly dawning on him - Father Peter was leaving too.

'I'll miss you Matthew,' but I'm afraid I have to go with them. 'There is one final journey I must make - Gerry O'Donnell and I are to tread a common path for a while.'

'I don't understand,' Matt said.

'Maybe you will one day,' the priest said, smiling at Matt, then he turned to Eddie. 'Are you ready my boy?'

Matt was speechless - he looked incredulously at his lanky friend. 'W… What does he mean, Eddie?'

'I'd nip that stutter in the bud, if I were you,' Eddie said. 'Such things can quickly become a habit!'

'You're leaving too?' Mel said. 'Why?'

'Because there's nothing for me here except unhappy memories. Father Peter thinks it will be good for me to start a new life across the water and he says he needs my brain for a while, whatever that means.' Eddie took the old priest's arm and together they walked to the water. 'Do me one last favour, Joe,' he said. 'Carry me to the boat; I'm really worried about my leg.'

Matt put his arm round Mel's shoulder. 'Well, I guess he's not changed that much,' he whispered.

As soon as the two men were aboard, Nic threw back the ropes, and Gerry hoisted the sails.

Matt sat on the warm sand next to Mel, watching the boat bob away across the water and again he wondered about

Gerry O'Donnell. The Irishman was as deep and mysterious as ever and he wished he had got to know him better. The enigmatic carpenter had always seemed to appear at their time of greatest need and without his help, they would probably have never survived the horror of Bala. From now on the evenings at Harlech would never be quite the same.

Matt watched Eddie waving from the back of the boat and he realised he was going to miss his friend even more, but it was the thought of never seeing Father Peter again that really scared him. Matt was truly the group's leader now and there would be nobody to share the burden with.

'Look at this,' Mel said - she had opened the ledger and was reading Father Peter's final passage.

"At last the impostor king is defeated, but the holy chalice has been lost. We cannot be mended now until a new king is born to Harlech; only then, will humanity return to the world. Our destiny lies under the walls of the great fallen city - this I know for I have seen it in my dreams. FP."

'What does it mean?' she said.

'Who knows,' Matt said, but he could feel the strange star-shaped pendant pulsing against his chest. He got up from the sand and helped Mel to her feet so that they were facing each other. He looked into her eyes and smiled. 'Here, I've got something for you.' He handed her a small bundle of cloth.

'It's my compass,' she said, her eyes filling with tears.

Then Matt kissed her. 'Don't ever get lost again,' he whispered.

THE END

The story continues in:

"The Sword of Fierbois"

Book 1: The Third Violation